Juno Rushdan is the award-winning author of steamy, action-packed romantic thrillers. As a veteran air force intelligence officer, she uses her background supporting special forces to write about kick-ass heroes and strong heroines fighting for their lives as well as their happily-ever-afters. Juno currently lives in the DC area with her patient husband, two kids and a rescue dog. Be the first to know about new releases, exclusive excerpts and contests by signing up for Juno's newsletter at junorushdan.com/mailing-list

Former naval intelligence officer and US Naval Academy graduate **Geri Krotow** draws inspiration from the global situations she's experienced. Geri loves to hear from her readers. You can email her via her website and blog, gerikrotow.com

D1386170

Also by Geri Krotow

Colton's Mistaken Identity
Her Christmas Protector
Wedding Takedown
Her Secret Christmas Agent
Secret Agent Under Fire
The Fugitive's Secret Child
Reunion Under Fire
Snowbound with the Secret Agent
The Pregnant Colton Witness
The Billionaire's Colton Threat

Discover more at millsandboon.co.uk

HOSTILE PURSUIT

JUNO RUSHDAN

COLTON'S DEADLY DISGUISE

GERI KROTOW

MILLS & BOON

First Published in Great Britain 2020
by Mills & Boon, an imprint of HarperCollins*Publishers*
1 London Bridge Street, London, SE1 9GF

Hostile Pursuit © 2020 Juno Rushdan
Colton's Deadly Disguise © 2020 Harlequin Books S.A.

Special thanks and acknowledgement are given to Geri Krotow for her contribution to *The Coltons of Mustang Valley* series.

ISBN: 978-0-263-28027-2

0420

MIX
Paper from
responsible sources
FSC® C007454

HOSTILE PURSUIT

JUNO RUSHDAN

To all the readers willing to take a chance on a new
Mills & Boon Heroes author, I am grateful.

Chapter One

For a year Lori Carpenter had stayed indoors, under constant watch, cut off from family and friends and everything familiar, in hiding.

Dread ate away at her every day. There was nothing she could do besides prepare. But it still wasn't enough, and now her time was up.

The arm lodged against her throat tightened.

"You let your guard slip," he whispered in her ear, his elbow locked under her chin, blocking off her airway.

Her lungs strained, clogged with fear as she flailed.

"Show me what you are," he growled.

Prey or a predator.

Adrenaline shot through her bloodstream, her heart beating like a snare drum. Survival instinct kicked in and the lead weighing down her limbs evaporated.

Lori thrust her elbow back into his ribs, once, twice. All the drills repeated day after day for fifty-five weeks came rushing to the forefront of her mind. To break away, she had to flip him. She slammed her heel down onto his foot. As she shrugged her shoulders, she hooked her foot behind one of his legs, seized the arm locked around her throat and bent at the knees.

His body rotated, going over her shoulder. Perfect execution of the maneuver.

But he grabbed her, taking her down hard with him to the concrete floor of the empty two-car garage. They rolled. Their arms and legs tangled.

She landed on top of US Deputy Marshal Nick McKenna and jammed her forearm against his throat. "I asked you to give me a challenging lesson. Not try to actually kill me."

Nick was tough, deadly. There was a darkness to him. The kind bred from dealing in the worst sort of violence. She appreciated that about him; it bolstered her confidence that he'd be able to keep her alive. So far he hadn't disappointed. But there was another side to him she preferred.

He tapped her arm, giving the cue their self-defense session was finished even though he was lethally capable of maneuvering free of her grasp.

Part of her wondered why he had let her flip him to the ground. No way she could've tossed him unless he'd allowed it. Besides the fact that he was powerfully built, he had years of training and experience she couldn't compete with.

She took her arm off his larynx, put her hands on his muscular chest and kept his body pinned with her legs, straddling his hips. Her belly fluttered with raw awareness, so close to him, pelvis to pelvis, their lips a breath apart. He took up all the oxygen in the room.

Rubbing his throat, he stared up at her with those intense, bourbon-colored eyes that seemed to see everything. Her fear, her pain, her loneliness.

Everything except her desire for him.

His devastating dark looks were even more tempting dotted with facial stubble and covered in a sheen of sweat. "I'm pretty sure attempted homicide is not part of my job description." The overheated gravel of his voice teased an itch that hadn't been scratched in a long, long time.

He flashed a heart-stopping smile that sent a tingle shooting straight to her thighs.

"You were right. I have been too easy on you and that's not doing you a favor." He swept a long lock of her hair that'd slipped from her ponytail away from her face, tucking it behind her ear. The brush of his fingertips, his touch lingering seconds longer than it should've, made her stomach bounce as if she were still a naive girl who believed in true love and the magic of chemistry, instead of the older, wiser thirty-two-year-old woman she was today. "You need to know what the fear and the panic would feel like in a real-world scenario so you can *think* and *fight* your way through it."

Nick had been an anchor during the bleakest months, her sensei, teaching her to punch, kick, throw a proper head-butt. And he had become a dear friend. A smart, steadfast, sexy friend she couldn't stop thinking about crawling into bed with.

Ted Zeeman crossed the threshold, strolling into the garage while typing on a laptop. Good ole Ted always popped up before Nick and Lori slipped across the line of propriety, like he could smell their pheromones from the next room.

Lori stood and offered Nick a hand up from the ground.

He took it, putting his palm on hers even though he didn't need her assistance, climbed to his feet and dusted himself off. Standing shy of six feet with broad shoulders and streamlined muscles that hinted at his leashed lethality, he wasn't a huge guy, but his magnetic presence dominated a room. Or perhaps he simply dominated her attention.

She dismissed the ridiculous crush she had on Deputy Marshal McKenna. If she liked him, then beneath the suits and badge was a quintessential bad boy.

In her experience, bad boys equaled heartbreak. Every

man she'd been attracted to had left scars. She wasn't in the market for another festering wound.

"Are you nervous about your big day tomorrow?" Ted asked.

Big day.

Weddings, funerals, your child being born…those were big days. Testifying in federal court against her in-laws' financial firm for laundering millions was inevitable once she'd discovered what Wallace Capital Management— WCM—had been up to.

After she took the stand tomorrow, marshals she'd never met would give her a brand-new name and whisk her off into a brand-new life in a brand-new city.

Hopefully, not one in backcountry nowhere.

"Yeah, a little." More like a lot. As in terrified.

"I'm about to file the morning report," Ted said to Nick. "Anything you want me to add?"

"Did you annotate our excursion?" Nick asked.

"Yep. You betcha." Ted nodded. "I reminded the boss, but I did the paperwork, too."

One hour a day, Lori was allowed off the premises. She usually relished the time jogging through the adjacent woods, but not today.

Ted slapped the classified US Marshals Services laptop closed. "I'm going to haul the trash out while you two get cleaned up so we can go *shopping*." He rolled his eyes.

Lori might've been living in yoga pants, jeans and T-shirts since her mad dash out of San Diego after spilling her guts to the FBI, but she'd be damned if she was going to face her no-good, cheating ex-husband and his lying, criminal family in anything less than the best professional armor.

"Fifteen minutes and we'll head out." Ted tucked the laptop under his arm. "Tomorrow can't get here soon enough. My last assignment will be done, and I can finally retire."

"Are you going to get a little hut on a powdery beach like you want?" Nick asked him.

"Boy, I wish. It's a one-bedroom condo in the Keys for me. You'll have to visit."

"Better believe it," Nick said. "We'll be out front in fifteen."

Ted strode back into the country house that was isolated on two acres of land.

"How are you holding up?" Nick's gaze found hers again, warming something inside her like it did whenever he looked at her that way. "It's the homestretch."

She should've been relieved. By noon tomorrow this nightmare would be over, but tension threaded through her, tightening her muscles. "My father-in-law, Sam, begged me to look the other way, keep my job at WCM and to forget everything." Lori almost kept talking, almost dared to unburden herself of the secret she'd been carrying.

One stupid mistake had pulverized her life like a sledgehammer crushed a walnut.

It wasn't as if she could hide it forever. The truth would come out in her testimony, but what would Nick think of her when he found out?

"Of course he did." Nick ran his hands up and down her arms. "Without you, there is no case. We're talking about millions of dollars a year. Billions. I'm sure whoever they launder money for are dangerous people and only care about their bottom line."

A shiver raced through her. Nick had no idea how dangerous, but she knew all too well. "Sam told me there's no way to win. That I'm going up against Goliath." And her father-in-law hadn't been talking about WCM. "He swore I wouldn't live long enough to testify."

The shiver deepened to a chill that seeped to her bones. The firm's biggest dirty client was violent and ruthless, had endless resources and people everywhere.

It was a miracle she'd lived this long.

"Goliath is big and ferocious. But not invincible. David beat him and so will you." Nick took both of her hands in his and held her gaze.

The gesture was small, but heated her cheeks and chased away her goose bumps. The space around them seemed to shrink, due to his proximity and the quiet strength he radiated. At times his tall, dark and brawny package was menacing, but he could also be…gentle.

"No matter what, I'll protect you and get you to court safely. Do you believe me?"

She believed he'd risk his life for duty and for any witness. "Yes."

Nick had kept her safe for three hundred and eighty-six days. What could possibly go wrong in the next twenty-seven hours?

NICK'S GAZE FLICKERED up to Lori's reflection in the rearview mirror of the car as he drove. Tension radiated from her slender body. Her expression was strained, her big brown eyes looking haunted. With her long chestnut hair loose and the flush of their workout gone from her cheeks, her fair skin was paler than normal. Somehow making the almost ethereal beauty about her more enticing.

The enormity of the transition she was going through wasn't lost on him.

He could tell she was doing her best to hold it together and not let nerves derail her. For a year he'd studied her. Paid attention to her body language and every nuance.

Witnesses tended to get antsy in protective custody, especially over a long period of time, and sometimes they made bad decisions. Tried to bolt when they should've stayed put. Deviated from protocol instead of adhering to the strict rules.

Buddying up to them helped him keep his finger on the

pulse of the situation, anticipate if things might go sideways because an informant was on the verge of unraveling.

What he hadn't counted on was falling for a witness.

Lori had totally blindsided him. Several hours a day, seven days a week, watching her, talking to her, touching her during their self-defense lessons, was winding him up tighter than a watch spring. He'd never been so viscerally attracted to a woman. Everything about her excited him—her voice, those doe eyes staring at him, her silky hair he wanted to feel sliding across his belly, the knockout body he wanted to—

"Finally, we're here," Ted said, intruding on his thoughts.

Nick put the brakes on the inappropriate fantasy and leashed his raging hormones. Having an infatuation with a witness that bordered on obsessive was a reason to have his head examined.

He turned into the mall parking lot and pulled into a spot close to the west side entrance. The trip had been approved by their boss and planned for two weeks. He and Ted had gone over the layout of the shopping center numerous times, had memorized the location of the security station and every exit, and had narrowed down the mall's peak hours. That was why they'd chosen the morning, shortly after the mall opened when it would be quiet, no crowds and easy to control the environment.

They entered the mall through a side door and walked down a short corridor with a few stores. Only the tea shop appeared to be busy at this hour. An apron-clad clerk stood out front holding a tray of samples. An elderly gentleman with a salt-and-pepper crown, hobbling with a cane, approached the clerk and asked questions about the different varieties available to taste.

As they reached the central part of the shopping center, Nick was at Lori's side and Ted at their six behind them. The entrance they used was the closest to the women's business-apparel store that Lori had chosen in advance. The walk was a short distance, but everything stretched before him, almost in slow motion.

Nick surveilled their surroundings, noting everyone in the vicinity. A couple, one pushing a stroller, the other with a baby in a carrier strapped to their body. Three fiftysomething-year-old ladies power walking while engrossed in a lively discussion.

Nothing stood out or struck him as unusual, but there was a subtle tug of caution in his gut, like he was being watched. Another furtive glance around still didn't pinpoint any cause for alarm. Why his pulse pounded, and his palms itched, he didn't know. They'd taken Lori on a few other outings, although never to the mall, and never to the same place twice.

It was probably just the buildup of stress and pressure from his longest assignment drawing to a culmination with her set to testify tomorrow. They were so close to finishing this.

As much as he needed to keep Lori safe and get her through her testimony, he also wasn't ready to let her go. She'd been the sole focus of his life for the better part of a year. Resetting and moving on didn't seem possible. It certainly wasn't desirable. If he had a choice, he'd keep on seeing her, talking with her, hell, sneaking in a permissible touch—every single day.

But that was the one thing he didn't have a say in.

He brushed the thought aside, concentrating instead on what he could control.

They reached the women's clothing store. As they walked inside, a chime dinged from a motion-activated PIR sensor he spotted.

An employee behind the register, wearing a blazer and sporting a curly bob, made eye contact and gave a perky smile.

One female customer perusing a row of blouses didn't glance their way.

"Hello," the young sales associate said, her warm voice rich with enthusiasm. "Right now we have a sale on accessories. Fifty percent off. Let me know if you need help finding anything."

"Thank you," Lori said.

"You've got twenty minutes." Nick looked at his watch while Ted swept the rest of the store. "We're in and out, okay?"

Lori went to a rack of suits. "You don't give a gal much time."

"One hour away from the property," he said, reminding her of the rules. "Not a minute more."

Nick's attention flickered to the other customer.

The woman was in her early forties, petite, olive complexion, coal-black hair pulled in a tight bun. No jewelry, wore slacks and a blousy top and carried a leather purse. She reached up, taking a shirt from the upper rack, and the frilly bell sleeve of her blouse dropped an inch, revealing a tattoo of a black rose on the back of her hand. The ink fit her. Beautiful. Elegant. Dark.

Reflexively, Nick pressed his arm against the Glock 22 in his shoulder rig.

"I don't see why I should be penalized because the house is thirty miles away," Lori said, checking the size on a navy two-piece.

The low chime at the front threshold rang. Another woman entered the store. Bottled-bleach-blonde. Tall and thin. Jeans and a buttoned shirt. Sneakers that squelched lightly against the tile floor.

"Eighteen minutes," Nick said, telegraphing with his hard tone this was nonnegotiable.

Lori cringed. "Yes, sir." She gave him a mock salute.

"Have I told you how much I hate it when you snarl orders at me like a drill sergeant?"

Snarl? And drill sergeants were the worst. No one liked them. "You're exaggerating."

"Try understating. When we're out, you have two speeds. Icy cool and this Judge Dredd persona."

Nick realized he sometimes came across as abrasive when he was in work mode, but that wasn't the impression he was shooting for. At all.

She picked a suit from the rack. "This should work. I better go try it on. Tick-tock."

Nick looked to Ted, where his partner stood at the entrance of the dressing rooms. Ted nodded, signaling the stalls were empty and he'd make sure no one followed Lori inside.

Blondie headed straight to some dresses hanging in the rear of the store, grabbed one almost mindlessly, or perhaps she'd been in before and knew what she was looking for, flicked a glance at a tag and made a beeline for the dressing rooms.

Ted lifted a palm, not letting the blonde in after Lori. The woman huffed and protested, raising a loud stink, but his partner held firm.

Show her your badge, Ted, and be done with it. Flashing the Eagle Top five-pointed star had a way of shutting down any complaints lickety-split.

"Who do you think you are?" Blondie asked with a fist on her hip.

"A US Deputy Marshal, ma'am," Ted said. "Sorry for the inconvenience and the wait."

"Listen, jerk. I need to get in there now."

Ted laughed in his self-deprecating way. "Sorry. Not going to happen."

The sales associate went over to the scene unfolding. "Hi," she said brightly, her sunny disposition almost disarming. "Is there a problem?"

Nick maintained his position, monitoring the rest of the shop and the entrance.

Black Rose circled silent as a fox around to an ornate display of scarves and ran her fingers across the silk. Not once since they'd entered had she acknowledged their presence in the slightest. Until now.

Her gaze lifted, meeting his, her face an expressionless mask, but her sharp eyes were those of a merciless predator.

Prior experience as an army ranger in Afghanistan before becoming a marshal had taught him the hard way never to underestimate a woman with a slight build, or even a child for that matter, and the deep scar under his chin was a testament.

For a chilling instant they stared at one another, sizing the other up. Not from a physical perspective. It was an assessment of will. And what Nick saw in her was fathomless.

Blondie threw the dress at Ted, dividing Nick's attention, and stormed out of the store.

The bell chimed. Black Rose's steely eyes narrowed before she turned and strode unhurriedly toward the door— as if she had all the time in the world.

Then he saw it. Her low-heeled boots that didn't make a sound.

His neck prickled the way it did when he was on a hunt for big game with his siblings. Nick followed. He had no reason to detain or question her, but something about that woman was *wrong*. From the tattoo, those rubber-soled shoes, to how she'd looked at him. As if she'd wanted to slice through him like a hot knife through butter.

None of it was evidence of anything and not cause for more than suspicion, but training and years of experience had taught him not to dismiss either.

The woman strolled away, lengthening the distance between them with each store she passed. One, two, three. But the tightening in his gut didn't ease.

Black Rose glimpsed back at him over her shoulder, caught his fixed stare and stopped in her tracks. Pivoting, she turned and faced him, leveling her icy gaze his way. The look she sent him was full of loathing and in a blink it changed. Her lips hitched in an ominous half grin and she winked. Almost daring him to pursue.

Old ranger instincts urged him to take up the chase, confirm what his gut screamed about the woman, shake something that made sense out of her, but his training overruled recklessness.

He looked back in the quiet clothing store, checking on things.

Ted no longer stood stationed at the entrance of the dressing rooms.

Nick touched his Bluetooth earpiece. "Ted? What's your position? Do you have eyes on Hummingbird?" he asked, using the code name for Lori.

Deafening silence.

Nick's pulse spiked, but he remained calm—never one to succumb to panic. He stepped past displays and racks, his gaze scanning, his mind assessing.

No sign of Ted. Or the sales associate.

Drawing his gun, Nick hustled toward the dressing rooms.

Anticipation coiled in his chest, adrenaline roaring through him. The weight of his backup piece strapped to his ankle was a small comfort. Nick's fingers tightened on his Glock. He reached the threshold, scanned left, then right.

Ted lay on the floor beyond the entrance in a corner. Blood soaked his white hair at the base of his skull.

Son of a—

Ted was down.

There was no time to check if his partner was unconscious or dead. A commotion deeper in the dressing room drew him forward. Two people struggled inside the second stall.

The horror in Lori's terrified whimper jolted his heart.

Chapter Two

Lori's blood turned to slush, but her brain didn't misfire in the panic swamping her.

If she froze, she was dead.

· If she didn't think, she was dead.

If she didn't fight, she was dead.

Lori had caught the glint of the door's lock moving in the mirror's reflection. But the sales associate had slipped inside the dressing room stall before Lori had registered what was happening or even had a chance to spin around half-dressed.

The next thing she knew, the young woman rushed up behind Lori and whipped some kind of cord around her throat. The sharp wire bit into her skin, pressing against her windpipe.

The pain from the instant constriction of her airway, the absolute terror, was mind-numbing. Her earlier exercises with Nick, despite how aggressive he'd been, paled in comparison. Deep down she'd known he'd never hurt her and that she was safe with him.

But the sweet-looking sales associate had morphed into a merciless killer and was strangling her to death. Every time Lori tried to throw an elbow back, the woman seemed to anticipate it, jerking her left and then right, spinning her in the stall as if Lori were a rag doll.

She fought with all her strength. Her attacker dug harder, not giving a second of reprieve.

Dear God! Where are you, Nick?

Lori sent her silent prayer up to some omnipotent being, the universe, to anything that'd listen. She was utterly powerless.

Her heart beat harder and harder against her rib cage. Her lungs squeezed as if caught in a vise, starved for air. She wasn't ready to die. Not like this.

She clawed at the wire tightening around her throat. Desperation welled in her chest. She tried to scream for help, to make any sound to draw attention. A guttural cry rose deep in her throat, but only the strangled wisp of air came from her mouth.

Her nerves ping-ponged as her mind surged for an escape. She kicked out, frantically.

At the same time, the dressing room door swung in. She glimpsed Nick for a split second before her bare foot—already in motion—knocked the door closed.

Pushing up and backward with both her legs, Lori sent her attacker slamming into the mirror. Glass shattered to the floor. Still clawing at the cord over her throat, her fingers slipped in the warm wetness of her own blood.

Her heart felt like it was trying to fight its way out of her chest, lungs burning for oxygen.

It was impossible for Lori to avoid the shards of broken mirror, and her naked soles were driven into the jagged pieces in the struggle. But only one thing mattered. Staying alive.

The door slammed open again. Nick used his hip and leg to keep it from swinging shut and aimed his gun.

He must not have had a clear shot because he didn't fire.

Lori's vision narrowed. Dark spots began forming in front of her eyes. Her panic-stricken heart squeezed.

Nick's voice rang in her mind. *Show me what you are. Prey or a predator.*

She had to do anything possible to give him a clear shot. *Right now!*

Lori threw her head back, smashing her skull into her attacker's face. Bone crunched and as the wire slackened a centimeter, she rammed her elbow into the woman's ribs.

With a grunt, her assailant's hold loosened enough for Lori to jerk away to the side.

Nick fired twice. The woman dropped to the floor.

Relief poured over Lori's soul.

Coughing, raking in air, tasting her own blood, Lori scrambled into Nick's arms.

He pulled her sideways against him. His hand clasped the back of her head, his fingers curling in her hair, and guided her face to his chest.

She broke down as sobs tore painfully from her throat.

"You're okay," Nick said. "I've got you."

The reassurance of his strong, solid form pressed close didn't do anything to loosen the knot of terror and anxiety twisting her insides. But she wasn't ready to put space between them. Not yet. She needed this. His warmth, his strength, his arms around her, a little longer.

"Nick. Nick…" she repeated again and again, unable to utter anything else.

She hated the neediness in her voice, the way she clung to him for dear life. Lori had never been a weak, whimpering damsel in distress. She took care of herself and never relied on others for anything. To do so only invited disappointment.

But this had escalated to the next level, to something that exceeded her deepest fears.

Someone taking a shot at her on the courthouse steps she'd braced herself for, but not *this*. Being attacked, nearly strangled to death in a dressing room with two armed deputy marshals within shouting distance.

How in the hell was that possible?

Oh, God. Oh, God. If they could get to her here, when her whereabouts and itinerary were supposed to be confidential, then they could get to her anywhere.

Panic swelled, building to hysteria. She was on the cusp of hyperventilating.

"Breathe. You have to breathe. Slow breaths, in and out."

Nick moved his head from side to side and she would've sworn his mouth brushed her hair. But she wasn't sure. Then his lips caressed her forehead in the barest touch, but the electric sensation was enough to burn through the mounting fear.

"I'm here. I've got you." He lowered his face to hers. His brown eyes—so authoritative and intense—anchored her. "I've got you, Lori. It's going to be all right."

NICK HELD HER tight to his chest, his heart sick with unfamiliar fear that threatened his composure. His muscles bunched, ready to blow a hole into anyone else who dared harm Lori. "Are you okay?"

She went limp against him, clinging to him with one hand and the other pressed to her throat. Her body shook so hard it was as if she might shatter into a million pieces.

He hauled her from the sight of the dead woman and inspected her neck. The garrote had left a laceration that would definitely scar if it wasn't tended to quickly. But she was alive and that was all that mattered. "Lori, are you all right?"

Nick needed to get her talking, make sure she didn't go into shock.

She sobbed into his shirt. Tears streamed down her face.

"Breathe," he said, gently. "Take deep breaths."

"If you had been ten seconds later…"

Brushing a finger under her chin, he tipped her face up to his.

Lori squeezed her eyes shut. "She would've killed me."

Seeing her hurt and distraught made his stomach clench. *Ten seconds.* Such a close call.

How many seconds had he wasted focused on Black Rose when he should've maintained his vigilance? The woman had been a deliberate distraction, goading him, to give the planted sales associate an opportunity to strike.

He'd give anything to rewind one damn minute and prevent this from ever having happened. How had he missed the setup?

Nick was no rookie. He didn't make wet-behind-the-ears mistakes. The bait to hook his attention had been clever, well played. They'd been ready and waiting for Lori to arrive.

But how had those killers known they'd be in the store?

He longed to hold Lori tighter, closer, and soothe her, but this was the wrong place and the worst possible time. Once Black Rose, or whoever the hell that woman was, realized the assassination attempt had failed, she could come back—with reinforcements.

"We've got to get out of here." His gaze fell to her bare, cut feet and exposed legs. Nick ducked into the dressing room, glass crunching underfoot, and gathered her things. "Here." He handed Lori her clothes. "Get dressed. There's a med kit in the trunk of the car. Once we're away from the mall, I can treat your injuries. But we're not safe here."

More tears welled in her eyes. "Okay." She brushed loose pieces of glass from her feet and plucked at embedded shards, wincing from the pain.

Nick took a knee beside Ted and put two fingers to his carotid.

There was a pulse, thready and slow, but he had one. Thank goodness.

The possible horror of losing both a witness and his partner at the same time flashed before him. No, it wasn't something he would ever be able to live with.

He had to make damn sure that never happened on his watch. Not today. Not ever.

"Oh, dear God." Lori peeked around the wall of the dressing room at Ted's body while tugging on her jeans. "Is he alive?"

"Yeah. She must've hit him on the back of the head." Nick loosened Ted's tie and undid the top button of his shirt. There was a lot of blood and no way to assess how bad his head injury was, not when Black Rose could pop up again at any moment. He hated it, but he had to risk waking Ted. Nick shook him hard. "Come on, Ted."

The old guy didn't move. Blood had trickled down, soaking the back of his collar.

Nick reached into his jacket pocket and took out smelling salts. As the middle child in a family of bounty hunters, he knew well enough never to leave without extra ammo, caffeine pills, condoms and smelling salts. Invariably, you'd need one or all of them.

He snapped the capsule of white crystals under Ted's nose, releasing the acrid punch of fumes. The ammonium carbonate tickled the membranes of Nick's nose and lungs, triggering his own breathing to increase.

Ted's eyes fluttered as he took a breath.

"There you go, buddy." Nick tapped his arm and helped him sit upright.

They had to get the hell out of there, but there was no telling what was waiting for them outside the store. Nick glanced at Lori. She'd mustered a brave face, her eyes wet with tears, but her stark vulnerability struck him.

"Take off your shirt," he said to her.

"What?" She gaped at him. "Why?"

Nick pulled off his jacket and holster and unbuttoned his

shirt. Lori stared at his bulletproof vest. It was regulation for the marshals to wear one out in the field. The beefed-up hard composite body armor had an extra protection plate.

She caught his intention and did as he instructed.

Even though Nick had fantasized about seeing Lori undressed more times than he was ashamed to admit, he averted his eyes while he unstrapped the vest to put on Lori. There was no way to conceal the fact she was wearing one with only the T-shirt.

He reached up to the rack of discarded clothes, grabbed a lightweight blazer, ripping the tags off, and helped her put it on.

Ted held the back of his head and wobbled to his feet. "What in the hell happened?"

"We'll talk in the car." Nick roped an arm around Lori, leading them from the dressing rooms. "But right now I want us out of here."

BELLADONNA STALKED ALONG the upper landing of the mall, drumming her fingers on the cold steel railing. The clothing store was fixed in her sights.

Tension crawled along the tendons of her neck. She rolled her shoulders once to ease it, maintaining her cool exterior despite her nerves.

This was taking too long. Something must've gone wrong.

The two deputy marshals rushed out of the shop with the target sandwiched between them, shouldering past passersby down the walkway. The target looked like she'd been through the wringer, but the problem was she was still breathing.

Trixie had failed. The talented young woman could flip from happy-go-lucky to jamming a fork into your eye in a breath. She would be greatly missed.

Things had not gone as Belladonna had hoped, but she

thrived on contingency plans and never accepted a hit without analyzing all the angles first. Not that she'd been given a choice in this situation.

Sixty contracts spanning over twenty years and three continents had taught her it was far easier to eliminate a target if they were on their own or simply had a private security team. Mishaps were more likely to occur when the target was in the protective custody of federal agents. Preparation for any possibility was key.

With the main money-laundering mechanism of the cartel at stake, it was imperative to have layers of contingencies this time. A web within a web, and she was the spider weaving the entire sticky trap.

After she was forced to take this job, her employer had made it crystal clear that a five-million-dollar payday, her reputation and her life all rested on the outcome.

Failure wasn't a consideration.

She had too much to live for. A family counting on her this time. She had to finish this job. No matter what.

Gritting her teeth, Belladonna slid a steady hand over her flawless bun, ensuring not a hair was out of place. The store had been the optimal location to take out the target. A controlled environment. No witnesses. Disposal would've been simple.

This setback was irritating, but temporary.

What had to happen next would be messy, far too public, making it harder to contain and to clean up. The likelihood of collateral damage would escalate exponentially. Belladonna abhorred the unnecessary loss of life. The hallmark of a true professional, one of the best in her humble opinion, was no accidental casualties.

But it had to be done. If a little innocent blood was spilled in the process, ultimately it was Lori Carpenter's fault. All that woman had to do was keep her mouth shut. Would've saved Belladonna so much trouble.

Now she had to go through the hassle, not to mention the sheer inconvenience, of killing that bitch.

Belladonna inserted her earpiece and activated it with a slight touch. "Bishop, you're in play. No knight stands in your way. Secure the queen at all costs," she said to another person on her team stationed in a prime position.

"Check," the low voice acknowledged.

The only other thing she wanted to hear was *checkmate*.

NICK GUARDED THEIR REAR, ensuring no one got the drop on them from behind. They hustled toward their exit. The mall left them too exposed. There were multiple sight lines for a sniper to take a clean shot. He glanced around, trying to assess where one could hide.

No, no. He shook the thought off. They'd considered that at least. That was why they liked this mall. There wasn't a suitable position for a sniper's nest. But the shopping center did provide opportunities for a hit man. They hadn't factored in the possibility of an open, up-close assault.

The couple with the stroller and baby carrier looped back around in their direction. There was no movement from inside the stroller or the carrier.

Were the kids asleep? Or were those dolls and the gear a facade, hiding weapons?

He had to consider everyone a potential threat.

Two feet in front of him, Ted escorted Lori toward the last short corridor. Both were injured and frazzled and needed time to recuperate.

Lori hurried along with a hand pressed to her throat. The back of Ted's head was still bleeding badly. His partner might need stitches and hopefully nothing else. Ted was literally hours from retirement and had almost bitten the dust.

Nick itched to have his weapon in hand until they were safely in the car, but he'd holstered it after leaving the store. The last thing they needed was to draw unwanted attention to themselves. Their scramble out of the clothing shop had probably already raised speculation among the onlookers, making them wonder if they'd robbed the place.

Nick spun on his heel, doing a quick three hundred sixty scan.

No sign of the woman with the tattoo. She'd vanished like a phantom. But that didn't give him a warm and cozy feeling, and it didn't mean there wasn't any danger.

Stay alert, stay alive, his former platoon leader used to say. There were no truer words.

They hit the west side corridor. The outer doors leading to the parking lot were in sight.

Ted held Lori by the elbow, keeping her moving at a rapid pace.

The older guy in front of the tea shop had progressed past asking questions to tasting samples. The nail salon and mobile phone shop were now a flurry of activity with customers.

A woman rummaging around in a large, bucket-size purse heading their way stole his attention. Nick slid his hand inside his jacket and gripped the handle of his service weapon, fingers tightening in readiness.

She pulled out a ringing cell phone and answered it, passing them by.

Nick exhaled the breath he'd been holding.

In fifty feet, they'd reach the doors and clear the mall. Then he'd reset from this epic disaster. Figure out how this could've happened in the first place.

All his senses were keyed up hot. Even his heartbeat had a machine-gun rhythm.

"I like the loose-leaf Dragon blend the best," the senior citizen said as Nick came within earshot.

The sales associate holding the tray smiled at him. "That's my favorite, too."

Only thirty feet to go.

The old guy pivoted, lifting his cane like a shotgun and aimed at Lori with shocking speed.

Taking him head-on was the only response.

Nick bolted forward in a rush and charged the guy. The AARP-card-carrier's eyes widened as he spotted Nick inbound and tried to redirect the aim. Nick knocked the cane up.

Bullets spit from the tip, spraying rounds on automatic. A plate glass storefront shattered. Rounds stitched up toward the ceiling. The air was split by the loud sewing-machine sound.

Ted pushed Lori up against a wall, out of the line of fire, and shielded her as he drew his Glock.

Bullets kept discharging in rapid fire. The gun concealed as a cane was such a thin, deceptive-looking weapon, but a stout recoil reverberated through Nick's arms.

The man fought Nick to regain control and almost succeeded.

Though the guy was older, he wasn't about to be put out to pasture. He had the strength of a bull and unleashed blinding martial arts moves.

Nick struggled to hold on to the cane through the assassin's lightning kicks until the weapon clicked. Empty. Nick threw a hard right punch, catching the older man full in the face.

To his credit, the man didn't stumble, but the blow stunned him a second. Maybe only a nanosecond before the man took a running leap into the air, screaming like a ferocious beast. AARP hoisted the cane up and swung it down.

Nick raised both arms, forming a triangle in front of his head to protect his skull. He took the brunt of the blow with his forearms and went for the man's knee with the heel of his foot.

The old guy was too quick and dodged it but left another body part vulnerable. Nick kicked the man straight in the gonads.

The cane slipped from AARP's grip and he doubled over in what must've been a world of hurt. But Nick wasn't gullible enough to think that man wouldn't recover in the next breath.

Nick grabbed the stainless-steel tray from the gawking clerk, letting samples of tea spill to the floor, and smacked AARP with the platter. A clang rang in the air as the man's head twisted. But he stayed upright, wobbling—still a threat. Nick threw his entire body into hitting the man with the steel tray again. Not once, not twice, hell, he didn't stop whaling on AARP until the guy dropped like a sack of potatoes and didn't so much as twitch.

Lori was safe behind Nick's partner, her face awash in renewed horror. Ted stood vigilant as a sentinel, determined not to let anything or anyone touch her, but his gun hand was shaking.

Not a good sign.

Ted was solid as a rock and Nick had never seen him tremble from nerves. Hopefully, his partner could make it to the car and Nick would tend to Lori and Ted later.

Right now there was a far more urgent problem.

The tingle in the back of his neck that slipped down between his shoulder blades told him he was being watched, and not by lookie-loo civilians.

He glanced around, barely taking in the carnage of broken glass and injured bystanders, bleeding and rolling on the floor from stray bullets.

One thing was at the forefront of his mind.

How many more hit men were there?

Chapter Three

Another bishop lost. Damn it!

Belladonna forced herself to stop staring at the target and turned, pretending to look at a storefront window display, in the opposite direction of the murmuring crowd that was gathering at the scene.

In another second or two, Deputy Marshal Nick McKenna would've sensed her surveillance and spotted her.

Unlike the older, softer Zeeman, McKenna was razor-sharp and capable. Traits she'd banked on in the clothing store when she'd lured the younger man away from the vicinity of the dressing rooms. She thought for certain he would've pursued her. The feral gleam in his eyes telegraphed his gnawing desire to do so, but he'd followed his protocol instead.

Something she bet he'd do again.

Even if she was mistaken on that account, she'd spent weeks planning, putting the pieces into place, waiting—down to the wire—for the final, missing element to fall in line.

There was nowhere they could go that she wouldn't follow. Nowhere for them to hide. She had a carefully hand-picked hit squad of more than a dozen left at her beck and call.

Belladonna whipped out her burner phone. First, she made a call to *housekeeping*.

"ETA on police?" she asked.

"They were just called," the whiskey-smooth female voice on the other side said. "A bystander in the crowd phoned it in. ETA six minutes. We've kept the mall security phone lines down and the video surveillance feeds to the clothing store and southwest entrance cut."

"Good. One less complication to deal with."

"You need to consider that someone may have filmed the altercation on their phone."

Exactly what Belladonna didn't need. Video footage slapped up on YouTube going viral. "I need cleanup. ASAP." She kept her own voice calm yet firm. "Two down. I don't want any DNA traces of my people left behind. Not a drop of blood. Not a single hair. No clothing fibers. Nothing. Do what you can to wipe the phones in the area clean. Are we clear?"

"As always. We'll monitor the internet in case any footage slips past us and pops up."

They'd clean that, too.

There wasn't a better housekeeping team on the planet, and they were worth their weight in gold. They would enter the mall disguised as paramedics and police officers, enabling them to move around unobstructed and unquestioned.

What they weren't able to get spick-and-span, they'd taint, making it worthless to forensics.

"Once you're done cleaning up this mess, restore feeds and phones before the media circus arrives."

Belladonna disconnected and sent a short text.

You're up, rook.

Standing by for a reply, she looked at the back of her hand and traced the lines of her tattoo—an inky rose. The symbol reinforced her resolve.

Tattoos or any identifying marks were a hazard in her industry, but she'd gotten it after her daughter was born.

The rose was meant to signify a fresh start, a path of her own choosing, a new identity.

Belladonna was the name the drug cartel had christened her when they took her in thirty years ago, smelted her down, trained her, forged her into the weapon she was today. It was Italian for *beautiful woman*.

And it was also the name of a plant. Every part of the nightshade from bloom to leaves to enticing berries was deadly.

Funny, she'd always loved the name and had embraced the purpose that had gone hand in hand with it until—

A response came back on her cell.

Ready to rock and roll. Set in ten.

She stowed her phone in her pocket. Lori Carpenter wouldn't live to take the stand.

Belladonna would make certain since her own life was staked on it.

"TED IS STABLE, and the bleeding seems to have stopped." Nick drove the sedan, headed in the general direction of the safe house, but with no confirmed destination yet.

His boss on the other end, Will Draper, would decide their next move. Nick continued to check his mirrors fifteen minutes later for any following vehicles. Using the skills that he'd learned from his family and reinforced by the US Marshals, he'd gotten on the freeway, gotten off and then immediately back on. Where traffic was dense, he weaved in and out of lanes.

He exited for the state road that led to Big Bear Lake. Rather than going to the safe house, he took a circuitous route, looping through residential neighborhoods, passing the camping gear store and veterinarian.

At every yellow light, he shot through and made sharp turns at the last possible moment. All the while staying vigilant and looking in his mirrors for a tail.

"But he'll need to be checked for a concussion as soon as possible," Nick said, finishing his update.

Until then, Nick needed to make a pit stop to get his partner some ice for his head and to treat Lori's wounds. He glanced at her in the back seat. Her arms were wrapped around her midsection, hugging herself, and her head rested on the window. A cloud of despair and fear hung over her. She looked so fragile and on edge and had every reason to be. He wanted to do something to restore her sense of safety, her belief in his ability to protect her.

The truth was he even doubted himself at this point for letting his guard slip. Something that never should've happened.

"Glad to hear Ted is fine. We've never had anything like this happen," Draper said. "Are you sure you didn't pick up a tail at the mall? You're not being followed, are you?"

"I'm certain. We aren't being followed." The road behind them was clear, but he hadn't loosened his death grip from the wheel or let his muscles relax in the slightest.

"Good. I'm going to have Intel get to the bottom of what happened." Draper heaved a hard breath over the line.

Nick didn't know Draper well. Six months after Draper had been appointed as marshal of the San Diego office, Nick had been banished to the remote mountains on this long-term mission.

This assignment was a punishment. For losing his temper and communicating with his fists rather than his words with a fellow deputy—a real bastard. His boss paired him with mild-mannered, easygoing Ted, figuring the two of them wouldn't clash. An accurate assessment.

Draper's track record as an ambitious hard charger and reputation for positive results were well-known and had preceded him. Zero mistakes on his record.

"In the meantime," Draper continued, "we have no reason to believe the safe house has been compromised. Based on your location and Ted's injury, it's the best place for you to go. Far better than holing up at a motel off the interstate that could easily be breached. And the nearest hospital is thirty minutes away, not that you'd be in a defensible position there. At least the safe house is stocked with provisions and has fortified safety features in a worst-case scenario. Go there, enter with caution and stay put until I have further instructions. I'll call in backup."

The safe house wasn't a perfect option. There was no way to know what information the assassins had, but Nick agreed that it was their best bet, for now. A haphazard decision made from fear without all the facts could leave him and Ted exposed and Lori vulnerable to another attack.

"All right. I understand." Nick disconnected. "We're sticking to protocol and heading to the safe house."

Protocol was everything. It had kept the US Marshals from losing a single person under active protection in the witness security program for decades.

"Not surprising," Ted said. "Did Draper have any ideas how they found her?"

Nick spotted a gas station convenience store, pulled over and threw the car in Park. "Draper doesn't know how, but he's got Intel digging into it." A fresh wave of tension churned in his gut. "I'm going to grab some ice for your head. Keep your eyes peeled."

Ted reached over and grabbed Nick's forearm, stopping him. "I messed up back in the store." He sucked his teeth, disgust stamped on his face. "Let that girl get the drop on me."

Ted had a perfect record, stellar reputation and was one

of the best to work with. Sure, he was about to retire, but he wasn't guilty of complacency.

"She was a professional," Nick said. "Looked perfectly harmless to me, too, and you were probably focused on the blonde as a possible threat."

The same way Nick had been focused on the brunette. Hell, he'd almost left the store to go after her, and if he had, Lori would be dead.

Ted grimaced. "Thanks for trying to make an old guy feel better, but I'll run in and get the ice. You stay with Lori. I couldn't live with myself if something else happened to her because of me. Don't let her out of your sight, kid."

At thirty-four, Nick was no more a *kid* than the assassin had been a *girl*, but Ted referred to anyone twenty years his junior as such. "All right. Two minutes, then we hit the road."

Ted gave a curt nod and climbed out.

Nick popped the trunk. "Give me a sec," he said to Lori as he opened his door, but she didn't acknowledge him with a glance.

He skirted around to the rear of the vehicle, grabbed the medical kit and slid into the back seat beside her.

She didn't look at him or shift his way or move an inch. Her blank stare stayed fixed outside the window, her limbs rigid with tension, a subtle tremble moving through her.

What he wouldn't give to make her stop shaking.

"Will Ted be okay?" Her gaze was still focused outside the window. "I feel awful that he was hurt because of me."

She was almost killed, twice, and here she was worried about Ted. Always showing concern for someone other than herself.

The more time he spent with Lori, the more he saw how she had a generous heart, one that he guessed had been hurt. He suspected it was the reason she was so guarded, but he admired her strength, too.

Tough as steel on the outside with a surprising vulnerability on the inside. An irresistible combination that had tempted him every waking hour in their close quarters.

Was the draw to her simply lust? Or something deeper, something more abiding?

The latter worried him senseless.

"Ted will be fine." He opened the med kit. "Is it okay for me to clean and bandage it?" He gestured to her throat.

She nodded.

Nick dabbed gauze doused with saline solution across the laceration.

Lori hissed, her pale face twisting in agony.

The last thing he wanted was to cause her more pain, but the wound needed to be cleaned. He applied triple antibiotic ointment to the raw wound and bandaged it.

"Hey, are you hanging in there?"

Another nod.

Ninety-five percent of the people the Marshal Services protected were some shade of criminal, endeavoring to evade prosecution by snitching on a bigger fish. That wasn't the case with Lori. She was a good person, a law-abiding accountant, no criminal history, who went to the FBI of her own free will. Most upstanding people didn't do that, believe it or not.

Turning state's evidence that qualified a person for WITSEC meant sacrificing everything. The vast majority weren't willing to accept a new identity without resources, credit or the promise of stability, all after being dumped in a strange environment. Their inclination was to look the other way instead.

While Lori's reward for doing the right thing by agreeing to testify against dangerous parasites was to risk her life, change her name, sacrifice her career, give up all her friends and accept a much lower standard of living. She didn't deserve any of this.

"Not much choice in the matter." She clenched her hands into fists, digging them into her thighs. "I refuse to roll over and give up."

Regardless of the horror and trauma of the past hour, she wasn't about to break. Her eyes were glassy from the strain. But beyond the tears there was determination. He could almost see her gathering her strength and he admired that about Lori.

She was a fighter. He'd seen her inner constitution during their hand-to-hand lessons.

No matter how many times he knocked her down or how hard she fell, she got back up. Sometimes winded and weary, but always with an easy grace, ready for more.

That took serious guts.

His mom had called her *incredible* in their weekly chats when he talked about Lori's compassion, her kindness, her courage—without mentioning her name or specific circumstances or anything to violate the rules.

"No. I wouldn't expect you to give up." Nick longed to touch her, as a man would a woman. Not as a marshal trying to put a witness at ease. He settled for setting his palm over her fist, and her fingers loosened instantly, taking his hand in hers. "But that doesn't mean what happened isn't overwhelming for you."

She wasn't a federal agent, hadn't grown up around a bunch of rough and rowdy bounty hunters, and had no self-defense training outside of what he'd provided.

This situation was bound to be tough for any civilian.

"I can't stop thinking about it," she said, her brow furrowed, "when all I want to do is push it from my mind."

His fingers itched to stroke away her worries.

When she'd asked to learn self-defense, he'd jumped at her request. Sure, he was eager to teach her skills he hoped she'd never need in her new life, but it was also a tad self-serving. All their physical contact, no matter how brief or slight, how accidental or deliberate, had only stoked his appetite for more.

"I don't think the garrote will leave a mark."

"The gar-what?"

"The garrote. What the assassin used to…" That woman had gotten so close to ending her life. Too damn close. And that was on him. "It'll take time to heal. On the inside as well as the outside." Temptation won, and he brushed his knuckles across her cheek. Satin didn't hold a candle to her skin. His breath grew shallow as she leaned into his touch. "But I'm here for you."

He wasn't exactly sure what he was trying to say, but he meant as more than a deputy marshal. He *liked* her. He *wanted* her so much that he ached, and he'd spent too much time wondering what it'd be like to kiss her. But staunch professionalism had always drawn a fine line in the sand, stopping him from doing anything they might both regret. That, and the ever-looming presence of Ted, if Nick was being one hundred percent honest.

Not that he should be thinking about that now, considering she was still in danger, but he couldn't help it with her sitting close enough for her warm breath to caress his cheek.

Averting her gaze, she put her palm on his thigh. "You mean, here for me for another day, anyway. Then you're off to your next assignment, next witness to protect, and before you know it, you'll have forgotten all about me."

Forgetting Lori would be like forgetting being struck by lightning. Totally impossible.

"No matter what happens after tomorrow," he said, cupping her cheek, and his heart pumped double-time, "never think you were just an assignment or a witness to me." *Because you're so much more.*

Her gaze lifted to his, and something sparked between them. Warm. Undeniable. Stronger than rapport. She wet her lips, and he was tempted to hold her in his arms the way he'd fantasized for months, reeling her flush against him, and kiss her.

Ted came out of the store with a bag of frozen vegetables pressed to his skull and headed for the car. Impeccable timing as usual.

"I'll never forget you, Lori. Never." Nick lowered his hand from her face. "When we get to the safe house, I can take a look at your feet."

She nodded. "Thank you, for everything."

Before Ted threw him a side-eye, Nick wasted no time switching seats back behind the steering wheel.

Ten minutes later they arrived at the safe house.

Rather than stow the car in the garage, he parked in the drive. Better to check the house and perimeter first, proceeding with caution like Draper advised and his gut insisted on.

"I'll do a sweep," Nick said. "Make sure it's all clear."

Ted scowled. "I'll take point."

Was he kidding?

Ted hadn't tossed his cookies or lost consciousness again, which were both bad signs with a head injury, but he had a tremble in his hand and wasn't quite steady on his feet.

Nick was all for tenacity—they needed it to get through these tough assignments—but pushing it was plain stupid. "You could have a concussion. What if you get lightheaded or pass out?"

"You're not leaving her side," Ted said, wagging a finger in Nick's face. "Got it, kid?"

"No, Ted. I don't *got it*. There comes a time when we have to acknowledge our limitations and concede. This is one of those times." Nick put his hand on Ted's shoulder. "It's no reflection on you or your record." He had admired Ted since he first started working at the San Diego office.

A lifer who hadn't grown soft or complacent, eager to help the newbies, lend an ear of support and offer good advice when solicited or not. Ted was like the caring, helpful uncle everyone wished they had. "You're not well. You need to stay off your feet. I'll clear the house."

Ted looked back at Lori like he was reluctant to speak in front of her.

She made it easier by looking out the window and pretending she wasn't privy to their conversation. A small consideration that spoke volumes about Lori's generosity, especially in light of what she'd been through. She had every right to chime in, shout her opinion, accuse Ted and Nick of falling short and failing her. But she didn't, always one to take the gracious, high road.

"I was with Hummingbird when that girl got close enough to almost—" he dropped his voice to a whisper "—kill her. Somehow, I didn't see it coming. That's on me." Ted shook his head, mouth pulled into a grim line. "I've got the feeling that this isn't over."

Nick had the same queasy sensation rolling in his stomach.

Black Rose hadn't shown herself again at the mall. But she was out there, somewhere, waiting for the opportune moment to strike.

Would that happen when Nick left Lori alone with Ted?

His partner was injured, less fit and capable now than he had been at the clothing store.

Nick wanted to clone himself into an army that he could rely on to keep Lori safe, but he didn't have that luxury. He had to work with what he had and stick next to Lori. No distractions, no being baited, no entertaining any other possibility.

"You need to stay by her side and make sure nothing else happens to her," Ted said.

His partner was well respected, senior and technically

in charge, but Nick could see it in his eyes—the need to get this right. No more mistakes.

Ted had made hard sacrifices over the years. His five tumultuous divorces were legendary. He wanted a committed, stable marriage and had tried multiple times to achieve it, and contested every dissolution, but this job demanded so much, sucked you dry. All he had left was his career and reputation.

Sure, it didn't keep a man warm at night, but he'd chosen to put duty first and accept the cost. Something all the deputies related to and commended.

To lose a witness was the one thing every marshal dreaded, but to have it happen on your last assignment would be a mark of shame none would be able to live with. Going down in infamy as *that* deputy marshal who'd lost someone in protective custody and becoming the focus of a lesson at the academy on what *not* to do.

No one wanted the torment of a tarnished legacy in their twilight years. It was all Ted had left.

"Got it," Nick said. "But if you start seeing stars, you let me know."

"Will do." Ted drew his weapon, switched off the safety and left the car.

As he jogged along the outskirts of the safe house, scanning the tree line of the surrounding woods, he did a quick perimeter sweep that must've made the old guy's head pound.

"All clear. Entering the house," Ted said over comms.

The security system gave thirty seconds for the code to be entered before sending an alert to district headquarters and the alarm sounded.

Nick stepped out of the car for a better vantage point, keeping his eyes peeled for any indication that the safe house had been compromised. He trained his gaze on the woods. Nothing beyond birds and squirrels stirred. No tingle down his spine like they were being watched.

"First floor, clear." Ted's voice was tight, strained. Through the open front door, Nick saw him cross the entranceway toward the stairs. "Heading to the second floor." A minute later he said, "Good to go. Cleared to bring Hummingbird inside."

Nick opened Lori's door and escorted her to the house. The crunch of the gravel in the driveway underfoot echoed in the stillness. He ushered her up the porch steps, inside and locked the reinforced steel door capable of withstanding a battering ram. The house was stuffy, warmer by about five degrees he estimated, but the smart thermostat was set for efficiency.

After a small adjustment, they could all take a breather and recover from the morning. Gain their bearings and assess everyone's physical condition. Lori needed painkillers and he had to examine Ted's head to see if stitches were necessary.

Nick had patched up a buddy or two in the field when he was in the army, a skill that had come in handy on more than one occasion, but he'd never treated a head injury before and wasn't qualified to try.

"Ted, what's your status?" Nick headed to the security system to arm it.

"Checking the crawl space in the attic. It's tight up here. And hot. But an ounce of prevention is worth a pound of cure."

This was why Ted was in charge, beyond seniority. The man might have a concussion, but he had the foresight and the fortitude to push through and check the attic. The assassins they were dealing with had proven to be resourceful and deceptive. On the off chance they had the location of the safe house, the attic would be a clever hiding spot.

Nick tapped in the code on the panel, activating the

security features of the house, from motion sensors that would alert them to anyone approaching, to video cameras giving them eyes for three hundred sixty degrees. If necessary, with the touch of a button, steel shutters would deploy, rolling down over the windows—a cheaper, more efficient alternative to bullet-resistant glass—turning the shelter into an impenetrable fortress.

Each safe house was designed to hold up under an attack and provide a secure environment where marshals could wait for reinforcements.

"Nick?" Lori asked, staring at the thermostat. Something curious in her voice tugged at him.

"Yeah." He turned, stepping up beside her.

"Look." She pointed to the Nest sensor.

He glanced at the round dial. Instead of the display showing the temperature, numbers were counting down. *Fourteen. Thirteen. Twelve.*

A raw, flaring pit opened in his chest as realization set in. The place was rigged to blow.

Chapter Four

Lori froze and blinked at the digital numbers on the thermostat rapidly counting down. The tiny hairs on the nape of her neck lifted. Her breath locked in her sore throat.

This couldn't be happening. One moment, the temperature had been displayed, showing seventy-four degrees. The next, Nick had set the alarm, and as she turned, she caught a flicker on the small screen from the corner of her eye.

Blind luck.

If she'd been standing at a different angle or two steps farther away, she would've missed it. But even now, her mind rejected what she was seeing.

Ten.

Her heart rate ticked up like a jackrabbit's.

Nine.

Oh, God. What was going to happen once the dial reached one?

A current of horror and dread surged through her, electrifying her.

Nick grabbed her by the elbow and hustled toward the front door. At the same time, he touched his earpiece. "Ted, get out of the house. Now. There's a bomb!"

His last word confirmed her worst fear. Echoed through her head on repeat.

Bomb. Bomb. Bomb.

A rush of dark energy overrode stark terror, blistering

across her nerves. Her feet moved faster than her thoughts. Not that there was time to think or barely breathe.

Nick flung the front door open. A deafening alarm blared.

They were across the threshold in a heartbeat and burst out into the glare of sunshine. White lights mounted around the house that would've been blinding at night flashed at a frenetic pace.

Heart racing, she held on to Nick's arm, her fingers digging into him as they ran as hard and as fast as possible down the porch stairs.

She tried to estimate where the timer was by now. How many seconds were left?

Whatever the answer, they needed more.

Her pulse throbbed in her throat. Everything was happening at warp speed. But it was as if her limbs moved in slo-mo, not carrying her away quickly enough.

How big would the blast radius be? Would they be in it?

They were at a breakneck sprint the instant they touched the lawn.

Still, they needed to be faster.

She glanced over her shoulder. No sign of Ted. Had he made it out of the attic, much less the house?

The ground shook and a searing clap blew out the windows in a shower of glass, spraying wood shrapnel followed by a roaring ball of flame. The force of the blast sent them hurtling forward off their feet.

Nick threw his arms around Lori in midair, using his body as cover. They both went down, the hilt of his gun jabbing into her ribs. A wave of hurt consumed her.

They'd landed with him taking the brunt of the fall and most of her weight on him. Her head would've slammed into the ground, but he'd tucked her skull against his chest, protecting her face with his hands when they hit the grass.

Nick rolled, blanketing her. His strong, muscular body

was as taut as a shield. She inhaled a relieved breath. They were alive. Barely. But they were both breathing.

For a dizzying moment she clung to him, her fingers gripping him so tightly she wasn't sure if she'd be able to let go. Lori's ears rang and her scrambled brain swam in a haze. Heat bore down on them, but her body was cold, skin clammy. She ached all over like she'd been slam-dunked by a bulldozer.

Agony rocked through every muscle, every cell.

Singed, smoldering debris rained on the lawn. Nick scooted upright, hauling her along with him. She was so shell-shocked the prospect of moving seemed unfathomable, but he yanked her from the grass in a sharp, urgent tug she couldn't resist until she was in a sitting position. He moved with such fluid quickness as if the explosion hadn't left him dazed in the slightest.

She sat, trying to gain her bearings. Her bones had been jarred by the blast. It was a wonder none were broken, but there was the sting of scrapes and scalding bruises.

Nick was on his feet, weapon drawn, scanning their surroundings in the same blink of time that Lori managed another cough and pressed a hand to her splitting head.

She braced for a squad of hit men to come storming out of the tree line any second.

When none did, Nick touched his earpiece. "Ted! Ted! Talk to me."

The sensation of the world rocking on a seesaw was subsiding, leaving Lori to deal with the pounding in her brain. She struggled to her hands and knees, finding the strength to stand.

Brushing hair from her face, she stared at the safe house, now engulfed in flames. Fire licked out of the broken windows, racing up the sides, tearing through holes in the roof. Black plumes billowed in the air. The roar of the blaze filled her ears.

Nothing could've survived that. Nothing and no one. It would've been impossible for him to have gotten down from the attic, climbed a flight of stairs and made it out of the house.

He'd been on the cusp of retirement about to start the next chapter of long, lazy days, fishing and drinking. Poor Ted.

Desperation elbowed aside her sorrow, putting her own predicament front and center.

"Ted!" Nick charged toward the house as if he intended to run inside and search for his partner.

A secondary explosion forced his feet to a sudden halt and his arm up, shielding his face. Lori's stomach dropped as she turned away from the blast, stumbling backward.

It must've been the propane tank at the rear of the house blowing.

Her feet froze, her legs trembled, helplessness swallowing her.

Nick ripped out his earpiece and let it drop to the grass. He stood there, daunted and gaping, looking as horrified and hollowed out as she felt.

Not once in the year she'd known him had he ever let raw emotion spill across his face. Every gesture, every expression, had always seemed so controlled, almost calculated. Like he never dared loosen the rein on his composure.

He hung his head a moment, shook it and then flipped right back into protector mode.

Turning to her, his face now inscrutable, he checked her over. "Are you okay?" His hands made quick work of patting her face and arms as he searched for any apparent injuries. "The shock wave from the blast could've caused internal damage," he said in a cold, detached tone. "Lori, are you okay?"

Aside from the fact that she'd almost been murdered three times in one day and it wasn't even noon… Aside from the fact their *safe house* was now a raging inferno, that everything was hanging in the balance—her life, her future, the prospect of growing old, all the things people took for granted every day like breathing... To boot, this nightmare was her own doing, and she kept making poor choices that turned a bad situation into an epic disaster. She had not only jeopardized her own life and Nick's, but also had gotten Ted killed. Now the only man left to protect her had hit the disconnect button and she cared more about whether or not he was all right than herself...

Other than that, she was just peachy.

"Nick, my God. Ted..." She wasn't quite sure what to say. Were there any right words in this situation? She swallowed past the lump forming in her throat as he stared at her, his face a hardened mask. "I'm sorry. He was a good man and didn't deserve..." She stepped closer, hoping the frost in his eyes might thaw. "Are *you* all right?"

Lori put a palm to his chest, and it was as if the gentle contact flipped a switch inside him. The ice in his eyes liquefied into a dark, molten fury that sharpened the angles of his face. His features contorted into something monstrous and murderous, his jaw tightening. His hands clenched. His bearing held all the menace of a junkyard dog ready to tear into someone.

The hair-trigger shift in him terrified her.

"Whoever is doing this, whoever blew Ted to smithereens... I'm going to rip them apart limb by limb." He spoke with unmitigated gravity that left her speechless. "They're going to keep coming. Let them. Because they have messed with the wrong marshal. No matter what it takes, even if it costs my own life, I'm going to kill every last one of them."

PERPLEXED WAS A DECENT word to describe how Aiden Yazzie felt.

Watching Will Draper strut around like this was any

other day, pretending that their office wasn't caught up in a CAT-5 crapstorm, left Aiden utterly baffled.

This wasn't about whether Draper was a good man or a bad man. Most people were a bit of both. This wasn't even about if he was making the right choices or the wrong ones. Everyone made mistakes.

Aiden wanted to know if the boss gave a damn.

Beyond how it affected his career. Draper was a fast burner with serious ambitions, but there was something about him that Aiden couldn't put his finger on.

Everyone had their way of dealing with things. Aiden glanced across his desk to his partner and best friend without benefits, Charlie. She ran around wearing armor made of ice, acting as if the only thing that mattered was the job and kicking butt. He was all in favor of being a fearless female, but even Wonder Woman wasn't afraid to love.

Aiden took after his dad. Still waters ran deep, and on the surface he usually wore an easy smile unless he was ticked off. Or perplexed.

He turned back to the break room. Draper filled his mug with coffee and walked back to his office with his sunshine-and-rainbows swagger.

Not to hate on pretenses, but that nonchalance was totally unsettling.

Granted, Aiden and Charlie had the scoop on what was happening with Nick and the attack at the mall. The worker bees at Intel couldn't help but buzz whenever something went wrong. Pretty hard to ignore the drone of disaster.

"We need to make our move now," Charlie said, "before they do." She gestured across the office to the only other SOG—Special Operations Group—members in their district.

For this type of dire situation, Draper needed to send deputies certified as elite tactical operators. Most SOG members worked full-time assigned to US Marshals Service's offices throughout the country and remained on call twenty-four hours a day for high-priority SOG missions. Only toughies made of steel endured the grueling training designed to weed out everyone except the best of the best—not that he was tooting his own horn. Okay, maybe he was just a little. Once they passed, it still took someone highly disciplined to make a commitment to respond to an emergency at the drop of a hat.

The list of potentials for Draper to choose from was short.

"Come on, before Tweedledee and Tweedledum beat us to it," Charlie said, always hungry for action and keen to shoot something.

They didn't let their skills get rusty, training four days a week—Krav Maga, long runs, practice at the range—but there was nothing like the zing of a real-world scenario.

Still, a part of Aiden couldn't help but wonder if her eagerness was a sign that she had unresolved issues with Nick.

Why did she have to mess around with someone from the office?

Especially Mr. Dark and Stormy, who had that carved-in-stone jaw.

Eck! Aiden shook it off and pulled on a grin. "Let's make it happen."

They raised their knuckles for a fist bump and then touched their wrists together in unity.

Spinning out of his seat, Aiden was on Charlie's heels.

By the time Tweedledee and Tweedledum caught sight of them, Charlie was knocking on the boss's door.

"Come in," Draper said.

"You snooze, you lose," mouthed Aiden.

Tweedledum threw him the bird.

Aiden blew him a kiss and gave him an *up yours* arm gesture.

"Hey, boss," Charlie said, leaning against one of the chairs in front of his desk and folding her arms.

Aiden closed the door and turned. He dragged his gaze up Charlie's svelte figure, appreciating the sight of muscle where there should be muscle and softness where there should be softness. It was a wonder Yazzie was able to work around her without getting sidetracked and a tragedy he was firmly planted in the friend zone—*without benefits*.

Cursing Nick in his mind, he stepped up beside Charlie.

"We heard McKenna and Zeeman ran into some trouble," she said. "Are you planning to send backup?"

Draper stared into those intelligent, sharp blue eyes of hers, playing his cards close to the vest, wearing his usual *everything's fine* expression. "What did you hear?" he asked, neither confirming nor denying anything.

Baffling. "Assassination attempt on Hummingbird at the mall."

Draper shifted his gaze to Aiden. "Word spreads fast. I'll have to rectify that."

In all fairness, it didn't spread so much as it was harvested. Most of the office was still clueless. Take Tweedledee and Tweedledum, for example.

"Everything regarding Hummingbird is need-to-know. Who told you about what happened to McKenna and Zeeman?" Draper asked, his gray eyes narrowing.

She flashed that trademark, megawatt smile that was pure Charlie Killinger and ran her fingers back through her sunny-blond hair cut in an angled bob. "I have my sources and my ways of squeezing information from a person."

"I'm sure you do," Draper said, "but I'm afraid I'm going to need you to be more specific."

Her smile evaporated, mouth flattening into a frosty expression. "Intel is in a frenzy. It's clear something happened."

"We both nosed around," Aiden said, tagging in. "Heard McKenna and Zeeman were attacked and are going to need backup. This *is* need-to-know for SOG personnel."

"Then why don't I have all my SOG personnel in my office right now?"

Charlie tilted her head to the side. "Because we're smarter, sharper and better looking."

Aiden couldn't disagree on that point and threw in a nod for good measure.

It only seemed to irritate Draper based on the sour look that slithered across his face.

"Yazzie and I want in," Charlie said.

"No surprise there." Draper drew in a deep breath, slipping his composed mask back on. "Are you sure you can handle supporting McKenna?" he asked Charlie.

She stiffened, those sapphire eyes turning to slits. "What's that supposed to mean?"

Did she really want Draper to spell it out? Not even Aiden wanted the debacle rehashed.

"You and McKenna had a thing last year," Draper said. "He broke it off. You weren't too happy about it from what I've heard."

With a wave, she dismissed the assessment. "I mean no disrespect when I say this, sir, but any issues between Nick and me is our business."

And Aiden's, unfortunately. It had been this weird lover-lover-best-friend triangle. Aiden had had to hear about it from both sides. He'd played it cool and acted neutral, offering nuggets of advice that made his gut burn with jealousy.

And the kicker?

Neither of them had listened to a word he'd said.

"That's a load of hogwash," Draper said. "It became my business when McKenna got into a fight with another deputy over you, which I'm told you instigated. The issues between you two went from private to public with the incident."

That fight had caused long-term waves in the office

that'd persisted after Draper had exiled Nick to no-man's-land for the use of excessive force.

Charlie scoffed. "Fine, let's clear the air and get on the same page. First—" she raised a finger "—Nick did break things off with me, but I was peeved because he beat me to the punch. I'm the one who pulls the plug on a fling. Not the other way around. Second—" another finger lifted "—I never instigate fights, but I'm more than happy to end them with words, and when that doesn't cut the mustard, I'll use my fist." Charlie stared at him straight in the eyes. "And third, I never allow anything in my personal life to get in the way of doing my job. Not ever. Sir," she snapped.

Aiden elbowed her. "You forgot one," he said to her in Navajo.

Fewer than a million people still spoke the language of his people and it was mostly only heard on a reservation. Charlie had taken an interest in learning when she'd accompanied him back home for his mom's funeral. Came in handy.

"What did she forget to add?" Draper asked, making it clear that he was no slouch and understood.

Aiden raised his brows and gave a nod that he was impressed. Because, come on, that was impressive and made Aiden even more leery of the dude.

"I'm quick on the uptake," Draper said, patting his own back, exuding that *me me me* attitude. "At previous offices I picked up a little Spanish, Russian and French. Call me paranoid, but I want to know what someone is saying in my presence."

Yeah, that did sound paranoid.

"She neglected to mention that Deputy Douche," Aiden said, refusing to sully his mouth saying the dude's name, "was talking smack about Charlie to Nick. She can screw who she likes and if she was a guy, that idiot never would've called her those foul things."

Tease. Whore. Slut. Aiden had made certain that every ugly, disgusting word had been documented in their statements. The other deputies had sided with Nick, Charlie and Aiden, and took to calling Jeff Snyder "Douche." Including the Tweedle duo.

After six months of constant disrespect, Jeff "Douche" Snyder transferred.

Good riddance, if you asked Aiden. There was no room for troublemakers on the team.

Aiden clenched his fingers to fists. "If Nick hadn't broken his jaw, I would've."

"I take it you would've broken his jaw, too?" Draper asked Charlie.

"Meh." She made a noncommittal sound and gave a one-shoulder shrug. "Sticks and stones. Right?"

"Okay. Fine." Draper raised his palms. "I take it you two aren't going to back down or back off until you get the assignment."

They nodded in unison.

"One question, sir," Aiden said. "How was Hummingbird's location compromised? Did the witness violate protocol?"

Draper squirmed in his seat, caught himself and stiffened. There was still a disturbing lack of consternation on his face. "We're not sure how the breach happened. It'll take Intel time to dig, unravel the knot of involvement and track any leads to figure out how we were compromised."

How an assassin had found their witness in the dang mall.

"You'll provide support," Draper said. "Zeeman is on his last leg, counting down the minutes to retirement of long, lazy days in the Key West sunshine. He's highly decorated, but short-termer-itis is real. Gear up, then head to Big Bear Lake and escort Hummingbird back to San Diego."

Charlie and Aiden exchanged confused glances. "Why are they way up at Big Bear?" she asked.

That was in the mountains. Hours away.

"I decided to use the LA office's remote safe house at Big Bear to keep Hummingbird as far away from San Diego as possible while awaiting the trial. Yes, it's an outside-the-box move. But I thought it the best way to ensure her safety. And," he said, straightening his tie, "Jack Foy himself commended and endorsed the idea."

Golly gee. The US Attorney for the Southern District of California himself.

Did Draper get tendinitis in his elbow from patting his own back so much?

"I'm going to call local police, or rather the sheriff's department," Draper said. "Have them send a car to the safe house and stay put until—"

Lynn Jacobs, Draper's assistant, hurried into the office without knocking, cutting him off. "Sir." Worry lines creased her middle-aged face and her watery, brown eyes were wide with shock or fear. "Nick is on the phone. There's been another incident."

Chapter Five

"We lost Ted. The safe house was wired with explosives. He was in the attic and didn't have a chance to get out. He's dead," Nick said in a rush, as soon as Draper had gotten on the phone. He had to get through it as quickly as possible. Ended up stringing the words so close together they sounded like one run-on sentence.

He prayed his boss wouldn't ask him to repeat it.

"What? Are you saying the safe house was compromised, too? Ted... Ted Zeeman was killed?" Draper's voice grew more and more agitated with each question, and the underlying shock in his tone was to be expected.

Nick hadn't had a chance to process it, either. He gritted his teeth, still beating himself up for letting it happen.

Not that he saw how he could've prevented it. Unless Nick had gone into the house first and cleared it. Then he might be the one dead and Lori left virtually defenseless.

He took the resurgence of sorrow and regret, stuffed it in a locked box and tossed away the key. Reflecting on it, hell, relaying the details to his boss, conjured feelings Nick couldn't handle. Not if he was going to focus on Lori and keep her safe.

Nick needed to be impervious and driven. Getting bogged down by anything else wasn't a luxury he had.

The prosecution's hard evidence had disappeared bit by bit or fallen apart. Two other witnesses had flipped, and Lori was all they had left. Her testimony alone was enough evidence and would be the nail in the proverbial coffin of WCM.

Justice would be served one way or another, but in order for that to happen, Lori had to stay alive.

"Yes, sir. That's exactly what I'm saying."

"What about Hummingbird? Is she—"

"Alive. Scared and a little banged up. But breathing."

"Well, thank the Lord for that." Draper's relief was palpable over the phone. "But how, damn it? How did that happen?"

Excellent question. "I was hoping you'd have some answers for me by now on that."

"I wish I did. But I'm in the dark here as much as you. I have intel on it, scrubbing everything. It's complicated with the LA office's involvement, but our analysts will turn up something."

Eventually, they would. "But will it be in time to prevent another attack on Hummingbird's life?"

"Whoever set the bomb might believe Hummingbird was killed. Why would you expect another attack?"

Experience. His gut. Everything inside him screamed this wasn't over. Not by a long shot. "I have to anticipate anything at this point, sir. The bomber might've been hiding in the woods, watching for firsthand confirmation. We have to assume they know she's alive and will try again."

Draper heaved a breath like he agreed, reluctantly. "Okay. Where are you now?"

Nick hesitated, suddenly uncertain how to respond. He wasn't exactly in a hurry to invite more danger to their current location.

Draper had made the decision to put Lori in a safe house in a remote location, hours away from the support of their own office. A site that required sharing her whereabouts with the LA station. They'd been required to submit twice-daily reports, detailing everything down to Lori's mood and what she ate. Draper had approved the trip to the mall, knew the specifics of what entrance they'd use, which store Lori had planned to shop in and at precisely what time she'd be there. To make an ugly situation downright insane, Draper had sanctioned them to return to the safe house.

It was true that at first Nick had been bitter and, truth be told, furious with his boss over serving a yearlong sentence. But if he hadn't been banished to Big Bear Lake, he never would've gotten to know Lori.

Hell, who was he kidding? He never would've fallen hard for her. Something he couldn't construe as a punishment.

The grudge Nick held was long gone and had nothing to do with his current doubts about his boss. Without concrete proof that explained exactly how they'd been compromised, the compass needle was starting to point to Draper.

"Sir, maybe I shouldn't say. With everything that's already happened, it might be best to restrict any further details regarding Hummingbird."

"That's not your call to make, McKenna. I have a responsibility, an obligation to keep Hummingbird safe. If you take this course of action and deny me the ability to send backup, then you're endangering her and this case. God forbid something else were to happen, the blame would rest squarely on your shoulders. Not to mention, the US attorney's office might feel inclined to bill you for the wasted man hours."

Nick didn't care about taking the blame or being billed. If they fired him, he'd go work with his family. And if the US attorney's office was stupid enough to bill him, well, they couldn't get blood from a turnip, so good luck with that.

The point that stuck in his craw was that Nick would essentially be tying Draper's hands with regards to sending reinforcements. Something Nick unequivocally needed based on the morning's events.

"All right, I'll tell you where we are." Some techie in the office was probably tracking Nick's phone for a geo-location as they spoke, anyway. "But sir, I need to speak frankly. If any other hit men come calling, I've got to go dark." Ditch any means for them to track him and end all communication. No more updates on their location. "And find a way to bring Hummingbird in under the radar for the trial. I won't have any other choice."

"Watch your tone with me," Draper warned.

Nick had let his frustration tip toward anger and get the better of him. Lost the capacity for a quiet, civil tone some-where between explaining his partner had been killed and trying to figure out if Draper had a hand in this somehow. He wanted to yell and smash things. He wanted to make the bastards responsible hurt and bleed.

Worrying about whether he'd ticked off Draper with his tone wasn't high on his list of concerns.

"Since you're such a fan of candor," Draper said, "I've got some for you, too. That's not your decision to make!" A string of curses followed. "You are not authorized to go dark. End of discussion. Now, I have two SOG operators sitting in my office at this very moment, ready, willing and able to assist you."

Tamping down the urge to punch the wall, Nick said, "We're just off State Road 38." He looked around the vet-erinary clinic.

His eyes glazed over the chairs in the empty waiting room, the displays of odor-masking candles and vitamin-enhanced treats that were for sale. The place was a glori-fied pet hotel.

Many of the upscale cabins and resorts around Big Bear Lake didn't allow pets, and folks wanted to board their furry, four-legged friends close by.

With no appointments on the books, it didn't take much to get the owner to close up shop while she tended to them. A flash of his badge. A vague explanation. Throwing out keywords such as *matter of life or death* and *discretion appreciated* did the trick. At his insistence, the owner had dismissed her two-person staff, lowered the storefront security gate—necessary for keeping local meth heads from breaking in at night and stealing drugs—and locked the doors.

"At Happy Paws and Wagging Tails," Nick said.

"What in the hell?" Disbelief sliced through his boss's voice. "Repeat that. Did you say you're harboring the US attorney's star witness at a damn veterinary clinic?"

"You heard me. Hummingbird had some injuries from the explosion, nothing critical, but I wanted her checked for internal damage to be on the safe side. I think you were right to steer us away from the local hospital." One good thing, but Draper's list of pros in this was woefully lacking. His credentials and reputation were solid, but something about this was thirteen shades of wrong. "Between the security surveillance cameras and their requirement to log the identity of all patients, we might be sitting ducks at the hospital. The owner here, Renee Holmes, hasn't asked for any identification and my badge has kept her questions to a minimum. Besides, this is the last place someone would look for Hummingbird."

At least, he hoped it was.

The safe house had been ablaze. Surely, the smoke had been seen for miles. He'd made a split-second decision to leave the scene. If someone had been in the woods, standing around waiting for first responders didn't seem like the wisest idea. He needed the most unlikely place where he could get Lori medical attention, and this was it.

"Nick, you've had a pretty intense morning, especially with losing Ted. It's good you're keeping your head and thinking clearly. Hummingbird needs you now, more than ever. Let the owner of Happy Tails, Ms. Renee Holmes, know that the US Marshals will compensate her for her services and that we appreciate her assistance. I want you to stay put. I'm going to notify the sheriff's department and have them send someone to your location."

"Please, don't do that, sir." Nick scrubbed a palm over his brow, struggling not to lose the little cool he'd regained as his thoughts raced. "I know that's a by-the-book decision and normally I'd be all for it, but too many people know about Hummingbird as is. We don't need to lengthen the list."

Besides, surely Black Rose was smart enough to monitor police channels. Zero in on a vague call to provide assistance to a deputy marshal. Even the use of something less transparent like a *federal agent* would draw the enemy's attention. Might as well broadcast the details about the witness in protective custody while they were at it.

Draper hemmed and hawed for a moment. "I see your point. Ordinarily, deviating from protocol is ill-advised, but I agree that an exception needs to be made considering the circumstances. Yazzie and Killinger are in my office now. You've been on speaker."

Nice of him to say something as an afterthought. Would've been great if he had mentioned it ten minutes ago when Draper had answered the phone. It was probably for the best to have others privy to both sides of the conversation. A lot had been discussed, an atypical course of action chosen and concerns expressed.

It was surprising to Nick that Draper had been willing to be so transparent with anyone else in the office. Then again, Nick had been at a severe disadvantage not knowing there had been eavesdroppers the entire time.

Damn. He tried to recall everything he'd said. Could anything be used against him later if things went from sideways to totally off the rails?

For the life of him, he drew a blank about most of it. But he'd been dead serious about going dark if necessary. As a last resort only.

"Hey, Nick." A smoky, feminine voice came over the line, the tone chummy-chummy.

Charlie.

"We've got your back, bro," Aiden said. "Hang in there, we're coming." Sincerity rang through loud and clear as a bell.

Some things never changed. After the hellish day he'd had, it was Aiden who had shown more concern than Charlie. Surprise, surprise.

"They're going to suit up in tactical gear and head your way," Draper said.

Charlie's ice-queen disposition and Nick's quick temper were the reasons he was in this situation to begin with. He was no longer upset with her for not being able to connect in a relationship beyond the physical. And even between the sheets, something had been missing. Yeah, it'd been hot sex, really hot, but there'd been no intimacy. Like she kept her guard up even while screwing.

He'd thought the mention of her name, hearing her voice, would raise a bunch of messy, conflicted emotions, but maybe time did heal all wounds. He felt absolutely nothing besides relief. Charlie and Aiden were both formidable, the epitome of warriors, and he couldn't name anybody else from the office he'd rather have at his side at a time like this.

"And I'm going to request to have a full SOG unit at the courthouse tomorrow," Draper said. "In the meantime, catch your breath and rest up if you can."

"Got it," Nick said. "We'll be waiting."

Draper disconnected and Nick put his phone away in his pocket.

He went to the bathroom, splashed cold water on his face, and stared in the mirror.

Crap. He looked like canned dog food warmed over—

felt like it, too. What he wouldn't give for a stiff drink to take the edge off.

Nick dried his face with paper towels and went to check on Lori in the back. Most of the dogs in the nearby kennels that were stacked along the wall responded to his presence. Some barked and yipped. A few panted and wagged their tails. Others simply stared at him.

Passing the cages, he spotted the open door to exam room two. Lori was right where he'd left her, sitting on a steel table.

This time, the body armor that had *US Marshals Service* written across the front had been discarded in a chair, her neck properly bandaged, and her scrapes and bruises had been treated and dressed down to her feet.

"Twenty-eight is pretty young to have your own veterinary clinic," Lori said.

"Technically, the place isn't mine. It belongs to Dr. Nguyen. I started interning when I was sixteen. When I finished my residency here, he just stopped coming in and let me take over. He spends all his time up at the lake now."

Nick stepped into the doorway.

"All done patching her up," Dr. Holmes said. "She doesn't have any broken bones, no internal injuries and no concussion."

Lori glanced up at him. The same wariness that had shone in her eyes when he'd ranted and raved like a complete psychopath about tearing people apart limb by limb was still there.

He'd let the darkest, ugliest part of himself show. A side few outside of his family had seen and lived to talk about. His gut churned at what she must think of him.

Lori lowered her eyes and wrung her hands.

"She's lucky," Nick said, "considering what we've been through."

Dr. Holmes sent him a sad smile. "Although I'm not

privy to the specifics, I gather it's a doozy. Would you like me to examine you, as well?"

"You've been so kind, Dr. Holmes. I wouldn't want to impose further and put you through the trouble."

"It's Renee, and it's no trouble in the slightest. I don't mind. Not every day I get human patients, you know."

"Thank you, but…" Nick shook his head. "Do you mind if we stay here a few hours?"

"Would I have to keep the clinic closed?"

"Yes. You would."

"What's a few hours?" Renee asked.

"Two to three. I have backup coming, tactical certified marshals, but they're on their way from San Diego. I know it's a big inconvenience. The Marshals Service will compensate you for your time."

"Money isn't the issue. I have to say this, otherwise, I'll kick myself later if I don't," Renee said. "I get the impression you two are running from something. I know this isn't my lane of expertise, but why don't you call the local authorities to help you?" Healthy suspicion crossed her face. "Wait for your friends to arrive at the sheriff's department instead of here. Unless whatever you're doing isn't legal."

The question and her supposition were both legitimate. Guess it was only a matter of time before he had to give her some real answers.

"I'm being hunted," Lori said.

Renee reeled back in surprise.

"I'm the material witness for an important case. There are a lot of people who don't want me to testify."

"Oh, hon." Renee clasped her shoulder, gave it a sympathetic squeeze and lowered her hand. "With you being a deputy marshal and the two of you showing up looking like you'd just been through World War Three, I figured it was something like that. But it doesn't really answer my question." She gave Nick a pointed look.

"No, it doesn't. My office was breached. Compromised somehow. At this point, the more people who know about her," Nick said, gesturing to Lori, "and her whereabouts, the harder it'll be to protect her. I don't know the sheriff around here or if he's got any crooked deputies in his office who might be willing to sell information. The people chasing her would pay a lot to get their hands on her."

"She. Not he. The sheriff is my mother and I know the three deputies that work for her. We grew up together. One of them is my cousin. They are honorable, good, trustworthy people. I'm talking salt of the earth. They'll help protect her until your tactical reinforcements arrive. I can't stay closed for three hours. One of the deputies will pass by in that time span and know something is wrong. So either you let me call my mom and ask her to come discreetly, no details over the phone, and you two can work it out in person, or you have to find someplace else to lay low until your friends show up."

Why couldn't anything be simple? "Do you mind giving us a moment?"

"Not at all." Renee tossed bloodied gauze in the trash and washed her hands. "I'll give you two some space to talk and decide. It's treat time for my buddies, anyway." The doctor went to shut the door.

"Please leave it open," Nick said. "Thank you."

He trusted the doctor. Sort of. She was a good-natured woman who only seemed to care about helping animals and people, but he'd prefer to know what the doctor was up to while they were in the clinic. So many unforeseen things had happened.

Renee nodded and left them alone.

Nick ducked his head into the hallway. Dr. Holmes grabbed a container of treats and went straight to the cages. All the dogs got excited, wagging their tails and jumping up on the metal doors.

Satisfied the doctor wasn't up to anything nefarious, he turned back to Lori.

Her coffee-colored eyes met his. Familiar desire to draw nearer and comfort her squeezed his chest, driving his feet toward her.

She hugged herself, hands gripping her elbows like she was afraid of him getting too close.

A wall seemed to lift between them. The one that had taken her months to lower before she had relaxed around him, started smiling, tossing out jokes, letting her humor and warmth shine. Gifting him with the pleasure of her laughter. There was no sweeter sound.

Nick stood still, hating himself for the way he'd lost control in front of her.

"What are we going to do?" Lori asked, averting her gaze.

"The idea of involving another office in this doesn't sit well with me. It could open a whole new can of worms. But if the sheriff and her deputies are truly as Renee described," he said, knowing they sounded a little too good to be true, "and her mother is willing to keep quiet about your presence, then we'd be ten times safer there than sitting at a restaurant."

"Okay. Whatever you think is best." She wrung her hands again and opened her mouth to say something else. A tense, silent moment passed, and she pressed her lips shut.

"Lori," he said, thankful that with the enthusiastic yelps in the other room the doctor couldn't overhear their conversation even though the door was open. "I'm sorry if I scared you out there with the things I said." He looked down at his field boots for a moment and then back up at her. "I was furious, and I spoke without thinking. I just want to reassure you that you're safe with me." When she didn't respond, he added, "I'll let Renee know our decision and leave you alone." He edged toward the door, his hands tightening at his sides.

"Nick, wait."

Chapter Six

"I don't want to be alone," Lori said.

As much as Nick wanted to believe that, her body language said otherwise. "Clearly, I'm making you uncomfortable."

"You did scare me out there. Seeing that side of you." She dropped her arms and scrubbed her palms on her thighs. "But I'm not afraid of you and you're not making me uncomfortable."

He gritted his teeth at that guarded glint in her eyes. "I can tell just by being in the same room that I'm making you uneasy. You have every right to be after my outburst. I don't blame you. I'm sorry you had to see me like that." *Completely unglued. Way to show self-control.*

"I wanted to talk to you about everything. What you said out there. I was nervous because I didn't know how to bring it up without you feeling judged and that's the last thing I want."

He slipped his hands in his pockets. "Look, you're fighting for your life. Judgment is natural. The dark place I have to go to sometimes is a hazard of the trade, but you shouldn't have to worry about the person assigned to protect you." *And whether I'm a raging lunatic who is two seconds away from snapping.* "I lost it out there. Said stuff that shouldn't have been said. It was unprofessional."

"I'm glad you voiced your thoughts. Relieved you

brought it up first. The men that have been in my life have tended to hide who they really are until I'm in deep and then they sprang their inner monster on me. I've been on that nauseating merry-go-round so many times I've come to expect it. But that's not what I want." She slid down from the table to her bare feet that'd been bandaged and winced, staying an arm's reach away. "You hold back so much of yourself with me sometimes, but I knew there was more to you than what you were showing me. I'd rather see it all up front. Even the parts that might terrify me. So don't hold anything back. At least that way I know who and what I'm really dealing with."

She was asking for honesty. Something he could handle. Something he could give.

He closed the distance between them. On impulse, he took her hand, then thought better of it and let go. "Leaving the army wasn't my choice. I was discharged, honorably only because my commanding officer saw fit to show me leniency. I killed an enemy combatant in custody."

Lori gripped the steel table behind her but didn't look away from him. "Was it an accident?" Her tone was quiet, gentle.

This was what he'd wanted from Charlie and she'd been unable to give. Care and concern as she showed genuine interest in him, asking the tough questions.

Now that he was getting it from Lori, he wasn't sure he liked it. No telling how she'd respond once she heard the answer.

"No. Not an accident." Didn't get more deliberate than what he'd done. "It wasn't premeditated, but JAG would've had legitimate cause to charge me with manslaughter, if not for my CO's intervention. The prisoner was trying to escape and while doing so, he murdered several people. One was this young contractor who'd worked in the kitchen. She was pregnant and scheduled to be sent back home in a week. But she was in the wrong place at the wrong time. When I caught him, I was enraged." Nick hesitated, deliberating whether to stop there or let her know precisely what he was capable of. "I bashed his skull in, against a brick wall." Saying the words aloud sounded just as horrific as his memory of that night.

Sharing it with her, he never felt more vulnerable than at that moment.

He took a deep breath, still ashamed of his actions, embracing the familiar pain and disappointment that flowed whenever he thought about it.

Deep down, Nick believed in justice. It was the reason he became a marshal. The balance of the scales and making the punishment fit the crime. What he'd done in Afghanistan had been a frenzied act of vengeance.

Sometimes the lines blurred. Sometimes he went too far. Sometimes he wondered, at his core, if he was a good man who did bad things for the right reason, or if he was simply rotten.

Watching Lori, he waited for the look of disgust to cross her face. Waited for the rejection.

It didn't come.

Maybe Lori's heart was so big and generous that she excused his eruption at the safe house and his confession surrounding his discharge from the army, but there was more.

Three strikes and she'd have to wash her hands of him. Accept that his inner monster was beyond redemption.

"I was given this assignment to protect you as a punishment. My boss, Draper, wanted to remove me from the home office because I got into a fight with another deputy and used excessive force. I broke his jaw. He had to have it wired and was in a lot of pain for a long time."

Sufficient time for that jerk to reflect and regret the things that he had said. Hopefully, he'd never talk about another colleague in the same disrespectful manner that he had used with Charlie.

Still, Nick had crossed the line. He owned that and took responsibility for his actions.

"The deputy, whose jaw you broke. Did he deserve it?" she asked.

Hell, yeah. "I should've used my head, not let emotion get the better of me, and shown more self-control."

She released the table and shifted closer. "In Afghanistan, your commanding officer protected you. Not only from being brought up on charges, but also from being given a dishonorable discharge."

He shrugged. "I got lucky. That's all." Different leadership could've led to a different outcome. One with him in an orange jumpsuit at Fort Leavenworth.

"Draper didn't fire you or suspend you for a reason, and it wasn't luck. This case I'm supposed to testify in is big."

Huge. *Major.* US Attorney Foy planned to use the win as a platform to run for governor.

"Yet, they put my life in your hands." She stroked a finger between his eyebrows as if to smooth out the worry line, and caressed his cheek. "What I saw in you at the safe house, the aggression, the thirst for violence, that's precisely what's going to give me the best chance to survive. Don't ever apologize for being who you are. I'm still breathing because of you."

Those words hit him dead center, healing something inside him that he hadn't realized was broken. She didn't see him as a monster. Lori wasn't afraid of him.

The weight of shame lifted, leaving him lighter. Liberated.

No woman had ever seen that side of him and understood it for what it was, trusted he'd never turn that darkness on her. Shown him affection in return. Lori was the first.

Forget professionalism and protocol. Overlook the fact

that she was a witness, an assignment. Lori tempted him like no other.

Right or wrong, he wanted her with an aching need that was wearing down his restraint.

She reached for his hand, drew it to her chest and held it in place. The gesture wasn't provocative but intimate, deepening the connection between them. Her gaze flickered down to his mouth and then back up to his eyes.

"You're like an onion, Nick McKenna—lots of layers. Some of them pretty dark. But I've got a funny feeling about you."

"Oh, yeah? What's that?"

"No matter how deep or scary those layers are, I don't think you'd make me cry."

THE AIR HUNG thick between them, electrified, damn near flammable, and they were two pieces of flint, igniting whenever they touched. One tiny spark and they might both combust.

"I would never make you cry," he said. "Unless they were happy tears. You're such a good person, so beautiful. I'd cut off my right arm before hurting you."

On some level, despite his bad-boy alter ego, she sensed he believed that to be true.

"What about you?" He caressed her cheek with his knuckles, those dark, exacting eyes taking her in. "You've been holding back pieces of yourself, too." A statement, not a question, that stalled the oxygen in her lungs. "I just shared my darkest, ugliest secrets. Quid pro quo."

The caress in his voice was more powerful than a physical stroke, tempting her to unburden herself. Nick was formidable and capable. He could handle anything.

Even the truth?

Don't be so naive.

She tensed and backed up against the table. If he knew...
No, when he found out...

Lori wasn't ready for that, to ruin this precious moment.
"What you see is what you get with me."

Nick flashed her a *come on* look and erased the gap separating them. "We all have secrets."

Sins to atone for. But hers wasn't wrath. Or up for discussion.

"You're safe with me, Lori," he said, and she knew he didn't only mean physically, but her heart was battered and bruised, more fragile than she dared admit.

He slid his hand under her hair at the nape, cupping the back of her head, and dragged her flush against him. Lori's body heated and her pulse kicked up at his proximity.

She didn't resist, surrendering to his maleness and sexiness and the take-charge side of him, the blend of which was intoxicating.

His strong arm wrapped around her waist. Protectively at first, then he planted his palm on the small of her back in possession, drawing her pelvis to his. Her gaze moved past his broad shoulders and fixed on his lips. He looked like the kind of guy who kissed and made love the way that he fought. No holds barred, pouring his all into it.

Life was too short. The god-awful events of the day had made her painfully aware of that, more than ever. She was done holding back, tired of denying her growing attraction to this man.

"All I've wanted since the day I was assigned to you," he said, "was to protect you, keep you safe." That smoldering gaze searched hers and she was tempted to confess everything.

He was a little dark, a little crazy, a little rough. Dangerous, but the good kind. She was a little damaged, a little pragmatic and a whole lot scared. Dangerous, too, but a different sort.

They were wrong for each other in a thousand ways.

Knowing there was no future for them, but having such powerful chemistry, it was impossible to be rational.

"Is that all you've wanted over the past year?"

She didn't want to die with regrets. Wishing she had seized the chance to taste Nick McKenna, just once. Her mouth watered at the thought. She'd never been so hungry for a man's kiss, for his touch.

"No. It's not." He fell silent then and cupped her cheek. His thumb brushed over her lower lip like a breath and caused a liquid rush of weakness in her knees.

He gripped her hips, lifting her up onto the table, and pushed forward. She let her legs slide apart to accommodate him.

"I've wanted *you* since I first touched you." He squeezed his eyes shut, an intensity she'd never seen in him taking over his features. "Those self-defense lessons, the grappling, the holds, my wandering mind taking me places it shouldn't go, the excuses to put my hands on you without enjoying you the way I secretly wanted was—" he broke off, bringing his face close, and finished in a rough voice "—pure torture."

His admission left her breathless, speechless, but her belly tightened and rolled in response. Nick McKenna had desired her all this time. She exhaled in relief and moistened her lips.

He pressed his forehead to hers and opened his eyes. Their gazes collided.

Her muscles strained with anticipation. The urge to hasten the contact that she craved swelled in her chest like a soap bubble and she had to act before it burst.

In the span of a breath, her arms twined around his neck and her lips were on his. The kiss was shockingly soft at first, closemouthed and languid.

His tongue glided along the seam of her mouth, teasing

it open. She melted against him and sighed as his grip on her tightened. The heels of his palms pressed into her hip bones, his fingers molding to the curve of her waist.

She tingled as though her body was waking from a long slumber with renewed circulation.

He growled, deepening the kiss, stroking her tongue with lush, greedy slides of his own. All the oxygen was sucked from her lungs, and her thoughts evaporated in a stab of pure longing.

With her breasts crushed to his chest, his heart raged against her sternum, the beat guiding her own pulse. He pulled her hips forward, making her achingly aware of every hard, hot, aroused inch of him.

She'd never needed anything more than to have the solid pressure of his body against hers, his sinewy strength and leashed control wrapped around her.

His hips rubbed against her inner thighs, the friction creating a deeper ache that made her forget about the pain in her body. Awakened a yearning for something wild and passionate, caution and reason thrown to the wind.

Nick was the perfect man to give it to her.

A throat cleared in the doorway. They both jumped, pulling apart and looking embarrassed. But Nick stayed close, keeping one hand on her hip.

Renee stood on the threshold. "Excuse me. I'm sorry to interrupt, but I wanted you to know that I tried to call my mother."

"You did what?" Nick snapped, his face turning furious. "I explained how precarious this situation is. Her life is on the line."

"I meant well. Yes, you're the professional, but I knew if you spoke to Mom face-to-face for two minutes, you'd know without a doubt that you can trust her."

Nick's jaw clenched. "You shouldn't have gone behind my back and—"

Lori put her palm to his chest. "Nick, you were going to ask her to call the sheriff anyway."

He turned to Lori, his brow creased. "That's not the point."

"No, it's not," Renee said. "If you'd let me finish. I said I *tried* to call her. I couldn't get through. The phone line is down."

A fresh wave of tension sloshed in Lori's stomach.

Don't overreact. It doesn't mean anything.

"Is that unusual for the phone to go on the fritz in this area?" he asked, taking out his cell.

"In a storm, sometimes it goes down. Otherwise, yes, it's unusual. And I couldn't get a signal on my cell."

Nick checked his phone. He looked up and shook his head. "No signal, either."

Her heart pounded hard as a fist against her sternum. The waking nightmare at the mall and the safe house resuscitated, engulfing her once more. The ache returned to Lori's throat on the next swallow, spreading with the next breath.

The apparatus the woman had used to try and strangle her was called a garrote. A word she wished she had never learned and now would never forget. Right along with the devastating force and heat of the explosion.

What new horror would be imprinted on her brain in the next few minutes?

"Do you have a two-way radio?" Nick asked.

Renee shook her head. "I don't."

A loud ding made Lori's pulse spike and she took a startled breath. "What is that?"

Nick went rigid. That internal switch in him had flipped and he was once again the icy, detached marshal prepared to annihilate anyone who sought to do her harm.

"Front doorbell," Renee said. "Someone's here."

Oh, God. Dr. Holmes had told them that she didn't

have any appointments this afternoon. What if it was another assassin?

Would an assassin ring the bell?

No one can protect you. It's only a matter of time. A matter of when and how they kill you. But they will, if you agree to testify. Her father-in-law's words came back to her in an insidious rush. She tamped down the hot bile spurting up her throat.

Nick drew his gun.

"It's probably one of the deputies," Renee said. "He must have driven by, maybe tried phoning to see why I'm closed, couldn't reach me and decided to ring the bell."

Yeah, maybe that was it. Lori prayed that it was the sheriff's department outside, but her luck today had been BAD. Beyond Altogether Disastrous.

The odds weren't in her favor.

"Let's take a look," Nick said. "Is there any way to see who is out front without going into the reception area?"

The accordion-style security gate was designed to deter breaking and entering, but whoever was out front could clearly see the reception area and front desk.

"We have a security camera. We can access the live feed and intercom from my office."

"Perfect," Nick said.

Renee led the way. Nick tried to get Lori to stay in the exam room, but she wasn't having it. She slipped on her shoes and followed them to the office.

They huddled around the computer screen on the desk as Renee brought up the footage.

A middle-aged lady, maybe late fifties, early sixties, stood outside holding a pet carrier with a dog inside. Behind her was an illegally parked black SUV with tinted windows. From the angle the car sat, it was impossible to tell if anyone else was inside.

"See what she wants and get rid of her," Nick said.

Renee hit a button for the intercom. "Can I help you?"

"Hello! Are you open? My dog is very sick. He's been throwing up all morning." She waved her free hand around as she spoke, gesturing wildly. "I'm worried he's dehydrated and might have worms or something. Can you check him out? It's an emergency." With her streamlined skirt and cute-as-a-button hat, the lady resembled an older Mary Poppins.

Relief ebbed through Lori, but Nick's eyes narrowed, his body coiled in readiness.

Renee looked to Nick.

"You can't open those doors," he said.

"But I have to. I'm obligated." Renee straightened in defiance. "There's a sick dog out there."

"Look," he said, taking on that hard-bitten, drill-sergeant tone that was worse than nails on a chalkboard. "I can't go into the details of what we've been through, but I'm telling you, not everyone is who they seem to be. You can't open those doors."

"Do you really think it's them?" Lori asked.

"Yes, it's them. It's no coincidence that the landline went dead and we lost cell service at the exact same moment that woman showed up."

Lori shook her head, not wanting to believe it, hoping there was another explanation. "How could they have found us here?"

"Damn Draper. It had to be him."

"Your boss?" Lori forced air into her lungs so her voice didn't sound so brittle. "You think he's a part of this?" Working for the cartel?

You have no idea who they own, who they've got in their back pocket working for them. Let this go. Otherwise it'll be your funeral. Her father-in-law had warned her, but she didn't listen.

"Excuse me!" the lady said. "Pepper already had one seizure today. Please, help us."

Renee put a palm to her stomach like the thought of turning away Mary Poppins and her little dog was too much to bear. "When I agreed to help you, I didn't sign on for turning away sick pets. The next vet is over thirty minutes away. I have to let her in."

"No, you don't," Nick said. "If she waited this long to bring that mutt in, she can drive thirty minutes. Renee, I'm asking you to trust me. Tell her to go to a different vet."

When Renee didn't appear persuaded to comply, Lori turned to her. "The people after me almost killed me three times today. Nick is the reason I'm not dead." She swallowed past the cold lump in her throat. "Please, listen to him."

Renee sighed, her gaze lowering like she was deliberating. Finally, she nodded and pressed the intercom. "I'm sorry, but we're closed because the computers are down. I hate to turn you away. Truly, I do, but there's another veterinary clinic not too far from here." Renee rattled off the address.

Nick stared at the monitor. They all waited to see how the lady would respond. Lori half expected the woman to pull out an Uzi and open fire.

The rear passenger's side door of the SUV opened. A brunette alighted from the car.

Lori's belly clenched. Was that the woman who'd been in the clothing store browsing earlier? Same chic bun, elegant movements, petite and pretty.

Oh, crap. It *was* her.

The brunette slammed the car door shut and approached the clinic in long, sure strides.

Queasiness took root in the pit of Lori's stomach.

"I knew it," Nick said. "Black Rose is behind this. It's another setup."

"Who?" Lori asked.

"That's what I've been calling her in my head from the tattoo on her hand. She's the puppet master pulling the strings of all the marionettes who've attacked you today."

Lori was too shocked to speak, her gaze glued to the monitor.

Black Rose walked straight up to the front door, looked up at the camera and waved.

Panic-stricken, Lori couldn't move. All the air whooshed from her lungs. A hundred different thoughts buzzed in her mind, but none fell from her lips.

On the monitor, Black Rose lifted her hand above her head and snapped her fingers. The lady holding the dog carrier did an about-face as a man hopped out of the SUV. He carried a briefcase, set flat atop both his hands, and walked up beside Black Rose.

"Dr. Holmes, do you mind if I call you Renee? So much more personal without the formality of titles. Don't you think?" Her tone was casual, freaking normal.

This couldn't be happening.

"Ask her name?" Nick said to Renee.

Renee pressed the intercom. "What do I call you?"

"Belladonna." A plastic grin tugged at her lips. She tapped the top of the briefcase next to her. The man opened it, revealing bundles of cash.

Renee and Lori gasped at the same time. Nick's hardened expression didn't waver, a flash of fury in his eyes. The heavy silence in the office seemed to press in on them.

"We can be friendly about this, Renee," Belladonna said. "Unlock the door, pull up the gate and step aside. Simple. Step aside and take care of those beautiful, innocent creatures. In return, the briefcase and its contents are yours. All I want is the woman."

What if the FBI was wrong and the cartel was too big to be stopped? What if the US Marshals couldn't protect her? What if Draper was in on this? What if Nick—

No, no. Lori squashed such thoughts. Fear was poison. She couldn't let it pollute her mind. Testifying was the right thing to do. She wouldn't second-guess her decision.

There was no way to turn back the clock, unring that bell, anyway. Her course was set.

Lori had to trust Nick to get her through this alive and she clung to that like a lifeline.

Renee hit the intercom. "The sheriff is on the way. I've just phoned her. Any minute, deputies will be here. I suggest you leave."

Nick clicked his tongue, irritation stretched across his face. "Why would you say that?"

Renee shook her head, her eyes wide with fright, and shrugged. "To make them leave."

Nick huffed an audible breath in response.

"That's not true." Belladonna wagged a manicured finger at the camera and tsked. "Seeing as how I've cut your landline and blocked your cellular reception. This friendship isn't going to work if we lie to each other."

"What are we going to do?" Lori asked, struggling to filter panic from her voice and failing miserably.

"I'm going to be completely forthright with you, Renee," Belladonna said. "You owe the two individuals you're harboring absolutely nothing. You have one of two choices. I'm a fan of option number one, where you open the doors, take the money and turn a blind eye. Or there's option two." Belladonna winced. "I set this clinic on fire. Think of all those poor, defenseless dogs inside. I will fry each and every one of them right along with you. If that's what it will take to see the woman that I want dead." She raised her palms in the gesture of a minister delivering the gospel. "I'll give you a minute to talk amongst yourselves."

The room spun. Lori clutched the counter to keep from falling down. She hauled in a deep breath in an effort to calm the frenzied pounding of her heart.

"You can't open the doors," Nick said. "She'll kill you either way."

Renee pressed a fist to her mouth and turned away from him. "The two of you have to leave. I have to let her in. I can't jeopardize the animals in my care. I'm sorry."

"It's suicide." Lori stepped around in front of her. "Those people out there are heartless. Ruthless. You can't trust them."

"That's a chance I have to take. I swore an oath when I became a veterinarian and I meant it. I can't allow those animals to die. Not when I have the power to stop them from being burned alive by opening that door. If that means trading my life for theirs, then so be it." Renee rubbed her forehead. "I couldn't live with myself otherwise. Go. Go now. The back door leads to outdoor space for the dogs. It's surrounded by a six-foot cinder-block wall. Go over the right side. It's adjacent to the parking lot of the gas station."

"That's where our car is," Lori said. Nick had thought it best not to park in front of the clinic.

"Come with us," Nick said. "It's the only smart play. The three of us get out of here together."

"I think we both know that's not going to happen," Renee said. "If I can stop her from burning down my clinic, from killing…" The words seemed to back up in her throat as she looked out at all the caged animals. "I have to stay."

Nick nodded. "I did know you'd say that, but I had to try."

"I'll stall, buy you a few minutes. As long as I can," Renee said.

"Is there a back way we can take to the sheriff's to stay off the state road?"

Renee nodded. She scrawled directions on a notepad,

tore it off and handed it to Nick. "Make it there and my mom, Sheila Holmes, will help you."

"Thank you, for helping us." Lori hugged her, hating that she'd not only endangered a kind veterinarian, but also defenseless animals. "I'm sorry we brought trouble to your door."

"I need your decision, Renee," Belladonna said. "I'm on a tight schedule and can't afford to wait any longer."

Renee pulled back from the embrace. "Go." She shooed them toward the back. "Hurry."

Nick grabbed the body armor, threw it on Lori, not taking the time to worry about concealing it, and led her to the exit.

Behind them, Lori heard Renee say, "Okay, okay! I don't want any of the animals hurt. Please."

"Excellent decision. I'm a dog lover, you know. Nothing against cats. But thank you for sparing me the moniker of The Pet Butcher. I mean, who wants to put that on their résumé?"

"No one, I suppose."

"Open up, Renee."

"I will. I swear. Let me grab my keys." Renee waved Nick and Lori out the back door.

They rushed through the noisy room that housed the dogs and cats, past the exam room, toward the exit. Lori glanced around for something she could use as a weapon. Anything could be waiting for them out back and she'd have to do her part to help Nick. To save herself.

She stopped in front of the fire extinguisher and hefted it off the wall. "I could swing it like a bat, clobber someone with it."

Nick pulled the safety pin from the extinguisher. "Better to spray someone in the face first."

Their gazes locked and something passed between them that didn't need words. A feeling, a jolt of understanding.

They nodded to each other. No matter what, they'd get through this together.

They hurried to the back door.

"Do you think Belladonna will kill her?" Lori asked.

"Renee is as good as dead, but I think the animals have a fair shot at making it."

GUN UP AGAINST his chest, Nick was ready for anything. His heart beat a slow, steady cadence. Adrenaline pumped in his veins, sharpening his focus and reflexes. He turned the key, unlocking the dead bolt, and flung the door open.

Nick crossed the threshold. Sensed movement from the right side before he saw it.

He caught the gun hand of a big man that was taking aim, and the meathead did likewise, seizing Nick's wrist. A standoff where neither could shoot.

A second man closed in on Lori. She let the fire extinguisher rip, spraying him in the face with a blast of foamy chemicals.

The massive guy in front of Nick turned out to be as slow as he looked. Nick went for one of his knees with his boot heel.

No matter how big or how strong an opponent, take out his knees and he was done.

The connection of the steel boot shank and kneecap made a god-awful sound as the man howled in agony and dropped.

Nick kicked the gun from his hand and threw a powerful knee into the big guy's skull.

Whirling around, he snatched the fire extinguisher from Lori and throttled her attacker. Without a suppressor, discharging his gun would only broadcast their escape.

Once Lori's assailant stopped moving, he turned back to the other guy to finish the job. Nick kept swinging the extinguisher—hoisting it up overhead and slamming it down full force—until he was one hundred percent certain that neither man would ever get up again.

He scanned one hundred eighty degrees. All clear.

Nick beckoned to Lori. She took his hand as they crossed the long, narrow run of the grassy play area. It wasn't until then that he noticed the air reeked of feces and rain.

Fat, dark clouds had moved in and the sky looked on the brink of opening any minute. All they needed was a downpour on top of everything else. As if the progressively worsening situation wasn't bad enough.

Things kept getting worse and worse as Belladonna somehow stayed on their heels.

If he found out for certain that Draper was behind this, so help him God, there'd be payback. Nick would make it slow and painful, make Draper want to weep and beg for prison, but first he had to make sure that Lori was safe.

Survival was the focus now.

They scrambled to the east wall. Nick holstered his Glock and took a running leap. He snagged the top of the wall, hopped up and glanced over.

No more goons in sight.

Nick straddled the wall and proffered a hand to Lori. "Jump up."

She did and he caught her arm, then he reached for her other hand. She put her feet on the wall, and he pulled, helping her walk up the slab of cinder blocks.

They hopped down to the ground side by side and duck-walked to the parked vehicle.

Once Lori was inside, he said, "Stay low. I'll be right back and have you in my sights the entire time."

She didn't ask questions and trusted him. "Okay."

He closed the door quietly and looked around for any signs of approaching danger. There was nothing. Still, his guard was up, and he didn't dare entertain relief.

Nick slinked around to the far side of the gas station and peeked around the corner at the vet clinic.

The steel security gate was up. A second SUV was parked in front, and one armed guard stood watch.

Belladonna must've been inside.

For Renee's sake, he hoped he was wrong and that she'd make it through this ordeal alive.

"PLEASE, HAVE A SEAT, Renee," Belladonna said in a tone that was sweet without pouring it on so thick it sounded phony. Even if it was. One caught more flies with honey than vinegar, yada, yada, and all those other pearls of wisdom that were true.

Belladonna gestured to the chair in the back office.

Renee sat, trembling, her gaze darting to the hall where armed men were searching the place. Belladonna had no doubt that her quarry had already fled, and her men would find nothing in the clinic. After all, McKenna was a slippery bastard, but he didn't realize that even though they were on the move, the noose was tightening around Lori Carpenter's neck.

Belladonna pulled out a chair and sat opposite Renee, crossing her legs. They'd have a civilized conversation. Woman to woman.

If all went as expected, not a drop of blood would be shed.

"Are you going to kill me?" The vet's voice cracked as she swallowed a sob.

"You did as I asked and I'm a woman of my word." Belladonna folded her hands in her lap. "The briefcase is yours, as promised."

Renee's face twisted in disgust. "I don't want your blood money."

Belladonna chuckled. "Well then, we have a problem. I

trust those who can be bribed to stay quiet. The self-righteous, who cling to their principles, not so much."

In the silence that followed, she let that sink in. Gave the vet a chance to see reason so they could come to a mutually satisfactory end.

Yes, Belladonna had been trained to be ruthless, to kill without discrimination, or hesitation. But time had seasoned her, made her wiser.

A smart assassin lived longer than a brutal one. And sometimes showing mercy wasn't the same as leaving a loose end. She only had to be prudent enough to distinguish between the two.

"Consider the money a donation to your clinic," Belladonna said. "And reassurance that you'll have a faulty memory about today. About what you've seen. What you've heard. Who you've spoken to."

"Fine." Renee nodded.

Two rooks entered the room.

"They're not here," Smokey said.

As to be expected. Belladonna nodded once in acknowledgment.

"I'll call housekeeping." Max took out his phone.

The new rook was an eager beaver, but he was jumping the gun. Did he think she was bluffing about letting the woman live and not torching puppies and kittens?

That kind of thing didn't even go over well in prison. Those who hurt children and animals had a tough go behind bars. Not that Belladonna was going to see the inside of a jail cell.

She raised her hand, stopping him from making the call.

Renee's chin lifted. "As you can see, they're not here. Please, I'm begging you to leave. I won't say a word to anyone."

"First, I have some questions."

Renee shook her head. "I don't know anything."

"That's not entirely true, is it?" Belladonna asked. "Where are they going?"

"Follow them and you'll find out." Renee shifted in her seat, gaze darting to the phone on the desk.

The line was back up and in working order. Little did Renee realize. Not that she would've gotten the chance to dial 911.

"Believe me, they are being followed." Once Belladonna had pinpointed their location to the veterinary clinic, she'd posted men at either end of the state road to intercept them in case McKenna and the woman managed to get out.

Then there was the fact she was tracking McKenna's electronic fingerprint and eavesdropping on all his cellular calls. As long as she prevented them from meeting up with those SOG operators, Belladonna had this in the bag.

"But I want to know their intended destination," Belladonna said, "and whether or not the men I have in position will be able to cut them off before they get there."

"I don't know where they're going. The second you showed up, they hightailed it out of here."

That was almost believable. *Almost.* "I'm a patient woman. Truly, I am." Sometimes Belladonna had to lie in wait for hours, days, for the opportune moment to strike a target. She had patience in spades. "But I'm short on time. I should mention that I have a keen sense of smell. I can detect BS from a mile out. So imagine how strong the stench is when you're sitting two feet away. Where are they going?"

Renee pursed her lips and gripped the edge of her chair.

The doctor knew exactly where they were headed.

"Friends cooperate. And I want us to remain friends," Belladonna said, annoyance leaking into her voice.

Renee seemed to make a split-second decision and opened her mouth.

Belladonna sensed the fib forming on her tongue and

stopped her. "Before you answer, understand that I will view a lie as cause to renegotiate our agreement. This *conversation* will turn into an *interrogation* and I'll be forced to introduce you to a level of pain you've never known. In the end, your life will be forfeit. Take a second to process that. Now, where are they going?"

Renee whimpered. "The sheriff's department. But there's no point in going there. You can't bribe or intimidate the sheriff. And it's not like you can have a shoot-out in the middle of the town. The State Police are only thirty minutes away and they'll respond to any report of hostile action."

Hmm. Renee was well informed. But it would only take the State Police ten minutes to pop up due to an inopportune three-car pile-up close by on State Route 18. Four squad cars were already on the scene.

Belladonna didn't have the luxury of engaging in a lengthy shoot-out with McKenna and the sheriff's department hunkered down to protect Carpenter.

Any action she took had to either be quiet or quick.

"I bet you thought you were above bribery and intimidation, too, until you weren't," Belladonna said.

"The sheriff is different. My mother won't negotiate with terrorists. Or whatever the hell you are. So you might as well give this up and leave that poor woman alone."

Mother? The plot thickened to the sublime consistency of pudding. "If only it were that simple." Belladonna licked her lips and leaned forward, resting her forearms on her thighs. "The marshal and the woman. Did there appear to be anything amorous between them?"

"What?" Renee stiffened in her chair.

McKenna had to have a weakness. Belladonna bet it was Lori Carpenter. Both of them were healthy, young, attractive, single, heterosexual, and they'd been in close quarters every day for a year.

"Oh, you don't understand the question?" Belladonna snapped her fingers and Smokey left the room.

Nothing more was required. Not a single word needed to be uttered. Her longtime rooks and bishops knew how she operated well enough to intuit what she wanted with the snap of her fingers or the lift of a palm. Smokey was practically her right hand. She was training Max, which was hard to do on the fly.

A moment later Smokey returned, holding a dog in his arms. An adorable poodle. Hypoallergenic, nonshedding; her daughter would love one exactly like it.

Smokey scratched the pooch's head and showered it with adoration.

Renee reared back with a hand flying to her collarbone. Tears welled in her eyes. "Don't. You can't. Please."

"Let's try again," Belladonna said, knowing the threat was sufficient, and that no animals would be harmed during this intimidation tactic. "Did they appear to be intimate, show any signs that their relationship was more than professional?"

"Yes, yes. I walked in on them kissing."

Interesting. Belladonna had expected to hear details of a hug, a comforting look that had lingered too long, the two of them holding hands. Kissing was better. Concrete.

"Please, don't hurt Bailey," Renee said, sniffling.

Belladonna gave a nod, and Smokey handed the dog off to someone in the hall to return to its cage.

"Thank you." Renee sobbed, looking overwrought from the conversation.

That one had a delicate constitution.

"No. Thank *you*," Belladonna said, standing up. The doctor had turned out to be a gold mine of information and would prove even more useful.

Max raised his gun and aimed it at the doctor.

Belladonna knocked his arm down. "What are you doing?"

"The boss doesn't want any witnesses," Max said.

Oh, hell no, those words didn't just leave his mouth.

A cold anger chilled her heated blood. "I need her, you idiot." She slapped him hard, backhanded, to remind not only him, but also all her people, of their place. "Who is running this mission?"

"You," he said through clenched teeth.

Dante Vargas, the west coast cartel cell leader, was technically in charge and was Belladonna's boss. But she called the tactical shots in the field.

"Who is in charge, right here?" she asked.

Max rubbed his red cheek and glared at her, murderous intent gleaming in his eyes.

Fury speared through her at having to ask twice. "Who?"

"You."

"Too bad you forgot that." Now she had to make him an example.

Leniency in this situation only invited insubordination. Perhaps even mutiny, where someone might stab her in the back, thinking they'd finish the job themselves, outshine her and earn a promotion.

Like she didn't have enough to worry about without that crap, too. She nodded to Smokey. He swept up behind Max, quicker than a blink, and slipped a garrote around his throat.

It took a lot longer than a slug to the brainpan to kill someone this way, but it was quieter and less mess.

Renee let out a horrified squeak, jumping out of her chair, and scurried back into a corner.

Good instincts.

Belladonna shifted out of the range of the struggle that ensued—not wanting to catch a stray kick from Max's steel-toed boots.

Drawing a fortifying breath, she took out her cell and made the call. "I need cleanup."

Another rook stepped into the office and grabbed Max's feet to help. The two of them wrangled Max's body taut and a gurgle came from him as he clutched his throat.

Belladonna smiled, her fury thinning to oblivion. *Teamwork makes the dream work.*

"Veterinary?" the female voice said over the phone.

"Yes." Belladonna ran a hand over her hair, ensuring not a single strand had been knocked loose. "One body."

"On it."

Smokey removed the wire from around Max's throat. The two rooks let the lifeless body hit the floor in a heap.

Crisis averted. Good thing she nipped that in the bud.

Belladonna turned to her rooks. "One of you, help the doctor into my trunk."

"B-b-but, you said you'd let me live." Renee squeezed into the corner as though trying to disappear into the wall.

"I'm afraid your life is no longer in my hands," Belladonna said, putting her cell away. "Whether you live or die today will be up to your mother. The sheriff."

Chapter Eight

Maybe going to the sheriff's department wasn't a good idea. Everything Nick touched turned to blood.

The thought of endangering more people kicked up a thrumming in his temples.

But that was the point of law enforcement; they weren't ordinary civilians like Dr. Renee Holmes, and the sheriff was the closest. Though he had a niggling suspicion that this situation exceeded the capabilities of the local sheriff, whose biggest problem was probably some meth heads pulling a little B and E in the area.

With Belladonna hot on their heels, and his SOG teammates hours away, the fact that they needed assistance was a dire understatement.

"Are you sure we should still go to the sheriff?" Lori asked as though reading his mind.

The only thing he was certain of was that he had to do everything in his power to keep her alive. "I was wondering the same thing. I don't think we have much choice."

If he kept Draper out of the loop and updated Yazzie directly about their new location, Belladonna shouldn't be able to find them. There was no reason for Belladonna to think that the vet had any clue of their intentions and unfortunately, Renee had probably caught a bullet to the frontal lobe two seconds after she opened the door.

He drove down the dirt path Renee had told them to take

in order to stay off main streets and looked for the fork in the road, where they needed to turn.

"Will her mother still help us once she learns we abandoned her daughter, left her to the mercy of assassins?"

"We didn't *abandon* her. Though we did leave her. Belladonna had threatened to burn down the clinic if Renee didn't open the doors. The doctor was hell-bent on ensuring those animals were safe." Not that he blamed her for following her conscience. Even if it was a reckless decision.

"That may be," Lori said, "but it doesn't feel like we made the right choice. I know we couldn't have fought them off there, but I hate to think about what might have happened to Renee. She was only being a good person, trying to help us."

There went Lori's big heart again, worrying more about others than herself. "We made the only choice we could." He reached over and took her hand.

Her thin, cold fingers closed around his, and the tension in her eased a bit. She rested her head on his shoulder. He pressed his lips to her soft hair.

Knowing how to console a witness and assuage their worries was part of the job, but this was different. Seeing the wave of fear recede from her at his touch filled him with an indescribable warmth.

He didn't date much. His job kept him so damn busy that it was part of the reason he'd hooked up with Charlie in the first place. She was attractive and it had been convenient for them both, but that train had never left the casual station. He'd had absolutely no affect on her. She'd treated him like a sexual Lego block.

With Lori, there was a bond he couldn't explain. Maybe it was a result of the time they'd spent together, with him not only attending to all her needs from groceries, to seeing a dentist, to reassurance about the trial, but also caring about her.

Somewhere along the way, he'd grown to need her, too.

His first thought in the morning and his last in the evening were of her. The most beautiful thing in the world was Lori's smile. He had vivid dreams about her and even more erotic fantasies of her writhing in pleasure beneath him, but what he craved was this closeness.

They hit another bump, jostling the car. He slowed from fifty to forty, working their way from one end of town to the other. The scenic route took longer, but it was smarter to stay off the main thoroughfare. Belladonna might have lookouts posted, waiting to ambush them.

The only problem was this road was narrow and unpaved. If another car came from the opposite direction, he had no idea what he was supposed to do. It wasn't as if there was enough room to pull over. It was a mystery how the locals managed.

One thing about this back road—it was quiet and removed from the touristy energy of town. It almost made it possible to push from the forefront of his mind that evil wasn't far behind, circling, poised to strike, to kill the beautiful, warm woman at his side.

That was precisely why he didn't shove the knowledge away and kept it front and center instead. Belladonna was cunning and sharp as a switchblade. If he let his guard slip, gave that assassin one inch, she'd take a yard and hang Lori with it.

He had to stay vigilant and on point. A single mistake could cost them both their lives.

"You didn't answer my question," she said, sitting up and looking at him. "Do you think the sheriff will help us?"

"Her mother sounds like a Dudley Do-Right. Duty first. If that's the case, she'll feel just as obligated to help us and to protect you as Renee did about the animals."

"I hope so." She gave him a weak smile.

The fork in the road was up ahead. Once they turned,

it was less than a ten-minute ride to the sheriff's dept. He gave her fingers a comforting squeeze and put both hands on the wheel.

His cell phone buzzed in his pocket.

Damn it. He should've gotten rid of it before they started their backwoods trek to the sheriff's department.

Nick fished the cell out from his jacket pocket and read the caller ID on the screen. "Draper." He cursed under his breath, weighing how to respond. Not thirty minutes after the last time they'd spoken, Belladonna had located them and made her move.

Experience, his gut—hell, common sense—told him it wasn't coincidence.

Draper didn't have to call Nick to track his phone, but he was going through the trouble of phoning for a reason. What did he want? What new angle was he going to play?

Nick answered. "McKenna."

"The working group I put together from Intel and IT to figure out how we've been breached finally came up with an answer," Draper said, excitement buzzing in his voice.

Now, that was unexpected and certainly worth taking the call, but could Nick trust anything Draper said?

He hit the speaker icon, letting Lori hear firsthand whatever explanation Draper was going to try to sell him. "Really. What did they find?"

"You're not going to believe this," Draper said, and Nick silently agreed that he probably wouldn't. "Our system has been hacked."

Talk about throwing him for a loop. Then again, it was the punch you didn't see coming that knocked you out.

He glanced at Lori. The mix of curiosity and wariness stamped on her face reflected how Nick felt but refused to show.

"Hacked?" Nick asked. "How? Are they sure?"

"They're certain someone has been fishing around in

our system, but they haven't figured out how yet. No fire-walls were breached. Whoever hacked us is smart, masking their point of entry, not staying too long at any given sweep, dipping in and out of the system, extracting data."

This was a digital world. Every report on Hummingbird was electronic, logged in the database. A breach of their system gave a plausible explanation for how Belladonna would've known in advance that they would be at the mall. What time. Which store. Even the entrance and exit they had planned to use had all been spelled out in the reports. Also, when deputies were out in the field on high-priority missions like this one, their cell's geolocator could be retrieved with a few keystrokes. Anyone with access could've tracked him to the veterinary clinic.

All of it was plausible. And convenient.

"Do they know how long we've been compromised?" Nick asked, dreading the answer. Hours, days, weeks, a month?

Jeez. The amount of sensitive, confidential information that could've been stolen was bone-chilling.

Long-term, this might impact more than Lori.

"They have no idea how long we've been exposed yet," Draper said. "They just discovered it. But once they have an opportunity, they're going to go over everything with a fine-tooth comb."

The USMS employed some of the best techies in the business. With such high stakes, they would run this to ground and ascertain their level of exposure. Hopefully, sooner rather than later.

"You said that our firewall wasn't hacked," Nick said.

"Right."

"Doesn't that mean whoever has been extracting data had internal access?"

Lori paled at his question.

Draper heaved a sigh into the phone. "Unfortunately, yes, it does."

"Is the person still in the system?"

"IT has closed all network nodes accessible from outside the building. We've enacted limited restricted access within the building. If the breach emanated from a computer in this building, IT will find it. I've instated a temporary lockdown. No one in or out until each CPU has been checked. But don't worry. Yazzie and Killinger are en route."

Nick could practically hear Draper's wheels spinning through the phone. The challenges had been identified and his boss was working viable solutions, but only half the problem was being addressed.

"What if it wasn't a computer inside the building that was used to breach us?" Nick asked.

Draper had access to the system from his home. It enabled him to work late, on weekends and to respond to any situation at a moment's notice.

"Then we may never know who breached us or exactly what data they stole." Draper's voice was solemn. "The good news is they no longer have access."

Good, yeah, but once again, convenient. For Draper.

His boss had a trailblazing record, utterly spotless. Other districts referred to him as Mr. Clean. No matter what trouble or scandal befell an office, Draper saved his own skin and always walked away without a speck on him.

Either Draper was just good at playing the political game and climbing the ladder, or he was as dirty as they came.

"No outside nodes will be reopened until Hummingbird has testified, the network has been scrubbed and patches installed to prevent this from happening again," Draper said, giving a textbook answer.

"Sounds like you've got your hands full, juggling lots of balls in the air," Nick said. "The blowback from this breach could be catastrophic."

"Yeah, well, heavy is the head that wears the crown. My problem and not yours. You worry about keeping Hummingbird alive."

"That's getting tough to do with assassins popping up at every turn."

"Don't tell me you've had more trouble," Draper said, almost sounding legitimately surprised and rather concerned.

Nick met Lori's weary eyes before looking back at the road. "As a matter of fact, we have. Assassins found us at the veterinary clinic."

Draper swore. "Hummingbird is okay, right? You're both okay?"

"Yes. We are. But sir, I have to go dark until I've made contact with Yaz and Killinger. I'll find an alternate location for the meet and notify them at the last minute."

"Hold on, McKenna. Don't be rash. If you're worried about your calls still being traced, get a burner phone."

"No. No more phone calls. No more updates."

"If you go *dark* and something happens to Hummingbird, after I'm done hanging your butt out to dry, you're fired."

Nick's blood pressure spiked at the threat. "And if I find out that you're dirty and had anything to do with our breach, you're dead."

He ended the call and stopped the car. Removing the battery from the phone, he got out of the vehicle. He dropped the cell and the battery on the ground and stomped both to pieces.

"We've got to pick up a burner," he said, climbing back in, and sped down the road. "I hope they sell flip phones in this small town."

"Why does it have to be an old-school flip phone?"

"Can't be traced."

"Could Draper be responsible for this?"

If Will Draper, the head of the San Diego office, was

the source of their breach, it complicated the situation. For starters, Draper had his fingers in everything related to this mission and had both the district attorney and the US attorney's office on speed dial since the case involved state and federal crimes.

Nick would need irrefutable evidence to get anyone to take the accusation seriously. "I hope not."

"But you really think it's possible your boss is the one who has been feeding information to the drug cartel?"

Nick's scalp prickled. He was aware that the financial firm Lori had worked for, Wallace Capital Management, had been laundering money for dangerous people. Not knowing who WCM's clients were, he'd assumed the mob or some other organized crime group. "Which cartel?"

"Los Chacales."

The Jackals.

His gaze snapped to her. "Is that who Belladonna works for? Is that WCM's biggest client?" The world's most powerful and violent drug cartel?

"Yes."

Holy hell.

The deputies assigned to safeguard a witness before a trial weren't privy to all the details of the case outside what was covered in the news and what was considered essential need-to-know particulars. And Lori wasn't supposed to discuss the case.

Now he understood how US Attorney Foy was going to leverage this into a platform to run for governor. Drug cartels, especially ones as powerful and brutal as *Los Chacales*, were considered the largest growing threat to national security.

A win against WCM would also be lauded as a win against the cartel. Talk about putting a feather in Foy's cap.

"How much of the cartel's money is being laundered through WCM?" he wondered aloud.

"Close to seventy-five percent."

Damn. This was insane.

The US attorney's office should've told the Marshals Service that Lori was going to be the biggest target in WIT-SEC in a decade. Hell, maybe ever.

What if they had informed Draper and that was the reason he had her squirreled away to a remote location three hours from San Diego, where there was zero chance of her being recognized?

But then somehow the cartel had gotten to him. Found out something about him they could use to coerce him, like gambling debts or deviant behavior?

Maybe it was as simple as greed, and they'd offered him more money than he could turn down.

With the breach of their database, anything could've been stolen, including the names, new identities and current addresses of all the people in the WITSEC program in the state of California. Not to mention the names and family members of every single deputy marshal and US Marshal in charge of a district office.

Forget about exploiting a person's financial troubles or hanging deviant behavior over their head. Snatch someone's kid and then ask that deputy or marshal what they were willing to do to keep their child alive.

Nick bet the answer would be *anything.*

Draper shared custody of his high-school-age son with his ex-wife. It wouldn't have been difficult for a skilled assassin to reach out and touch them.

The cartel would go to extraordinary lengths to stop Lori from testifying if it was going to hem up seventy-five percent of their money-laundering operation.

Seventy-five. "How do you know WCM was cleaning seventy-five percent of the cartel's money?"

Her eyes shifted away a second. "I was the accountant assigned to that client's portfolio."

That gave her access to everything the cartel would've invested, but something about Lori's explanation didn't jibe. "Yeah, okay, but you would only know how much WCM cleaned for them and how much was the firm's cut. Not what percentage that was of the cartel's entire bankroll."

Unless she had information from inside the cartel itself.

If he hadn't lifted his gaze from the road to glance at her, he might have missed it. Hell, even though he'd seen it, that flash of alarm in her eyes had popped up and vanished so quickly, he doubted his eyesight.

"What are you suggesting?" she asked, reeling away against the passenger door. "Are you accusing me of something?"

"I'm not accusing you of anything. I'm trying to understand because this isn't adding up."

"I don't know what you want me to say."

"How about the truth." He didn't think she was lying per se, but she wasn't being completely forthright. She was hiding something from him. The question was, what?

He was aware she had an immunity deal, but he'd assumed it was to protect her if she had unwittingly done something that she could be charged for later. Now he wasn't so sure.

"Why do you have an immunity clause in your deal to testify?"

She narrowed her eyes, lifting the wall between them. "Aren't the specifics of a witness's deal supposed to be confidential? Not even deputy marshals are supposed to know, right?"

Whoa. Her throwing in his face that she was a witness and he was a deputy hurt worse than a kick to the gut. She was correct and entirely justified if she felt he'd violated her privacy. But the sting of her words told him that he'd lost professional objectivity.

"Yes, it's supposed to be confidential." Nick only knew

because he'd overheard Draper at the tail end of a conversation with the US attorney's office. "But answering a question with a question isn't really giving me an answer."

Lori shook her head, withdrawing into herself. "I went to the FBI when I didn't have to. I was doing my civic duty, trying to do the right thing. This is a job for you, but it's *my* life that's being ripped to shreds. Those assassins are hunting *me*. So why do I feel like I'm the one on trial here?"

Forget a kick to the gut; this was a boot heel to the teeth. "I didn't mean for you to take it like that."

"I took it the way you intended, and don't use that tone with me."

"What tone?"

"Oh, please." She waved a hand at him in disgust. "As if you don't know. It's one thing to use it while barking out orders to protect me. It's another thing to unleash it to intimidate me."

He smothered the frustration simmering inside. Snapping at her wasn't going to achieve anything.

"Look," he said, making his tone Charmin-soft, "knowing exactly what we're dealing with will help me protect you."

"I found out WCM was laundering money for *Los Chacales* and went to the FBI. The cartel put a price on my head. Now Belladonna and her merry band of killers are gunning for me. End of story. What more do you need to know to keep me alive?"

He was on her side. The only thing standing between her and a hot slug to the back of the head. Yes, she was an assignment and he was professionally obligated to protect her, but he meant it when he'd told her that he'd rather cut off his right arm than hurt her. He sure as hell would jump in the line of fire and take a bullet for her and that didn't have a damn thing to do with his job.

If she didn't have anything to hide, then she wouldn't

be so defensive. Evasive. Throwing out the reminder of her confidentiality clause like a yellow flag on a football play.

"I get that this is personal for your in-laws." He did his best to bottle his rising anger. "But I need to know if this is also personal for the cartel?"

Lori folded her arms across her chest and straightened. She wasn't budging.

"Hundreds of millions of dollars are at stake," she said. "I don't think it gets more personal than that. Do you?"

She did it again. Used a whole lot of words to avoid giving him a straight answer.

He pulled into a spot in front of a mobile phone store down the block from the sheriff's department and threw the gear into Park. As much as he wanted to continue this discussion, she didn't give him the chance.

Lori jumped out of the car and slammed the door.

Chapter Nine

Fuming, Lori stood on the sidewalk.

How had the conversation in the car spun so far out of control, so freaking fast? She'd let one little thing slip, and Nick picked it up and ran with it like a contestant on *The Amazing Race*.

That stubborn, willful, *gorgeous* man.

She was overwhelmed and scared and didn't need him ambushing her, too. Not when she was trying to catch her breath and make it through this the best way she knew how.

Nick shut his door and stalked over to her. "We can table the conversation for now, but don't think it's over," he said, irrepressible as always.

She rolled her eyes. "Of course not. Your ego couldn't handle that."

Incredulity eclipsed the banked indignation on his face. "My ego?"

"Yup. Because you weren't the one to decide *end of conversation*. You're like a dog with a bone, digging around in my business. My life." *Trying to unearth my secrets.* They were hers for one more day and then all her dirty laundry would be aired. "You and I both know full well that you don't need any of the answers to your questions to protect me."

He huffed at that. "You're right. I don't need the answers to do my job. But I do need them for my peace of mind."

Lori's brain was spinning to keep up with Nick's words. "What are you talking about?"

"To hell with the trial and the Marshals Service for a second. This—" he gestured between them "—is the first time I've had that *I give a damn* feeling for someone." His voice lowered, resonating with a gravelly heat that turned her center molten. "Yes, it's ill-timed and inappropriate, but if that bothered you, then you wouldn't have kissed me back. And woman, you kissed the hell out of me."

He pulled her into his arms, and she was tempted to run her fingers through his thick hair and absorb the security of his embrace, to yield to him in every way. But she couldn't.

"What I'm saying is, I'm crazy about you, Lori."

He wrapped an arm around her waist and caught her chin, forcing her to look at him. His thumb feathered across her cheek.

Heart racing, she gaped at him, overcome by his words and the uncharacteristic emotion that shone on his face.

"I know you like to dunk your peanut butter sandwiches in milk," he said. "That you won't eat Chinese food without chopsticks. That you hate carnations because they remind you of your mother's funeral. That charity work uplifts you, renews your spirit. It's your way of giving back since it was the Helping Hands Foundation that saved you during those rough years with your dad."

This was killing her. She pressed her trembling fingertips to his lips to silence him. If he didn't stop, he was going to turn her into a mess. A big, sappy mess.

But he kissed the pads of her fingers and kept talking. "Your favorite book is *Wuthering Heights* and Heathcliff ruined you for life. Now you're only attracted to the dark, brooding, dangerous type. Lucky for me." He stared down at her, his smile sexy and devastating.

Deep in the pit of her stomach, she knew that no other man would look at her as he did right then. She wanted to burn this moment into her memory so she would never, ever forget it.

"But I have to know what I'm dealing with, who you are," Nick said. "All the cards on the table. It's the only way we can tell if this is real."

For a long, breathless moment, she was too choked up to speak. He wanted to see her layers, nothing more than she'd asked of him, but voicing the truth would snip this connection between them. Like cutting a tether. She couldn't bear that on top of everything else going on.

She couldn't breathe past the knot in her throat, but she forced herself to swallow down the ache. To ignore the hot flutter of desire.

"What difference does it make?" Desperation flooded her. "If I survive, after I testify, I'm gone and it's over, anyway."

Why put themselves through unnecessary heartache?

Better to leave well enough alone. She wrenched free of his grasp, hating the way she had been softening in his arms, and stormed into the cell-phone store. Spotting a small display of flip phones, she hurried to the rack.

Nick went up to her, drawing her attention like a tractor beam. "It matters to me. And I hope like hell that it matters to you, too."

Of course it mattered. No man had ever been so honest with her, shown her so much respect by opening up the way Nick had back at the clinic. It couldn't have been easy, and she admired his courage. The trust he'd shown her was a gift and a miracle rolled into one.

She understood what it meant. What it was worth.

Her reluctance to do the same made her the biggest hypocrite.

For someone who detested double standards, her omission sickened her, but she didn't have the strength for the cold slap of rejection that she'd face from him.

"There's no point," she said. "Please, drop it."

He nodded, his eyes growing cold. "Well, that's the most disappointing response I've ever heard." His tone was hard enough to crush a diamond, reminding her with blinding clarity that there was nothing soft about this man.

Not his body, or his mind, or his personality.

"Welcome back, Deputy Marshal Dredd. Did you have a nice ten-minute vacation?"

Regret stung her tongue. She wanted to hit Rewind and take those ugly words back. The man just told her he was crazy about her for goodness' sake, and instead of being honest, she pulled the rejection rip cord first and parachuted out.

"Wish I could say it was nice to see you, Lori 'The Chicken' Carpenter, but I'm not a liar. I had a fantastic vacation with an incredible woman until she lost her suitcase full of courage. Too bad she's not here now." He grabbed a phone and went to pay for it.

What in the hell could she say to that?

He was right. She was a coward.

Even more surprising, through the anger and the argument, the sexual tension arcing between them was a live wire crackling with heat.

She went up to the register where Nick was paying. The clerk cut the plastic packaging open for them and tossed it in the trash. Nick pocketed the phone.

They walked to the sheriff's department in silence. He opened the door for her, and she entered the vestibule on rubbery legs. She found she couldn't look at Nick. Not that he had done anything wrong. She'd probably have a harder time looking in the mirror.

He held the inner door for her, as well, and they approached the front desk.

"Hi, how can I help?" the twentysomething receptionist asked.

"I'd like to speak with Sheriff Sheila Holmes." He flashed his badge to the receptionist.

Lori glanced past the four empty desks spread out behind the receptionist to the sheriff's office. Through the office window, Lori spotted the sheriff engrossed in a lively conversation with a man about ten years her junior who was holding a pie.

The physical similarities between the sheriff and the vet were plain. The same slender build, olive complexion, friendly, heart-shaped face, mahogany hair—the sheriff's was pulled into a loose French braid.

"Certainly. One moment," the receptionist said.

Apparently, the office was so small and informal, she just spun around in her seat and beckoned the sheriff over with a hand.

Sheriff Holmes clasped the man on the arm and said something to him that caused him to nod and hand her the pie.

She took it and walked him to the front. "Thanks again, Gerald, but if you keep bringing me these delicious pies, I'm not going to be able to fit into my uniform."

A tantalizing aroma curled around Lori and she realized that it had been more than six hours since she'd eaten.

"I've got to win you over some way, Sheila. I figured my best bet is through my baking. So, I'm not going to stop until you agree to have dinner with me. I've got a huckleberry recipe that'll knock your socks off." He winked.

The sheriff chuckled at that, the bright smile emphasizing the fine lines around her eyes and mouth. Then she caught sight of the bulletproof vest Lori was wearing and her laughter died.

"You better say yes," the receptionist said, still giggling, "before one of us gains fifteen pounds from eating all that sugary goodness."

"Thanks again." The sheriff's tone flattened as she gestured to the pie.

Gerald took the hint. He slipped on his ball cap, tipped the bill to her and was gone.

"Hello, I'm Sheriff Holmes." She set the pie on the counter and proffered her hand.

"Deputy Marshal Nick McKenna." He shook her hand. "Do you mind if we speak privately in your office?"

Up close, Lori noticed the same smattering of freckles across Sheila's nose that Renee had. They were both approachable and welcoming, but where Renee had been sweet, there was a discernible toughness to the sheriff.

"Not at all. Can we get you two anything?" the sheriff asked. "Water, coffee, strawberry-rhubarb pie?"

Lori's stomach answered with a loud rumble. "All three for me, please."

"I'll just have a water," Nick said.

The receptionist nodded. "I'll bring it in a moment."

"Thank you, Suzie," the sheriff said, and then led them to her office.

She invited them to sit in chairs opposite her desk and closed the door.

Once the sheriff was seated behind her desk, Nick said, "Ma'am, what I'm about to tell you is extremely sensitive and confidential. I'd appreciate your discretion."

"Okay." She folded her hands on the top of her desk. "I'm listening."

"This is Lori Carpenter. She's been in WITSEC for a year and is supposed to testify in an important trial tomorrow down in San Diego. My office has been compromised and her whereabouts leaked to *Los Chacales*. The drug cartel."

The sheriff's face hardened as she took everything in. "I'm familiar with them. A pretty dangerous group."

Dangerous? That was like calling a hurricane gale a breeze.

They seemed unstoppable and relentless. If the sheriff didn't help them, if this plan didn't work, Lori had no clue what they were going to do.

"Yes, ma'am. They are," Nick said.

The receptionist knocked and entered. She set a tray down on the desk, passed around beverages, handed Lori a piece of pie and a fork.

The sheriff thanked Suzie again, and the receptionist left.

Lori dug in, scarfing down the slice of heaven in five bites before Nick got to the grisly parts and she lost her appetite. The sheriff studied her intently, gaze bouncing back to Nick every few seconds as he continued to explain.

"Four attempts have been made on her life since this morning, including at our safe house, which was rigged with explosives and killed my partner."

The sheriff's eyes narrowed, and she straightened. "The explosion on Mill Creek. That was you?"

Nick and Lori both nodded.

"Two of my deputies are out there now. The fire department recovered a body. I take it that was your partner," Sheriff Holmes said. "I'm sorry for your loss."

Nick hung his head. Guilt over Ted must've been heavy as sandbags on his shoulders by the looks of him.

"We barely survived," Lori said. "If it hadn't been for Nick, I wouldn't have. I owe him my life." She turned to him, but he refused to meet her eyes.

Lori owed him much more than that. A debt that couldn't be repaid.

At the very least, if they made it to the courthouse, she'd tell him how much he meant to her before they parted ways forever. Tell him that she was beyond crazy for him, totally over the moon and lost. Hopelessly lost in the sense of comfort and security his touch brought; lost in his incredible magnetism when they were in the same room; lost in his dark eyes when he looked at her. And if she stared into them now, she'd drown in the bourbon-brown depths.

She ached at the thought of never jogging together again, no more long conversations, not playing board games, not watching movies, not cooking together and taste-testing recipes.

He'd given her so much, shown consideration for things in ways that Ted hadn't. Still, it might've just been him fulfilling his job duties, but the time they'd spent together had shown her how much she'd tolerated from others, how little she'd expected for herself and thought she deserved.

Although she was seated, she felt off balance. Her heart was breaking. The world was unraveling. She was going to lose her best friend.

Lori had had a handful of lovers and been married once, but none of those men had been her best friend. Or knew her as well as Nick did.

She couldn't hold back the tears welling in her eyes.

"Here." Sheriff Holmes handed her a box of tissues. "I'm sure today has been quite an ordeal for you."

"Yes, it has," Lori breathed.

Nick placed his hand on her shoulder and gave her a long sideways glance, the affection in his eyes saying he was there for her. The silent gesture was all he could do in front of someone else.

"Sheriff," he said, drawing his hand into his lap, "the cartel is still here. Close by."

Lori and Nick exchanged a look. She held her breath, waiting to see if he was going to mention Renee and what happened at the clinic.

"Special Operation Group deputies are coming up from San Diego to provide assistance," he said. "We need a safe place to wait and to keep Lori's name out of your system until then."

"Why hasn't the LA Marshals' office been notified?" the sheriff asked. "They're closer."

"I'm not a hundred percent sure. My boss, Will Draper, made the decision. Possibly to limit their involvement since we don't know if the leak could've come from their office. But ma'am, I have reason to believe that Marshal Draper might in fact be the breach."

Sheriff Holmes pursed her lips and leaned back in her chair, the leather groaning with the movement. "That's a pretty heavy accusation. Do you have anything to substantiate it?"

"No, ma'am. I'm afraid I don't."

Lori chugged a little water and then traded it for black coffee, bypassing the cream.

"Is there anyone who can corroborate your story?" Holmes asked.

"The marshals on their way up here can."

"Give me a number." She picked up the phone and waited.

"I'd prefer to hold off on notifying them until they're closer to the area," Nick said.

The silence that followed was tense.

Sheriff Holmes studied him a moment, looked to Lori, then back to him. "Why is that exactly?"

"As I've told you, we've been compromised," Nick said. "I think it might be my boss. He is the only person who has been aware of Lori's location up to thirty minutes ago, where the cartel last found us. But as you pointed out, I don't have proof. Therefore, I could be wrong. If we wait until my teammates are closer to Big Bear Lake, then we've risked nothing. Tipping our hand sooner opens the door to the possibility of sabotage."

Holmes drew in a deep breath, seeming to weigh her

options. The whole back-and-forth process agitated Lori's nerves.

"How about I ask the State Police to send a few squad cars over? Precautionary measure," the sheriff said.

"Would that request entail notifying them that a deputy marshal is in your office along with a star witness?" Nick asked.

"It would. To tap their resources requires a darn good reason. You have one, but to get them here means I have to share that reason."

"Then that's not a course of action I can endorse. No one can know we're here. The moment you make a call, it could be intercepted."

"I want to help, but you're not giving me much to work with while asking me to have a bucketful of faith in your story." She folded her arms. "What was the last location where you were attacked?"

Nick's gaze fell, but apart from that, Lori wanted to shake whatever he was thinking loose from his lips.

She didn't want to spoil any strategy he had planned, but Renee's situation, the predicament they had left her in, was eating Lori up inside. She couldn't stand it any longer and opened her mouth to confess what had happened.

"Sheriff," the receptionist interrupted over the intercom of the phone on the desk. "US Marshal Will Draper is on the line for you."

The sheriff raised an eyebrow and looked to Nick. "Anything you want to change about your story before I take that call?"

"No, ma'am. But I would ask that you put it on speaker and refrain from mentioning that we're here."

"How about we start by putting it on speaker and see how it goes?"

A quick nod from Nick. "Your house, your rules."

Lori's stomach flipped over and knotted.

"Sheriff Holmes, here. How can I help you, Marshal Draper?"

"Hello, Sheriff. I have reason to believe that a rogue deputy of mine, Nick McKenna, along with a witness who is in protective custody, is on his way to see you. If he's not there already."

One silent beat passed, followed by another as the sheriff eyeballed Nick. "What makes you think that, Marshal?"

"The transceiver in his car shows that he's very close to your location," Draper said. "A quick stroll away."

Sheriff Holmes tilted her head, gaze bouncing between Nick and Lori.

Nick clenched his jaw and Lori could tell he was beating himself for leaving the car so close. But it wasn't as if they'd had time to switch cars and she hadn't been up for a trek through the woods on foot. The longer they were exposed in public, the easier it would be for Belladonna to find them.

Lori wanted to reach over and take his hand, tell him that it was okay.

"You said Deputy McKenna has gone rogue. In what way?" Sheriff Holmes asked.

"He just lost his partner and has faced several near-death experiences today."

That was all true, Lori thought. Maybe Draper wasn't the traitor and had no intention of throwing Nick under the bus.

"But McKenna has shown signs of being unstable," Draper said, shattering Lori's fragile hope. "I'm afraid this has sent him off the rails."

Lori shook her head, wordlessly pleading with the sheriff not to believe a word of it, but Draper went on.

"First, he violated protocol, endangering a very important witness by taking her to be treated at a veterinary clinic," Draper said, and the sheriff's eyes flared wide.

"Then he abandoned his government-issued phone. He's paranoid, delusional and exhibiting rash behavior."

"You son of a bitch." Nick jumped to his feet. "You're just trying to cover your own ass. Isn't that right, Mr. Clean?"

"Listen to me, you hotheaded, impulsive, insubordinate bastard," Draper said.

"Which veterinarian?" Sheriff Holmes interrupted, her face darkening with alarm.

Draper didn't respond, and Nick hung his head.

The sheriff stood up. "I asked which clinic." Her voice was cold steel.

"Happy Paws and Wagging Tails," Lori said. Regret and guilt snaked through her veins. "Your daughter's clinic."

Sheriff Holmes blanched.

"Draper, you still there?" Nick's brow furrowed. "Draper?"

The sheriff picked up the receiver, putting it to her ear, paused, then stabbed a few buttons on the dialer. "The line is dead."

Lori and Nick turned toward the front door at the same time.

Four black SUVs pulled up and parked.

Lori's stomach dropped to the floor. "Oh, God. They're here."

Chapter Ten

"Who's here?" Sheriff Holmes asked.

"The cartel." Nick drew his weapon. "They're here for Lori." *Draper strikes again.* Nick and Lori had to make it through this alive, so he could beat Draper to a bloody pulp.

A deputy walked in from the back door next to the sheriff's office. He ducked his head inside the room. "Hey, Aunt Sheila—I mean Sheriff. As I was coming in, I noticed a suspicious van and SUV pull up out back."

The sheriff hopped to her feet. "Suzie! Lock the front door. Now!"

The receptionist wrenched open a desk drawer and fished out a set of keys. She scurried out of her seat and hustled to the door. Fumbling with the keys trying to find the right one, she dropped them, and they fell to the floor in a clatter. She scooped them up and scrabbled for the right one. Shoving the key into the dead bolt, she locked it.

Suzie clutched the keys to her chest and backed away from the doors.

The deputy looked around, his eyes clouded with confusion. "What's going on, Auntie?"

"The *Los Chacales* cartel is here."

"The Jackals? Are you kidding me?" He rocked back on his heels. "What are they doing around here? Vacationing at the lake?"

"No, Denny," the sheriff said, flatly.

"Wow." He folded his arms. "You're serious."

"Nick, what do we do?" Lori asked.

Belladonna exited one of the vehicles, walked up to the front door, slipped her hands into her pockets and waited.

Nick reached out and drew Lori close, putting her behind him. "We need to prepare for heavy action."

"Denny, go to the armory," Holmes said. "See if you can contact the State Police on the two-way radio. Then bring everything you can carry, locked and loaded—extra ammo, too."

"I can help you carry weapons," Lori said.

Nick nodded for her to go with him. "But stay away from windows."

"There are none back there," the deputy said. "Come on, miss."

"That woman is called Belladonna." Nick gestured to the dark-haired, lethal-looking lady out front. There wasn't a stitch of concern on her face. The air of confidence about her was unnerving. "She's not here to talk. She's here to kill Lori Carpenter. Anything she says or does is with that singular goal in mind."

Sheriff Holmes nodded. "That may be, but this is my house. My rules. And we'll play it my way."

Nick followed the sheriff to the receptionist's desk. "Suzie, if I give the signal, you hit the emergency button. Understand?"

The receptionist's gaze flickered to a big red button on the wall next to her desk, then she looked back to the sheriff and nodded. "I understand."

"Then what happens?" Nick asked. "A bunch of flares launch, and someone responds to the distress signal?" He wasn't trying to be funny, but he did want to know how the red button was going to save the day.

"No flares. This place gets locked down tighter than a

chastity belt with four-inch-thick reinforced steel, capable of withstanding the impact of a truck. Nobody is getting in."

He wished he shared her confidence, but Belladonna was full of surprises, and underestimating her might be a mistake they wouldn't live long enough to regret.

"No joy on the two-way, Aunt—" Denny stammered. "I mean Sheriff," he said, setting down an armful of weapons on one of the desks in the rear of the station. He had everything from assault rifles, shotguns, to M84 stun grenades. But the last item he dropped on the table was unexpected.

"You have a machete?" Nick asked.

Denny grinned and nodded. "We confiscated it two months ago from a hunter going after big game in the area without a license. I shudder to think what he planned to do with it. Hack up a mountain lion or a bear?" Grimacing, he shrugged.

Lori dumped boxes of extra ammo beside the stash.

"Hang back there," Nick said to her, not wanting to give Belladonna the chance to take a potshot at Lori or give a possible sniper a clear line of sight.

Pressing her palms to the bulletproof vest, Lori gave a quick nod.

"What's the plan?" the deputy asked.

"That woman is standing there waiting to talk," Holmes said. "So I'm going to hear her out and make it clear that Ms. Carpenter is under the protection of this department. Then I'll take it from there."

"I'd advise against talking to Belladonna at all, much less winging it." Nick didn't think the sheriff was being naive, assuming it would be quite that simple, but she was way out of her depth here. "Dealing with the cartel isn't the same as handling a few meth heads or some drunks in a bar fight."

"This may be a small town, but I'm not a dumb hick.

And this is my house." The sheriff looked at Suzie. "If it comes to it, on my mark, hit the button. Don't hesitate."

"I won't let you down, Sheriff," Suzie said.

Holmes squared her shoulders and straightened her spine like she was shoring herself up. She turned and pulled open the inner door, stepping into the vestibule.

Nick kept his weapon ready and stood on the threshold between the small antechamber and the rest of the station so he could hear the conversation and cover the sheriff.

With his gun aimed at Belladonna, he wondered if chopping off the head would stop the war-beast hunting Lori. Or would two new heads spring up?

Belladonna clasped her hands in front of her as if preparing to do business. "Good day, Sheriff."

"*Los Chacales* aren't welcome in my town. What do you want?" Holmes asked through the door.

"I think you know the answer to that question already." Belladonna's gaze cut to Nick before falling back to the sheriff.

"It's not going to happen," Holmes said. "You'll have to go through me, my deputy and that deputy marshal in there first to get to that woman. Not to mention the State Police who'll show up if you start any trouble and cause problems. It isn't worth it. I suggest you get back in your vehicle and leave with the rest of your *Jackals*."

"I'm willing to wager you'll open that door for me within the next two minutes."

The sheriff hooked her thumbs on her utility belt. "I'll take that bet and double down."

"I like your spirit." An amused look spilled across Belladonna's face. She glanced at her wristwatch, then lifted her hand and snapped her fingers.

The rear passenger's side door of the SUV on the right opened. A man got out, tugging someone along with him.

Renee. She was alive.

A jolt of relief that the young veterinarian hadn't been killed was quickly submerged in a wave of dread. Gut-churning, get-a-head-start-running, they're-screwed dread.

Belladonna had the ultimate leverage.

"Renee?" the deputy asked, stepping closer.

A harsh audible breath rushed from Sheriff Holmes. Her hands flew to the door, palms pressed to the glass. "Oh, God, not my baby," she said in barely more than a whisper, her voice cracking.

As the sheriff's composure dissolved from staunch professional into terrified parent, that sense of dread morphed into something deeper, scarier. His instincts might be misfiring, and maybe he was overreacting. It was possible that Sheriff Holmes was so principled that her response would be aboveboard.

But Nick was no idiot. It was possible, but not probable.

Renee was gagged and her hands bound, but didn't appear to have any injuries. Her tearstained faced looked younger, more innocent, than it had an hour ago.

Belladonna took Renee by the elbow and hauled her up to the door. "Sheriff, I understand that you have an admirable sense of duty and a moral constitution that I never will, but nonetheless respect. You can keep your principles, your conscience unsullied. Or your daughter can keep her life."

A sob came from Sheriff Holmes and she covered her mouth with her hand.

"Don't do it, Mom," Renee said, the words muffled but the meaning crystal clear. "Don't."

"If you listen to your daughter, tomorrow you'll be planning her funeral. Deciding between a casket and cremation." Belladonna's grave words hung there.

The tension stretching throughout the station pulled tight as a rubber band ready to snap.

"Aunt Sheila, it's Renee, for crying out loud," the deputy

said, trying to get closer, but Nick raised a palm, keeping him back. "We've got to open it, don't we?"

Trembling, Holmes shook her head, like it was an impossible choice ripping her apart on the inside. Nick could only imagine what was going through her mind.

His gut twisted with worry.

Sheila Holmes was an upstanding sheriff, but she was a mother first. A mama bear who wasn't going to let anyone hurt her cub. To hell with the law. To hell with having blood on her hands. To hell with aiding and abetting murderers.

Nick had from that very moment until the sheriff admitted the very same to herself for him to figure out what to do.

The wall clock ticking into the petrified silence told him he didn't have long.

"If you open that door," Nick said, "Lori is dead, and the Jackals win. More people will die at their hands."

"Lori's testimony may hurt the flow of our money for a little while, but it will *not* stop us. More people will die at our hands regardless." Belladonna was all business. "If you don't open the door, I'll snap your daughter's neck like a twig, and I promise you that I will still get inside your station. You'd gain nothing, and lose your daughter for what? To protect Lori Carpenter, a woman who isn't as innocent and sweet as she might lead you to believe."

Lori's eyes had grown wider and wider as the assassin had spoken.

Belladonna's gaze flashed past the sheriff and collided with Nick's. In his peripheral vision, he saw Lori backpedaling away.

"A year is a long time to spend watching over someone. Isn't it, McKenna? Easy to understand if you've developed a soft spot for her. Did she tell you how she became the accountant for WCM's largest client?"

"Her in-laws own the firm," Nick said. "She was given the promotion as part of the settlement of her divorce."

They'd both been briefly married before. He'd gleaned tidbits from their conversations about their ex-spouses, but that was as much as Lori had shared. Deflecting with how she couldn't discuss the case.

"Is that what she told you? And, of course, you believed her. It's a good story. Not as sordid as the truth. Did she happen to mention that she was my boss's lover for almost a year?"

It was a blow, hitting Nick in the chest like a sucker punch.

"Oh, yes." Belladonna nodded. "They were hot and heavy, lived together, your Lori and a *jefe* of *Los Chacales*. When the accountant handling our portfolio *retired*, my boss is the one who saw to Lori's advancement. He gave her quite a lot. A promotion. Jewelry. Luxurious trips. Payoffs. She took all of it. Including our hush money. To say the least, he's not happy with her. You're protecting a liar. A thief. A traitor. The mistress of a drug lord."

His heart stopped for a beat. Nick stood there, reeling, his head hung low. A part of him had suspected that Lori was hiding something. But this...

This was too ugly. Too repugnant. Too much.

He had to detach, be all focus and purpose. Not take the bombshell personally.

Nick looked up and caught the smirk on Belladonna's face.

This was what she wanted. To drive a wedge between them. Divide and conquer.

"You're very good," Nick said to Belladonna. "Quite silver-tongued."

"Thank you. I had an excellent teacher."

"But it won't work." Nick shook his head, clinging to cautious hope that none of this would influence the sheriff.

"Really?" Belladonna's face softened and her voice lowered as her gaze returned to Holmes. "This is a small town,

Sheriff. No one will know that you opened the door. No one will care because Renee will still be alive."

Nick's pulse quickened, his body registering the fight-or-flight need. "Lori may be all of the things you said. Hell, most of the people in WITSEC are, but she is still a material witness."

Justice had to prevail.

"Sheriff," Belladonna said, "what's it going to be? Lori Carpenter? Or your daughter? You have ten seconds."

"I can't do this." Holmes looked back at Nick and Lori over her shoulder, her expression stricken, her voice anguished. "Forgive me." She reached for her keys that were hooked on her belt.

Damn. Nick had expected it, but shock still slammed into him. He spun, vaulting toward the wall, and lunged for the red button.

He slapped it as hard as he could.

Steel shutters dropped in front of the door and windows, zipping down with a deafening thud.

"No! Renee!" Sheriff Holmes cried. "That's my daughter out there!"

Nick's gut burned. Renee Holmes was an innocent, only guilty of helping them. The last thing he wanted was to throw her to the wolves twice. "I'm sorry."

The shutter rattled as though someone on the other side had kicked it. "Pull it up!" Belladonna said.

"I can't," the sheriff sobbed. "It's on a thirty-minute time lock and sends an automatic distress signal to the State Police. Please, don't hurt my daughter! Please! Renee!" The sheriff sobbed, screamed, pounding on the door.

Her nephew rushed into the vestibule and threw his arms around her. From her trembling mouth came more wild, primal cries as she kicked and flailed.

Nick stood there, stunned to silence. The outpouring of

her pain was worse than if he'd taken physical blows on his head and shoulders.

Lori turned away from the sight, hugging herself, and leaned against the desk.

Five minutes ago he would've gone to Lori and put a re-assuring hand on her back. Now, renewed shock and anger flooded his mind, churning and growing into something so raw he wasn't sure he could ever stand to touch her again.

This is just a job. She is just a witness.

And he'd keep telling himself that until it was true.

Denny dragged his aunt away from the door. Suzie went to her, as well. The two of them tried to console Holmes with words; they tried to comfort her by holding her, but nothing worked to stop her tears.

Once the sheriff's movements slowed and she caught her breath, she stared at Nick, glaring daggers at him. "What did you do?"

It was a rhetorical question, but in a low voice, he said, "Stopped you from making a terrible mistake."

"You son of a bitch." She lunged for him as though she meant to claw his eyes out.

Nick swung his gun in her direction.

Her nephew wrangled her back. "Aunt Sheila, don't. Please, calm down."

"Trying to save my daughter wasn't a mistake! Are you a parent, McKenna?"

The combination of the sheriff's tormented tone and the reality that he'd never had anything in his life as precious as a child gutted Nick. "No. No, I'm not."

Shaking her head, she squeezed her eyes shut and sobbed. Suzie hugged her back, crying along with her.

Everything the marshals had taught him kicked in. "Sheriff, they have nothing to gain by hurting Renee now." It was the only thing Nick could think to say. His point was valid, but he didn't have a clue whether Renee would be unharmed. "She'll be okay," he said, using that well-practiced, comforting tone.

It wasn't his intention to make false promises. Witnesses fretted all the time about loved ones that had been left behind and needed reassurance. Sometimes hope had to be enough when there was nothing else to cling to.

"What if you're wrong," the sheriff snapped, "and they kill her out of spite? Those merciless monsters don't even need a reason to shed blood, but you gave them one. Didn't you? You ticked that woman off and she's going to take it out on my baby." She cut her eyes from him in disgust.

If he was wrong, and he prayed that he wasn't, then Renee's death would be on his conscience and he'd have to find a way to live with that.

"Lori, remove the sheriff's and deputy's sidearms," he said while keeping his gaze on the distraught mother.

"You can't do that," the nephew said.

Nick gestured for Lori to get on with it. She removed both guns from their hip holsters.

"It's just until you calm down." Incensed people in great distress did the stupidest things. Sometimes when they came to their senses, they had no recollection of what they'd done. "I think you should go back into your office and try to see reason." Nick motioned for them to start walking, keeping the gun pointed at them.

The trio shuffled to the office and Nick followed, to be certain no one made an irrational grab for one of the loaded guns on the table along the way.

"All we have to do is stay calm and wait it out," Nick said. "The cavalry will be here in less than thirty minutes."

DAMN!

Belladonna roared on the inside, thirsting to rip Nick McKenna's head from his body with her bare teeth. She'd been so close, so damn close, to sealing the deal and getting the sheriff to cooperate that her damn pulse throbbed in her temples.

Her first inclination was to exorcise the rage and frustration by shooting Renee in the face.

Then Belladonna thought of losing her own daughter to senseless violence, no open casket… Did she still have the nerve to do this job?

But it was more than just a trade. It was a culture of brutality.

Robin Leach never would've hosted a show called *Lifestyles of the Fierce and Dangerous.*

She needed to find a way out, for the sake of her family.

Love had planted seeds, taken root deep, and over the past three years, she'd sprouted a deplorable heart. It made her weak. Soft.

But in this moment, her determination was on fire.

She shoved Renee to the side. The young woman tripped and fell. Belladonna kicked at her to get going, but Renee cowered like a miserable, beaten dog.

Pulling on a tight, stoic expression, as if this fiasco didn't faze her in the least, Belladonna spun on her heel and crossed the street.

While her men backed up their vehicles, repositioning near her, she touched her earpiece. "Converge on my location. Now," she said to her people who were stationed at the rear of the building.

She was done playing games. The pressure was about to get cranked to the max.

Once her men poured out of their vehicles, armed to the nth degree, and huddled around her, she looked at Smokey. "Go get Big Ben."

He turned and marched to the van, like a loyal soldier.

"The State Police will be here in less than nine minutes," Belladonna said to the rest. "We need to get in there and eliminate the target in eight. On my mark, set your timers. In five. Four. Three. Two. One."

A series of digital beeps resounded.

Smokey returned carrying an anti-tank rocket launcher loaded with a high-explosive warhead. He propped it on his shoulder, aimed at the sheriff's department and prepped the RPG.

Across the street, Renee's eyes flared wide. She scrambled up from the ground and took off like a bat out of hell.

Finally. *Stupid bitch.*

With the snap of her fingers, Belladonna issued the wordless order, *Smokey, make a hole.*

He smirked. "My pleasure."

Chapter Eleven

Darkness. Lori's head swam in a sea of darkness.

Her eyelids fluttered open. She lay facedown, her cheek pressed against the tile floor. Dust and acrid smoke tainted each breath, clogged her throat.

Her ears rang above the pounding in her head. Her lungs were like heavy, wet sandbags. She coughed, barely able to breathe, the throbbing ache remaining.

Nick!

A terrifying blast had torn through the front of the sheriff's department. The intensity of the explosion had hit the building like a magnitude-ten earthquake. Nick had grabbed her and shoved her down behind a desk. She would've sworn he'd been right there beside her.

Nick!

She wanted to move, to find Nick. But it was as if she'd been displaced from her body and had no control over her limbs.

On a primitive level, she knew she had to get up—had get out of there. But her brain was full of static, blaring white noise.

One thought broke through. Belladonna was coming for her. That assassin wouldn't stop until Lori was dead and permanently silenced.

Her mind staggered at the grim reality.

She had to move. Now. Lori mustered her strength and

pushed up to her knees. The movement made her head spin and her sluggish body ache in places that had been numb a moment ago.

"I've got you." Nick clutched her shoulders, his voice bringing instant comfort.

He was alive.

"Can you stand?"

She had to try. "Think so."

Holding her by the arms, he hauled her onto her feet. Her chest heaved with the harshness of her strained breathing.

Pain ripped through her side and she pressed her palm to the area. It was tender and sore.

Lori swayed and staggered, desperate to orient herself. "What happened?"

"My best guess, it was an RPG. We have to move before they come in and slaughter us all. The smoke and the flames at the front are the only reasons that they aren't already in here."

His words were the adrenaline-fueled shot of reality that she needed. Survival instinct kicked in, jump-starting her brain and snapping her out of a stupor.

She gave a weak nod and turned to him. His appearance rattled her. Plaster dust and ash covered him, his face peppered with cuts and bruises, but he was alert. Closer inspection made her freeze. Blood dripped from his temple down along his cheek. The breath locked in her lungs. She touched a gash on his head above his brow.

He hissed in pain, reeling away from her fingers.

The sound gripped her heart, reminding her of the secrets Belladonna had spilled and twisted. Not into lies, but into an oversimplified, convenient version of the truth.

"Nick, are you okay?"

His lips thinned, the look in his eyes savage. "Yeah, I'm fine," he said in an uncompromisingly male tone. "You?"

Her skin was hot and damp with perspiration, and every

muscle throbbed like a wound. "I'm walking and talking, so yeah. I guess." She looked around.

There were too many things to register at once. Plaster was still crumbling around them. Ashes rained down. Sparking electrical wires hung from the ceiling. Everything was in ruins—shattered glass, twisted steel, chunks of concrete. The reinforced shutter that had been shielding the front door was decimated. A gaping hole ringed by a jagged line of fire was left in its wake.

Nick rushed to the far rear of the station and checked on the others inside the sheriff's office. Lori tried to catch her breath and stayed close behind him, battling the dizziness.

The sheriff, the deputy and the receptionist were in shock, but managed to climb to their feet.

Suzie's bleeding arm appeared to be the worst of their injuries, but she didn't look too good. She swayed, unable to find her balance.

Lori wondered if she might have a concussion. Hell, they all might.

Suzie doubled over and vomited.

That wasn't good. The receptionist needed medical attention.

"We've got to pull it together, quickly," Nick said to the room. "Time is the enemy and it's working against us."

The deputy hurried and made sure his aunt was okay. Once she nodded and waved him off, Denny grabbed Suzie's arm, slung it over his shoulders, and helped steady her.

"They're about to storm in here and kill everyone." Nick's tone was as grave as their situation. "We need to be ready. In position to open fire first and not let them in."

"No!" The sheriff shoved off her desk and pushed forward. "We can't use lethal force. What if Renee is still alive and they use her as a human shield? Or she could get hit by a stray bullet. We can't fire unless we have clear shots."

The possibility of Renee taking friendly fire hadn't occurred to him. The idea was more than he could swallow. He'd left her to hang out to dry twice already. This wasn't going to be the third time. If she was alive out there, then he'd take every precaution to see that she wasn't harmed. He owed her for how she'd helped them when she didn't have to.

"All right," Nick said. "With all the smoke and dust, the only way to get a clear shot is to go outside, which might work to our advantage better than staying cornered and letting those murderers pick us off one by one." He went to the stockpile of weapons on the table a few feet away. Slinging a rifle over his shoulder, he also took the machete. "I'll start with nonlethal force." He snatched the stun-grenade launcher from the table and held it up. "The rest of you, arm up."

Propelled by a sense of urgency and self-preservation to evade, to escape, they each grabbed weapons.

Lori took two handguns and made sure the safety was off. Nick had taught her the basics of gun safety, even though they'd never practiced shooting.

If her skill at carnival shooting gallery games was any indication of her skill level, then her aim was lousy. But she reasoned that if someone got close enough, she'd be able to put a bullet in them.

"Okay, move it, people." Nick gestured and it got them all in gear, shuffling along. "We've got to hurry."

They made their way through rubble toward the front of what was left of the station. Stumbling around a block of concrete, Lori narrowly avoided an electrical wire that dropped and sizzled when it hit the floor.

Nausea bubbled in her stomach, but she kept going, hurrying along. One step in front of the other.

At the ragged, charred entrance, they separated and dispersed on either side. They all crouched down low behind what walls were left, staying out of sight. The billowing smoke and falling ash helped to camouflage them.

"I know it's called a stun grenade, but will it be strong enough to slow them down and give us a chance?" Lori asked.

Nick took her hand, his thumb brushing over her skin, and just as quickly let go as if he'd touched an exposed electrical wire. The spark of awareness hit her hard and deep. Then his gaze turned glacial, his features shuttering.

She wished they had thirty seconds alone, hardly enough time to explain how complicated things were for her, but enough to apologize for disappointing him. For hurting him by not being a better person.

"Each grenade will issue a flash of around six million candela—a huge pyrotechnic charge that will cause immediate blindness—and one hundred eighty decibels that will render them deaf. It'll knock them on their butts for a few minutes and give us a shot." He looked to the sheriff, letting Lori's hand go, and she rubbed her palm, surprised by the residual tingle. "Getting outside is the only way to see what's what. Right after I unleash a can of fury, or rather three, we make a break for it. We'll have minutes at best. Seconds at worst. We'll need to make each and every one count."

"Everybody watch your aim, in case Renee is out front," Sheriff Holmes said, and the group nodded in response. "You two should take off, get out of town. No offense, but if you leave, then maybe the trouble will follow you."

The sheriff wasn't wrong, and Lori wasn't offended. The trouble, aka Belladonna, would most certainly follow them.

"Fair enough," Nick said in response. "But we won't get far on foot. Does anyone have a car we can use?"

"I do." Denny fished keys out of his pocket and tossed them to Nick. "My Bronco is parked out back. It's an old beater, but it runs."

Nick gave a nod of thanks and stuffed them in his pocket. Turning, he took a knee and peeped around through the opening.

"Damn. They're coming across the street," he said low, raising the hair on the back of Lori's neck.

Her pulse skyrocketed, beating too fast, adrenaline soaring in her blood. She could do this. She had to do this. No other choice.

He lifted the launcher, lowered his eye to the sights and pulled the trigger. Three cans discharged with a soft *pssh* sound.

"Everyone, take cover," he whispered.

A hard lump of ice dropped in her gut, blipping out the nausea. Lori pressed her back against the wall. She closed her eyes and covered her ears.

THE CLATTERING SOUND was soft, barely perceptible over the car alarms blaring in *dee-do, dee-do* succession. The others had missed it. Three small canisters that had dropped, rolling on the asphalt in front of them. Putting them dead center in the kill radius of the grenades.

But Belladonna was several paces behind them and saw it.

She turned and shouted, "Grenade!" as she ran and dove for cover behind a nearby pickup truck. But it was too late to save them.

Brilliant flashes of light erupted behind her and at the same time two-hundred-decibel teeth-rattling bangs cracked the air.

Flash-bangs designed to disorient and confuse anyone in the vicinity. Not high-yield explosive or incendiary grenades meant to kill.

This was law enforcement she was dealing with. Stun grenade should've been her first thought, and if it had been, she would've covered her ears. But she had reacted on pure instinct.

She had been turned away from the flashes and had shut her eyes the second she processed what was happening, sparing her retinas the worst of it. Her vision was a little blurred and she saw stars.

Her ears were a different story. Forget about hearing at all.

The concussive blasts and deafening bangs turned her brain to mush. Ruptured her tympanic membrane. Disrupted the fluid in her middle and inner ear.

She tried to stand. The ground became a Tilt-A-Whirl ride, her balance obliterated.

Before she looked at her men, she knew what she'd find. The agonizing bursts of light had fried their eyes and since they had been farther ahead of her, they had absorbed the full brunt of the brain-hammering pops.

She peered around the rear of the truck. Her rooks and bishops were disabled and useless, writhing on the ground, holding their heads. Easy pickings.

Smokey and another rook were the closest to her. Both outweighed her by a good one hundred pounds. She grabbed Smokey by the collar and heaved with all her might, dragging him behind the vehicle.

Daring to go for the other one, she snatched his arm and hauled him across the pavement. Everything was off center and spinning. She stumbled and fell. There was no shaking off the effects of the stun grenades. She just had to muddle through it until the brain-caught-in-a-blender side effect wore off. Gripping her rook by both his wrists, she heaved again.

It wasn't team spirit and it certainly wasn't compassion that spurred her on.

Replacing them wouldn't be simple or easy. The more

she had to do on her own, the more risks she'd have to take, and the less likely she'd be to survive this assignment.

She was acting out of sheer practicality.

Nick McKenna was the first one to emerge from the smoke and ashes of the building, a semiautomatic rifle at the ready. Lori Carpenter was behind him, wielding a gun in each hand.

What was this? The OK Corral?

McKenna opened fire. There was only a high-pitched ringing in her ears, but the flashes from the muzzle were unmistakable. She registered the gunfire as distant muffled thuds. Each one she felt more than heard as it resonated through her.

Two of her men on the ground stopped moving. Shot and killed.

Panting, she released the second rook, content that his head and torso were out of danger of being hit by a stray bullet.

She took a beat to recover her breath and duckwalked toward the hood of the pickup.

Her vision had cleared. She didn't see white spots fading in and out any longer. Belladonna drew her suppressed 9mm and rose. The world still seesawed and her gun hand shook. Lining up her sights, she aimed for Lori Carpenter's forehead and pulled the trigger. Her HK VP9 snapped twice, and she took comfort in the familiar recoil if not the sound.

A bullet struck the target.

In the damn vest, of all places.

The force of the projectile knocked Lori Carpenter backward and she dropped.

McKenna trained the barrel of his rifle on Belladonna and opened up on her.

She ducked behind the truck.

With the loss of her hearing and the disruption of the

fluid in her ears, Belladonna's equilibrium was toast. Her normally perfect aim had been thrown way the hell off, but this was ridiculous. She'd had the woman in her sights and only caught her in the chest near the collarbone.

The target had fallen from the impact, but the vest had taken the bullet, and Lori Carpenter was still alive.

A red haze of fury filmed Belladonna's vision, anger flooding her limbs like battery acid. This wasn't what she needed right now. Her eyesight was the one thing going for her and she needed to get a grip.

She cursed her luck and checked her watch. Four and a half minutes left. The game was still on.

The target would be dead weight. McKenna would have to carry her. And he wouldn't be able to fire behind him at the same time.

Taking a breath, she took her chances and stood.

Precisely as she'd forecasted, McKenna had the target slung over his shoulder and was hightailing it east.

She leveled her gun at them, took a steady breath, strained to focus the sights on Carpenter's dangling head and—

The truck windshield in front of her exploded, struck by a fusillade of bullets that drove her down behind the frame of the vehicle.

She pivoted and peered around to see the sheriff, Deputy Barney Fife and Aunt Bee taking potshots at her as they maneuvered down Main Street.

In what upside-down world was she playing defense instead of being on the offense?

Not the OK Corral, but *The freaking Andy Griffith Show*!

If she wasn't worried about getting shot, she'd look around for Ashton Kutcher to jump out and say, "You've been punk'd."

The trio was headed in the opposite direction from McKenna and the target, but Belladonna would have to expose herself to have another go at Carpenter.

She growled her frustration, preparing to do something reckless and impulsive, totally against the grain, when her men started to recover enough to shoot back and lay down suppressive fire.

Before she could draw a relieved breath, the second rook she'd saved lurched back and twisted like a spinning top, falling on top of her and knocking her to the ground.

Blood poured from his face. His cheek had a gruesome hole in it. He was a goner and nothing could be done for him, but even worse, he was leaking all over her, getting her filthy and leaving the worst mess.

This was a DNA nightmare that housekeeping wouldn't have time to clean.

They needed to pull the plug on this gunfight and get back on point, tracking the target.

She shoved the corpse to the side and sprang to her feet. Catching the eyes of Smokey and a handful of the others, she motioned for them to follow her. She returned fire as they fled, but the three locals, who'd ended up being an effective distraction, slipped inside an establishment.

Glancing around, she counted four men dead and two more wounded. McKenna and the target were nowhere to be seen.

They'd gone east but couldn't have gotten far. Especially on foot. McKenna's car was still parked two doors down. They'd go for a new vehicle.

She checked the time. Two minutes until the State Police arrived on the scene.

Gritting her teeth, Belladonna and her team split up into two different SUVs. They would find the target and McKenna.

They weren't called *Los Chacales* for nothing.

Jackals were fast, deadly hunters, and the primary reason they weren't an endangered species was because of their resourcefulness.

Chapter Twelve

The hustle to the Bronco left Nick winded. He got Lori into the passenger side and climbed in behind the wheel. Keeping his Glock holstered, he chucked the rifle and machete in the back to get them out of the way. They hit the seat and floor in a clatter. He cranked the engine, backed around and hit the gas. Heart pounding off the rails, he sped out of the parking lot behind the sheriff's department, the tires squealing.

He checked all his mirrors. Belladonna and her crew wouldn't be far behind. It was a small town. One way in and one way out. At least, as far as he knew. Only a matter of time before they found him, and he couldn't waste time looping around and backtracking. That would give the chance to form a roadblock and box them in.

Best to make a beeline straight out of town. The great race was on, but they were at a disadvantage in the beat-up, late-model Bronco. Flooring this thing to seventy might be pushing it past its limits.

He checked his mirrors again. All clear behind him.

Lori groaned, opening her eyes. She went to sit forward but winced and dropped back in the seat. The pain must've been excruciating.

In Afghanistan, he'd taken a bullet once. His vest had saved him, too, but his chest had ached for days.

"Can you take off the vest?" His gaze bounced between

the road ahead and the road behind in the mirrors, and then over to Lori. "I need to make sure you aren't injured."

The slug had snapped Lori's body to the ground with such violent force, it was as though a steel fist had gripped his heart. The bullet had struck dangerously close to her throat. If Belladonna's aim hadn't been off, another couple of inches higher, and Lori would be bleeding out. But her collarbone could still be broken.

Nick made a sharp left turn, hit the next corner and made a right onto SR 18.

Removing the Velcro straps, Lori wheezed through the agony her poor body had endured today. She was taking it like a real trouper. No complaints. No whining.

"You okay?" she asked, groaning as she pulled the body armor overhead.

Lori's worrying about him when her clavicle might be broken and her chest must've been throbbing revealed another quality about her that he found endearing. He wanted to wipe his mind clean of the ugly things he'd learned. Turn back the clock to when she had been his Lori.

Not that she had ever really been *his*, but his heart didn't seem to realize it.

"Let me see," he said, pulling down the collar of her shirt and inspecting her with his fingers.

She winced, shrinking back from his touch. The blunt force of the bullet would leave a nasty bruise.

"It's not broken. But the area will start bruising soon."

"Where are we going? To meet up with your tactical teammates?"

Nick shook his head, gaze flickering to the rearview and side mirrors. "No. Doing so means putting you in the palm of Draper's hands." He trusted Yaz and Charlie with his life, but Nick didn't trust Draper as far as he could throw him. "He'd decide which San Diego safe house to put you in overnight and who'll be on your protective detail. Odds-on certainty that Draper will pull me."

Alarm crossed Lori's face. "I don't want that."

Neither did Nick. He gritted his teeth, wishing the only reason was to finish the mission.

"So what are we going to do?"

"Plan B. Or is this C?"

"Honestly, I think we're up to D." She flashed a sad, weak smile.

He clenched his fingers, resisting the urge to caress her cheek, and pulled the phone from his pocket. Most numbers he didn't know by heart, so used to having everything saved on his cell and at his fingertips. Other than the office, he had two other numbers memorized.

His mother's and his older brother's.

He dialed and was relieved when his call was answered on the third ring.

"Hello, this Bowen McKenna." His brother's voice, deep and powerful, the way Dad's had been, resonated over the phone.

"Hey, Bo. It's me."

"What kind of hot water are you in this time?"

Nick groaned. "Why would you assume I'm in trouble?"

"Because you call Mom when everything is fine," Bo said, "and you call me when you're in trouble."

Fair enough. "I need help."

"See. What do you need?"

"Airlift. Can you fly into Big Bear Airport, pick me and a witness up?"

"A witness? That sounds like a violation of USMS protocol."

"It's a long story, but I promise my reasons for asking are solid. If you don't do this, I'm pretty sure my witness won't live to see the sun rise." He exchanged a glance with Lori, and the trust in her eyes, the affection she had for him, shredded him. If he could just get through tomorrow, his life would go back to normal, the way it was supposed to, and this temptation, his anger, the gut-wrenching disappointment, would fade, and he could work on forgetting her. Reestablish the line in the sand that he'd never cross again. "And no guarantees that I'll make it, either."

"No pressure there." Bo chuffed a deep laugh. "You're lucky it's my day off. I'll get the helicopter fired up and head out. Is this a good number to reach you?"

"For now, anyway, yeah. Be sure to use Mom's maiden name for the logs. I don't want any record of a McKenna flying in and out."

"Got it. Be there as soon as I can."

He owed his brother one. Bo was the most reliable, dependable, bail-your-butt-out-no-matter-what person Nick knew. His brother never considered the blowback from helping, simply dove in and gave an assist whenever needed.

"And don't say you owe me one because you owe me like a million."

Nick smiled on the inside. "Who's counting, right? Thanks, Bo." He disconnected. "We'll spend the night in Nevada at my family's compound and fly into San Diego in the morning." Going totally dark was for the best. Too many coincidences and unanswered questions surrounding Draper.

His family was trustworthy. The compound was fortified. And they had a *working* relationship with the local law enforcement. Most important, no one in the USMS would know that they were there.

Hope bloomed in his chest. As he looked up in the rearview mirror again, that hope withered. He spied a hulking black SUV speeding up behind them. His fingers itched in warning. The road headed out of town was flat, and the SUV whipped around the sparse traffic in sight, eating up the asphalt and closing the distance.

"We're being followed."

Lori turned around and looked through the back windshield. "It's her. Isn't it? Belladonna, the damn terminator. She keeps coming and won't stop until I'm dead."

Protective instincts flared hot. "Well, she's going to have to come through me to get to you." He had to separate the personal from the professional, like church and state. "Because I won't stop until you've testified. Then you become some other deputy marshal's problem."

Lori sucked in a shaky breath, emotion burning in her eyes. "Right."

He hurt at the pain he saw in her features. Pain that he'd caused. But there was no time to worry about bruised feelings, not when the much higher priority was keeping them both breathing.

Letting out an irritated groan, he refocused.

When the SUV behind them cut around a minivan, he spotted two vehicles following them. Not one.

Great. The more, the deadlier.

The lead SUV roared up, eating the asphalt between them. If that beast of a vehicle was armored, they were screwed.

Nick gripped the wheel hard enough to make the leather groan, preparing for anything.

They crossed the town limits. He floored it, hitting seventy-five before the engine protested.

The SUV rammed them, jostling the truck forward.

A squeak of surprise left Lori's lips. "Oh, God. They're trying to run us off the road."

"No, they're not. But we'd be lucky if they did."

She shot him a perplexed look. "Huh?"

"If they wanted to run us off the road, they'd be alongside us."

The car raced closer. Rammed them again, this time hitting the left corner of the rear bumper, confirming his guess. Belladonna's team was executing the PIT maneuver—precision intervention technique—he had learned from Bo when he was on terminal leave from the army deciding between joining the family business and the US Marshals Service.

"They're trying to knock us into a spin and force us to a stop. Surround us from there."

"How is being run off the road better?" Her voice was frantic. "We could die in a crash."

"Could, yes, but—" Another hard ram interrupted him. "We'd have a chance of making a run for it. They force us to stop. Box us in. We're dead. There's no bulletproof glass or armored plating on this vehicle. All they'd have to do is open fire to turn us into Swiss cheese."

"But what about all the stuff in the woods? Aren't there mountain lions, bears, snakes?"

"Better the wildlife in the woods than the Jackals behind us."

The SUV bulldozed up from behind to take another swipe at them. This time Nick hit the brakes. The antilock braking system kicked in. Then he cut the wheel hard to the right. The Bronco gave an ear-splitting squeal as the rear end fishtailed. Another ram from the SUV sent both vehicles into a wicked spin.

But their Bronco went spiraling off the road over to the left, sideways and downhill. The car flipped and bounced. The rough terrain of an embankment rushed up to greet them.

Down the car went again at a sharp angle and in a long, fast slide.

If not for the seat belt that cut into his chest and abdomen, he would've gone out the windshield. The car's frame shrieked as it contorted.

Metal grinding, glass shattered and imploded, the vehicle came to an abrupt halt as it slammed into a tree.

An airbag inflated, knocking him back in his seat. Dust saturated his airway. Dazed, he pulled his Glock and shot the deployed airbag. It deflated instantly. He looked over. Lori was in the same predicament. One bullet rectified the problem.

His brain kicked into gear. He processed that they were upside down.

The thought of time hit him next. They had no time.

Belladonna and her people would swarm down the hill as soon as possible.

He fumbled with the seat belt and depressed it. Bound by gravity, he dropped down to the roof of the car. His hands landed atop shards of glass. But he had to keep moving. No pain. No weakness. Driving forward no matter what.

Lori was conscious, but stuck. He helped unbuckle her, making sure to keep her hands out of the glass. The soles of her feet were already damaged from earlier. He'd spare her any further suffering that he could.

He kicked out what was left of the windshield, not simple in the cramped space, and steered her out. But he didn't follow right away. They needed weapons.

Turning back, he smiled at the one thing in their favor. With their being inverted, every weapon in the truck was on the roof in plain sight and he didn't have to scavenge for them.

He handed Lori his Glock. She seemed reasonably comfortable with a 9mm when she was shooting like Annie Oakley earlier, but she'd dropped both guns when the bullet hit her vest. "Here."

She took it and her gaze was drawn uphill. "Get out of the truck."

Nick slung the rifle over his shoulder, shoved another 9mm in the back of his waistband and grabbed the machete.

"Get out, Nick! Now!"

He crawled through the open windshield and scrambled to his feet.

At the top of the hill, a man stood on the crest of the embankment. A rocket launcher rested on his shoulder and he flipped up the sights.

Nick grabbed Lori's hand and they bolted into the woods. He shoved branches out of their way, guiding her under larger limbs as they wound around old, massive trees.

Behind them, a jarring explosion shook the ground. There was no need to look back to see that the Bronco was a ball of fire. Or to know that Belladonna's team was headed downhill after them.

Nick pulled Lori, forcing her tired feet to move faster. They were both exhausted, mentally and physically, but he prayed that adrenaline fueled her system hot as jet fuel, the same as his.

He wasn't sure how long they had until Belladonna's team dispersed and attacked from various flanks. They wouldn't all come head-on.

"Keep going. Head northeast."

Her eyes flared wide in alarm. Ragged breaths tore from her mouth. "No. We should stick together."

"We separate or we die."

"I'm slowing you down. Aren't I?"

She was. "No. If you keep going, then I can hang back and take a few of them. I swear to you, I'll catch up. I won't leave you alone. If you run into trouble, fire the weapon. I'll hear it. I'll come for you."

Lori's eyes were clouded with fear and doubt, but she nodded. "Don't die on me."

"I won't. Go!" he said in a harsh whisper, and Lori took off.

Nick repositioned the sling of the rifle across his body and slipped behind a redwood. Rotating his neck, letting the joints pop, he got ready for war.

Rangers were shock troops. Quick strike force and highly trained at capturing, securing and killing.

THE SKY HAD darkened to the point that you couldn't tell if it was dusk or day. Distant thunder rumbled. The air smelled of rain. And something bad.

Something close to failure.

Belladonna shrugged it off. Failure wasn't an option.

Her people had scattered, fanning out to encircle McKenna and the target. But Belladonna slowed her pace, hanging back a bit. She knew something the others didn't. McKenna's history. His military record.

He used to be a ranger. Trained to operate in mountains similar to these. Skilled in taking out the enemy in Iraq and Afghanistan, in someone else's backyard and at the disadvantage.

As if making her point for her, a bolt of lightning illuminated a wide, sharp blade swinging out, taking the head of the bishop twenty feet in front of her.

Belladonna raised her suppressed weapon and fired away. Bullets struck bark.

McKenna was gone. Vanished like a phantom.

Fat indigo clouds swelled on the horizon and the wind changed, along with her forecast.

On her right, she glimpsed McKenna dart out from behind a redwood, snap a neck and disappear again. Seconds passed. One of her men screamed thirty feet ahead. She was on the move, slinking around trees. By the time she got there, another bishop was down. In pieces.

McKenna was pretty good at killing. Too bad he wasn't on her team.

Alas, he worked for the opposition, and two kings couldn't remain on the same playing board much longer.

Movement on her left. A tortured scream. McKenna

sliced through another like a searing blade through softened butter.

Her pulse kicked up, but her focus was laser sharp.

A breeze whispered past her. She spun three hundred sixty degrees, ready to pop a cap in anyone who wasn't on her side.

Where the hell was Lori Carpenter? Squirreled away inside a hollowed-out tree trunk?

Belladonna wouldn't put it past McKenna.

She crept through the woods, tracking her quarry, determined to remain the hunter and not to become the prey.

Thunder roared, but over it a shot was fired. Wild and telling.

McKenna had been doing his best to remain silent, not using his government-issued gun that lacked a suppressor and would give away his position, opting for a machete instead. The target, Carpenter, had discharged the gun. A stupid civilian unaware of how the loud report would echo.

Belladonna took off in the direction of the shot at a controlled pace, eyes on the lookout for any booby traps, just in case it was an ambush. She wouldn't be the one ensnared.

Coming into a clearing, the light was dim. The sky dark.

Twigs snapped behind her. She pivoted and spotted one of her few remaining rooks. Her numbers were rapidly dwindling. She could execute any job on her own, but backup was better on an assignment such as this.

In the clearing she spotted McKenna, hacking away another of her brethren like a bloodthirsty butcher. Behind him the target stood, holding her neck, raking in air as if she'd come within inches of losing her life. Yet again.

Belladonna's teeth ached to make it happen and be done with this.

As she took aim, stepping into the meadow, McKenna spotted her.

Belladonna had them, finally, and she couldn't contain her smile.

Lori Carpenter gasped and reeled back. McKenna raised his hands, still clutching the bloody machete. Standing in front of the target and blocking a clean shot, he backed up, slowly, head lowered.

It was the oddest thing. Rather than reveling in the posture and cowered look, Belladonna's skin crawled.

A roar blasted behind her, rattling her to the marrow. It wasn't thunder. It was feral.

She pivoted, slowly, cautiously, training her weapon in the direction of the sound.

A black bear charged the rook behind her. He screamed and ran—toward her.

What the hell? It was every soul for themselves.

She wasn't an outdoorsy person and hated camping, but she'd picked up a thing or two. Never run from a bear.

Then it dawned on her that McKenna had spotted the animal and had responded to its presence, not to hers.

There was no time to check if McKenna and the target were still behind her—only a fool would be standing there. She took aim on the bear.

The charging beast swooped down on her rook. She fired. A claw ripped through the arm, connecting with human flesh. A double tap from her gun. Her rook's screams died. The bear growled and bellowed. Then it stormed toward her.

Her heart flew into her throat. Fear wasn't new. She embraced it, owned it and stood her ground. Taking a deep breath, she pulled the trigger twice.

The beast gave a whimper and dropped.

Belladonna whirled and took after McKenna and the target. She was a hunter, not a tracker, but she could tell what direction they had headed.

No matter the developments in her life, taking time off

from work, becoming a wife and a mother, she'd never let herself go. She was in peak physical condition and could run a marathon if the mission necessitated it.

She leaped over a log and ducked under a low-hanging branch, her footfalls light and sure. Running all out at full speed, she'd trained herself not to take noisy breaths.

It paid off. She heard them.

One hundred feet ahead. Two running and a river—water rushing fast, something large. Not a babbling brook.

She wound around trees, sending little creatures scurrying. Faster. She needed to be faster and close the distance. Not let them slip through her fingers again.

Pumping her arms, driving her legs, ignoring the burn, she pushed even harder to close the distance. She glimpsed McKenna and Carpenter. This time, Carpenter wasn't wearing a vest.

They were hand in hand. Smart enough not to run in a straight line. They cut around a large redwood that obscured them.

Belladonna lengthened her stride, tasting victory on her tongue. Her heart pounded so hard, she thought it might explode. But she didn't care. There was only the chase. And her prey.

Her blood thudded against her eardrums. She was so close, could smell their sweat and fear in the air, the distant roar of the river amplifying the jolt firing in her muscles.

She burst through the tree line that opened onto a rugged dirt trail. Gun raised, vision clear, mind steady, the sweet rush of adrenaline singing in her veins.

They stopped to take a breath, and Belladonna stopped to take a shot, her finger on the trigger.

A twig snapped beneath her foot. The sound sent the two scurrying to the side and diving down a hill.

She took off after them, sprinting to the spot where they'd been standing only seconds ago. They skidded and tumbled in a wild descent down a steep grade. Belladonna squeezed off a few rounds, narrowly missing the target's head each time and hitting dirt, or rocks, or a damn tree.

Maybe Carpenter would break her neck on the way, or at least her leg to slow them down.

Belladonna redirected her aim, approximating where they'd stop. Have a steady, clean shot. The two reached the bottom, precisely where she'd calculated—as if landing on a marker—but soft earth gave way.

They both went in a violent whoosh as the river snatched them both, ripping them downstream.

Shock and frustration roiled hot through her, building and spiraling until it exploded. Belladonna screamed, raging at the air, at the storm coming in.

Taking a breath, she pulled in control. Battened down all emotion tight. They might drown. But *might* wasn't good enough. She needed Carpenter's head on a platter.

The river led somewhere. She'd find it. Then what?

They were hunters, not trackers. It wasn't the same thing at all.

There was also the possibility that McKenna and Carpenter would find their way out of the water before they reached the mouth of the river.

Belladonna tapped her earpiece. "Who is left?"

Smokey was the first to respond, followed by two others. She'd started the day with fifteen. Now the target was in the wind.

Things couldn't get much worse.

Then her phone rang. She'd programmed a ringtone for anyone who might call this number. "Tubular Bells" played. The theme song for *The Exorcist*.

Her day just got worse.

Sucking in a calming breath, she answered the phone.

Chapter Thirteen

The shock of cold water exploded through Lori's body the instant they tumbled into the river. Icy water rushed into her and over her, stealing her breath. She flailed at the surface with her hands, trying to keep her head above water.

Nick was there, combating the current alongside her. One second they were close enough to almost touch. The next they were jostled apart. In this together but fighting their own separate war.

She went under, swallowing water, gagging. Lungs straining, near bursting. The current teasingly thrust her up. Her head popped out and she raked in a desperate breath. Keeping her chin above the surface was a battle she'd win and then lose.

The bank of the river was within reach. She struggled to grab at slippery rocks. To snatch hold of loose roots. But the current sent them hurtling downstream. Her fingers had no chance to find purchase.

She drew a breath, then another. The brutal assault was relentless. On a manic gasp for air, she took more water into her mouth. Her lungs. The weight of her clothing only dragged her down.

If she was still wearing the bulletproof vest, she would've surely drowned.

And she still might.

The rushing water sucked them both forward. Sheer momentum and the heavy current became the greatest threats.

"Branch!" Nick sputtered over the roar of the raging river, and it was a ferocious beast, more merciless than Belladonna.

She spotted it. A large branch that hung over the water. A lifeline.

The river tossed Nick into the lead, the current catapulting them faster and faster toward the fallen log. But they couldn't afford to miss it.

This was their only chance. The one possibility to get out.

Desperation beat through her hotter and harder than a pulse.

Almost there. Almost. *Now!*

Nick reached up, growling, revealing that he was pure warrior. Down to his soul. He snatched hold of the log.

With only seconds to reposition, he shifted and latched on to her jacket.

Hold on. Hold me!

She grabbed on to his arm and did her best to fight the current as he hauled her up to the log. They shimmied toward the bank. The river yanked insistently, clinging, like an angry lover that wouldn't let go.

The fallen branch was wedged into the bank. But with the two of them, their weight was too much. Spindly limbs snapped and broke. The soaked bark of the log began to crumble.

She clawed into the earth, grappling to find purchase, and this time her fingers did. Using what little strength she had left, she pulled herself up.

The branch gave way, falling to pieces. But she grabbed Nick's hand and tugged at him, her muscles burning and her neck straining from the effort.

Water beat against his body, making her temper flare.

She pulled harder and helped drag him from the snarling current.

Her heart pounded against her ribs as she coughed up water and crawled over rocks and damp dirt and reeds to get as far from the bellowing river as her body would allow.

They both dropped on the ground. Soaked. Exhausted. Panting. But they were alive.

Huzzah!

She'd never had a greater sense of accomplishment. A stronger desire to jump up and dance for joy. But she was totally wiped.

"Now…what?" she asked between ragged breaths.

"We find the road. Avoid the Jackals. And hitch a ride."

Sounded like a plan.

"Ready?" He extended his hand to her.

Hell. No. She wasn't ready. Her limbs were heavy, and her lungs were finally starting to function properly again now that she'd expelled the water. Couldn't he give her one minute to catch her breath, revel in the fact that they hadn't drowned?

But she said, "Yeah. Let's go."

THE LIST OF reasons why Nick admired and, yeah, was crazy about Lori, had just gotten longer. Beautiful and kindhearted, tough yet vulnerable, funny and courageous, but she was also resilient. And girl-next-door sexy. He'd never met a woman like her. Damn near perfect.

Except for the other list of reasons that had landed her in WITSEC. She was not a victim here. She was a criminal.

He clenched his jaw and dropped her hand the second she was steady on her feet.

They were shivering from the cold and staggering along like they'd been on a weeklong Vegas bender, but he quickened his step. "Come on. Keep up. We've got to find help and get out of these wet clothes."

Huffing and puffing, she held her own, matching him stride for stride. Thankfully, they'd come across a trail. It'd lead to the road or civilization. He'd take either.

They'd gone at least two miles before her lips turned blue. First time that beautiful bow-shaped mouth of hers had stayed closed for so long, leaving him to the torment of his conflicted thoughts.

"Thank you," she said, as if picking up on his need to end the quiet. "For getting me out of the sheriff's department, away from Belladonna in the woods."

"No need to thank me. It's my job."

"If it hadn't been for you, things would've played out a hell of a lot differently. Thanks for not turning your back on me after what you heard, without knowing my side."

Now he had the torment of dealing with her thoughts. The quiet would've been better.

"Your side?" he snorted. Her side of the lies, the betrayal. Her side of shacking up with a vile, despicable man. Accepting his jewels, trips, payoffs, his hands all over her body. His stomach roiled. The whole *sordid* thing sickened him. "You had a chance to come clean, tell me your version of the truth, and all about your kingpin sugar daddy. Instead, you clammed up and pulled away."

"Is that what you call your interrogation in the car? A chance?" Her angry eyes flashed up at him. "When I asked you to share who you are with me, I was calm, gentle, patient."

True, true, true. He growled on the inside. No way was he going to let her turn this around on him. He stopped and pinned her with a glare. "Before we walked into the sheriff's department, I was calm. And gentle. And as patient as you're ever going to get from me." He'd told her what was in his heart, only to have her reject it. "Still, you didn't say a word!"

She swallowed hard, her eyes watering, lips quivering.

"Because I couldn't bear to put myself out there, peel back the layers, and have you look at me the way you are right now. Like you loathe the sight of me."

Guilt reared inside his chest. He clenched his jaw, not knowing what to say.

He could never loathe Lori. But he wasn't sure he could accept what she'd done, either.

A rumbling sound up ahead drew his attention. "Do you hear that?"

"Is it a truck?"

"Come on."

They ran down the trail, and through the tree line was a state highway. An eighteen-wheeler was just about to pass them, when Nick sprinted into the road on the lane opposite the oncoming truck and waved his hands. Lori ran up beside him and helped flag down the driver.

The truck passed them in a whoosh. Then the semi slowed to a stop.

They ran to the passenger side.

Nick climbed up, wrenched the door open and flashed his badge. "We could use a ride to the Big Bear Airport. It's official business and it'd be much appreciated."

"Sure! That's only a ten-minute detour. I don't mind helping you out."

They had a ride. Relief sliced through his chest.

Nick helped Lori up and inside.

The driver blasted the heater and gave them a blanket from the back.

"Very kind of you," Lori said.

The driver asked questions born of curiosity. It is to be expected when two people resembling drenched cats run into the middle of the road and one has a badge.

Nick gave brief, vague answers and luckily, the driver didn't push and the ride was short.

"Mind dropping us off here?" Nick said, gesturing to

the tourist shop that sold souvenirs and clothing. The airport was only one block down.

"No problem." The driver came to a stop and let them out. "Good luck!"

"Thanks." They'd still need it.

The store was kitschy, crammed with cheap souvenirs, but they had dry clothes. Sweats were the simplest, warmest choice. Nick opted to keep his shoes on, even though they were soaking wet and squeaked. Lori picked flip-flops, not that there was much in the way of choices for footwear.

Nick set everything on the counter and threw in two pairs of sunglasses. "I've got limited cash. What kind of discount can you give?" he asked, once again flashing the badge like it was a black-and-white hypnotic spiral that could bend people to his will.

"I can offer a two-for-one law-enforcement deal."

He pulled out a few wet bills from his wallet. "Thanks, buddy," Nick said to the clerk.

Lori changed first in the single fitting room, and Nick went in after.

The clerk was kind enough to give them a large plastic bag for their stuff.

Dry, more or less, and reasonably warmer, they pulled on their hoodies and headed to the airport.

One city block. Six hundred and sixty feet. That was how far away the airport was. And all it'd take was for one Jackal to spot them and another exit strategy would go up in smoke and they'd be back on the run.

The hoodies and sunglasses helped disguise who they were, but at the same time it drew attention to them. An unavoidable trade-off.

Two hundred feet from victory, he spotted Charlie and Yaz leaving the airport and getting into a silver SUV parked out front waiting for them. They'd have to drive past Nick and Lori to go deeper into the town.

Nick grabbed Lori and shoved her into the doorway of a mom-and-pop bookstore. He tried the handle, but the door was locked. His gaze homed in on the be-back-in-15-minutes sign.

"What's wrong?" Lori asked.

"Deputy marshals. My guys are about to pass us."

"Why not talk to them, explain everything?"

They'd ask questions, doubt his plan, perhaps even his sanity after he mentioned his concerns about Draper. Nick wasn't taking any more chances with Lori's safety. Draper be damned.

He pressed close to her, nudging them both into the corner. "It'd be a hell of a lot easier if they didn't spot us. We can just hang here a minute and pretend to be—"

Lori took Nick's face in her hands, and rising on her toes, brought his mouth to hers.

It wasn't a soft peck, but a greedy, openmouthed kiss that incinerated every thought in his head. Her tongue slid over his as her fingers dove into his hair. His lips burned and his body tingled. Without his permission, his mutinous arms wrapped around her, his treasonous hands clutching her closer.

He breathed her in, sucked down her flavor and squirmed to get even closer. The plains and valleys of their bodies fit and aligned like two halves of a whole. Before he realized it, he was the one deepening the kiss. Nick couldn't get enough of her mouth. The taste, the texture of her tongue, the sense of rightness despite the warning blaring in the recesses of his mind.

Need stirred inside him, an animate, living thing awakening with ravenous hunger.

His control was spinning, slipping away from him with each caress, each silken stroke of her tongue, and the only thing that mattered was the feel of her curled around him.

The sound of a throat clearing startled them, making them jump apart.

His heart jackhammered in his chest.

A thirtysomething woman with wide eyes and a wider smile, holding a takeaway coffee cup, jangled keys in front of them. "I can open up if you want to come in. But I kind of got the impression you two might prefer to be in a room at the B and B three blocks over." She waggled her eyebrows.

Lori blushed and hung her head.

"Sorry, ma'am." Nick took Lori's hand and led her away to the airport. "What were you thinking back there, kissing me like that?"

"I thought you wanted us to pretend to be intimate. You know, lovers, so no one would notice us. I was just trying to sell it."

Sold! He'd bought it lock, stock and barrel. "Don't do it again."

"You kissed me back, you know."

He wrenched the airport door open and carted her inside.

"You're hurting me," she said in a tight voice.

He looked down at their joined hands and only then did he register that he was not only holding her hand but also squeezing all the blood from her fingers. "Sorry." He let her go.

Pushing back his hood, he removed his shades, and she did likewise.

"Are we going to be okay waiting here for your brother? What if your colleagues come back?"

"Trust me, they'll be busy. After they see the devastation at the sheriff's department, they'll speak to her, find out that Ted's body was recovered, and they'll swing by the safe house to see it firsthand. Then their last stop will be the morgue. To bring Ted's body back to San Diego. There'll be lots of paperwork and it'll take hours."

"Okay. What do we do while we wait for your brother?"

He pointed to the only restaurant in the small airport and headed over.

The hostess greeted them with a smile and menus the size of poster boards.

"Booth, please," Nick said. "Can we get that one?" He pointed out one in the far rear, close to the kitchen, where the lighting was dimmer and no one else was seated. It'd also give him clear lines of sight to the front door and restrooms. If anything was coming for them, he'd know.

He flashed a wheedling smile instead of his badge.

"Sure," the hostess said and led them to the table he'd requested.

Nick ushered Lori with his palm at the small of her back, thought twice about the unnecessary contact and dropped his hand.

They sat across from each other with his back to the wall. A quick perusal of the menu showed him breakfast and lunch were both available until three.

A waitress came over and set two waters down. "Are you ready to order?"

"We have ten bucks and we're starving," Nick said. "What do you recommend?"

"Are you sharing?" the waitress asked.

"Yes," they said in unison.

Old habits die hard. Whenever they ordered takeout at the safe house, he and Lori always shared. It'd started with wanting to try the other's dish and morphed into standard practice.

"Then I suggest either the cheeseburger or the Reuben with fries."

"Reuben," he said.

At the same time, she said, "Cheeseburger."

Nick bit back a grin. "I know Reubens are your favorite."

"And I know you love to try the cheeseburgers at a new place," she said.

Why did she have to make it so hard to hate her and so easy to love her? "The Reuben, and feel free to be generous with the fries." He smiled and winked at her. "Pretty please." It wasn't often that he whipped out his charm card and played it, but he was starving and could wolf down an entire plate of fries on his own.

The simpering waitress nodded and withdrew.

He leaned back, folding his arms and looked at Lori. No smile. No wink.

If she thought that she could ambush him with a kiss— granted, it had been a full-scale bombardment on his senses, the definition of shock and awe—and sharing a meal was going to change his perspective, then she was sadly mistaken.

She wrung her hands and bit her lower lip like she was gearing up to say things he'd rather not hear. "I owe you an explanation."

"You don't owe me anything. There's nothing between us besides my sworn obligation as a US deputy marshal to protect a witness."

"Stop it," she said in a harsh whisper. "I may not have told you everything, but I have never lied to you. Please, don't start pretending like there's nothing between us. It's not fair to either of us."

"Fair?" He leaned forward, putting his arms on the table. "I admitted how I felt about you two hours ago. You told me it didn't matter. So why are you so hell-bent on explaining anything?"

She took a deep breath, looking as rattled as he'd felt after that insurgent-attack kiss. "Because you deserve to know."

That he found difficult to argue with. He didn't invest his heart lightly. And a piece of his belonged to Lori. He did deserve to know. "I'm listening."

Chapter Fourteen

Lori dug deep, trying to tap that wellspring of courage hidden somewhere inside her. "Things weren't quite as Belladonna had portrayed them. The divorce from my ex took a long time. Two years. While we were separated, hashing everything out, I met Dante Vargas at a company party. I knew he represented our biggest client, but I didn't know anything illicit was happening then. He was a little older. Very charming and debonair at first." Probably in the same manner Satan had been when he tempted Eve with the apple.

Nick squirmed, his face pinching with a sour look.

"Do you remember the things I told you about my dad?"

He nodded. "How he beat your mother and verbally abused you, called you worthless. The names he called you." His mouth flattened and his hands balled to fists.

"After I found out that my ex-husband was cheating on me, with so many different women in the office, and I confronted him, he told me it was my fault. For not being good enough. Not being better. That I should dress more provocatively like this one... Or not fight back, when he'd force himself on me."

Tears stung her eyes, but she had to reel them in, stuff the sadness and pain and grief down. She didn't want Nick thinking that she was trying to manipulate him by crying. Some women did that. Lori wasn't one of them.

"I didn't know." His voice was brittle. "That he raped you."

Her heart throbbed in her chest. "Took a long time for me to even see it as rape. I mean, he was my husband. Right?"

"No, Lori." He reached for her hand.

But she pulled back. She wasn't telling him to get sympathy, only to help him understand her choices.

"Dante came into my life at my lowest point. He said all the right things. Swept me off my feet with lavish gifts and trips. That part is true. Here was this businessman who made me feel desirable and special. But it was all a facade."

God, she'd been so stupid, so blind to the truth. As ignorant as Eve.

"Didn't you suspect that his business wasn't legitimate?"

"No. A lot of our wealthy clients had personal security, the same as him. There were never any drugs around, no violence. He took his phone calls in private and I was never in his office."

The waitress brought the food to the table. She set the Reuben in front of Lori and a cheeseburger in front of Nick. "The cook made an extra by accident." She winked and strutted off.

Her appetite was gone. Nick must've lost his, as well, because he pushed his plate to the side.

"How did you get the new position?"

"It was Dante's idea. He said that the accountant handling their portfolio was retiring. Short notice. Looking back, I think he meant that the accountant was *being retired*." With a bullet to the back of the head. She swallowed down the bile rising in her throat. "I told him that with the messy divorce, I didn't want to rock the boat. He told me he would take care of it. Then my ex said that the promotion would be a part of the divorce settlement along with a lump sum of alimony five times the amount that he'd initially specified."

"How much?"

"Two million dollars. When I asked him why, he said it was for my pain and suffering."

"Why did you stay with WCM after you found out about his affairs?"

"I had a good position I enjoyed, but my in-laws convinced me. They said I was still family and that I'd always have a job there."

He nodded like he got that part. "And you found out about the money laundering once you started the new job."

"The weekend before I took over the new position, Dante insisted on moving me in with him. It felt rushed, too fast, but he's the type of person who is so persistent you can't say no to him." Her gut clenched thinking back on it. "It wasn't until we started living together, day in and day out, that I saw he didn't have relationships with people. To him, I wasn't a girlfriend. I was a possession. A piece of property. And the only reason he moved me in to begin with—"

"Was to watch you," he said, finishing her sentence, and she nodded. "Did you confront him about the money laundering?"

She shook her head. "No one confronts Dante. I *broached* the subject." Dante wouldn't even discuss it until he'd stripped her naked and ensured she wasn't wearing a wire. That conversation had made her top five of all-time most humiliating. "He made it clear the money from my divorce settlement came from him and it was to keep quiet. Then he warned me never to discuss it again. So I didn't."

Nick's eyes narrowed. "Warned you how? Threatened you? With a gun? Knife?"

How could she explain it? "Dante is evil and insidious. He's like cancer. He didn't need a gun or a knife. Not with someone like me, anyway. You say the big C. Stage four. I get it. No explanation necessary."

"Did you keep sleeping with him?"

"I was in a different trap. Playing a different role. Acting in my own life. None of it was real. None of it brought me happiness. Not like what I found in spending time with you."

He looked away from her. "You call it spending time. I call it WITSEC. A part of my job."

She put her hand on his forearm. "Was kissing me part of your job, too?"

"No, but it was a mistake." He pulled his arm back and straightened. "How long did you launder their dirty money? How long did you let him touch you after you knew the truth?"

The heat of shame and embarrassment crawled up her face. "Six months," she said, low, the two words sour on her tongue.

His mouth twisted in disgust and she saw it again. The loathing in his eyes.

Her skin crawled remembering those six months with Dante the devil. The tense meals with her head in a guillotine, the awkward kisses that tasted of fear, forcing herself to detach as they had sex like she was having an out-of-body experience while her soul screamed for her to get away. Six months of dread ballooning in her chest, trying not to lose her mind, or her life.

"I needed time to come up with an exit strategy," she said, desperate to explain, for it to make sense to him, "and figure out how to pull it off."

The quiet air between them was weighted. She felt his gaze on her, his judgment, when she yearned for his understanding.

"Too bad you can't take all of that money with you into your new life." The more Nick said, the deeper Lori felt the cut.

She shook her head, her heart bleeding.

Where was her Nick? The one who could be gentle, comforting, compassionate?

"I never wanted their blood money," she said. "I gave it away. As soon as I found out it had come from Dante, I wrote a check to the Helping Hands Foundation." Her favorite charity that had kept the darkness from swallowing her when she was a teen. "They needed it. Not me."

The fact seemed to sober him, but it didn't soften him. "When I'm in the presence of evil, I sense it. Like an icy finger moving over my spine. How come you didn't feel it, that Dante Vargas, the biggest drug lord on the western seaboard, was evil?"

She'd asked herself the same question every single day for the past year. Dissecting her choices, analyzing her mistakes, so she didn't repeat them.

But Lori didn't think there was any answer that she could give that would satisfy Nick.

TWO HOURS LATER, Nick and Lori were still picking at their food, content not to force the conversation further.

He kept turning it all over in his head.

Lori wasn't like ninety-five percent of the people who entered the WITSEC program—bottom-feeders. She was trying to get herself out of a bad situation and to survive. But how she'd gotten into that situation with Vargas to begin with niggled at him.

Had a part of her been tempted by his money and his power? Her ex-husband had been the same, but with Vargas, she'd gone from bad to worse. A cartel boss, a reputed psychopath.

As much as it unsettled him, he couldn't dismiss all the good things about her, either. She was the best thing to happen to him, even with *Los Chacales* on their asses. And he had never desired any woman the way he hungered for Lori.

He yearned to kiss her again, hold her, have her body molding to his—

But his brain kept spiraling back and snagging on Vargas.

"Hello there." Bo slipped into the booth beside him, catching him in a headlock and ruffling his hair. "I didn't expect to find you two moping and wearing matching his and hers outfits."

Damn it. How had Nick let his older brother get the drop on him? He'd never hear the end of it.

Nick wrangled his head loose. "Get off."

"You're slipping. No wonder you had to call me for help." Bo turned to Lori and extended his hand. "Bowen at your service, ma'am. Have no fear, the smarter, stealthier, more charming McKenna is here."

Nick rolled his eyes.

"Wow. That rhymed." She shook his hand. "I'm Lori. Nice to meet you."

"Listen, there is serious stuff going on," Nick snapped. "We need to stop shooting the breeze and get out of Dodge. Plenty of time to talk at home."

AIDEN STOOD, STARING at the charred remains of the Big Bear safe house. "What do you think of everything the sheriff said?"

Charlie shrugged. "It's hard to say. Nick is taking a big leap by accusing Draper of being the leak without any proof. And he is a hothead."

Aiden nodded. "And impulsive."

"And stubborn."

"But he's never been *unhinged*."

A one-shoulder shrug from Charlie. "It's not for us to reason why."

"It's for us to keep witnesses alive," Aiden said, finishing her sentence.

"As long as Hummingbird is still breathing and Nick gets her to the office tomorrow, so we can escort her to court on time, I don't think we should worry about the rest. For now."

"Agreed." Aiden's phone rang. He knew who it was before he answered. "Hello, sir."

"Did you find McKenna and Hummingbird?"

"Negative, sir. Both birds appear to have flown the coop."

Draper swore into the phone. "Who the hell does he think he is? Going dark! What is he thinking?"

He's probably thinking about keeping a witness alive. "I'm not a mind reader, sir." He exchanged a knowing look with Charlie.

"He's endangering a witness. If anything happens to Hummingbird, it's McKenna's fault. Do you understand?"

Aiden let out a low sigh that wouldn't telegraph over the line. "Zeeman's body was found in the safe house."

"Go to the morgue. Bring his remains home with you. If you have any trouble, give me a call and I'll take care of it."

"Roger."

To be summoned was never good.

Dante Vargas had summoned Belladonna.

The director of the cartel's west coast branch—made him sound like he was a civilized banker instead of a psychotic drug-lord butcher—had packed up his entourage, driven two hours from San Diego to Laguna Beach, and set up shop in three adjacent oceanfront villas at the five-star Montage.

All to receive face-to-face confirmation as soon as possible that Lori Carpenter would no longer be a problem.

Belladonna had failed to deliver, and Dante wasn't happy.

Smokey pulled up in front of the center villa. "Should I wait for you?"

Translation: *Are you walking back out alive or being carried out wrapped in plastic?*

"Wait for me." She was walking back out, even if it meant she had to kill Dante to leave.

Belladonna opened her door and slid out gracefully, wearing a white silk suit she'd changed into. A guard let her inside.

The first thing to greet her was a breathtaking, panoramic view of the ocean.

The second was a squad of armed men. She counted a baker's dozen.

Dante had obviously anticipated her enthusiasm to keep breathing.

Well, good on him.

Belladonna smiled, aware of the unnatural pull in her cheeks that contradicted the tension surging in her veins. She sauntered deeper into the foyer, her three-inch heels clickety-clacking across the marble floor. The place epitomized relaxed class and stellar beauty. Always nothing but the finest for Dante.

Rapid-fire, she formed an exit strategy.

That was her gift. To assess. To forecast.

Unfortunately, all scenarios she visualized left her wounded. The vast majority mortally, considering she only had one concealed weapon on her. But if she counted her right and left shoe heel each as deadly instruments, that'd give her three.

No matter how many times they patted her down, they never found the third.

Men.

But none of those weapons were as effective as a bullet. She was outmanned, outgunned, but not outsmarted. She'd have to talk her way out of this.

Belladonna raised her hands and assumed the position.

Beefcake Number One patted her down, copping a generous feel of her breasts, butt and had the gall to leer in her face when he cupped her sex.

Compartmentalizing, she stuffed her fury in a box and tucked it in her mental closet right beside a beautiful pair of Louboutins to offset the ugliness.

Then she thought about her innocent daughter, Lily, growing up and one day facing such humiliating treatment from some man who sought to bully and intimidate her.

To hell with that.

Belladonna punched him in the throat and slammed the heel of her palm up into his nose, breaking it with a delicious crunch.

Watching him crumple to his knees, gagging and bleeding, turned her smile from artificial to genuine in a snap.

The others surrounded her, semiautomatic HK MP5s at the ready in their meaty grasps.

She extended her bloody palm. "A napkin. I can't go in there looking a mess." Thankfully, she didn't seem to have any blood on her pristine white suit.

Dante was a stickler about appearances.

Beefcake Two ran and grabbed a napkin for her. She wiped off her hand and tossed it back at him.

"Señor Vargas wants you to remove your shoes," he said. "Please."

This shouldn't have surprised her—Dante had taken over as her mentor and commander when his father passed—but it did.

She slipped off the deadly, stainless-steel spike heels.

The marble floor was cold beneath her bare feet. She welcomed the sensation, hoping it would cool her temper, too.

Beefcake Two escorted her through the villa to the living room.

Dante sat on the sofa, legs crossed, an arm stretched across the back of the couch, sipping a drink. The tall glass was filled with ice, a pale liquid and mottled mint. She assumed it was a mojito.

For a man in his midfifties, time had worked in his favor. Like a fine wine, he aged well. He possessed the fit physique of a man in his prime. From a distance, he oozed sex appeal and charm and had this mesmerizing way of hooking you. But the closer you got to him, the easier it was to see the illusion. It was plain to see how the wolf had fooled the sheep, Lori Carpenter.

"Would you care for a beverage?" Dante asked.

"No, thank you." She kept her expression soft and her voice polite. "I'm working."

"Come now. I won't offer you a last meal. But surely I can give you a last beverage."

She scanned the floor for a polyurethane tarp. A telltale sign he planned to put a bullet in her head. There was none.

"I insist." Dante smiled with all the sweetness of battery acid. "What will you have?"

"Calvados," Belladonna said, brightly.

Dante pointed his finger at her and chuffed out a laugh devoid of humor. "Cheater." He wagged his finger.

Champagne, single malt scotch, rum, vodka, gin, bourbon and beer, Dante traveled with. He only had Calvados on hand at his home, but never had the apple brandy on the road. And it wasn't something he could simply send a goon to the local liquor store to fetch.

She shrugged, mustering her most charming smile. If she had to beg, steal, cheat or lie to get back to her family, then she would.

Before she met her husband, Alessandro, her life had been full—of violence and bloodshed—and she'd been fine. Perfectly fine. Then he drifted into her orbit. More like crashed and there was no stopping the collision. She became painfully aware of the emptiness inside, of how he made her ache to be better.

Only fools fell in love, but she'd fallen anyway.

Only those who got out of this bloody business—free and clear—were safe to saddle themselves with a defenseless child. But there was no *out*. Not for people like her.

And she'd had a kid anyway.

She was still fine, better than before, but if she lost them, or if they lost her…

What had she been thinking? No one could have it all and it had been greedy of her to try. But once you experienced the warm intoxication of love, tasted happiness, it changed everything.

So yes, she stood in front of Dante Vargas, trying to cheat death.

"Why isn't that bitch dead?" His smile evaporated.

"Nick McKenna has proven to be more formidable and resourceful than expected."

"But that is why I brought you in, Bella," he said, making her skin crawl. "You foresee and adapt."

"It's not over. I still have time to eliminate her."

"You've lost lots of rooks and bishops, but I don't see a scratch on my strongest piece. I don't think my king has seen much action, gotten up close and personal with this Nick McKenna. Why have you been playing it safe?"

Getting up close and personal on other jobs hadn't scared her. If she had died back then, it wouldn't have mattered. But now…

The faces of Alessandro and Lily floated up in her mind's eye. Now she had two miraculous reasons to live.

"I have a contingency plan," she said with genuine confidence. "But I'll need more men."

The USMS was nothing if not predictable. McKenna might be rogue, playing it his way, but Marshal Draper would bring him back in line.

Dante picked up a remote control from the coffee table

in front of him and turned on the TV that hung above the lit fireplace.

A video came on. Of her husband, playing with their daughter.

Dante knew about them. Knew where they were and was making a point that he could reach out and touch them. At any time.

Her heart withered and the taste of ash saturated her mouth.

"Your daughter is beautiful. She looks so happy. Carefree. I want her to stay that way. And your husband. Handsome, but I never would have imagined that you would've fallen for a college professor. Biology, no less."

And that was when the game flipped, and hope sparked anew.

Her husband's cover was intact.

Dante had no clue that Alessandro was deadlier than she was. That meant only one man had been sent to keep an eye on them, two at the most, since there was no perceived threat.

She looked back at the video, playing on a loop.

Their daughter wore the garish two-piece she'd regretted buying, the one Alessandro hated with a passion. Seeing Lily run across the beach wearing it was a message.

Alessandro was aware they were under surveillance and he had it under control. She would've taken a relieved breath if not for the fear that Dante would've registered it.

"Please, don't hurt them," she said as if reading from a script. Alessandro would rip out the carotid artery of anyone who got close to their daughter.

"Believe me, that is not what I want." Dante stood and walked up to her. He grasped her chin between his thumb and forefinger and tipped it up. *"Belleza deslumbrante."*

Ravishing beauty.

It made her want to puke.

"Why should I give you another chance?" Dante asked. "Why should I let your family live?"

Fury bubbled inside her, but she masked it with a sly grin. "Because I brought you a gift."

Dante released her and stepped back. Way, way back like he was afraid.

After threatening her family, he should be.

"Unless it's Lori Carpenter's head in a box, I'm not sure I want it," he spat.

She considered going for her concealed weapon, the hairpin that secured her bun in place. It was as lethal as an ice pick. She'd have time to cross the room and stab him in the jugular before his guards entered. But then she would be stuck.

"Trust me, you'll want it." Belladonna raised her palms.

His shoulders relaxed at the conciliatory gesture.

Slowly, she reached inside her silk camisole, into her bra, and retrieved the USB drive tucked under her breast. She was a generous C cup. Between the ample padding in her push-up bra and her fleshy tissue, the guard never would've felt it.

Belladonna offered him the drive in her palm.

"What is it?" he asked, taking cautious steps, closing the distance between them.

"The California WITSEC list and the name of every deputy marshal in the Golden State."

Dante beamed. That was right; she was walking out of there.

"How did you get this?" he asked, taking the drive.

That was for her to know and for him never to find out. "It's like you said. I foresee and adapt."

He cupped her cheek and lifted her face, bringing her lips to his, and kissed her. Closed mouth, but nonetheless revolting.

Her stomach cramped and she wished she'd worn her poisoned lipstick.

"There is no one else in the world like you, Belladonna." He kept his face close, the stench of rum brushing over her skin.

She couldn't wait to take a shower.

"Kill Lori Carpenter and I will let you go."

Her heart leaped, but her mind spun like a pinwheel. "What?"

"Kill her for me and I'll set you free. You can go and live your life with your family without looking over your shoulder."

He is the prince of lies, a maestro of manipulation.

But what if he meant it? What if she could be free?

"I want that bitch dead before she testifies. Fail me, I'll make you watch as I skin your husband alive, and then I'll kill you and take your daughter. Train her to be your replacement. The same way my father took you when yours failed him. I have a lovely name already picked out for her. I shall call her... Oleander."

Chapter Fifteen

The storm stalked them from California to Nevada, thunderclouds darkening the early-evening sky. No rain yet, but it would come.

As the bright lights of his family's compound came into view, a sense of peace washed over Nick. The mountains rose up behind the property set on five acres, and to the east was a partial view of the Vegas strip in the distance.

There was no safer place on earth for Lori. He'd imagined bringing her here during his conversations with his mother. What it would be like having her in his childhood home, surrounded by people who knew him best. Sharing the other side of himself with her.

But none of his delusions had been under such horrible circumstances. It was the dose of reality he needed.

The drone of the helicopter's engine had smothered his anger and quieted his mind on the ride. If he thought of Lori only as a witness, then it was possible to keep his emotions in check and his perspective objective. So that was what he decided to do.

Bo landed on the helipad and shut the chopper down. As the rotor blades slowed, Nick took Lori's hand and helped her climb out. The small touch sent electricity firing across his nerves, wreaking havoc on his brain.

As long as he didn't touch her, he might be able to think of her as only a witness.

Nick broke the physical contact between them, and the striking loss of heat was immediate. She drew in a sharp breath, her shadowed gaze capturing his, and wet her lips.

Had she felt it, too, that spark of connection?

His pulse pounded in his veins for reasons that had nothing to do with danger.

He paused to take in the sight of her set against the backdrop of his family home. Those doe eyes, her fine-boned features, that pale, rose-colored mouth he longed to kiss until they were both breathless. Even though they were outside, the space around him seemed to shrink, condensing to her. She was everything he'd always desired, and he wanted her.

Not only to have her in his bed and appease this craving that was as terrific as it was terrible, but also he wanted her to be his, to hold and protect and love.

Maybe he was fooling himself to think objectivity with Lori was possible, or maybe loving her made him a fool.

He wished he could tell the difference. The one thing there was no denying—he wasn't just crazy about Lori Carpenter. He loved her.

It was the only explanation for his jealousy over Vargas and why her past grated on him.

Coming up alongside them, Bo whistled. "So you're the hottie my brother is sweet on."

Nick squirmed on the inside but didn't dare let Bo see it. "I never called you that. Not that you're not attractive." Lori was a knockout, but it wasn't her beauty that had stolen his heart.

The ache in his chest returned at the thought of her with Vargas. He wanted to strangle the man.

Lori blushed, her gaze lowering.

"In his defense," Bo said, "he never referred to you as a *hottie* to our mother."

Her eyes and her brows lifted. "You talked to your mother about me?"

Nick elbowed his brother in the ribs to keep his mouth shut. "I may have mentioned you in vague terms, once or twice."

Bo laughed. "Yeah, once or twice. Anyway, Nick only falls for hotties. So we all assumed."

"Your family has talked about me?" Lori asked, wrapping her arms around herself.

"Once or twice. Come on," Bo said, spurring them to walk to the house. "The moment I told Mom that you were bringing your witness here, she went to the kitchen and started cooking. I'm sure she's got a feast waiting inside. Hope you're both hungry."

"I'm starving," Lori said.

Nick's appetite had also returned with a vengeance.

"Good," Bo said. "Because not eating would offend her."

They ascended the front steps to the wide wraparound porch.

Bo marched inside with his usual bravado. "They're here!"

Nick ushered Lori inside ahead of him and closed the door. The large house smelled of turmeric and coriander and saffron. Scents he equated with safety and love.

Whenever he came back home, after he'd decided to carve his own path separate from his family, it was always strange but comforting at the same time. Like putting on your favorite pair of worn-in shoes that no longer fit.

Speaking of which, he pulled off his still-wet shoes and socks and put them in the row of other footwear by the door. Bo did the same and Lori followed suit.

His mother, Pamela Maadi-McKenna, drifted into the foyer barefoot, wearing a long kaftan in a dramatic print of jewel colors, mostly sapphire and emerald, her jet-black hair in a messy-chic top knot. She always made flawless perfection look effortless.

Lori did, as well. She didn't have to try. Sans makeup, windswept hair, sweats that hugged her lean, curvy frame, she was absolutely stunning.

His mother wrapped him in a tight hug, then kissed his cheeks three times. She bracketed his face with her palms and looked at him as if she hadn't seen him in years.

"You did right to come home," his mother said, bypassing pleasantries and lightening his heavy spirit with the very first words from her mouth.

Mom swung her bright-eyed attention to Lori like Nick was now yesterday's news. "Welcome." She clutched Lori's arms and kissed her cheeks. "I'm Pam."

"Lori. Nick talks about his family all the time with such great affection. It's a pleasure to meet you. Thank you for allowing me to come. I'm sorry to put you through all this trouble."

"It's no trouble." Mom took Lori's hand and held it between both of hers.

Lori threw him a questioning glance. He hadn't thought to explain his mother's peculiar ways before they had entered the house.

Flashing a shallow grin, he shrugged.

His mother stood there, smiling at Lori, holding her hand, doing her *thing* that made newcomers uneasy at the five-second mark based on the comments and questions that came afterward.

Explaining why his mother held someone's hand while staring at them in silence didn't help. In fact, it tended to push the awkward meter closer to unsettling. Girlfriends declined to come back to the house. Not that he'd brought anyone home in nearly a decade.

Pamela Maadi-McKenna had a gift. He wasn't sure what

to call it. His father had said she had a sixth sense. Could touch a person and tell things about them.

She shook my hand, stared in my eyes for ten seconds, his dad had said, *and told me that she didn't mean to scare me, but that I was the love of her life, that we were going to get married on a beautiful spring day, have three children and be happy. I thought she was a sandwich short of a picnic at the time, but she was so gosh-darn gorgeous and confident. Instead of running for the hills, I asked her out on a date, and it was the best decision of my life. Always listen to your mother, boy.*

Nick clasped his mother's shoulder and gave a squeeze that signaled *please stop.* "Whatever you cooked smells delicious."

"Yes, yes," his mother said, taking the hint and releasing Lori's hand. She gave his cheek a pat. "Show Lori to the bathroom so she can freshen up and we'll eat." His mother drifted off to the kitchen.

Nick guided Lori down the hall. "I'm sorry about my mom."

"Sorry about what?"

"Her holding your hand and staring at you. I promise she's not crazy."

"I didn't mind. I liked it. A very warm, intimate way to greet someone."

It was intimate all right, bordering on invasive, but it pleased him that she felt welcomed because he knew that she would be. He stopped in front of the bathroom. "Take your time. Mom keeps basic toiletries in the cabinet. The dining room is through there." He pointed to his right. "You can't miss it."

"Thanks. I'll only be a minute." She held his gaze a moment, and he wanted to say more but couldn't find the right words. Then she closed the door.

He went the way he'd indicated and found Bo talking to his sister Julie.

"Hey, Jules." Nick hugged his little sister, relaxing a little more. "I wasn't sure if you'd be in or out skip tracing."

"Just finished an hour ago. We had a guy jump bail, but when I heard your mysterious witness that you've been safeguarding for a year was coming, I couldn't miss the chance to meet her. Kicked down the right doors, knocked around the right heads and found him. So where is she?" Jules's eyes danced like those of a giddy teenager.

"Bathroom." Nick figured it was best to address the elephant in the room before it turned and stampeded him. "Look, I don't know what Mom told you guys, but Lori is not my girlfriend. She's just a witness. Let's keep it professional."

Jules winked. "Right, sure. *Professional*." Her gaze lifted somewhere behind him and by the gigantic grin spreading on his sister's face, he guessed Lori had entered the room. "Hi, I'm Julie," she said, shoving him to the side, "but everyone calls me Jules. It's so nice to meet you."

Jules hugged Lori and thankfully gave her room to breathe.

"I'm Lori. It's nice to meet you, as well."

His mom came in and set platters down on the set table. "Let's eat. Lori, please." She gestured to a seat beside her.

Everyone sat. His mother outdid herself preparing all his favorites. Kabobs, *fesenjoon*, *kashke bademjan*—eggplant dip—tamarind-stuffed fish, saffron rice, *dolmeh*, stuffed grape leaves, and yogurt cucumber sauce with rose petals.

"This spread is incredible," Lori said.

"Thank you." His mother encouraged her to help herself.

The table hung in quiet anticipation waiting for Lori to taste the food.

"Oh, my God. This is beyond delicious, Mrs. McKenna.

I can see where Nick gets his love of food. I wish I'd had this growing up."

"Call me Pam, please. I'm happy you like it."

"Love it." Lori practically had a food orgasm with each bite.

Nick couldn't help but wonder what face she'd make with him buried deep inside her, writhing in pleasure as he brought her to the brink and pulled her back before letting her orgasm.

Lowering his gaze, he shook the wicked thought from his head.

"Red wine?" his mom offered, and when Lori nodded, she filled her glass and passed the bottle.

"I have to tell you what an amazing son you've raised," Lori said between bites. "I owe him my life. He's the bravest, most honest man I've ever met and is kind enough to share his food with me. Doesn't get much better than that." She turned her sparkling gaze to him, and he wished the circumstances, all around, had been different.

"Keeping you alive is my job," Nick said, his tone harsher than he'd intended.

"But sharing your food with me wasn't. Or your mom's recipes."

"Really?" his mom asked. "Nick never seems interested in cooking here at home."

"We cooked all the time together. Three or four times a week. But I have to confess, the *fesenjoon* we made wasn't half as good."

His mother gave him a knowing look and smiled at his scowl. She liked Lori a lot. It was hard for anyone not to.

"So how's the bounty-hunting business going?" Nick asked, eager to change the subject.

"Good." Bo stuffed more food into his mouth.

"What else did you and Nick do together tucked away in a safe house for a year?" Jules waggled her eyebrows.

"We talked a lot, went jogging, played board games, watched movies, but cooking was the best."

It had been the best. That was when they swapped childhood stories. Hers had been dark and his had been complicated, but happy. It was the most sharing he'd ever done in any relationship.

"What was Nick like as a kid? Saint or hellion?"

Glances passed between his family members. "Hellion," they all said together.

Nick grimaced. "Lori doesn't want to hear about that."

"But I do." Her eyes shone with curiosity.

"Well then, I don't want to hear about it," Nick snapped. "Okay?"

Blessed silence.

Everyone ate and Nick hoped no one spoke another word during the entire meal.

Of course, it only took two minutes before his mother said, "Lori, what do you do?"

"I'm an—"

"She can't talk about it," Nick interrupted, and his mother responded with a glare of daggers.

"You all have your mom's coloring and soulful eyes," Lori said. "I've seen pictures of your dad, and I can see the resemblance in the boys, but Jules, you're a spitting image of your mom. So beautiful."

"Thank you!" Jules sat a little taller in her chair. "I love you already. I can see what Nick sees in you."

"So can I," his mother said.

Did his mom mean that in the way a regular person would, or had she *seen* something?

He'd learned long ago it was best not to wonder and certainly not to ask.

Forks finally lowered to the plates as the last of the wine was poured.

"Nicky," his mother said. "Help me in the kitchen with dessert."

They cleared the table of the platters of food and plates.

Carrying the nine-inch hand-painted gilded plates that had been set out, he joined his mother at the counter in front of his favorite dessert. The most delicious thing in the world. A three-layered chocolate cake with ganache and mascarpone pistachio filling.

She only made it on his birthday. A time for celebration. But he wasn't feeling festive.

"What is wrong with you? Why are you so cranky?" she asked.

"Cranky? What am I, a damn toddler?"

"Language."

"Sorry." He hung his head. "It's been a tough day. I've earned the right to be grumpy."

"You both look like you've been through hell. But I don't understand you. For a year you've talked to me about the woman sitting in the other room. Fifty-two conversations about all the things you admire and adore about her."

Nick shot his mother a *cranky* look. He'd never used the word *adore*. Even if he did on some level.

"You've never spoken about any woman with such affection. Not even that *girl* you married."

Nick winced. "Mom. Don't bring that up." They had only been twenty-one, both of them had been drunk and wrong for each other. It had only lasted twenty-seven days. The shortest marriage in McKenna or Maadi history.

"My point is, you're enamored," his mother said. "I dare go so far as to say in love with her. Yet, you are so cold and distant with Lori. Why?"

"You wouldn't understand."

She tapped him hard on the nose with two fingers.

"Ouch!"

"Don't be such a baby," she said, slicing the cake. "And don't be condescending. I understand more than you think."

"I meant you wouldn't understand because you're not in the USMS and have never worked with a witness."

She cupped his cheek. "I may not be a marshal, but I am a mother." She returned to plating the cake.

He put his hand on her forearm before she cut a fifth piece. "We only need four. I'm not having any."

"You could use a little sweetness. Trust me on that." She cut a fifth slice anyway. "What is wrong, *azizam*?" his mother asked, calling him *my dear* in Farsi.

"I found out some things about Lori that I'm having difficulty with."

She clucked her tongue, plating the slices. "You're always so hard on everyone. Expecting people to meet some impossible standard of perfection that they can't live up to. And when they don't, you pull away and cut them off. It's almost as if you only want what you can't have and once you get it, you find fault. If you continue like this, you'll deny yourself happiness and live a lonely life."

He had put Lori on a pedestal and crowned her with a halo when she was human and fallible the same as him. Rather than showing her compassion when she was at her most vulnerable, baring her soul, he'd gifted her with anger and jealousy. Completely disregarded how she'd been manipulated and used.

Nick gritted his teeth, hating himself.

"I have sat with her, touched her, *read* her." His mother let that sink in. "Lori has a good heart. And it is plain to see that she loves you. Have you ever done anything that you've regretted, that you were ashamed of?"

Horrible things. Things he'd shared with Lori and she hadn't turned her back on him or judged him. She'd shown him affection and acceptance instead. Love.

"I thought so," his mother said, wagging a finger.

"Did you read me? Is that how you know?" He stiffened, hoping she hadn't.

"No, *azizam*. I didn't have to. We've all done things that we regret. That bring us some measure of shame. The choices you two have made, the roads you've each taken, have led you both here, together. It's okay to be a fool for love, so long as you are not a damn fool."

The difference suddenly struck him, and he had his answer. "Mom, *language*."

She dismissed him with a wave of her hand. "Help me serve dessert."

They carried the cake into the dining room, where Bo was pouring brandy and Lori was laughing with his siblings. The sound of her joy warmed his heart.

He had all the people he cared about most in the world in one room and somehow, he'd been too narrow sighted to enjoy it.

"Nicky, why don't you and Lori eat outside?" his mother said. "Enjoy the view and the fresh air."

LORI TOOK NICK's nod to his mother's suggestion as a hopeful sign. He'd been tense and terse during dinner. The opposite of what she'd expected.

They strolled out onto the porch and sat side by side on the patio sofa. Another hopeful sign. Watching the storm roll in, lightning flickering in the distance, the low rumble of thunder, the air heavy with the promise of rain, they ate dessert and drank brandy together the way they had so many times at the safe house without the alcohol.

Tomorrow she'd testify, and they'd go their separate ways. She didn't know if she'd have an opportunity to tell him all the things in her heart after she took the stand, much less in private. This was her chance and she was going to take it. "Nick, you're the first real thing in my life. Our friendship. What I feel for you. The happiness, the safety, the…love. It's all real for me."

He set his plate and brandy glass down. "I think I know why you fell for your husband and didn't see that Dante was evil."

She braced for some harsh retort, her stomach muscles clenching. All the men in her life had disappointed her, ultimately objectifying her and not seeing her as good enough. To receive the same rejection from Nick, in his home, surrounded by his caring family, might be more than she could handle.

But he took her hand in his, brushing his fingers across her knuckles, like they were a couple, bound together by more than his job. "They were abusers, like your dad. Their tactics were subtle and insidious at first. That's why you didn't see it. I know Vargas is a psychotic scumbag because I'm trained to see it. It's my job to know, but it wasn't yours."

"A part of me realizes that I was set up and manipulated. But another part feels like I should've seen it coming. Or to solely blame my ex-husband and Dante is shirking responsibility."

"The vast majority of people are happy to shirk responsibility for their mistakes and problems. Not you. But you're not at fault for what they did to you and I shouldn't have gotten so bent out of shape over Vargas. I was jealous."

If only he knew how little there was for him to be jealous of. "I'm sorry for not confiding in you sooner."

An odd vulnerability softened his eyes. "No, I'm the one who's sorry. For disappointing you when you finally tried to explain. You needed me to listen, to be the best version of myself, and instead I gave you Deputy Marshal Dredd."

She snickered, loving him even more for owning up to it.

"Our pasts have made us who we are. It's what brought us together. To get sidetracked by anything else is foolish.

You're the best thing that's ever happened to me, knowing you, falling in love with you. No matter what happens tomorrow or the day after, I need you to know that this is real."

"I don't want to think about tomorrow. Only about right now. Spend the night with me." Her request dangled between them, leaving her feeling exposed.

His eyes gleamed in the moonlight. Lori held her breath, waiting for his response.

He gave a sultry smile that stirred butterflies to take flight in her belly.

Pam came out onto the porch. "I know it's been a long, exhausting day for you both. I've made up the bed in your room for Lori. Jules set out some things for you that should fit. Nicky, you can stay in the spare bedroom in the basement."

"If it's okay with Lori and you, Mom, I'd prefer to be upstairs in my room."

Lori smiled, her cheeks turning pink. "I'd prefer that, too."

His mother folded her arms. "I don't know about that."

"I'm not supposed to let her out of my sight," Nick said, his tone matter-of-fact. "No funny business."

"No. Funny. Business." She wagged a finger. "Come in before it starts raining." His mother picked up their dirty dishes and went back inside.

He waited a beat or two and said, "I'm going to make love to you. And if I do anything that remotely comes across as funny, then I'm doing it wrong."

Lori laughed.

Cupping the back of her head, he leaned in, closed his mouth over hers in a long, lingering kiss. "Tonight I want to erase the past, everything that came before us."

An exorcism of the darkness and a possession of something beautiful. She wanted that, too, for it to be carnal pleasure and sacred communion.

"Take me to bed," she whispered across his lips, "but I have no intention of us getting any sleep."

"Good. Neither do I."

Hand in hand they entered the house. The aromatic delight from dinner was still rich in the air. Chatter came from the kitchen.

"Should we go say good-night?" she asked in a low voice.

He shook his head, giving her a sly grin, and led her upstairs.

The wall along the stairwell was filled with family pictures. Pam and his father on their wedding day, Nick with his siblings as children playing, their father teaching them how to shoot. Smiles, hugs, laughter and warmth radiated from each one. A wall of love.

Lori's heart squeezed and she tightened her fingers around Nick's.

At the top of the landing, she asked, "Where's your mom's room?"

"First floor." He gave her a quick, light kiss. "Wait here a sec."

Nick disappeared down the hall and crept into another room.

Lori turned to see more photos. Pam sat in a rocking chair; an older toddler stood beside her knees with his head in her lap, she held a baby in her arms and her belly was round with more life. There was a look of utter contentment on her face.

An ache blossomed in her chest. She thought about what it would be like to have Nick's baby in her belly, in her arms. She'd never felt safe enough to ever entertain the idea of motherhood. The danger still hadn't passed, yet if it did, this was what she wanted, children and a house full of warmth, with him.

Nick hurried back, carrying condoms, and whisked her into his room.

Before she had a chance to take in the bedroom he'd grown up in, he kicked the door shut and pulled her into his arms, his face coming down to press a kiss to her lips.

Butterflies swarmed in her belly, and her arms made their way around his neck, her fingers tangled in his thick, cool hair.

Their tongues met in an erotic slide. In the gentle cage of his arms, his hands, the pressure of his mouth, there was the sublime balance of tender roughness. His desire for her was unmistakable as well as his awareness of her comfort. He took care not to agitate her bruises while conveying the intensity of his passion.

Magic.

The smooth, slow licks of his tongue were deep and intoxicating, teasing her with the promise of what was to come. She could kiss him for hours, getting drunk on this foreplay alone. The desire for that, hours, days, a lifetime of his kisses, made her chest constrict.

He guided her to the bed in a sensual dance, their bodies swaying to music meant only for them, and lowered her down.

The evidence of his desire, the impressive thickness, nudged against her belly. Need for him pulsed between her legs.

Taking her face between his hands, he fused their mouths, pressing his tongue deep, unleashing her hunger for more intimate penetration.

When he pulled his lips away, she was left panting for breath and melting around him.

He peeled her clothing off, taking care with her injuries, and she helped him, eager to have every inch of herself exposed to his touch. "You're so beautiful. Not just your body, but your soul. I'm so lucky."

His words made her heart squeeze and soar at the same time.

As she stripped him, her fingers sifted through the dusting of hair on his chest, lingered on the ridges of his sculpted abs. Absorbed the heat of his bare skin. After months of flirting and wanting and craving, to finally have him was glorious.

Cupping her breasts, he took one nipple into his mouth and toyed with the other. Every wet tug of his mouth and sweep of his tongue drove her wild.

She clutched him tighter, pressed her belly to the thick, straining shaft between them, and rubbed her body against his with matching urgency.

It was like stoking a fire, and a maddening yearning took over. She was so aroused; she might die if she didn't have him inside her.

Taking his hips, she guided him to the cleft between her thighs. "I need you." She fumbled for a condom, ripped it open and rolled it down over his shaft.

"I wanted to get you there with my mouth first." He nibbled on her earlobe, and she tingled at the thought.

"How about we take each other there later? I need you inside me right now. I can't wait."

He slid his hand to the place that ached for him; his fingers tested her readiness and spread her open.

Anticipation was a white-hot rush in her veins. The blunt tip pushed at her core, breached it, stretched her. She clutched his firm ass and pulled him into her to the hilt. He was hot and thick, and the searing kiss he gave her was a claiming. Soul to soul.

It was ecstasy.

Each slick thrust, each passionate brush of his lips,

healed something inside her. Showed her what it was like to make love. To be cherished.

Agonizing need coiled tight in her core. Her whole body went taut as whimpers spilled from her, eyes squeezing shut, her nails digging into his back. She fell to pieces in his arms, doing her best to be quiet. And failing.

Just before the last rippling aftershock, he followed her over the edge. One last thrust, he stiffened and collapsed on top of her.

He held her close—his fingers in her hair, her cheek to his chest—and rolled them onto their sides, staying buried inside her.

For the first time in her life, she was completely connected to another, in every way possible. The closeness, this love, was everything she'd been missing but needed.

Chapter Sixteen

"I'll have Hummingbird there this morning," Nick said over a new burner phone he'd gotten from Bo.

"You better," Yaz said. "Not only will Draper have your ass if you don't, but he'd be justified."

"I'm not asking you to buy stock in what I've said about Draper, but the fact is we have been compromised. All I'm asking is that you tell him I'm bringing her in at ten-thirty by car. But I want you and Charlie to meet us at the heli-pad on the roof at ten." That way if Draper planned to sab-otage her arrival, the misinformation would be enough to still protect Lori. "We'll bring her inside and you and the rest of the SOG unit that's coming in can make sure she gets to court safely."

The tactical team would be locked and loaded with an arsenal of firepower and prepared to handle absolutely any-thing on the one-minute drive from the US Marshals' of-fice to the federal courthouse.

"The support unit is here. They got in last night."

"Good. I'm not asking you to stick your neck out. I'm just asking for help with the added precaution. I've kept her alive thus far. Help me get her through the homestretch."

"It's a small ask. We can make it happen."

"Thanks, Yaz."

"You realize the moment Hummingbird is in the build-ing and Draper sets eyes on you, you're fired, right?"

"I figured as much. But I'm not going to stop digging until I find proof that the SOB is involved. And when I do, it's his funeral."

"I totally didn't just hear you threaten a US marshal."

Nick raked a hand back through his hair. "Thanks. See you in a few hours." He hung up.

Aiden and Charlie could be trusted, and it'd be easy to explain the small deviation in plans as a last-minute change. Bringing Lori to the district office first was part of their protocol that Nick agreed was in her best interest.

A full SOG unit would have personnel posted outside the courthouse, in front of the US Marshals' district office, and escort her across the street to the federal courthouse using ballistic protective shields to cover her as the vehicle entered the courthouse.

The procedure was solid. The only opportunity Draper would have to sabotage things was as Nick delivered her to the office. But he wasn't going to give him the chance.

Nick finished his breakfast and his coffee, setting the dishes in the kitchen sink. Lori was still getting ready upstairs and said she couldn't eat with her nerves kicking up.

"You don't look well rested," his mother said, making a fresh pot of coffee.

He wasn't. Blissfully exhausted and thoroughly content was more like it. He and Lori had made love through the storm and the rest of the night. If he'd been a gentleman, he would've let her get more sleep. But he had to release a year of pent-up longing and lust. Taking her in the shower, licking his way down her delicious body and feasting between her legs back in the bed.

Her appetite had matched his rapacity, only heightening his arousal. They'd consumed each other and once their need had been temporarily slaked, they'd spooned.

They managed to doze for all of two hours.

Nick grabbed another piece of bacon from a platter. "It was hard to sleep with the storm."

"The storm outside or inside?" his mother asked.

Nick averted his gaze and stuffed the bacon into his mouth.

"I trust there was no *funny* business."

"No, ma'am," he said in total honesty.

"Good." She shot him a knowing glance. "If there had been, you would've been doing it wrong."

Nick choked on the food sliding down his throat.

Bo walked into the kitchen from the dining room with his empty plate and patted him on the back. "Are you all right, Nicky?"

"Your brother has never been better." His mother flashed a wry smile. "Isn't that right?"

It was true. Better. Happier. Lighter. His heart was like a hot-air balloon taking flight in his chest. "I should go check on Lori."

"She'll be down when she's ready. Jules wanted to make sure Lori had an outfit for today that she'd be comfortable in."

As if they'd talked her up, Lori entered the room. Wearing one of his sister's practical dresses—since Jules wasn't a suit gal—a pair of his mom's heels and a stunning smile, Lori looked beautiful.

Her dark hair was fashioned in a style he'd never seen on her, swept up in a twist off her shoulders. It flattered her, highlighting her features, warm eyes, high cheekbones, those kissable lips. But he'd prefer to see it loose and spread across his pillow again.

Their gazes collided and stuck. His pulse quickened and his heart grew even lighter. It was all he could do not to whisk her into his arms, hold her close, tight, and kiss her.

They'd been perfect together, fit like they belonged. Not

just physically. It'd been the most satisfying carnal experience but also the most intimate.

God, why had he denied himself, them both, this pleasure for so long? Why didn't he make love to her sooner?

"Excellent choice," his mother said. "You look ready to take on a titan."

Lori's brow wrinkled, and Nick could practically hear her thoughts. Did his mother know Lori was about to go up against Goliath, a titan?

Nick had no clue whether his mother knew. He appreciated their unspoken *don't ask, don't tell* family policy.

"Are you sure I can't fix you something to eat on the flight?" his mother asked.

"No, I'm fine. With the jitters, I won't be able to eat until after I've testified."

"Good luck, my dear." Hugs and kisses were exchanged. "Nicholas," his mother said, pressing a palm to his cheek, "it's not over. Stay vigilant. I fear the worst is yet to come."

If there was more his mother could've said to help him, she would've.

No MATTER HOW frightening, no matter how risky, there was only one thing she could do.

Belladonna checked the time again. 9:50 a.m. She didn't know when the target would arrive at the US Marshals' office, or how. In a car driven down Broadway, entering through the garage, or by helicopter on the roof.

But the marshals would follow protocol down to the letter, and the target would be brought to their headquarters and then escorted to the federal courthouse. A full Special Operation Group contingency team was on the ground and waiting. They'd be geared up in body armor, locked and loaded to blow away any threat.

Belladonna was counting on the SOG not to disappoint. Her plan depended on it.

She'd positioned the replacement pawns, bishops and rooks in their respective places at the crack of dawn while the city was still sleeping. Each had their role to play. Everyone was under strict orders not to deviate from the plan.

A gambit if ever there was one to be played.

The carnage would be devastating, splashed across the news headlines for days. Many lives would be lost. But the only ones she cared about were hers, Alessandro's and Lily's.

It'd be nice if Smokey made it, too.

She clenched the burner phone in her hand, her knuckles whitening. The text message would have to be perfectly timed. She patted the messenger bag in the passenger seat. Her ace in the hole. It would work. It had to.

Glancing at the back of her hand, she was pleased the body makeup covering the rose tattoo hadn't smudged. Her gaze flickered up to the rearview mirror of the parked sedan she sat in. Her short blond wig looked natural. She almost believed the disguise herself.

"Helicopter inbound," Smokey said over her earpiece that was hidden by the wig. "Civilian. ETA two minutes."

"It's them. I need synchronized execution of the fireworks. Wait for my mark."

"We're ready. The next time you radio in, the entire team will be able to hear you."

Excellent.

She took out her burner cell and sent the text.

Time to trim the bonsai.

Within thirty seconds she received Alessandro's response to her code for him to neutralize any threats, take their daughter and run to their contingency location.

Clippers in hand. See you soon.

Belladonna removed the battery from the phone, snapped the SIM card and chucked everything out the window. If things went as she expected, then she would indeed see them soon.

She put the car in Drive and turned down Broadway.

Nick McKenna was playing hide-and-seek, oblivious to the real game. This was an Armageddon match and he was blind to her next move.

THE GREETING LORI received from Nick's teammates was hurried. She got the feeling they didn't want to have her exposed outside for too long. Besides catching their names, Aiden Yazzie and Charlie Killinger, the rest had been a blur as they hustled her inside and down to the third floor.

The reception from Will Draper had been even colder. He threw a scowl at Nick and cut his eyes to her. "Ms. Carpenter, it's good to see you again," Will Draper said to her, escorting her to his office without so much as a handshake. "I was under the impression you wouldn't arrive for another hour. By car." His sour expression deepened to a pointed glare he turned on Nick and his two teammates.

Nick closed the office door. "We had to change the plan at the last minute."

"Not one word out of you. You're an embarrassment to this office and you're fired. I want your badge, your gun and you out of my sight," Draper snapped in a rush as though he'd been holding the words in and couldn't keep them bottled up a second longer.

"Excuse me, Marshal Draper," Lori said, the anger firing in her veins spurring her to step forward. "But Nick McKenna deserves a decoration, not a reprimand. The only reason I'm alive is because of him. Considering how the breach in this office jeopardized my safety several times, and not your deputy's actions, I'm shocked you're not showing more gratitude to someone who has gone above and beyond the call of duty. If he's not part of my protective detail to the courthouse, then I won't be testifying today."

Draper's jaw dropped and his face turned beet red. "Ms. Carpenter, with all due respect, you aren't privy to our standard operating procedures and the various rules Deputy Marshal McKenna has broken."

"Marshal Draper, you weren't almost killed multiple times and on the run for your life over the last twenty-four hours. You don't know the first thing about what we endured or survived out there. If that man," she said, pointing to Nick, "isn't properly commended and promoted for his efforts, then you either have your head up your butt or he's right and you're a traitor to justice. And I want you to know that I intend to share my perspective not only with the US attorney's office but also with the attorney general and my congressman."

BELLADONNA PASSED THE front of the US Marshals' office, where deputies in full tactical gear stood out front. She drove up to the parking garage of the building and spoke to the armed security guard, flashing the star pinned to the outside of the black badge holder that hung around her neck. "Hi, I'm Deputy Marshal Sharon White down from the LA office. I have an appointment with Marshal Draper."

The security guard turned to his laptop, verified her appointment, and waved to two more SOG deputies kitted in armor from top to toe to let her through.

Belladonna's hacker had planted the fake appointment while in their system.

She entered the garage and picked the first available spot. Getting out of the car, she touched her earpiece. "Stay on your objective, no matter what, until I say Echo Sierra." The siege would end, and Smokey would do one last thing for her. "Begin in thirty."

Counting down in her head, she tapped the device once more so nothing else could be heard on her side.

Twenty-eight. She walked through the lot and entered the building.

Twenty. Her heart pounded hard against her ribs as she crossed the lobby to the reception desk, but she had nerves of steel.

Sixteen. She repeated the same thing she'd told the guard outside, all the while keeping the count in her head.

Eleven. The man seated behind the desk eyed the badge prominently displayed and waved her through to security to have her bag checked.

Eight. Belladonna sat the messenger bag on the security table and flashed a smile. Nothing sexy, no teeth showing— a casual *hey, how are you* grin.

Five. Opening the main compartment, the armed guard returned the smile. *Four.* He took out the laptop, looked it over, noting the US Marshal Services label—*three*—and slid it back inside. *Two.* Then he turned the bag over and reached for the zipper of the back compartment.

One.

Thunderous gunfire erupted in front of the building.

At the same time, the rest of the coordinated attack began. A truck crashed into the security gatehouse by the entrance to the parking garage. The SOG deputies posted in front of the federal courthouse across the street were swarmed. A van exploded on the corner of the San Diego Police Department one mile away. Perched on the hotel rooftop diagonal to the US Marshals' building, a sniper took aim with a high-powered semiautomatic Barrett M82 .50 caliber rifle that was going to pack one hell of a punch. He let loose on the tinted, bullet-resistant windows of the third floor using black tips—armor-piercing rounds.

None of this would kill the target. None of this was intended to kill her.

It was all a distraction.

As the guards in the lobby ran to assist the tactical deputies out front of the US Marshals' building, Belladonna took her messenger bag that hadn't been fully searched, leaving the main compartment open, and headed for the stairs.

The elevators were about to fill up and she wanted to avoid the crowd.

According to their protocol, every available SOG member and deputy trained for field duty was mobilizing to assist team members under direct fire outside: in front of the building, at the parking garage and by the courthouse. It would bleed them dry, leaving none inside.

The remaining personnel on the third floor, mostly analysts, IT and management, were moving to the conference room away from the windows. Huddled together where someone could eliminate several birdies with one stone.

For a witness, the procedure was different. They were to be isolated with a deputy in a holding room that had reinforced walls. The door could only be opened using a personal identification number.

Belladonna drew a deep breath, opened the stairwell door and walked onto the third floor. Her sniper was peppering the office space with high-caliber bullets meant to tear through armor. Making a beeline for the conference room, she unzipped a compartment on the side of the bag and removed a canister of halothane.

She hurried to the room and opened the glass door. Catching Will Draper's surprised gaze, she pulled the pin, dropped the canister and shut them in. The effect of the colorless, sweet-smelling sleeping agent was almost immediate, neutralizing fifteen people in a snap.

Turning on her heel, she marched toward the holding room. As soon as her sniper was out of ammo and McKenna had been baited and hooked by the lull in gunfire, she'd make her move.

Chapter Seventeen

Inside the holding room, Nick finally managed to get Lori to sit. He stood beside her, rubbing her back in small circles. Her body was taut with tension.

Even in the room with reinforced walls that reduced outside noise, it sounded like all hell was breaking loose.

The high-caliber rifle—a real humdinger of firepower—was still making mincemeat of the third floor. An explosion rocked the building, he gauged somewhere out front. There had also been reports of an attack at the parking garage and on tactical personnel stationed at the courthouse. Yaz, Charlie and all the others were properly swamped.

It was a war zone on multiple fronts. Damn. Had Belladonna mustered an army?

Lori was an hour from testifying. They'd gone through so much to keep her alive and get to this point, Nick wasn't going to let anything happen to her now.

The police would respond. SWAT would be on the scene to assist any minute. They were going to get through this.

Quiet fell, and Lori's shoulders relaxed. The fusillade of semiautomatic gunfire had stopped. Maybe it was over, or being handled by SWAT.

The police were less than a mile away. They had to be here by now.

A series of beeps resounded in the hall. Someone was probably coming to give them the all clear.

The door opened and Nick's blood turned to slush.

Even with the blond wig and stodgy suit, he recognized Belladonna in the flesh.

As he went to draw his Glock from the shoulder rig, she tossed a black bag on the table and lunged for him.

Her elbow caught him in the cheekbone, twisting his head to the side and sending pain grinding down his face and into his teeth.

Lori gasped, hopping up and scrambling back against the wall.

With a lightning move, Belladonna torqued his gun hand, threw a knee to his gut and disarmed him. His weapon clattered to the floor. In the struggle, he reached out to grab her, but only ended up with a handful of the wig and ripped it from her head.

She launched a fist at his windpipe, stealing his breath. But he managed to throw a quick jab to her face.

Belladonna reeled back into a reverse flip. Her rising feet, coming up like pistons, caught him square in the chin, snapping his head up. Momentum threw him backward into the wall.

Nick took a ragged breath, marveling at how badly he'd underestimated Belladonna's fighting skills. She landed softly on the balls of her feet, whipping out a left hook at his head.

A raw-numb tingling exploded in his eye, leaving him dazed. Instinct kept him moving and blocking. Belladonna pressed her advantage, unleashing a blitzkrieg of punches and kicks.

Somehow, he shoved her off, gaining space to defend himself.

They hammered each other with bare-knuckle blasts. Nick outweighed her and had more force behind his blows. But she was faster and better trained at hand-to-hand. He wouldn't last much longer before she trapped him in some deadly grip. Broke his arm. Snapped his neck.

Then that would be the endgame.

Getting to his gun was the only answer.

He spotted it under the table. Flinging a chair at her, he dove for it, his fingertips grazing the handle before Belladonna drove a heel into his kidneys and sent the gun skittering.

Nick's back throbbed where he'd been kicked. His eyes watered from the blow.

Lori made a play for the gun, the floral dress fluttering around her legs. Nick pushed up from the floor.

Belladonna was a blur of movement, rolling across the table.

Lori grabbed the gun and lifted it to fire. But the assassin kicked it from her grasp and sent it flying in the air.

As Nick jumped up and to the side for the weapon, Belladonna whirled, snatching Lori.

They faced each other in a standoff, panting.

Nick had the gun, safety off, finger on the trigger. And Belladonna had Lori positioned in front of her like a human shield and a dagger-sharp hairpin to Lori's throat. The assassin's black hair had tumbled loose, falling freely, almost curtaining what little of her face was exposed.

Belladonna pressed the pointed tip of the deadly instrument to Lori's carotid artery.

Nick made eye contact with Lori. Her face was stark with fear.

Panic swelled in his chest. He held the gun rock steady, but he didn't have a clear shot.

He shifted his gaze to the assassin. "Kill her and I kill you." He issued the imperative statement of fact without letting the fear flooding him leak into his voice, his tone glacial.

"I know." The utter lack of concern from Belladonna

sent a trickle of cold sweat down Nick's spine. Then she said, "But I don't want to die today. I have a proposal."

It was some kind of trick, had to be. "I'm just supposed to trust that, after you've relentlessly pursued us with every intention of ending both our lives?"

"I used halothane on the people in the conference room. I could've used it on you two instead. Once you were out cold, I could've killed Lori and fled."

Nick narrowed his eyes at her. "Then why didn't you?"

"My personal circumstances have changed. I have one chance to break free of Dante Vargas. And this is it, but I need your help."

His heart stuttered at the turnabout. "What? You're insane if you think I'm going to help you."

"I have a family and he's threatened their lives unless I kill her." Belladonna nudged the sharp tip against Lori's throat, drawing a drop of blood.

Starbursts of red exploded behind his eyes, and he clenched the gun tighter, praying for enough clearance between the two women to put a bullet in Belladonna's head.

"Dante has promised to release me from his service if I follow through, but he is the prince of lies," Belladonna said. "He'll never free me. And if I don't get out, then one day, he'll claim my daughter, too. I can't let that happen. So I have a proposal. One where we both win."

"You made several attempts on my life, her life," Nick said through clenched teeth. "Who knows how many good people are dying right now under the siege you started outside? And you've already murdered one deputy at our safe house. I don't see a scenario where we can both win."

Mentally, he sifted through options, his mind scrambling to think of a way to get Lori through this alive. Even if he signaled Lori to take some action, throw an elbow back into Belladonna, anything to get distance between them so he could get a shot, it wouldn't work.

Belladonna wasn't flush to Lori, leaving her ribs exposed to an attack. She stood at an angle as if anticipating some countermove.

"Lucky for us both, I do," Belladonna said. "Lori lives and testifies. That's the win you want. I leave, you put the word out that a female suspect meeting my description was killed making an attempt on her life, and I give you the name of your traitor. That's the win I want. You should want that, too."

"I know who the traitor is. Will Draper."

"Really?" Her granite expression shifted. "Do you have proof?" A ghost of a smile stretched across Belladonna's tight face. "I do. Look in my bag. Middle compartment."

Nick kept the gun raised and backpedaled to the table. Not taking his eyes off Belladonna, he felt for the compartment. It was open. He pulled out a laptop.

"Do you recognize the serial number?" she asked.

His gaze bounced between the assassin and the computer. He turned it over and checked the number. His blood turned cold.

Belladonna flipped open the badge hanging around her neck, showing him the ID. "Your traitor is Ted Zeeman. Not Will Draper."

His mind reeled, the breath in his lungs stalled. "We have Ted's body in the morgue."

"No. The body you have in the morgue was planted in your safe house by one of my people. On the laptop, I've downloaded Ted's dental records and the records for the person in the morgue."

Nick shook his head in disbelief, blowing out a shaky breath.

"Who do you want more? Me, someone who is being coerced and threatened? Or Ted Zeeman? Someone you trusted, who betrayed you for money. The morning of your trip to the mall, Ted gave me the address to the safe house and left his badge and laptop for one of my people in the trash bin outside. When the attempt at the mall failed, he called me from a convenience store to find out the contingency plan. He let you walk into that house, thinking neither of you would be walking back out.

"We used his laptop to breach your system. Dante Vargas has the WITSEC list and the names of every deputy marshal. Ted facilitated that. He's the one who put a roving bug on your cell phone for me, so I could not only track you but also listen to all your calls. He also gave me the details about your protocol and procedures. How do you think I was able to get in here? Whose PIN do you think I used to open that door?"

Fury beat in Nick's chest like the wings of a startled bird. "You know where Ted is?"

"Yes. I arranged his transportation out of the country and can tell you exactly where to find him, a beautiful white sand beach. I want Lori to live. I want her to testify, to hurt Vargas and the cartel. I also want to disappear with my family. So I'll ask you again. Who do you want more? Me? Or backstabbing Ted?"

If he had to make a choice, there was no contest. This was personal. He wanted to rip Ted's head off.

"A draw is a good thing," Belladonna said with that silver tongue, in her honeyed voice. "No more bloodshed. I'll stop the siege outside."

And he could end the assault going on outside, possibly save lives? It was the only choice. "Deal."

"Put your gun on the floor. Kick it away and I'll release her."

Belladonna could've used halothane on them, killed Lori and left. But she hadn't because maybe her story about her family and wanting freedom from Vargas was true. Nick did as she instructed and raised his palms.

"If Will Draper gives you a hard time about going along

with our deal and my death isn't reported in the news as we've agreed, tell that bastard I'll come for him and I promise he'll die screaming."

Nick nodded. He was okay with that.

"Ted is in the Maldives. I downloaded his address and imagery of the island onto the laptop, as well."

"How did you know how this was going to play out? That I'd agree?"

"It's a talent of mine." She punched in the code, unlocking the door, and opened it.

Releasing Lori, Belladonna touched her ear. That was when he spotted the comms device.

"Echo Sierra," she said, letting the door close.

Nick grabbed his gun, contemplating going after her. A second later the power was cut, trapping them inside the room. Effectively eliminating that option.

In the darkness, Nick found Lori and hauled her into his arms. "When she had you with that spike to your throat, I died a thousand deaths."

He felt her tears on his cheeks. Then again, he couldn't be certain he wasn't the one crying. Gratitude and relief tangled through him and he squeezed her tighter, not wanting to ever let her go.

The power came back and he stared at Lori in the light. Her eyes were glassy and her face damp. He cupped her cheeks and pressed his forehead to hers.

"Oh, God," she said on a catch of breath. Lori nestled closer, her fingers clutching his back. "I wasn't ready. For this to be it."

"I know." He kissed her lips, tasting the salt of their mingled tears. The thought of her coming so close to death still made his heart contract.

"You saved my life again." Her voice was rough with emotion.

"Didn't really have much choice. That's the job."

She laughed and cried at the same time. "Stop saying that."

"Okay." He wiped away her tears with his thumb. "You're more than a witness to me. You have been for months. I can't say exactly when it happened, but I'm so in love with you that—"

Beeps chimed in the hall.

Nick and Lori pulled apart but stayed close.

The holding room door opened, and Yazzie crossed the threshold, eyeing them both. "You two are both okay, good. Charlie is helping the others in the conference room. They were hit with some kind of sleeping gas, but they're waking up." His voice was hesitant as his gaze flickered between them like he was picking up on their energy. "The attacks stopped. They just pulled back and left. The police are in pursuit."

"I gathered," Nick said. "We lose anyone?"

"No. Lots of injuries, but everyone is going to live. Draper is conscious. He wants eyes on the witness right now."

"Yeah, okay. I need to talk to him anyway. There have been some developments."

Testifying had lifted a great load from Lori's shoulders. But when new marshals waited for her outside the courtroom, the weight was quickly replaced by a different strain.

"Can you give us one minute?" Nick asked the deputies there to relocate her.

They both nodded and stepped a few feet away.

Keeping her alive, getting her on the stand, was always going to lead here, but she hadn't had time to think about it. Until now.

"They won't tell me where you're going," he said low. "Protocol." He slipped her a piece of paper, his fingertips brushing hers, lingering. "When you're able to, provided you want to, call me."

She'd spent every day with this man for a year and didn't even know his phone number. Something about that made her heart ache. "Of course I want to. I will as soon as I can."

"I won't be able to come to you right away. It'll be a little while before I can see you."

Her chest tightened. "Why?"

One of the deputies waiting leveled a reproving glance at them, and he dropped his hand from hers.

"I'm on a plane to the Maldives tomorrow. We don't have an extradition treaty with them, but Draper doesn't give a damn any more than I do. I'm going to bring Ted back and he's going to answer for what he's done."

"Is Draper going to honor Belladonna's request?" She discreetly tucked his phone number in her bra.

Nick nodded, a ghost of a smile on his lips. "It didn't take much convincing after I passed along Belladonna's message."

"Once you bring Ted back, you'll come to see me?"

Nick glanced over at the deputies coming toward them. "No. I need to wait until they have you settled and back off. A few weeks at most. I swear."

Earnestness gleamed in his whiskey-brown eyes and echoed in his words.

"McKenna, we can't give you any longer. The SOG unit is waiting to escort us to make sure we don't run into any problems along the way."

"Okay," Nick said, taking a step back, his brow creased. "Lori…*kharabetam.*"

She knew the word was Farsi but didn't have a clue what it meant.

With a deputy positioned on either side of her, Lori put one foot in front of the other and walked away from the only man she'd ever truly loved.

Each step she took deepened the ache swelling in her chest. A torrent of emotions whirled through her and she didn't know how much more upheaval she could handle before falling apart. And for the next few weeks, she'd have to hold it together without Nick.

Nick.

Lori spun around, breaking away from the deputies, ignoring their questions, and ran back to Nick. She stopped short of grabbing him and kissing him and making an even bigger spectacle. "*Kharabetam.* What does it mean?"

He gave her a warm smile, his eyes radiating love. "I'll tell you the next time we're face-to-face and I'm free to kiss you."

"You sure do know how to leave a woman hanging."

"Well, I've got to keep you thinking about me someway."

"Trust me. No effort at all on your part is required."

One of the deputies took her by the elbow, and they escorted her away.

Epilogue

Nick had found Ted Zeeman seated on a powdery white sand beach beside a hut, fishing, drinking beer and canoodling with a woman.

His female companion had been a surprise. A prostitute he'd fallen for who happened to work for *Los Chacales*. The cartel controlled much of the prostitution in California, so it was only two degrees of separation.

Pillow talk had been Ted's undoing. After a particularly glorious evening, he'd let it slip that he'd be out of town for a year, guarding a high-profile witness for the big WCM case. He'd arranged to meet his lady friend in a motel near Big Bear to have his pipes cleaned every three months. Turned out the cartel offered money for information about Lori's whereabouts. Every month, the bait for a tip had increased. Once it had gotten to a ridiculous sum, the woman blabbed.

At his last scheduled rendezvous, Belladonna had been waiting for Ted.

Zeeman had offered the confidential laptop, his credentials and information about the marshal's protocol in exchange for Belladonna giving him a clean exit strategy.

Slapping handcuffs on Ted had been ten times more satisfying than Nick had imagined.

But absolutely nothing topped this moment. Standing under the warm Phoenix sunshine in front of Lori's apartment door. Her last name was Washington now, but one day he'd hoped to make it McKenna.

Nick knocked, excitement buzzing in his veins.

Lori opened the door and his world righted.

Her hair had been lightened to the color of melted caramel, doe eyes sparkling in the light, gorgeous in a form-fitting white sundress that clung to her curves like a second skin.

She was a sight for sore eyes that immediately got him hard and set his heart on fire.

He silently promised he'd be a gentleman and not pounce on her until after lunch.

Lori launched herself at him, wrapping her legs around his waist, and kissed him.

He supported her weight with an arm beneath her rear and carried her inside, kicking the door shut behind them.

After dropping his suitcase, he curled his fingers in her hair and deepened the kiss.

She was vibrantly alive in his arms. Her lips were petal smooth, her tongue coaxing.

"You smell so good, feel so good," he said in a rough whisper. "You're making it tough for me to be a gentleman."

"How about you be the natural hellion that you are and make love to me until I can't remember my new last name?"

"Happy to oblige."

He pressed her back against the wall and tore open the front of her dress, sending tiny pearl buttons skittering to the floor.

No underwear. *Oh, man.*

There was only creamy bare skin inviting him to touch and play. He kissed and licked and nibbled her neck, over the faint line from her old wound, down to her breasts. Sucked on her nipple.

Arousal kicked him hard, his skin tightening with anticipation at the pleasure that awaited them both.

She unfastened his belt, lowered his zipper and grinned at his rock-hard erection. "Have I told you how impressive you are?"

"No, but feel free."

Her hand closed over him and squeezed, spurring him to shamelessly moan.

He cupped her sex, finding her hot and wet and equally ready. "Condoms are in my bag," he said, proud of himself for remembering.

"Can't wait. Been thinking about this for days." She positioned him precisely where she wanted him. "I need you now."

Their union was quick but all-consuming. Urgency drove each unrestrained thrust. They moved as one, stroking and groping, their coupling of love and lust. Need gathered fast, painful as a bruise. It was wild and mindless, but achingly beautiful.

Shoving his hand down between them, he circled the right button, making sure they came together. The world turned stark white as pleasure shot through him hotter than a bullet. Her scream of satisfaction filled his ears, and he couldn't help but smile.

He carried her to the sofa, more of a shuffle, really, with his pants around his ankles. Thankfully, it was a short distance. They dropped in a tangle, still connected. He soaked up the contact, the sweet brew of sensation, like a greedy sponge.

She ran her fingers through his hair and tugged his head back, meeting his gaze. "I've waited five hundred and..." She looked at the clock on the wall. "And thirty-five hours to know. What does *kharabetam* mean?"

He gave her a deep, soul-wrenching kiss. "It literally means I'm ruined for you." Cupping her face, he brushed his thumb over her cheek.

Happy tears glistened in her eyes. "Good, because you're stuck with me."

He laughed, stroking her hair. "Do you like living in Phoenix?"

She shrugged. "It's okay. Better than backcountry nowhere."

"I'm going to put in for a transfer, but before I do, I wanted to see if you were open to moving."

"I'd love to. It's not as if I've found a job yet, but can I?"

"Sure, as long as it's not a city you've lived in before or have family. I was thinking about Vegas."

A bright smile spread across her face. "Yes!" she squealed with absolute delight. "I love your family and it would be amazing to be close to them."

"There are some bounty hunters I know who could use an office manager. Someone capable of balancing the books. Interested?"

"Of course."

"And I was thinking, maybe we could get married, next year. In the spring. Mom says the weather is perfect for a wedding."

Her eyes grew wide and she looked choked up.

Way to go for moving too fast. "We can take it slower if you like. I didn't mean to rush you."

"You're not. It's just that you're giving me everything I've ever dreamed about and hoped for, making wishes I didn't even know I had come true."

His heart rolled over in his chest. "I love you, Lori. I want to give you the world. I want you to be the mother of my children and grow old with you. I really am ruined for you."

"Ditto, *kharabetam*."

"Now, I've got a really big question for you."

"Bigger than me moving and marrying you?"

"In a way, yes. How do you feel about me taking you on a proper date? We've never had one."

Her smile blossomed, growing wider and deeper and filling him with the loveliest sensation he'd ever known. He would do anything for this woman.

She brushed her lips against his, soft and sweet, and said, "I thought you'd never ask."

His cell phone rang, and he was tempted to ignore it, but she fished it out of his pocket and handed it to him.

He answered without looking at the caller ID. "This better be good."

"It's me, Charlie. Aiden and I are in a world of trouble. We need your help."

Why couldn't they have waited to call after his first date with Lori?

Nick sighed. "What do you need?"

* * * * *

COLTON'S DEADLY DISGUISE

GERI KROTOW

To Alex
It's such a joy to see the thoughtful,
compassionate man you've become.

Chapter One

Isabella Colton pulled up to Mustang Valley High School fighting a sense of urgency that wasn't usually her gig. Normally she absorbed every mile of scenery as she drove between her home nestled on the outskirts of Mustang Valley and into the town proper. Saguaro cacti sprinkled spots of green across the southeastern Arizona desert; many of the desert flowers were abloom, their hues of fuchsia, crimson and cream a stark contrast to the constant cactus green. But she'd noticed none of them today, and barely even registered the way the deep blue sky contrasted with the pale coral, violets and browns that made up the sandstone horizon.

Why, when she'd finally settled into her career as a journalist, was she all of a sudden feeling so stressed? Was it because she knew so much was riding on this assignment? Or the fact that she'd deliberately lied to her triplet brothers—Spencer, a Mustang Valley PD sergeant, and Jarvis, a businessman currently working as a ranch hand—when they'd asked why she couldn't meet them today for lunch.

Could it be because you're going against every principle you hold closest to your heart?

Maybe. Choosing to sign up as a contestant in the

Ms. Mustang Valley Pageant was certainly out of her wheelhouse. As in, out in space from her true beliefs. But she was willing to do whatever it took to get the story, this story, right.

She'd been a reporter for the Lifestyle section of the *Mustang Valley Gabber* for over three years. It was time to break out, to write about subjects she was passionate about. More than anything, Bella longed to get to the truth of life, subject by subject. This was who she was, and she'd known it ever since she'd lost her parents when she was ten years old. There were a lot of things she couldn't control in life, but when she could, she wanted to get to the bare facts.

Since she'd accepted that reporting was her talent, she didn't want to waste another minute on articles that no longer interested her. It wasn't fair to her readers or to her. She'd written enough lifestyle and fashion pieces for the *Gabber* to last her lifetime.

It was time to make a change. Bella wanted to make a difference.

For years, she'd had to watch her best friend, Gio, do everything to fit what she believed to be the pageant lifestyle; from starving herself to paying thousands of dollars she didn't have for unnecessary collagen and Botox injections that began in her early twenties. Last year, Gio paid the final, irrevocable price when she died due to malnutrition and other effects of her eating disorders. At first glance, deciding to enter the exact culture that had killed Gio seemed counterintuitive. But not when she reminded herself why she was doing this—to out the people who had killed her best friend.

Bella needed the inside dirt on this pageant, and the only way to catch this fly would be with a generous dollop of honey, according to what Gio had told her over the six months before her death, just under a year ago.

Heartache mingled with grief at the reminder of Gio's death and Bella's irretrievable loss. Tears swelled and blurred the view of where the Arizona horizon and blue sky met in Mustang High School's parking lot. Bella's heart constricted at the natural beauty she and Gio had often shared on long hikes through the desert, or to the local lake, next to an abandoned silver mine that they both loved so much. Until Gio's disease weakened her too much to make the treks. Gio's precipitous demise had been a shock, the years of illness finally ending her too-short life.

Bella owed it to Gio and every woman. Too many, including Gio, had suffered from the constant dieting and negative body image that pageants—and society as a whole—had so vilely infected them with. Bella owed it to them to expose the people and institutions that perpetuated their suffering. While she couldn't go after the entire pageant industry, she was able to delve into Ms. Mustang Valley, where Gio's problems, according to her friend, had all began. If she could keep this in mind, instead of her constant grief for her bestie, she'd get this assignment right.

What hurt the most right now was that all Gio had wanted from this particular pageant was the scholarship prize to Mustang Valley Community College. Gio would never go to school again, ever.

"Stop this right now. Pull it together, Colton." She flipped the decrepit old station wagon's visor down to use the mirror and dabbed at her tears, grateful she'd chosen the makeup with a waterproof label on it. She bolstered her spirits by sniffing the inside of her wrist, where she'd applied her favorite perfume. The soothing floral scent was a signature Parisian brand she'd noted on Kristi Sparkle, the supermodel who'd passed through Mustang Valley just a few weeks ago. It had been a fun gala at Mustang Valley town hall, where Bella had been able to interview the not-yet-thirty-year-old woman for a good fifteen minutes. It had made Bella grateful that in all of her thirty-one years she'd never held a job that required her to be anyone but herself. And while she'd maintained her weight she worked hard to do it. Healthy eating and lots of physical activity. Except when she had a pressing deadline, when Bella's coworkers knew to stay out of the line between her and the chocolate-chip cookies at the local bakery.

Bella's job as a journalist for the paper and blogger for its website afforded her an inside glimpse into the lives of the more affluent citizens of Mustang Valley, Arizona. It often put her in the position of experiencing events she'd only ever seen on television as a child. The only girl of three siblings, her first two decades had been tumultuous with Mom's and Dad's deaths when she and her brothers were only ten. Then, Aunt Amelia had raised them, but she never let them forget that she'd sacrificed *the best years of my life* to do so.

It'd taken a while for Bella to let go of the guilt her relief at Aunt Amelia's passing ten years ago had caused. At twenty-one, Bella hadn't comprehended that her sense of relief was absolutely normal.

Her professors at Arizona State had expressed their sympathy and compassion for her loss, for not having a parental figure at her graduation the following May. But to Bella, Aunt Amelia's death had been when her true life began. When she was able to make her own decisions without the looming negative comments Aunt Amelia doled out like thistles on a hiking trail. Those thorns were able to sneak into the oddest places such as the sole of a shoe or inside the back of a shirt; their sting was always guaranteed.

"Okay. You've got this." She spoke to her reflection, popped the visor back up and got out of the car. It'd been thirteen years, but MVHS still had the aura of countless life lessons about it, including when she'd tried to sneak a cigarette in the girls' restroom and skipped out on lunchtime. In both instances her nemesis Mrs. Maple had caught her and none-too-compassionately marched her down to Principal Kenner's office. Bella grinned, remembering the expression on Aunt Amelia's face when she'd been called in over Bella's truancy. It'd only been over one lunch period, to get a tattoo with her best friend. Bella reached up to rub her shoulder for good luck, where the small angel rested, but stopped herself. She'd put professional concealer over the symbol of her friendship with Gio, as the Ms. Mustang Valley Pageant did not allow visible tattoos. Bella sniffed. Another good reason to eschew the event.

You're doing this for Gio.

The building itself had undergone a recent facelift; bright teal roofing and matching painted trim stood out against the dark bricks and highlighted the elegance of the grand dame of Mustang Valley. Originally the town market during the mid-nineteenth century, the building had been expanded upon and modernized over the last century and a half. It truly was a beautiful piece of Mustang Valley charm. Had she really managed to avoid this place for the better part of ten years?

Bella teetered on the kind of espadrille wedges she

probably hadn't worn since high school, either. She bent down to tighten the ankle strap, not needing to make a fool of herself by twisting an ankle before she even submitted her application.

Today was the last day to enter the competition. A quick glance at her phone confirmed that she had a full fifteen minutes to turn in her application with attached résumé, photos and birth certificate. A certificate she'd thought long and hard about forging, but would it really gain her the edge she desired? She was well within the eighteen-to-thirty-five-year-old limit. She'd been working for the *Mustang Valley Gabber* long enough. It'd been Bella's goal for the last couple of years to move out of the *Gabber* and get to a bigger news outlet. If she were ever to be the kind of reporter she believed she could be, this was her most realistic chance.

She had to convince the pageant board that she wanted to do this, for real.

The front entrance of the school was clean and bright, as she always remembered. The relentless Arizona sun beat on her shoulders, bared by the strapless red-and-white-striped top she'd chosen to go with the white capri pants. The outfit was totally out of character for Bella; she preferred simple lines, be it in jeans or a sundress. But she had to come across as a serious contestant, and that meant she had to scream "glamour." She'd even had red highlights woven into her ash-blond locks, something she'd never considered previously. Tattoos, piercings, sure, but her hair was something she'd never dyed before. To her initial chagrin, the highlights had blended into her hair to make it all appear red, a strawberry blond shade. Gio had had red hair, and Bella decided her matching color was a good-luck charm from beyond. Tears again threatened and she sniffed them away, lifted her chin and straightened her spine.

Bella opened the school's front door and walked into the lobby.

She gave herself a moment to take it all in. A lot had changed over the past several years. The first thing her gaze landed on was a metal detector, but before she could assess the rest of the entrance she was stopped by a police officer.

"Excuse me, ma'am. I need to see inside your bag." The man was tall and fit, not unlike Spencer. Dark hair, and what looked like even darker eyes but she couldn't be sure as they were downcast, his gaze following his hand as he moved a stick through her large white leather designer bag. As he searched, she checked his name badge to ask Spencer about him later. Or, maybe strike a conversation now. She was on the clock as far as her undercover report was concerned.

He didn't have a name badge, and a closer look revealed he wasn't MVPD at all but rather, private security. The dark blue uniform was so similar in appearance to Mustang Valley PD's that it was an easy mistake to make.

"I thought MVPD had an officer here at all times." As soon as she spoke her mind she wanted to bite her tongue. She was here on an undercover assignment. Not the time to reveal her knowledge of the local community. Be a pageant contestant, not a blogger.

"When the students are present, yes, they do. But not during weekends and spring break. I'm pageant security."

"Oh." She looked at him and wished she had some handy banter. He was undeniably attractive, but with an air of stiff reserve. She opened her mouth to start a friendly conversation but he wasn't interested.

"Name?" Cold brown eyes assessed her and she stiffened, fighting the urge to take a step backward. An aura of authority exuded from this man and she couldn't help but wonder if he did something else.

"There's not a visitors' list—no one knows I'm entering." She wasn't about to be intimidated.

He held up a handwritten logbook. "I'm required to enter each name, for the pageant authorities to verify that they have received every application."

"Isabella Colton." His heavy, albeit well-sculpted, brows didn't budge from their place that reflected his intense focus as he wrote her name on what looked like maybe the twentieth line on the page.

Bella ignored her anxiety over how many contestants there might be. More would be better, as it would allow her to blend in more readily. If there were only twenty, she'd have to work at participation while gathering information for her report.

"ID?" He held out his hand without looking back up. She retrieved her Arizona driver's license, placed it carefully on his palm.

"Is this a part-time thing for you?" She smiled as she imagined a beauty contestant would, fluttered her lashes, ignored the two that stuck together. This glamour gig was not as easy as it had looked in the several pageants she'd studied online during her preliminary research. Her research yielded enough ammunition to warrant her entering the pageant. Of all the Arizona pageants, the Ms. Mustang Valley competition reflected the highest number of winners who'd later admitted to having mental illness, an eating disorder, or both. Most had gone public with their struggles once their year's reign was up, in order to both keep their scholarship intact, yet also provide public outreach to young women who found themselves in the grips of the same vicious diseases.

The security guard cleared his throat and she all but physically shook her head.

Worry about the research later. You're a contestant right now.

She still wasn't certain about which talent she'd choose. It was a sad competition between oratory skills, i.e. reading a Samuel Clemens Langhorne or Mark Twain poem, or performing a Hula hoop routine she'd choreographed in seventh grade with Gio to their favorite bubblegum pop hit.

He handed her ID and bag back, the tips of their fingers briefly making contact. "You can step through the metal detector now. The pageant committee is on the stage, in the theater, through the second doors on your right." His deep voice revealed nothing but professionalism. The security dude wasn't going to be an ally in her quest to uncover this pageant's deepest secrets. At least she knew from the start. She wouldn't waste any more energy on him. There were more important sources to mine.

Bella walked under the metal frame and when the detector didn't sound, she didn't look back. Forward was the only direction to achieve some kind of justice for Gio.

Wondering why the fleeting contact with this man moved her more than it should have wasn't worth her time.

Except, if she found out what else he did for a living, other than work as a pageant security guard, it might make an interesting side item for her investigative piece. She chuckled under her breath as she headed for the auditorium.

FBI Agent Holden St. Clair took a swig of water as he took his post offstage in the high school theater. The area between the side curtains allowed him to watch each contestant as they were interviewed, observe the pageant board members and keep an eye on the contestants who'd already been interviewed but now were seated on the stage, waiting until the entire process was over. The early birds got to see all of the interviews, which he supposed was some kind of pageant advantage. Holden didn't care. His job was to keep the building secure. He'd gone back and forth between here and the school entrance for the last eight hours.

It had been a long day.

After all contestants had finished today they'd be asked to leave and then only the ones who received a callback would return tomorrow for the start of the pageant preparation.

He'd had to stifle a laugh when his supervisor had told him he was assigned to work undercover at the Ms. Mustang Valley Pageant. His life experience to date included serving overseas while still in the army, and several different investigations as an FBI agent, including a few serial killer cases, not working as a security guard—even though he was hunting a murderer now.

Something about Mustang Valley was bothering him, ever since he'd driven into the modest-size town. His assignment was straightforward: observe and protect the pageant from the possibility of a serial killer who'd struck at two previous pageants earlier this year in Arizona. He was doing this undercover, with minimal other Law Enforcement Agency, LEA, involvement for now. Besides the director of Arizona pageants, who'd hired him, Holden had an inside LEA connection in town: his army buddy Spencer Colton, who worked at Mustang Valley PD with his K-9 companion Boris. After he'd spoken to Spencer on the phone, they'd met up at a restaurant in Tucson, so that Holden's cover as a security guard wouldn't be compromised. Spencer had given him the scoop on Mustang Valley and in particular the high school's blueprints, security footprint and the background on each of the Ms. Mustang Valley Pageant board members. The pageant board included Hannah Rosenstein, a MVHS Spanish teacher, Selina Barnes Colton—Colton Payne's ex and a rabid socialite who frankly, from what he'd read, was going to be a real pain in the neck—and several local business owners. So far he'd not found any reason to suspect any of them of wrongdoing but it was his job to remain alert.

Spending time with Spencer had been great and he'd been delighted to find out Spencer had fallen for a woman he planned to spend the rest of his life with. Spencer teased him, said Holden's turn was coming. Holden blew off Spencer's sentiments. After being so badly burned by his ex he had no room for anything more than short-lived hookups. Working a serial killer case left no time for that, either.

As much as Spencer assured him that he'd be a perfect fit in Mustang Valley, and that the openness of the citizens would hopefully expose the killer sooner, Holden had been on edge ever since he'd driven into Mustang Valley's historical downtown. Surrounded by so much Southwest American history, it was easy to forget he was here to investigate a serial killer who preyed upon beauty contestants, redheads in particular. So far all of the Ms. Mustang Valley contestants had been blonde or brunette, and he'd wondered if this pageant might escape the notice of the predator. Until Isabella Colton walked in with those red streaks in her hair. And green eyes, eyes he'd find attractive if he didn't know they'd be like bull's-eyes to the killer. Both of the previous victims had red hair, and green eyes.

He made a mental note to let Spencer know that Isabella was applying to compete in the pageant. He assumed it was Spencer's sister, Bella, that he'd talked about. While the Colton name was huge throughout the country, and especially in Mustang Valley, where one part of the family had made itself a billion-dollar oil empire, he doubted there were many Bella Coltons in this two-horse town. The pageant director, also a Colton, was a typical rich socialite, and he didn't think she was a close relation to Spencer or his probable sister. Like any other large, extended family, the Coltons had many branches. Spencer was from a modest background, and had been quick to let Holden know it when they were serving together.

"Thank you, Marcie." The pageant committee chair dismissed the second-to-last contestant to make it in by the deadline. Isabella Colton was the only one who remained.

He'd locked the front doors after scanning Isabella through security. All he had left to do today was observe as the last contestant hopefuls submitted their applications, and survived the board's initial interview.

It wasn't an easy task to remain focused. Isabella Colton's appearance made his gut tighten and put his instincts on high alert. Until the minute she walked through Mustang Valley High's doors he'd been hopeful that he'd be able to move on to the next Arizona pageant, scheduled for Scottsdale next month. He knew the serial killer he was after had only ever murdered redheads.

All hope that this pageant might be spared what two smaller towns in Northern Arizona had experienced— the brutal deaths of redheaded contestants—evaporated with the swoosh of the school's front doors behind Isabella Colton.

Holden wished for the first time in his career that he wasn't undercover. That he could snap his fingers and be the real Holden, for just one conversation with the woman who'd just walked into Mustang Valley High School's theater. To warn her away, to tell her that she should find another way to pay for her college or whatever she wanted to do with the winner's prize. But he was undercover, and since his guise was a security guard, his job was to stay quiet and observe. Isabella Colton still had to pass the scrutiny of the pageant review board, so at least there was a chance she'd be turned away either for her age or an incomplete application. She didn't look older than the thirty-five-year limit, but she wasn't too young, either.

"Isabella Colton?" Mimi Kingston, the pageant director, called out for the redhead and Colton couldn't help but do his job thoroughly and make sure he had a good description of Ms. Colton in his mind. At the security checkpoint he'd been focused on the possibility of any of the contestants bringing in a weapon, checking to make sure they weren't a potential suspect. He'd never investigated a female serial killer but the bureau had several over the years. It happened.

"Bella?" Mimi squeaked out the second syllable, clearly surprised to see the other woman.

"Surprises never cease in Mustang Valley. You know that, Mimi." Bella placed her application packet on the table that was center stage before returning to the single chair, and sat. He didn't see her bag; she must have left it in the theater seats. Since no one was left other than those onstage, all part of the pageant, it'd be secure. He was impressed. Bella Colton looked more put-together than the majority of the other contestants.

Her golden-red hair was tied up behind her head in one of those fancy styles he'd only ever noticed in the movies. What caught his attention was the creamy pale skin of her nape, where a few wispy tendrils curled. Her top bared her shoulders, revealing a prominent but not unhealthy collarbone. His mouth moistened as his tongue practically experienced how smooth it'd feel under it.

Holden bit down on said tongue and reminded himself he was on duty, and Bella Colton was most likely Spencer's sister. Holden's job was to protect the pageant, and if Bella was indeed his buddy's sibling, it raised the stakes on this operation. Since Payne Colton had been targeted, no Colton was safe.

He watched Bella cross her long legs at the ankles and rest her hands in her lap, her shapely knees fitting perfectly together. Her ankle-length pants were form-fitting and brokered no complaints from him. He liked that her nails were short, though painted bright red. Holden wasn't a fan of those long, fake nails, and he wondered what Bella did when she wasn't trying to rustle up a scholarship to Mustang Valley Community College.

"Thank you for your application, Bella. We're taking turns reviewing it." Derek McDougal spoke up, the only male on the board. He rustled the second page. "I see you're a Mustang Valley High graduate. So you've known about the pageant, as this is its thirtieth year." He passed the application packet to the next board member. "While we're reviewing everything to make sure you qualify, please tell us why you're here." Derek looked at Bella as though she were the canary and he the poised house cat.

Holden's sense went on high alert, as while McDougal didn't appear to have any connection with the previous pageants and murders, he was an anomaly. Two of the committee members, the Spanish teacher and Selina Barnes Colton, had been involved with at least one if not both of the ill-fated pageants and while they were automatic suspects, the outliers had to be examined, too.

"Certainly." Bella beamed. If she noticed Derek's leer she didn't show it. "As most of you know, I'm a lifelong Mustang Valley resident. I've been lucky enough to go to college, where I received my bachelor's in journalism. It's there on my résumé." She nodded at her application packet, which was being passed down the row of seven pageant board members. "I've fallen on hard financial times lately. I'd use the scholarship to MVCC to begin a new career that would have a more reliable income than freelance writing."

"But you're employed by the *Mustang Valley Gabber*, aren't you?" another board member called out. Holden made a mental note to check up on Bella's supposed dire straits, but all *thoughts* screeched to a halt. Wait—Bella Colton was a reporter? His gut twisted and he knew his mouth probably did, too.

Holden had nothing more than disgust for reporters.

Not for the usual reasons he knew other agents detested the media. Holden's distrust of reporters was very personal in origin, thanks to his last girlfriend, someone he'd thought might be with him for the long haul. Nicole, his ex, turned out to be dating him because she'd hoped to glean confidential information about the Coltons from him. This was last summer, when he'd investigated a crime in Roaring Springs, Colorado during its annual film festival. By the time the last film premiered, Nicole admitted her motive for wanting to wait all day in the hotel room for Holden. They were through. In the two years since, he'd dated on and off, but never anyone serious. And the bad taste in his mouth from being duped by a reporter had never washed away.

"I still work at the *Gabber*, but it's a modest wage, supplemented by freelance work that's also been drying up. It's time for me to face facts—I've got to find another type of job or starve." Bella smiled as she continued the interview. Her entire face lit up and dang it, it ignited something deep inside his chest. Holden's breath caught at the exquisite shade of peach on her cheekbones, the bright hue of her irises. But her green eyes didn't sparkle to match the dazzling of her white smile. Instead, Holden had the oddest sensation that Bella Colton was in the midst of a huge act. And the board was her audience. But why?

"With the scholarship to MVCC, I'd be able to become a nurse."

"The medical industry? A Colton?" Maeve Murphy, who'd worked as the school nurse for decades, spoke up.

Bella's foot began to shake at the end of her long, shapely leg, but her smile never faded, her chin remained uplifted. Holden gave her ten points for composure and the pageant had yet to begin, her application yet to be accepted.

"I'm not clear on what being a Colton has to do with a career choice." He heard the challenge in her tone even as she delivered her response so sweetly. It only served to make him admire her more. He really didn't need to admire anyone right now, though, and definitely not a journalist. He was here to find a serial killer.

You still have to live.

Maeve's plump face turned red. "It's just that, you're from a family of lucrative businesspeople. Why medicine, why now?"

Bella leaned forward, never breaking eye contact with Maeve. "I'm sorry—I think you're mistaking me for one of the other line of Coltons, the ones who own Rattlesnake Ridge Ranch and run Colton Oil. My brothers and I are from a different part of the family. In fact, I don't even know most of my Colton cousins very well." Her voice had turned to ice and Holden watched both her and the pageant committee's expressions. Most of the people on the board were career educators, including Maeve, an RN. If Bella was in her late twenties, maybe early thirties, she, Spencer and Jarvis must have gone to school here while Maeve and the others were on staff. They had to know her and her brothers. He'd read that Mustang Valley had a population of ten thousand. In short, Maeve knew Bella and her brothers.

And for some inexplicable reason, he was relieved to receive confirmation she wasn't familiar with the larger branch of her family.

A woman with pouffed-out brunette hair and large dangling earrings raised her heavily braceleted arm, waving at Maeve. "I can personally vouch for Bella and her desire to make something of herself. She's a lifelong resident, as she's stated, and her aunt raised her and her brothers after her parents' deaths in an auto accident. Tragic, I tell you. Yet you've survived the odds and are here to present yourself as a contestant. And, may I add, Bella was the brightest student of her class when I had her. Brava." Hannah Rosenstein nodded in encouragement toward Bella. Hannah was the school Spanish teacher and Holden had witnessed her vouch for exactly one other contestant, also a former student. If she said Bella was solid, he suspected the board would accept her application.

"*Muchas gracias*, Señora Rosenstein." Bella responded in a decent accent.

Senora Rosenstein grinned. "De nada. It's heartwarming to see you've remembered your Spanish."

Holden sat still until Bella's interview was finished and she was released to leave the building. Only after she exited the auditorium's back door did he stand and head for the back of the stage to begin his last inspection of the building before he locked it up for the night. Until next week, when the contestants would be called in to start the pageant prep.

A movement on the other side of the stage caught his attention. A tall figure in dark clothing, his face covered with the shadow from the brim of a baseball cap, the man wasn't anyone Holden had allowed in the building. Holden had memorized the exact number of people who should be here—board members, contestants, plus Bella, who had left the building by now—in the high school. This was a stranger, an interloper.

Holden drew his weapon from its hidden place in an

ankle holster and deliberately made his way to the back passage behind the stage, to avoid detection by the suspect. No one was going to be hurt—not on *his* watch.

Chapter Two

Offstage, Bella quickly slipped out of the espadrilles and shoved them into her oversize tote. Her feet made no sound on the old, highly waxed corridor floor that had borne thousands of teenaged feet through the years.

Looking over her shoulder, she made sure that the way-too-intense security guard hadn't followed her, but he'd been pretty settled in his chair on the stage, observing the pageant committee's discussion. The members had been deep in conversation as she and the other contestants exited. Bella had made to leave with the group, then peeled off as the last of the women exited through the main door.

The memory of his gaze on her made her skin heat and her anger rise. Did he think she couldn't see him as the pageant committee grilled her? And what was his job here, exactly? She thought security guards just manned doors and entrances.

Memories swiped at her focus as she ran to the teachers' conference room. She'd been in several musicals during middle and high school, all performed in this very building, on the same stage where she was going to have to pretend to compete for Ms. Mustang Valley. Bella knew these corridors and rooms as well as the house she'd grown up in until their parents had died. Some buildings were imprinted on a heart as firmly as the memories that were created in them. She sighed. Even the not-so-great memories—the ones of Aunt Amelia, who had single-handedly raised Bella and her brothers after the accident—were here. Bella recalled Aunt Amelia at back-to-school nights, frazzled as she found getting to three different class sessions impossible. She'd taken it out on the triplets later, complaining about how her life could have been so much easier if Bella's parents had lived.

Bella hoped that tomorrow she'd be asked to report back to participate in the pageant. She knew it depended on the interview, the personal essays, answers to a total of five written questions that covered her views on charity, community and personal excellence, and her "contestant resume." The resume had to include current contributions to Mustang Valley, her service hours outside of work, and her place of employment. She'd cringed at the glamour portion of the submission package, which required a headshot as well as an "athletic pose." Bella used her tripod to take the photo of herself in yoga pants and workout bra. But it'd all be worth it if she made the cut. She'd learn more about the selection process and any "advice" doled out by the committee that might include starving oneself. She was looking for this kind of evidence against the pageant, but Bella needed more proof that this pageant in particular encouraged the women to be as thin as possible, or any other trigger that would have set off Gio's issues. Gio had mentioned Señora Rosenstein as being particularly snide in her comments about any plus-size contestants, forcing them to weigh in each day, sometimes twice per day. As the pageant's self-appointed volunteer choreographer, Selina had made nasty, derogatory comments to Gio and other contestants more than once, and Gio told her there were transcripts of the actual pageants where Selina cut contestants for such subjective transgressions as not being "dancer-like." Gio's claims weren't enough to write an investigative report with, however. Bella needed to establish a pattern of wrongdoing for as far back as it existed, if possible.

The records of the previous pageants were reportedly stored in a single, locked file cabinet in the corner of the teaching-staff room which doubled as a group dressing room. Gio had gone over all of it with her as she lay dying, her spent body nearing its end on the hospital bed.

Gio's last smile to her had belied her wasted state, and Gio's spirit buoyed her with each step closer to the staff room. Reaching the steel door, she peered through the small, high window, but it had been papered over from the inside. Probably a security move due to the ever-present threat of school shootings. It was a harsh reality Bella's generation had only begun to come to grips with. She sucked in air as quietly as she could, listening for anyone else in the area. It was impossible to tell if someone was in the room until she entered, and she had no idea how much time she had to find what she wanted.

Holding her breath, Bella opened the door and pasted a smile on her face. If anyone was here, she'd make up a stupid excuse and skedaddle.

No one was in the room and she scanned it with her reporter's-eye view. The worn furniture and wood-paneled walls had been replaced with contemporary ergonometric chairs, sofas and laptop desks. The walls were a pale shade of lime, the white trim of the huge picture windows creating a crisp, clean, calming effect. If she weren't a Mustang Valley native, she'd be stunned by the unparalleled view of the Mustang Valley Mountains.

Bella would have plenty of time to appreciate aesthetics later, while running through the pageant. Right now she needed the files Gio had told her about. The files held the transcripts of previous pageants, priceless evidence. Her chest felt heavy as she remembered Gio's insistence that the Ms. Mustang Valley pageant was the most tortuous, demeaning experience of all the pageants she regularly competed in. Sure, Ms. Mustang Valley held the highest prize—a full, four-year ride to the local college. But it came at such a high price. As part of her prep for going undercover, Bella had interviewed a couple dozen Ms. Mustang Valley pageant entrants from the past decade. She'd found their names in the archives of the local newspapers, as all contestants were announced before the final night.

While all described the competitive environment she'd expected, with the stakes so high, none gave her the specific details Gio had in those last months before she died. Bella needed the pageant's written history, and if she was lucky, she'd find out what Selina Barnes Colton and Hannah Rosenstein had really said to Gio.

Acutely aware that she could be interrupted at any second, Bella searched the room for the file cabinet. Nothing resembling Gio's description or her memory existed in the staff room. Tears of frustration and rage threatened and she blinked. She refused to have her attempt to find justice for Gio stymied this early into her efforts.

Calm down. Think.

Hands on hips, she took one more look around the

room, beginning and ending with the stage door. Her mind's eye saw the stage beyond the double doors, the dressing area to the left—

The dressing room! The space beyond the room divider where the cabinets had been placed. She recalled Gio's offhand comment about how crowded it was in there, with twenty-four women changing for swimsuit and evening-gown competitions.

She slowly opened the double doors to the stage, aware of each tiny creak and squeak. The voices of the pageant board floated through along with the unmistakable scent of the stage. Pinewood, varnish, decades of sweat and joy that had been expended through performance after performance, tryouts and auditions. To her left the sun's rays filtered through dust from the dressing room. Sweat beaded on her upper lip and trickled down her spine, even made her palms wet. Apparently air-conditioning wasn't in the school's weekend and evening budget.

As soon as she could close the doors without a sound, she made haste toward the side room. Before she reached the threshold, her gaze landed on her prize: the old, battered metal file cabinet sat in the far corner of the room, laden with props resting atop its rusty finish.

Yes.

She reached into her pocket for the key that she'd found in the box of treasures Gio had left for her. A favorite pair of earrings Bella had always admired, photographs going back to elementary school, the tickets from a summer concert series they'd scrimped and saved to afford. And a small, sealed envelope.

Gio's mother brought the box over to Bella's home two weeks after her daughter had passed. She expressed again how much Bella had meant to Gio and how much Bella's support helped her during the awful grieving process.

Bella wasn't surprised to find a small note in Gio's unmistakable neat print addressed to her. Her bestie liked to have closure and loved writing letters. The surprise had been the file cabinet key tucked inside the exquisite stationery.

Bella had expected that she'd have to do a lot of digging and research before getting enough evidence to take to the police in the hopes of obtaining a search warrant, to get official access into the files. Gio's claim that certain pageant officials had caused her eating and mental disorders needed to be substantiated.

The pageant files from years past would tell Bella not only who the judges had been, but bear witness to their thought processes and training methods. Methods that Gio thought still existed even today, with all the knowledge about eating disorders and mental illness.

Bella looked at her watch. She figured her time was running short, as the security guard was bound to get up and check the backstage area. Did she have enough time to finish her theft?

No time to worry about it.

The key was in her pocket and she wrestled it out, jiggled it into the lock. For one heart-stopping moment she feared the key might break before she was able to turn the lock as both were practically ancient, the metal spotted with rust.

Finally the lock turned and she grasped the handle, used her thumb to slide the drawer stop to the right.

The sound of fabric against fabric was her only warning before a strong hand clamped over her nose and mouth. She was pulled up against a person behind her. She fought to turn but her attacker was stronger and yanked her hair, hard.

"Don't move or I'll snap your neck." The low, taut voice vibrated with menace and sounded like a horror-film villain's. Spots started to float in front of her vision and she kicked backward with her heel, hoping that the blows against this maniac's shins and feet would make him loosen his hold on her.

He tugged harder on her hair and she cried out in pain but with her air supply cut and in such agony it came out as a whimper.

"You're not being very smart. You'll never win this pageant. If you want to live, you'll quit before you start."

Focus. Observe. She tried every tool she'd ever read about to capture a solid description for the police. And most of all, she fought for her consciousness. Victims who passed out didn't always fare well.

"Stop!" A loud, booming voice echoed through her rapidly fading awareness. Bella tried to hold on to that voice, its strength, its promise of safety.

But her world crashed into nothingness.

"STOP OR I'LL SHOOT." Holden had his weapon aimed on the man in black, whom he'd gone after when he saw him in the shadows. The creep held an unconscious, drooping Bella Colton with one arm, her head up next to his as protection from Holden's bullets. At least, Holden hoped she was unconscious and not dead.

"Never." The assailant turned and faced him. He wore a ski mask and sunglasses under the black ball cap. A mouthpiece revealed how he disguised his voice. "I will crush her throat if you don't back off."

Holden stood his ground, praying for extra time. For this suspect to make a mistake, to move enough so that he could get a clear shot without risking Bella's life.

Unless the killer had already claimed his next victim. He risked a quick look at her face and its pink tinge assured him her heart was at least still pumping.

Moving his gaze back on the enemy, he slowly lowered his weapon. The other man had no visible weapon. But the serial killer had poisoned or shot each of the other two victims, so his comment about crushing her throat didn't match. But it might be part of his thrill—using different MOs.

"You'll never get out of here alive. Turn yourself in now and you live." Holden had to be careful to not betray his real identity to this lowlife. The less the killer knew, the better. It wouldn't matter if he could apprehend him right here, right now, but Holden had been in this situation before. Bella's safety came first. He watched the man's hands for any sign of movement toward Bella's throat. Right now his arm held her neck up against him.

"You don't own me, you pathetic excuse for security." The killer's voice sounded like a space alien and that added an extra creepiness to his words. Holden itched to cuff him, to get him to confess to what he'd done.

"What do you have against this woman? Drop her."

"Everyone is not what they seem." He was backing toward the exit, dragging the still unresponsive Bella with him. "If you were doing your job, I wouldn't have been able to get to her. She's mine."

Not on Holden's life.

Holden took one step toward the assailant and allowed himself to fall forward, as if he'd tripped. The man jerked, saw the clear line Holden had to shoot him and let go of Bella, then ran out the exit. Holden took off after the man, but when he entered the large corridor he was gone. Holden pulled out his cell and called 9-1-1, identifying himself as pageant security to keep his cover. He requested police backup, informed them of Bella's unconscious state and asked for EMT support ASAP. He continued to run through the school in all directions the man could have gone but it was fruitless. And he had to turn back to protect Bella until the other LEA arrived on scene.

The man behind the stage, who'd rendered Bella Colton unconscious, had disappeared as if a stage trapdoor had opened and swallowed him whole.

Sirens sounded and he rounded back to the staff room, to check on Bella. As he neared, he saw EMTs rush in and decided to stay back until they'd treated her. If she regained consciousness here, he didn't want to be the first person she saw. Better to stay in the background of all that had happened. His cover was vital to keeping the pageant contestants safe, especially the single redhead with green eyes, Bella Colton.

He slipped into an empty classroom and called Bud Langston, the Arizona State pageant director, one of the few people who knew about Holden's undercover role besides Holden's handler at the FBI office in Phoenix. Bud had contacted Holden, who got permission from his supervisor to work the case that the FBI began investigating after the second pageant murder. Bud's son had been Holden's college roommate and Bud had jumped at the chance to have Holden work undercover during the Ms. Mustang Valley Pageant. Anything to keep the participants safe.

"Bud."

"Talk to me, Holden."

"It's a rough start to Ms. Mustang Valley, Bud." Holden recapped what had happened.

"Thank God that Bella Colton wasn't harmed—or was she, besides being knocked out?"

"I don't know for certain, but I'll find out and get back to you. She was out the entire time I was there, so there's slim to no chance she knows of my involvement."

"That's something, at least." Bud swore and Holden bit back a grin—Bud was a navy veteran and *salty* came to mind. "I wish you'd caught him."

"I do, too. But, Bud, we can't be certain this is the same man we're looking for. Beauty pageants attract all kinds, and are the perfect target for anyone who's off-balance and looking for a sick thrill." Criminals had all kinds of motives.

"I get that, and I'm glad you're on the case. What will it take to call in more federal agents?"

"That's above my pay grade, but to be honest, we're stretched thin at the moment. Plus, the risk of anyone figuring out we're here will prevent us from operating with the freedom we need to apprehend the suspect." Holden was fairly certain the criminal only saw him as a bumbling security guard, which was how he wanted it. It might make Holden the man's first target, if and when he came back. Holden would be ready for him.

"Thanks for what you did today, and please keep me informed." Bud's sincerity was tangible in his voice.

"Will do." When Holden disconnected, he put in a call to his FBI supervisor, who expressed the same disappointment that Holden hadn't apprehended the criminal, and added an additional task that Holden had already figured into his work in Mustang Valley. He'd call Spen-

cer later, after he got out of here. Spencer and he had
agreed to not communicate unless absolutely necessary
while Holden was on this case, undercover. And now
his buddy's sister was smack dab in the middle of the
case. She'd been hurt on his watch, not something he
relished telling Spencer.

He had to keep tabs on Bella Colton at all costs, without her figuring out he was FBI. Holden had trailed suspects and victims alike, all in the line of duty as an agent.

So why did the prospect of keeping her safe fill him
both with anticipation and dread?

Chapter Three

Bella squinted against the bright light the ER doctor shone to measure her pupils' responses. "I'm fine, really. I think he knocked me out with one of those pinches, you know, to my jugular." She felt silly, especially after she'd realized the ER doc was none other than Shawn Trembly, a boy she'd briefly dated in high school. They parted ways after school and ended up being friends. "It's great that you were able to fulfill your dream, Shawn. You know, to be a doctor."

"You mean a sleeper hold, a choke hold." Shawn nodded as he kept to business, evidently not as ready to dismiss Bella's attack and loss of consciousness as anything near normal. "That could be true, and the bruises at the base of your neck support it, but I want an MRI to confirm. You hit your head when he dropped you, and there isn't a lot of swelling at the contact spot. We need to rule out a concussion. And yes, I got to follow my dream. But I'm not a doctor, I'm a physician's assistant with a specialty in trauma."

"That's still great." Could he talk about anything other than how she'd been knocked out? Bella didn't want to dwell on her attack. She had a case to investigate.

"Let's keep the focus on your treatment, Bella. You've

been through a traumatic event." He tapped into a laptop, his expression grave. Shawn was classically handsome, with deep blue eyes and dark hair she remembered being curly, but was now in a tight crew cut. But she felt zero chemistry between them now. And for reasons unknown to her, the mental image of the security guard at MVHS popped into her brain. The man had been so intense. She stiffened. Could he have been the person who attacked her?

In truth, it could be anybody. It gave powerlessness a whole new dimension, and she'd thought she'd already been through it after watching her best friend die.

Anxiety rushed over her, and she knew one thing. She had to get the heck out of this hospital. Researching the guard was her first priority. Maybe he wasn't on the payroll for the protection of the contestants but to keep the pageant's legacy intact by guarding that file cabinet.

"I'm not nauseous, or dizzy, and I don't remember seeing stars."

"But you were unconscious. Give me the benefit of the doubt, Bella." Shawn wasn't going to budge and she let out a long sigh.

"Fine." Sometimes giving in was the quickest way to a vital goal. Bella had to get to the bottom of this pageant's history and apparently continued abhorrent ways, and she was running out of time. She had the length of the pageant to bring this investigation to fruition. And Bella had to get back to those files before they disappeared. Her gut sank at the thought. By getting caught trying to open them, she may have alerted the bad guys that they needed to destroy them, or at least hide them elsewhere. And who used paper files anymore these days, anyway?

She needed to get back to the school and into the staff room when the rehearsals weren't in session, and when no security was on premises. It was the school's break, but certainly the principal and senior staff had to come in to take care of administrative duties? She could pose as herself, doing an article on MVHS and how it had changed over the years. A profile on Shawn, from being her high school physics lab partner to becoming a trauma/ER physician's assistant, would be a great cover.

The sense of dread in her stomach lessened, but not when she thought of walking back into MVHS.

Bella wasn't a gambler, but she'd bet that the mysterious security guard was definitely a key to finding answers.

Two HOURS LATER and with assurances that she didn't have a concussion, Bella pushed through the hospital exit doors and ran smack into a tall, hard mass of man in a blue uniform.

"Spencer!"

Her brother was almost a foot taller than her and kept himself in top shape as a sergeant for MVPD. In uniform, he usually exuded authority, a no-nonsense countenance. Since he was her triplet and she knew him better than most anyone, save their brother Jarvis, Bella could tell Spencer had more on his mind than police business.

"What the heck, Bella?" His blue eyes sparked with concern and not a small dose of frustration. He looked at her, then pulled her to him in a big-brother-style hug. Which technically was correct as he'd been born two minutes ahead of her. "I about flipped when I found out you'd been brought in."

Bella soaked up the love, as her brothers were her closest friends and only immediate family. Despite the Colton name and the hundreds of distant relatives who shared it, Bella and her brothers had only ever been able to rely on one another, as had their parents before they died over twenty years ago.

"I'm fine." She pushed back and looked into Spencer's eyes. "Seriously. I had a scare, by some jerk who's probably involved with the Ms. Mustang Valley Pageant. He knocked me out with one of those Vulcan-grip maneuvers."

"Do you mean a choke hold?" His worry was evident. "What were you doing at the high school, Bella?"

"Where's Boris?" She sought to distract her brother as she looked around for his K-9 partner, a beautiful chocolate lab they all considered part of the family.

"With Katrina. They're working on some more in-depth maneuvers. And stop trying to avoid my question." Spencer might be in overprotective-big-brother mode, but it didn't stop the warmth in his eyes from blossoming at the mention of his love and local dog trainer, Katrina. They'd recently fallen in love and gotten engaged.

"Let's talk while you drive me home."

"You don't have another ride arranged?"

She shrugged as they headed for the police K-9 SUV parked in front of the entrance. "I was going to call for a ride with my app." Actually, she'd planned to walk back to the high school to retrieve her vehicle and maybe manage to sneak back inside. Nothing she'd willingly share with her cop brother.

"Why wouldn't you call me or Jarvis? We're your family, Bella."

"I know, but you're also both a bit controlling about what you think I should be doing with my life."

"It's no secret that something's afoot in Mustang Valley." He got behind the wheel and moved a laptop out of the passenger side. She slid onto the leather seat and realized how hot it was.

"Air, please."

"Sure thing." He flicked on the engine and put the SUV in Drive. "Where to? The high school?"

"Yes. I left my car there earlier."

"And why exactly were you there?" Spencer's attitude was all casual but she knew it was from years of experience interviewing victims and criminals. Her brother could be as patient as needed when he wanted information.

Bella sucked in a breath, held it and slowly released it. The technique was part of her daily meditation to keep her tendency toward anxiety at bay. If the day's events hadn't triggered her, she'd bet Spencer's reaction was about to.

"Don't get mad. The last thing I need right now, after such a, a traumatic experience," she silently thanked Shawn for the description, "is you coming down hard on me. I'm doing an undercover exposé of the local beauty-pageant circuit and I need to participate to get my story. But no one can know about this, Spencer. You can't tell anyone at work. Promise me."

"Of course I won't." She knew he would though, if he thought her safety or anyone else's depended on the information. "Why would you do this, Bella? Is it about Gio?"

Her throat tightened and she squeezed her eyes shut. This was going to be more difficult than she foresaw, the constant reminder that her best friend and confidante of twenty-five years, ever since first grade, was gone.

"Partly, yes. Mostly I want to dig deep and find out who's really in charge of these things, why they still have categories like evening gown and talent competition. I mean, it's the twenty-first century. What gives, you know?"

"Save the flip tone for your readers. I'm your brother and I'm telling you, this is a bad idea. You've heard about the other two pageants in other Arizona counties, right?" He took the slow way to the high school, through the back part of Mustang Valley that cut through pastures and gave the best views of the mountains in whose shadows they'd grown up.

"I have heard. But the murders are unrelated. One was poison and the other a gunshot. Probably disgruntled boyfriends or overzealous competitors."

"They haven't found the killer in either instance. You need to be very, very careful, Bella."

"There's a security guard employed by the pageant. He'll keep it safe. According to the EMTs who took care of me, he's the one who called it in."

She wondered if he'd found her on the floor, unconscious, or if he'd gone after her attacker—or both. As fit and strong as the mysterious guard appeared, bottom line was that he was a civilian, nothing more. He hadn't prevented her attack.

"There is, and he's got a superb résumé from what Chief tells me, but it's not good enough for me at this point. Since you won't carry your own protection, Bella, you need to consider dropping out of the competition. Can't you get the information you need by interviewing the contestants?"

"No. Not the same. Look, I don't tell you how to police. I appreciate your input, but don't tell me how to do investigative reporting. I promise I'll let you know the minute anything fishy turns up. But I have to be able to do my job, Spencer."

"I hear you're in financial trouble."

"What? From the interview the board did?" Anger spun in her stomach like a heavy rug in her dryer. "Is nothing confidential in this tiny town?"

Spencer laughed and she wondered what amused her brother. Of course, he'd been a lot happier lately, and smiled more than she'd ever remembered. "Not a whole lot, I'll give you that." He pulled into the high school parking lot and up to her car. "Just do me a favor and be extra careful."

"I will. I promise." She said goodbye and got into her vehicle. There was no chance of Spencer departing before she pulled out, and he'd no doubt follow her for a bit to make sure she not only drove capably but got home safe and sound.

Sometimes having a big brother put a big, wet damper on her investigative reporting.

HOLDEN CAREFULLY FOLLOWED the K-9 SUV through Mustang Valley back roads, promising himself he'd take a bike ride out here when the case wrapped up. Not if, but when, because he had to catch the Pageant Killer before anyone else got hurt.

He'd pulled up Bella's bio, then her blog, then had his colleague back at the Phoenix field office do a background search on Bella. She was smart about her security protocol, but his agency had ways of ferreting information. Holden already knew that Spencer was a highly decorated police officer, but he hadn't heard that Spencer had recntly saved his fiancée from certain death with the help of his K-9, a chocolate lab named Boris. Boris, along with the other MVPD K-9s, had his own Facebook fan page. As an FBI agent Holden stayed off social media, but he knew it was an important way that the local LEA could communicate with their community.

Holden suspected that Spencer had no idea that his sister had entered the pageant. Finding her in the staff room after she'd made it look like she'd left the building raised all kinds of red flags.

As the car dipped around a bend, he realized they were heading back to the school. As he'd predicted, Spencer was taking Bella to get her vehicle. Was he really going to allow his sister to drive after such a traumatic event?

Not that it was his problem. Keeping Bella safe from the killer was all he was tasked to do. Besides finding and arresting the murderer.

Holden continued to follow Spencer but couldn't help the flashback images that he associated with the words *traumatic event*. He'd worked a case in which a serial killer that the agency had tracked for nearly a year had taken him hostage. In what he'd expected to be his first successful apprehension, he'd miscalculated and the killer had trapped him in an abandoned silver mine in southeastern Arizona, not far from Mustang Valley. He'd still caught the killer, but it had taken its toll. The experience had been harrowing and life changing. Instead of deterring his desire to do investigative work, fortified it.

Spencer signaled a left turn into the school drive and Holden quickly turned right, down a side street where he wouldn't be detected by either Colton. He'd taken the time to change out of his security-guard uniform and into plain street clothes—cargo shorts, dark T-shirt, running shoes and ball cap—as soon as Bella had been taken away by the EMTs. He hated not being completely open with Spencer about this, but he had to figure out what Bella Colton was about.

He'd also had to accept that the attacker had gotten away. For now. If indeed Bella's attacker *was* the killer.

Holden knew that since he traded his security uniform for street clothes right after he left MVHS, he wouldn't be readily recognizable by most people he'd worked with earlier today. He didn't want to have to explain why the pageant security guard was hanging out around the school after hours.

He parked his car on a quiet street and got out, hoping to appear as much a part of the scenery as possible. Lucky for him there was a walking path that ran past the subdivision, the school and out to the desert beyond. Mustang Valley gave every appearance of being a beautiful place to live, to settle, to raise a family.

Except for the possible serial killer who stalked the pageant.

Holden walked until he was close enough to make out Spencer's SUV cruiser, which was parked next to the most beat-up, ugly station wagon he'd ever seen.

Bella Colton must not have been telling a total lie when she'd informed the pageant committee about her dire financial situation. No one with a decent paycheck would drive such a jalopy. He wondered how it passed inspection, then remembered her brother was a cop. His handler in Phoenix had filled him in on Bella sporadically over the last couple of hours. The psychological profile he was steadily building of her didn't fit a person who'd cheat on her auto inspection, though.

Bella had a decent blogging career in hand, but much of her freelance work reflected the expertise of someone with a lot more talent than just writing for the local, small-town blog. Holden's colleague was female and apparently Bella's articles were receiving a lot of play on social media and had even found their way into print here and there.

From all indications, Isabella Colton was a woman on the verge of a career breakout. Holden knew the feeling. If he nailed this case, he'd be that much closer to his next rank. Not only would it be a pay raise, but he'd be achieving the goal he'd set out for right after graduating from the academy in Quantico, Virginia. Holden wanted to be career FBI.

The white stripes on Bella's top reflected the lowering sun, and turned her hair a golden shade of copper that reminded him of the pots and pans his grandmother polished and hung over her wide farm stove in Kansas. Grandma St. Clair had served as a WASP—a Woman Airforce Service Pilot—in World War II and she was his most ardent supporter when he'd been selected for Army ROTC at Kansas State. Grandma had sent him letters the entire time in the army, and had attended his promotion to captain two years before he resigned his commission to become an FBI agent. Sadly she'd passed before he'd left Quantico but she'd known the path he'd chosen. Like Grandma St. Clair, Holden wanted to make a difference in the world. Protect it at all costs from the most evil acts.

Bella walked the short distance to her car, and gave her brother a quick wave before getting behind the wheel.

Please don't follow her home.

If Spencer trailed Bella, Holden would be unable to tag along at all this evening. He couldn't risk Spencer spotting him, as his army best friend would recognize him immediately. Bella shouldn't see him either, to be on the safe side. He had no reason to think Bella had the military background Spencer did but in truth had no idea if Bella had ever served or engaged in any kind of LEA training. The background information he had wasn't complete.

You could confront them both, let Bella know who you really are.

He wasn't ready to. Not yet. His gut was telling him to lay low. Besides, Spencer was going to be angry when he found out that Bella had been attacked on Holden's watch. Holden deserved the rancor but wasn't going to let it be a distraction. Not until he figured out what Bella Colton was up to. She wasn't just a regular pageant contestant. She'd better hope the committee didn't read too many of her articles or they'd question her motives for competing, too.

Holden turned and walked the short distance back to his car. As he did, he heard a siren. By the time he was in his car and at the corner of the side street, he saw Spencer's unit fly around onto the main street and head away from the school, siren flashing. Counting to five, Holden pulled out and slowly drove by the school. He expected to see Bella's car heading out of the parking lot but instead saw the back end of her vehicle as she drove toward the school, then turned left onto the inside perimeter road.

Bella Colton chose to come back onto school property after surviving a close call with a possible serial killer.

Not that she knew about the serial killer, but she'd been attacked. Why would she do that?

Holden knew only one way to find out.

Chapter Four

Bella's head pounded and she grabbed her water bottle from the worn adjustable holder she'd found at the dollar store.

"Yuck," she spoke to herself at how warm the liquid was, but at least it was some kind of hydration. Thank goodness the hospital had told her she didn't have a concussion, or she wouldn't be able to return so soon. If she was accepted into the pageant, she'd get an email or phone call tonight and have to report again tomorrow morning for the indoctrination process. It'd be too late to search the file cabinet by then, with so many people around.

As she drove past the main building and then around to the backstage parking lot entrance, she let out a huge breath of relief. Yes! The first responders had all left, so she didn't have to either lie or sneak her way back in. The stage entrance loading dock stood out, the massive concrete block reminding her of the piers she'd once seen when she and her brothers went to the Pacific Ocean with their aunt. Aunt Amelia hadn't been a very loving or demonstrative woman, and in fact had made it clear that she'd been saddled with raising Bella and the boys at the most inconvenient time of her life. Bella had wanted to tell her aunt, even when she was only ten, that there probably wasn't ever a good time to have your sibling up and die and leave you with triplets, but she'd thought better of it. Aunt Amelia had a short fuse and Bella never liked to be on the receiving end of her verbal lashes. And at least Aunt Amelia did love travel and they made yearly pilgrimages to places she had visited as a young woman, fresh out of college.

Since the school's rear lot was completely empty, she turned her car around and backed in, butt against the loading dock, to facilitate a quick exit if necessary.

Please let me get in and out of here okay.

She was prepared this time, as she shoved her cell phone in a back pocket with one hand and held her pepper spray in the other. No one would sneak up on her again if she had anything to do with it.

The pavement under her wedge heels had cooled and a soft breeze came in from the mountains, a gift. When she looked north she saw why—a cloud bank held tight over the range, promising rain in the next day or so.

She smiled and despite the attack, made a conscious decision to stay positive. This was all about exposing a vast, far-reaching, decades-deep pageant practice that had left too many young women with very adult mental and physical illnesses, from body dysmorphia to eating disorders. A sliver of doubt niggled at her premise and she tried to brush it away. In her research she'd discovered that it was widely believed that eating disorders, like addictions, occurred in people predisposed to such diseases. That might mean that Bella wouldn't be able to definitively blame a particular pageant board member or group. Gio's mother had admitted their family members suffered from mental illness for as long as she could remember. But the pageant board had planted the seeds for Gio's disorder to sink its claws in deep, hadn't they? Would she be able to definitively state that the pageant triggered Gio's genetic tendencies? She decided to not worry about it in this moment, and focus on getting back inside the building. More information could clarify Gio's nightmare.

Bella hadn't thought about the prospect of climbing atop the loading dock. The back garage-type door was her only way in, from what her reporter's group informed her. Her editor-in-chief and supervising editor knew what she was up to, as did her closest reporter friend, Fred Jameson. Fred had never let her down, was always there for her and didn't hesitate to speak up if Bella was crossing a boundary. Like the time she'd tried to stake out the local drugstore to catch underage teens purchasing vaping paraphernalia. She'd nearly been arrested as the shop owner wasn't impressed with her credentials and positive motives. Fred had given her the passcode for the loading dock's security pad, procured from "a friend of a friend." Bella suspected Fred had paid someone off for the information but didn't ask for details.

She silently thanked the years of video workouts she'd done as she climbed atop her car and then leaped up to the loading dock, no small feat in capris and sandals. Euphoria began to sing in her veins until she eyed the keypad lock next to the sliding door. Her colleagues had failed to mention this. It must be a new addition.

Still, she was this far. Bella decided to go for it and pressed the main button, hoping that maybe she'd luck out and the door would rise at once. All she got was a "please enter the passcode now" message, given in a disembodied female voice.

"Drat. Drat. Drat." She muttered as she looked over her notes and emails from her trusted reporter circle. There, in bold letters, was the password that Fred had insisted she write down.

MUSTANG#1

Without hesitation she punched in the code. Hitting Enter, she held her breath. Until the grinding gears engaged and the door rolled up.

Bella hunched to get inside as quickly as possible, and once past the entrance hit the close button, ensuring no one would see the open door and call the police. That's all she needed, to be caught breaking into the very school she'd been attacked in mere hours earlier.

Darkness immediately surrounded her so she pulled out her Mag-Lite and made her way through to the staff room, behind the stage. There hadn't been any cars in the front lot where Spencer dropped her, and none back here, so she was comfortable in the thought of being alone. For now.

She still had to be careful. Not that being a journalist didn't involve a modicum of wariness each day, but this time it felt different. Not only because she was attacked. She was getting herself more embedded than she ever had before, and the stakes were higher, now that she knew Spencer suspected the two pageant murders were related. His belief had been written all over his face.

No one would blame her if she decided to quit.

Never. This was for Gio's sake.

Light still came through the staff-room windows and allowed her to see what she'd tried to breach before—the antiquated file cabinet. Except something was off. She squinted, tried to deny what she saw. Each and every drawer was open. Rushing to the cabinet, she couldn't keep her groan from morphing into a cry as she saw all of the drawers had been emptied. If anything had ever been in there at all. Grasping the corners of the rusty metal cabinet, she bowed her head and for the first time since Gio's funeral allowed herself to weep.

After a good cry, she'd be ready to make an even better plan. No one or nothing was going to keep her from justice for Gio.

HOLDEN GAVE BELLA Colton credit. The woman was as intrepid as any agent he'd ever met. As much as he wanted to discredit her motives due to her job description, he couldn't. She wanted something in the school, most likely the staff room, and wasn't going to let a mere attack get in her way.

He waited to see her disappear through the cargo entrance before he used his fob to enter the building. It'd show up on the security system as him, as the guard, and he'd explain it as having seen the cargo door being opened after hours. If Bella had a key code she might have some kind of legit reason for entering. But if she were entering the school again for a valid reason, why wouldn't she use the front entrance? His internal radar wasn't happy with what he'd witnessed. It was time for Bella Colton to answer some questions.

It took him a few minutes to get to the stage, as he had to move quietly. He drew his weapon as a precaution against the attacker returning, not to protect himself from Bella. She was an aggressive reporter but had no criminal record. Once again he thanked his lucky stars for his investigative team at the Bureau and the training he'd received. This case was growing more complicated by the second, as if the evil surrounding it was molten lava seeping into every crack and crevice of Mustang Valley.

An odd sound made him halt backstage, behind the curtain that allowed for undetected passage from stage left to stage right. The sound was from the staff room, he was certain. But he had to get closer, to make sure it was only Bella in there. As he crept along the cinder-block wall, the black curtain to his left, he heard his breathing, his heartbeat. But no more sound from off-stage. Had Bella already left?

He cleared the curtain and saw the light pour out of the staff room a.k.a. stage dressing area. A few more steps and he'd put Bella's journalistic snooping to a quick end.

But when he looked into the room, cleared left and right, it was empty. He stepped inside the open door and saw that the LEAs had done their job—swept for finger-prints, opened all drawers and file systems to rule out explosives, left everything as they'd had to.

The attacker had held an unconscious Bella near the old file cabinet, before he'd dragged her to the side exit and made his escape. Holden holstered his weapon and walked to the cabinet, the dusty behemoth's four deep drawers wide open.

"Stay right where you are or I'll spray!"

Female voice, to his rear, dead center. Voice—Bella Colton.

Crap.

Holding up his arms, he spoke. "You're safe. I'm the security guard."

"Don't turn around or reach for your gun. I will take

you down. You're not in uniform." She paused and he wondered if she was calling the police.

"This is Bella Colton. I want to speak to my bro—"

"Heck no!" He turned and faced her, ready to explain why he was here and find out why the hell she was. "You're okay, I'm—"

Wet liquid heat hit his face, his eyes, his nostrils and then his mouth. And oh, by the love of heaven, it burned. As if microscopic shards of glass were cutting his face wide open.

Bella Colton had just pepper sprayed him. He, an FBI agent, had been bested by a reporter.

Again.

Chapter Five

Bella watched the security guard, in plain clothes, wince against the sting, while his hand reached into his back pocket. She kept her grip on the spray canister, ready to hit again.

"Hands in front." But he didn't pull out another weapon, and his pistol remained holstered. He held out what she thought was his wallet, until it flipped open, displaying a badge and credentials.

"Holden St. Clair, FBI." His voice was remarkably steady for someone who'd just been hit with burning pepper-oil solution.

"Really." She leaned forward and grabbed the ID holder from him. It looked real enough. "I'm going to verify this through my brother." She called Spencer's cell.

"Go ahead. Tell him you're with me."

"Bella, you there?" Spencer's voice broadcast over her phone's speakers, from the side table where she'd thrown it when she decided to use the pepper spray. No longer seeing Holden as a threat, she grabbed her phone and turned the speaker off.

Spencer sounded stressed. A twinge of guilt made her feel like the bossy sister he teased her about being.

"Do you know an FBI agent named Holden St. Clair?"

"Maybe. Why are you asking?" Spencer's voice was guarded.

"I just pepper sprayed him."

"For crying out loud, Bella, he's on our side." Still, Spencer didn't say how he knew Holden, if he did. Or why.

"What do you mean by that?"

"Put him on the line, Bella."

Grudgingly she handed her phone to Holden. "He wants to talk to you."

Holden took her phone and she absently noted she'd have to clean it, so that she didn't get any pepper oil on her.

"Holden here." He looked at her but it was short-lived as he squinted his eyes closed again, tears pouring from them.

"Yes, I'm with her. She's safe. Uh-huh. Yes, it's true. She did. I'm buying next time. I'll let you know." Holden's one-sided conversation with her brother was impossible to follow, but she thought she heard the roar of Spencer's deep belly laugh when Holden said *Yes, it's true*. Apparently she'd brought down a Goliath with the pepper spray.

"Trust me, Spencer. Thank you." He handed the phone back to her. She gingerly held it to her ear, careful not to touch it directly on her skin until she cleaned it. Holden's hands were probably full of pepper oil.

"Yeah?"

"Listen, Bella." Spencer's voice was lighter, but still serious. "For once in your life you have to follow everything someone else tells you. Holden is the real deal—we served together."

"Wait—he's *that* friend Holden?" Shock pulsed through her. Spencer had mentioned a Holden, the man who'd saved them both from certain death during one training mission gone wrong. Spencer always spoke with awe when he talked about Holden. "As in your bestie, your army buddy?"

"Yeah."

She'd just pepper sprayed her brother's best friend, and a war hero.

Way to begin your investigative journalism career.

"Did you know he was working the pageant? Why didn't you tell me?" Bella knew her face was red. At least Holden's eyes were too sore to notice.

"Why didn't you tell me or Jarvis you were getting involved in the pageant, much less entering it? You don't tell me a whole heck of a lot about what you're working on, Bella. You let us think that you're doing home-decorating stories." Her brother's frustration was tangible over the phone's connection.

"Give me some credit, Spencer. I do more than life-style pieces." Although his comment left a stinging barb. She was doing this article precisely to get away from her current kind of story. But it was secondary to finding clarity on, and maybe even the original triggers for, Gio's eating disorders and mental illness.

His sigh would have bounced off the walls of the arroyo they played near as kids. "Just listen to whatever Holden says, Bella."

"Will do. I've got to help him out with the pepper spray cleanup, then I'll turn in for an early evening to binge-watch my favorite shows. All safe and sound."

"Bella..."

Holden had moved to the staff refrigerator, and she

saw his large, strong hand grab a quart of iced tea instead of what she assumed he wanted, the quart of milk next to it. "I've got to go now, Spencer. Thanks for verifying Holden's identity and you have a good evening."

Bella disconnected and looked around the staff room. No sign of her previous attacker, or anyone else. They were alone, she and Holden. His low groan drew her back to him. The man was in a lot of pain but she supposed he was swallowing most of it, keeping up some stoic front he'd learned in the military and perfected in the FBI.

"Wait, let me help you." She took the quart of tea from him and handed him a bunch of napkins from the pile on the counter. "You grabbed the iced tea. I think you want milk, am I right? Come here, I'll fix you right up."

"Sure you will. Just like you sprayed me?" His words came between pants, indicating the depth of his discomfort. Regret tugged at her but she brushed it aside. Nothing she could do to change the past, but she could help Holden now.

She set the milk on the counter and grasped his forearms and ignored the warmth that emanated from his skin. It had nothing to do with physical attraction or any notion of romantic chemistry. The heat was his reaction to being attacked by a nasty chemical, right in the face.

"Here, kneel down with your back against the counter, and lay your head back on the edge of the sink. I'm going to pour the milk directly on your eyes. You're going to have to open them."

"And I should trust you because…" He lowered to the floor, his discomfort obvious but he was for the most part quiet. As much as one can be when tears and mucus were running like an Arizona spring rainstorm. As soon as his head tilted back, she opened the milk.

"Okay, here's the first dose." She poured the white liquid over his forehead, eyes, nose, mouth, then dabbed at his face with more napkins. She had no desire to get the oil on her hands. "Now, open your eyes as soon as you feel the milk again. We have to get it on your eyeballs."

"Got it. Hit me." His grim expression as he braced himself for the next round was almost comical. She bit her lip.

"This will make it feel better, promise." She poured directly on the bridge of his nose, and when he lifted his lids she splashed milk into each eye, and he made sure he blinked several times instead of screwing his eyes shut again. "You've done this before, Agent St. Clair."

"There are a lot of things I've done before, Bella Colton."

"I'm TALKING ABOUT the milk, and pepper spray." Her hands shook and he didn't think it was from the weight of the carton. She was the wrong woman during the wrong investigation, or he'd enjoy the thrill of knowing he'd gotten under her skin.

Thank goodness she'd insisted on helping him with the milk. His eyes still hurt but at least it didn't feel like fire ants were crawling over them and up his nose any longer.

"To answer your question, I've had training in countermeasures for everything from pepper spray to chemical warfare. Where did you learn the milk antidote?"

"My brother, of course. Lean back again." She waited until he was in position and then poured more of the cold elixir on his eyes, his skin. "I made him tell me about everything he learned at the police academy, and he still fills me in about his more interesting cases, as much as he's able. He doesn't reveal any confidential material, of course. He had to take tear gas and pepper spray at the police academy. Do you do the same at the FBI Academy?"

"Yes, in Quantico. Virginia. But your brother and I went through a lot of combat training together in the military, and in particular we did the tear-gas training at the same time." He remembered meeting Spencer and admiring how cool he stayed under high-pressure situations. They'd both gone on to reach US Army captain, before leaving for their respective careers in law enforcement.

"I know where Quantico is. I visited an old boyfriend there once, to see him finish Officer Basic. He was a marine."

"Uh, I know who else trains at Quantico." He couldn't help the tiny dig. "What happened to him?" He hadn't missed her *old*-boyfriend reference.

"He deployed overseas for nearly two years. I waited, but by the time he came back we were kaput. Too young to survive that many miles for so long. Plus, I happen to have two very overprotective brothers. No man has gotten past their scrutiny yet."

Holden shook his head, wiped his face with the paper towels she handed him, letting the last of the milk drip off him and into the sink. He lifted his head, stood up and took ahold of the milk. "Thank you." He looked at her with a clear gaze for the first time. And saw her brilliant green eyes wide and…aware. Of his every move. Heat roiled in his gut.

Can it. She's Spencer's sister.

"No problem." She threw the empty milk container out, cleaned up the sink. He moved to help but she waved him away. "Are you going to tell me why you're on assignment here, during the Ms. Mustang Valley Pageant?"

His eyes were calming down and he couldn't stop his gaze from resting on her. And imagining the direction this conversation would go if they hadn't met in the middle of a probable serial-killer case, if she wasn't related to the one man he trusted with his life. He couldn't give any woman more than today, not after how his ex, Nicole, had burned him. Long-term love wasn't in his cards.

And Bella Colton was the kind of woman you didn't mess around with to ease an itch. Bella struck him as a forever woman—either you gave her everything, or didn't start anything.

Holden knew where that left him.

HOLDEN'S SILENCE UNNERVED Bella as she threw the last of the wet paper towels away, the scent of milk still clinging to the staff-room air. But how could she blame him? He'd survived a pepper-spray attack only minutes before yet he was already in control of himself, and clearly demanded control of their discussion. Bella wanted to be annoyed, angry, furious at this stranger who, in some ways, knew her brother better than she did. Yet Holden exuded a sense of realness, a grounded energy she hadn't experienced with another man. As if he was a man she could truly trust.

Whoa, girl, back it up.

Bella trusted no man besides her brothers. She didn't know Holden from a hole in an Arizona butte. Just because being alone with an attractive man wasn't something she'd done in a long while didn't mean she could let her physical needs dictate her reaction to him.

"Don't make me ask again, Holden. Please."

"Tell me why you entered the contest first." He volleyed the query with complete equanimity. Oh, yeah, Holden St. Clair was a man with his stuff in one sock.

She blinked, ignored the shiver of awareness that was getting too familiar around him. "Why do you think? You heard my interview. I need the scholarship prize."

"So you said. To go to nursing school. And as much as you just handled my injuries with ease, need I remind you that you inflicted them? I'd think someone who wanted to go into any kind of medicine wouldn't want to hurt a fly."

"You were stalking me."

"I was protecting you from your attacker."

"Give me a break, Holden. If that's true, you must have seen me earlier with Spencer. You knew he'd keep me safe. Yet you followed me in here. That's pretty creepy, if you ask me." Her hands began to shake and she didn't have to question why. The mere mention of the attack must be triggering an unconscious memory.

"I was going to call Spencer and tell him that I was concerned about your personal safety. Today, in fact. But I, ah, was waylaid by a person very competent with pepper spray."

"Wait a minute—my attacker, did you see him again? Around here?" Fear continued to rise in her gut and she tried to squelch it but couldn't stop the tremor that rolled through her skeleton.

Holden's hand was on her shoulder, warm, protective. And she didn't bristle, but accepted it with a smile that she knew must look wan at best. Exhaustion poured over her and she sank onto the nearest seat, a sofa cushion.

"No, and if I did, I would have already had you out of here. I'm sorry I didn't catch him earlier." A tendon on the side of his jaw clenched and she knew he was annoyed. At her, at losing track of the attacker, probably both.

"I thought it might be you." Except she'd heard his voice telling the attacker to stop. His voice had steadied her, even in the grips of a probable killer.

He chuckled. "I don't blame you. No, it wasn't me. You can verify with your brother or any other MVPD officer. I called in the incident as soon as your attacker took off."

"After you made him let go of me."

"I can't take credit for that. It was the circumstances."

"Of you forcing him to flee. My brother told me when he brought me back to my car. All of MVPD is in awe of how you handled the situation. You stayed cool and forced the attacker's hand."

She regarded him, liked how he didn't so much as twitch under her scrutiny. "You followed us from the hospital, didn't you? I knew I saw you there." She saw him again in her mind's eye, how he'd leaned up against the nurses' station and kept his face averted as she'd walked out of the hospital. But she hadn't trusted her memory, not so soon after being knocked out.

Holden nodded. "I did."

"How did he knock me out?"

"You don't remember?"

She shook her head. "One minute I was at the file cabinet and the next I heard this awful voice, then all went black."

"He had a voice box on, over a facemask and hoodie. I saw it."

"Terrifying." But it didn't answer how he knocked her out.

"He used a sleeper hold on you. I saw it as I came into the room. You were already out—there was nothing I could do to protect you from being knocked unconscious."

"You kept me from a lot worse."

"Maybe."

He was being modest but she wasn't going to call him on it. Not yet, not until she figured out why he was here, now. The FBI was interested in the pageant, confirming her suspicions that there was more going on here than a scholarship contest.

"I'm a reporter. I'm not hiding my motives for being here from you. Unlike you." She knew she really needed to back off the accusatory attitude but it was hard. Federal agents had a reputation of not looking fondly upon the media.

"True on all accounts. Answer my question, Bella. Why are you here?"

She ran over all the reasons to not tell him but they didn't make sense. Not when she was looking up at him, the red, blotchy skin of his face a reminder that he'd calmly taken an all-out attack from her, yet remained cool and calm. The ultimate professional. No wonder having him as a security guard had seemed like overkill. He looked and acted like he was tops in his field at the Bureau. Whatever Holden was, he appeared to be a man who got what he wanted.

"I'm doing an undercover report on pageant practices, specifically Ms. Mustang Valley. Not just this year's, but the last ten pageants or so." The time span that Gio had participated. Before eating disorders and resultant poor health had taken her, too soon.

"What kind of 'practices'?"

"I want to find out if they ever made, or still do make, the contestants diet or be a certain size or weight. If they encourage any kind of unhealthy behavior that had a long-term effect on the contestants."

"You look down in the dumps about it. I can't say that I'd find that surprising. Would you?" His astuteness rattled her. How did a stranger see right through her?

"I, I'm doing it because I lost a friend who spent half of her life competing in pageants, including this one. She never won, but never gave up. And it killed her."

"What killed her? Exactly?" His voice, low and deadly, unexpectedly buoyed her. Holden was a man who sought justice every day, who probably understood her motives better than she did.

"It wasn't foul play, if that's what you're asking. Not with a visible weapon, anyhow. To be fair, I don't know what really took her. In the end it was classified as malnutrition due to an eating disorder. No matter what the death certificate said, she's gone forever and while I blame the pageant industry as a whole, I'm especially furious at Ms. Mustang Valley. I can't rest until I know the persons who tortured her the most, who bullied her to turn herself into someone she wasn't by alternatively bingeing and starving herself. I suspect the pageant board and maybe some of the judges are to blame."

"Do you have any idea exactly who? Names?" Holden's interest buoyed her. Maybe she would get her answers more quickly with his help.

"Gio mentioned both Selina Barnes Colton, and Hannah Rosenstein. And I want to state, for the record, that I'm no relation to Selina, not by blood, anyway. And that branch of the Coltons hasn't had anything to do with me or my brothers in decades." Vulnerability flared but relief that someone else believed her suspicions, didn't think she was stringing together random events, outweighed any sense of risk.

Holden watched her for a long moment, then walked to the sofa and pointed at the spot next to her. "May I?"

"Of course." She shifted to the side a bit, but there wasn't a lot of room on the two-cushion sofa. As she realized that she didn't mind being so close to the man she'd been wary of all day, the man she'd attacked, the silliness of the situation hit her. Laughter bubbled up and she let it out.

Holden looked at her and a wide grin split his face, swollen, red-rimmed eyes and all. His pepper-spray injuries didn't keep her from seeing the spark in his dark irises, though.

"I'm so sorry I pepper sprayed you. I'm not known for being the most gentle of persons around these parts, but I don't usually attack complete strangers."

"I'm not a stranger. I'm a federal law enforcement agent who needs answers. It sounds like you do, too. We can accomplish a lot more together than we can separately."

Anxiety rumbled in her gut. She was a reporter first, not some kind of wannabe cop. "I'm working on an article, a report. Wouldn't it be a conflict of interest for us to work side by side?"

"Only if you plan on breaking the law, or to keep anything from me that legally I need to pursue my case.

I'm ignoring how you got back into the school tonight, of course."

She considered it, considered him, blew her bangs out of her face. "Fine. But I don't want you restricting my participation in the pageant at all. I need to be able to function as a regular contestant, to get into all the events." She groaned as she thought of evening-gown competition.

"To be clear, you're trying to pin your friend's death on a particular person on the pageant board? And right now you've got Selina and Hannah as suspects?"

"Yes. No. I don't know." She hated this part, the fact that she really didn't even know what she was searching for. It stirred up her worst fears—that she'd never find out why Gio had to die. "What I'm trying to do is expose this pageant's culture for what it is. Find out what triggered a beautiful young woman to turn to a life of self-mutilation and experience severe body dysmorphia at such a young, malleable age."

"You aren't going to find any one person to blame, Bella. You don't really believe that you will, do you?"

Holden's gaze cut through her and she shivered, then was awash in heat. Yeah, there was chemistry here. The kind that could and would not only derail her undercover investigation, but get her heart into deep waters. But something more played out between them. Holden was taking her seriously, not mocking her for entering the pageant.

He seemed to respect her, even though he gave off waves of disdain whenever she said the words *reporter* or *story*.

"I don't know what I believe right now. I won't until I

read the pageant archives. Which I may never find now."
She cast a glance at the empty file cabinet.

"Fair enough. But I'd hate to see you risking your
safety to find there's no answer that will satisfy your
need for closure. Trust me on this, Bella. Sometimes we
don't get all of the answers." The loneliness in his tone
wrapped around her. She wondered if he was talking
about the service but didn't want to go there, not with
someone she'd just met.

"Where do you live, Holden? When you're not out
investigating beauty pageants?"

He blinked, caught off guard by her change of subject. She liked that she did that to him, made him think
on his feet. Or on the sofa. Most men didn't reveal that
she'd made them do a mental double take.

"Right now I'm staying at the Dales Inn, much to the
consternation of my boss." He grinned and it was as if he
really did consider her a trusted colleague, adding oxygen to the warm glow in her belly. "We don't usually get
put up at luxury hotels on our government budget. But
there wasn't any other place to stay, not close enough to
do my job well. When I'm not on the road for a case, I
live in Phoenix. I work out of the field office there, and
fly back to DC as needed to give reports."

"Are you an agent or a profiler?"

"Agent. Profilers don't generally work in the field,
not on an active case, unless it's exceptional and has
involved a larger number of victims. Why do you ask?"

"I already know why you're here, Holden. There were
two deaths in two previous Arizona pageants this year.
They're under the same promotions-company umbrella.
You must think they're related, and that Ms. Mustang

Valley is next on the list. Am I right? Don't worry, I'm not putting any of this in my exposé."

He stared at her for a second before looking away, out the window at the setting sun. "Partially. But I'm not privy to talk about all of it."

"What, you want me to work with you but you're not going to fill me in on what you find? That's not a good deal for me. Spencer told me more in a three-minute car ride than you have over the last half hour." She stood up.

"Bella, wait." He grasped her hand and she looked down at the sight of their hands together. It should feel wrong, or out of place, considering their stations in life and here, now, in the pageant. Yet it felt right.

Bella tugged her hand free. Falling for an FBI agent was not the path to getting what she needed for her exposé. No matter how much her brother trusted him.

Chapter Six

"I'm sorry." Holden wasn't fond of apologizing and the fact that he was doing so to someone who'd been no more than a stranger only hours earlier should concern him. But a serial killer was on the loose. He knew Bella's brother, a man he would trust with his life during lethal missions. All of that, combined with having witnessed what Bella had suffered through so far today made polite social conventions superfluous. There wasn't time to "get to know" her. Holden was committed to keeping her alive.

She turned, her narrowed eyes flashing jade fire. "Sorry for what?"

He sucked in a quick breath. "For sounding like a jerk. Large parts of the investigation, of my job, are classified. I know you understand this, since Spencer is your brother. He can't tell you all of his police business."

She nodded. "I do understand. And you must understand that since I'm back here, today, willing to risk running into the suspect who knocked me out earlier, I mean business, too. I'm willing to do whatever it takes to split this pageant wide open."

"It's at the risk of your life, if we're dealing with the same killer."

Her eyes shimmered and he caught a wave of grief as it pulsed off her. "I don't expect this story to come without a price."

"Nothing worthwhile ever does. But is it worth it for a story?" His phone buzzed and he checked the text. His supervisor. "I have to take this. Will you wait for me, let me take you to dinner? We can talk this over and come up with an actionable plan that will suit both of us." And keep her safe.

Bella's wariness couldn't be more evident in the way she eyed him as if he were her worst enemy. "Fine. But it's dessert, not dinner. At the local diner downtown. The one with the hitching post out front. Do you know it?"

He nodded, held up his index finger. "Right. Do not leave until I do." He took the call. "St. Clair."

"What's going on? I've got MVPD reports in front of me that an assailant attacked one of the pageant contestants?" His boss, in Phoenix, didn't sound pleased.

"Yes. I'm on it. With the victim now."

"Who is she? And you shouldn't be with her, Holden—she needs to be in protective custody until we catch this killer."

He turned his back to Bella, searching for a modicum of privacy. "Agreed. She's a reporter on undercover assignment, entered the pageant for her story on another topic entirely."

"That makes this even more dangerous, Holden."

"Or it'll bring it to a close sooner." He looked over his shoulder and saw that Bella was talking to someone on her phone, using earbuds. "I will make sure she's safe, boss. Her brother is the only other civilian, besides the statewide pageant director, who knows my identity. Spencer Colton and I served in the army together. I can't convince her to quit, and if being knocked out and almost abducted didn't do it, we're better off having her on our side." His gut churned at the memory of his ex and how he'd been duped by her journalistic goals. At least Bella was up-front about why she was here, and unapologetic about her career goals.

"I completely trust your judgment. It's just that we've got a very intelligent killer this time, Holden. He's willing to use different methods as long as he gets his victim."

Holden didn't have to be reminded that a killer who didn't stick to their own protocol, who kept changing things up, was the most dangerous and hardest to catch. A vision of Bella, bloody and inert, forced its way through his logic and he had to fight to stay present, in the reality that she was safe and he'd keep her that way.

"All the more reason for me to keep a close eye on Ms. Colton."

"What is she investigating, by the way?" His supervisor's question was tinged with impatience edged with curiosity.

"Pageant methods, possibly their influence over young women at critical ages, how the methods can encourage eating disorders."

His supervisor let out a low whistle. "That's a tall order from just one competition."

"Not for this reporter." It was natural to defend Bella and her work.

Another red flag. He was too close to making this

case personal. Or had it been personal from the moment he'd realized the killer's number-one target was his buddy's sister?

BELLA AGREED TO allow Holden to inspect her car for any intruders and explosives, and only after he was certain she was safely locked inside, the engine running, did he get in his vehicle. He followed her to the rustic Western diner that was off the town's tourist path, a place she often came to work on her laptop when the *Gabber*'s offices were too busy or she needed to be out of her house. Bella prided herself on her independence, to a fault. It surprised her that she found comfort in knowing Holden was behind her, that if the attacker jumped out from in back of one of the many parked cars around the diner, Holden would be there.

The attack, remembered or not, must have shook her more than she realized. Vulnerability choked her ability to think as clearly as she needed for this job.

Once inside they sat at a booth in a far corner of the restaurant, able to see patrons arrive without unnecessarily exposing themselves.

"Are you sure you just want dessert? I'm starving and plan to have a full meal." Holden was courteous in the way she'd seen other LEAs behave, including her brother. Holden seemed to see her as part of his case, although his demeanor toward her had an icy frosting to it she couldn't put her finger on. Yet.

Her stomach grumbled and she let go of her stubbornness. "You're right. I could use a decent meal. It's been a long day." Her admission came easily. It was the first time since earlier today that she'd been hungry. The events over the last several hours had doused her appetite.

"You're probably coming off the adrenaline rush of surviving the assault. It's your body's natural reaction to what you went through."

A laugh escaped her. "Your words are so compassionate, agent."

He scowled. "Don't refer to me as anything other than my name. That's for both our safety. And I'm sorry if my manners need polishing. I'm hungry."

"More like hangry."

"Excuse me?"

"Hungry, angry, mix in tired, and you get hangry."

His scowl deepened but then miraculously morphed into a grin. "Heck, I've been called worse, I suppose."

"Hi, ya'll. What'll you have?" Angelina, a woman Bella had gone to school with, stood at their table.

"Hey, Angelina." She gave the waitress her order. "Are you still in law school?"

Angelina grinned. "I am. Getting ready to graduate and take the bar. I'm working here at night to help out my parents." Angelina's family owned the successful and cherished local.

"That's wonderful! Congrats."

"I'm Holden. I'm a friend of Bella's." He was polite and Angelina evidently thought he was hot, too, from the way she arched her brow and shot Bella a grin. "I'll have your biggest hangry burger and fries, with a strawberry milkshake on the side." Holden flashed a wide smile at Angelina. "I've been told I'm hangry."

Angelina snorted. "I'm hangry all the time." She winked at Bella. "Hank and I just found out we're going to be having twins."

"Oh my goodness, I had no idea you were pregnant! Congratulations."

"Thanks. We're pretty excited. I hope I can pass the bar before the baby comes." She smiled at Holden. "And I'm hangry by the end of each shift. I'll ask the cook to give you an extra helping of fries."

"Thanks."

Holden conversed with Angelina as if he'd known her as long as Bella had instead of for the last three minutes. As she checked him out, Bella's first impressions of Holden stood; he was strong, poised and exuded confidence that could be intimidating if the one facing him didn't have a spine. But he was kind and didn't seem to think being an FBI agent made him better than anyone else. The opposite, in fact. Holden had a healthy humility she found very attractive.

She sat straighter on the red-leather-padded bench. One thing Bella prided herself on was her strength of character, no matter who she was sitting across from. As he asked for mayonnaise instead of ketchup for his fries, he smiled at Angelina again and the flash of white stirred something Bella had kept quiet for a while, since she'd helped Gio through her sickness and those last awful weeks. Bella's last boyfriend hadn't been able to handle her needing a break to care for her best friend and she'd flat out dumped him.

"I'll be right back with your drinks. Nice to see you, Bella."

"You too, Angelina." She smiled at the expectant mother. It must be baby season for MVHS alumnae. Angelina was the third in two weeks she'd heard was having a child. It stirred something in Bella that she knew to be her biological clock ticking. She wouldn't mind kids someday, but only after she found the right man, and was certain she was up to the task. Being orphaned and left with Aunt Amelia so young had left a stamp of reality on any urge for family, save for her brothers.

"You know the waitress, I take it? Is this the kind of town where everyone knows one another?"

"She and I are high school classmates. We haven't kept in close touch, but yeah, it's a fairly tight-knit community. To a point. It's not like I'd be able to tell you how her marriage really is, whether or not she's living her dream."

"Meaning?" Holden's expression was back to badass FBI agent. She felt as though she was being inspected, and realized she was.

"Let's get something straight, Holden. I'm willing to work with you, even help your investigation if I can, but I'm not beholden to you because you work for some big government LEA."

"Fair enough."

"And it's pretty clear you have some issues with me, though you're not saying what."

His brows rose and she knew she'd surprised him.

"I don't care for reporters. I find your profession revolting." His words didn't surprise her. What stunned her was that he flat out admitted it.

"Then why the heck are you looking to work together? I'm in the pageant solely for my story. I haven't misled you about that." She'd taken a risk by telling him anything to begin with. It was too late for self-recrimination, though.

"To keep this aboveboard, between us, you need to understand that the pageant may be shut down at any point."

"I'm kind of surprised that you haven't done that already." She smiled at Angelina when she slid a large diet soda in front of her.

"I don't know who it was who attacked you. If I did, and if I could prove it was the same killer from the other two pageants, I'd do it in a heartbeat."

"Would you, though?" Anger simmered low and hot in her belly. "You want to catch a killer. Take away Ms. Mustang Valley and you have no bait, no means of attracting him."

"Tell me about the files you were looking for."

"Pageant records. They've been in that old file cabinet since I went to Mustang Valley High."

"The drawers were empty. You saw that."

"I assumed that MVPD took them. For evidence." She spoke to him as professionally as she could muster this late in a day that had included her first physical attack, ever. It was a blessing she had little memory of any of it, other than the creepy voice behind her before she was knocked out.

"The person who attacked me—did you see him?"

"I did. But he was completely disguised."

"His voice sounded odd."

Lines appeared between his brows and on the bridge of his nose and her fingers twitched. It'd be so easy to reach across the table and smooth those out for him.

What was she thinking? She shoved her hand under her thigh.

"The voice disguiser… That's pretty high-tech, isn't it?" It sounded like a seriously committed criminal to her, to have special disguise equipment.

"Not at all. You can buy them from five dollars on upward to hundreds of dollars. They're available in party stores for Halloween, and online. There are even apps that do it for you."

A shiver ran up her spine and down her front. She crossed her arms against the involuntary response. "I can't see someone trying to protect the pageant files going to such lengths."

"Nor can I, unless…"

"Here you go." Angelina was back and set their platters down in front of them. The aroma of her hot meal made Bella's stomach growl. Holden's surprised glance, then that quick grin, let her know he'd heard it, too. Red-hot embarrassment assaulted her cheeks but she kept a smile pasted on her face until Angelina left.

"I haven't eaten since early this morning, over fourteen hours ago. I'm allowed a stomach noise or two."

"Hey, I'm not saying anything." But the grin was still there.

"You were saying why you think my attacker used a voice disguiser?"

He chewed his hamburger for several moments, wiped his mouth, took a sip of iced tea. "It's not just the voice disguise—it's the lengths he went to, to completely hide his identity. It points to someone local, and if it's someone from Mustang Valley, it could be related to the pageant. Who holds this competition so dear that they'd hurt others to keep it running?"

"That's my question to answer, isn't it?" She munched on a fry. "I'm keeping all avenues open. My first thoughts are to find the evidence for the extreme weight and diet restrictions that Gio told me were assigned as a matter of course for every contestant. I'd hoped to have that in hand already, in those files."

"You don't. So until you get the files?" He didn't miss a beat.

"I have to keep going, play along as if I'm really a legitimate contestant."

"Which you are. Does it bother you, the lying?"

"Not as much as my trust being compromised."

"How so?" One brow up, his intense chocolate gaze on her. Did his lids lower a smidge as he checked out her lips?

She shivered, but not from temperature. This chemistry had to be in her imagination. Maybe it was part of surviving the attack. She may have been unconscious but her brain had witnessed all of it; isn't that what her friends in medicine told her?

"Cold?" He'd seen her shudder.

Bella shook her head. "No. Annoyed is more like it. I told you what I was working on in confidence. And then you told someone during your phone conversation. I couldn't help but overhear it."

"That was my supervisor—I'm obligated to keep him informed about all aspects of this op, especially since I'm working solo here. It won't go any further."

"You're forgetting an important detail, Agent St. Clair."

"What's that?"

"You're not alone. We're in this together, remember?" She couldn't say why but she relished the look of what she interpreted as disgust crossing his face. He hated reporters? Great. She'd be sure to not disappoint.

"Speaking of that, there's something we have to absolutely agree on or I'll be required to disqualify you from the pageant."

Bella's blood stilled, and she swore it lowered in temperature. "Are you threatening me, Agent St. Clair?"

"No, but I'm going to have to make you promise to allow me to protect you."

"I don't ne—"

"Hold it." He held up his hand, a smear of ketchup on his palm. This man enjoyed his meals as much as she did. "Before you spout off about your brother being able to take care of you and provide security, forget it. We might be facing two criminals in my estimation. A possible serial killer, and someone additional, someone who wants the pageant's workings protected at all costs. If it's all just one criminal, that's enough. MVPD is already strapped to the max with its current investigation, and as a Colton you're that much more visible. You either need to hire 'round-the-clock security with the utmost credentials, or trust my expertise in keeping you safe through the pageant."

"Or else." She waited until he met her eyes again. "Let me guess, ultimatums come in your job description." Her vision narrowed in on his gaze, his confidence prickling her self-esteem. Anger simmered in her gut although it wasn't at Holden, but herself.

Isn't it your ego, your pride that's being hurt?

She ignored her conscience. She had to. Otherwise she'd have to admit that she found the prospect of allowing FBI agent Holden St. Clair to guard her at the least interesting, and at the most, sexually exciting.

"Actually, no. I don't hand out ultimatums or live in the black and white as much as you might think. Criminal investigations are messy, and rarely do they move in a straight line. Do I find the bad guy? Yes, most of the time. And it's pretty straightforward, as far as who a killer is. But getting there, uncovering the evidence, that's different each time."

"Don't expect me to commiserate with you. Reporting—accurate, with verifiable sources, protected or not—is always difficult. When it isn't, I know the subject matter isn't what I'm supposed to be doing."

"You'll get no commiseration from me on journalistic technique." He finished the last of his burger and eyed her over the votive that Angelina lit when she brought their drinks.

If she saw a flicker of humanity in his gaze, she credited the candle. Holden St. Clair was as hard-boiled as any LEA she'd met in her job, and as stoic as her brother. His demeanor was what really frightened her, though. As tough as his statements and matching views were, he spoke without animosity or judgement. He was calm, the strength of his personality driven by integrity, if she had to guess.

Just like her long-deceased father. Not a day went by that Bella didn't think of her parents and the awful loss she and her brothers and okay, even her not-so-dear old Aunt Amelia, had suffered. But she had a feeling that while she was in Holden's company she was going to be remembering Dad a lot more.

Thinking about her dad and the years she'd lost with him only ever accomplished one thing. It made her vulnerable.

Bella didn't do vulnerable—not again, anyway.

Chapter Seven

Holden watched the light play across her face, narrowly illuminated by the tiny candle. This greasy spoon was a far cry from the linen tablecloths he was used to sharing with beautiful women, in Phoenix. Yet he couldn't remember having a meal with anyone as attractive as Bella in eons. Not in the physical or chemical way, but intellectually. And maybe a bit more. Bella's intelligence was reflected in her keen wit, dry sense of humor—which he adored—and her willingness to totally submerse herself in the pageant.

"Are you pro beauty pageant or not?" He'd learned long ago it was best to be direct if he wanted the truth. "I can't tell if you're supportive of the other contestants or silently judging them."

"I would have answered this differently, immediately after Gio passed away." She weighed her words. "I have nothing against the pageants that have a valid award, like the scholarship with Ms. Mustang Valley. I absolutely don't support requiring women to adhere to a construct of beauty or certain physical attributes, though." Again, doubt tugged on her conscience. The possibility that Gio's eating disorders had been triggered but not caused by the pageant was something she was going to have to reckon with by the time she finished her exposé.

"Yet this pageant's prize is scholarship driven, as you've mentioned."

She nodded. "It is. Which is why I'm able to stomach entering. Trust me, if the prize had been no more than a tiara and sash to wear in the annual Mustang Valley parade, I'd still have had to consider it to get to the bottom of my investigation. But it would have come at a much higher price. Plus no one would have believed me, or trusted my motive for entering. With the scholarship prize it's easy to pose as a legit competitor."

"Thank you for being so honest in your response. I appreciate that you didn't just give me a politically correct line." He didn't want to hold her feet to the fire as he rather enjoyed their conversation and getting answers meant it would end sooner than later. But Bella Colton was a woman of substance and integrity—he imagined she'd never settle for anything less than complete transparency—and from what he'd already witnessed, wouldn't waste time squandering her energy on circular questioning.

"It's hard to not be in awe of the contestants. They appear incredibly vested in the process," Bella said. As did the pageant board, which he was watching closely, and now knew she was, too.

As if she were a balloon and he held the air passage, he heard the long swish of breath as it left her lungs, her chest raising and falling in sync.

"That's what's so difficult in this case. When the other pageant contestants, and especially the board, find out I did this for an investigative report, they're never going to forgive me. And I don't blame them. I'm not responsible for anyone else's feelings but my own. Yet I saw the other applicants all waiting for what I was going to say, when I came in the school and they were in the folding chairs just off the stage. They weren't only waiting for me to screw up, which I'm sure most of them were—I'd expect that in any competition. What was different is I felt as though they were cheering me on, showing me that I can do it, that my goals matter. And most of them don't even know me."

"You believe they're supportive of you, even though they'd do anything to win the scholarship themselves?"

"Yes." Her head tilted slightly and revealed the length of her neck that her ponytail bared. She'd put the long locks up before they came in the diner and he longed to see her hair down around her shoulders again.

Definitely not a thought an FBI agent should be entertaining during a lethal investigation.

"You sound like you were surprised."

"Of course I was! You were there—didn't it seem a little bizarre, to have the other contestants see my interview, watch for my weaknesses, yet give a big show of support?"

"No." His one-syllable reply sounded harsh and even though it wasn't his concern, he wanted her to know that he understood her observations. He'd had them, too. "Yes, the fact that they were so ready to cheer you on seemed odd to me, when only one person is going to win that scholarship. Which, may I observe, is a hefty amount of change. It's local, a community college, but still, that's got to be worth at least several thousand dollars."

She named the figure without hesitation and a warmth

lit his insides. Bella wasn't a fly-by-night reporter or blogger; she'd done her homework.

"It's enough to either pay for the full four years at Mustang Valley Community College, MVCC, or at least four semesters at the closest Arizona state school."

"I did find it odd that you were in financial straits after working in your field for so long." He didn't want to give away how much he knew about reporters, not to this beautiful woman who didn't remind him one bit of his ex, save for her job description. He still felt foolish that he'd allowed his ex, Nicole, to lead him on for as long as she had, all for a story.

"I'm not in bad financial straits, not really." She grinned. "I'm not stupid. If they research my earnings over the last two years they'll see a significant drop-off from the *Mustang Valley Gabber*—like all newspapers and blogs, we're struggling. I've relied on extra free-lance work beyond my full-time *Gabber* position, and it's enabled me to put a good amount in savings over the last five or six years."

"Any reason why?"

She shrugged. "Why not? I'm single and I came up with enough to put a down payment on a house. My mortgage is manageable and I live pretty simply."

He couldn't help check out her clothes, still the same striped top and white pants from earlier. The sparkling jewelry. She seemed as though she was doing more than getting by paycheck to paycheck.

"Hey, don't judge me on how I appear now. Or how I looked earlier—it's been a rough day, right?" She let out a throaty laugh and he felt it shoot right to his crotch.

Yeah, working with Bella Colton was going to be a

challenge. Not the working part—the keeping it to business only piece.

"I have to ask how far you're willing to go for your writing, Bella."

"What do you mean? Haven't I already showed you I'm willing to do just about anything to get the answers I want?"

"Are you willing to have me protect you, offer to be your bodyguard, for the duration of the pageant?"

"Sure. I mean, that's why we're meeting here and now, right? To agree to share information."

"I need more from you, Bella. I can't let you out of my sight until we apprehend the suspect."

"I'm not going to your hotel room with you. So where will you stay?" She was so determined, and he found her independence incredibly sexy. But as he took in her beauty he didn't miss the bright red highlights in her hair—bullseyes to the killer.

"No, you're not coming to the hotel with me." She'd figure out his intention to not leave her side soon enough. "I've been hotel hopping, up until the last couple of days, as I've spent more time in Mustang Valley." He wasn't going to share that he was a naturalist who counted a night under the stars with no edifice to block them more luxurious than the swankiest hotel on the planet. He'd be able to keep her safe in a tent.

She nodded. "Makes sense. So that no one catches on to your routine. You're the one who's supposed to be determining patterns, right?"

"Exactly."

"We'll exchange phone numbers, and I'll text you each time I leave my house, and tell you where I'm going." She pulled out her phone and her fingers hovered over the face. "Give me your number and I'll call, then we'll have one another's info."

He went along with it, until his phone vibrated, her number illuminating. The buzz went farther than his hand where he held his cell but he'd worry about his attraction to her later. He had to keep Bella Colton safe.

"There you go." She slid her purse onto her shoulder. He reached out and stilled her by touching her forearm.

"Wait."

She stared at him and when their eyes met the claws of her searching need reached him in places he didn't know he'd opened to her. Bella wasn't just another woman or citizen he was trying to protect. There was something more between them. Something he'd been missing in his life for a long time.

"You keep asking me to slow down, Agent St. Clair. I'm concerned you're not going to be happy until I stop my investigating entirely." He heard the threat in her words. Not a frivolous barb, but a show of her steely strength, the determination to do right by her best friend.

"I have to be with you, Bella." As soon as the words left his mouth he saw her eyes widen, her lips part. And darn it, he looked down at where her breasts pressed against her shirt, the hard nipples pushing her response through the thin material.

"That sounds like a personal issue, Agent St. Clair."

"No, I don't mean it that way. I mean yes, there's clearly some chemistry here, which is to be expected. I mean, we're adults, both single, on an intense case." As he bumbled he watched her and instead of being revolted by his faux pas she appeared…delighted. Bella Colton let out a belly laugh that proved her lack of self-consciousness and her ability to live in the present moment. Good traits for someone who was a potential target of a serial killer.

"You're refreshing, Holden. I've no doubt you're a crack agent or you wouldn't have been sent here. But you're real. I like that."

He ignored his embarrassment, the racing thoughts that he'd never be worthy of this woman's attention. Holden considered himself too devoted to his job to deserve a woman like Bella, a woman who deserved a man who'd give her nothing less than one-hundred percent. He stopped his thoughts with expertise gained from years of investigative work that required complete focus. Had he forgotten that she was a reporter, just like his ex?

You're on the clock, man. Get it done.

"You're a target, Bella. The killer likes women with red hair and green eyes, and you're the only one with both."

"I have blond—" She fingered her ponytail and her face crumpled. "Crap. I forgot. I do have red hair. I thought it'd help me stand out from all the other contestants, especially the blondes."

He nodded. "It does. And it was smart, for the pageant. Except you may have drawn the attention of the killer already."

"I'd say I did by getting attacked." She spoke matter-of-factly and he let it go. It wasn't the time or place to remind her that he wasn't so sure her attacker was the serial killer. The killer's modus operandi was to lay low until he either poisoned or shot his victim. It made Holden think that the killer didn't seem to care how his quarry died, just that they did. Something he wasn't going to let happen to Bella.

"The truth is, Bella—I need to stay with you. At your

house, and possibly elsewhere if we decide you need to move. It'll probably amount to nothing more than me sleeping on your floor by the front door for the next few weeks, with no further interruption from any bad guy. But we can't take the risk that they know your identity or where you live."

Her face stilled, then she laughed again. "Oh, just wait until Spencer finds out that his buddy is sleeping with me."

"Ah, not with you, specifically—" All he needed was Spencer coming down on him for moving in on his sister.

"Chill out, Holden, and let me have my sibling fantasy. My brother means well, but he's always telling me how to stay safe and live my life. He's absolutely livid I signed up for the pageant, as I'm sure you figured out already."

"I don't blame him. There are a lot of moving parts here. And another thing—you can't tell your work colleagues or supervisor who I am, or that you're working with me. No one but you, Spence, and the state pageant director know I'm on the case. No one on the Ms. Mustang Valley Pageant board knows who I am. I'm deep undercover here."

"Not so deep, Agent. I know who you are and I'm a member of the press, remember?" She looked away, lost in thought for several moments. He let her process his request. It was a lot. Sure, she'd seen his badge, Spencer had vouched for him, they'd survived a possible abduction attempt already.

He'd helped her—she knew that. But she was about to let a strange man into her home, no matter that he was Spencer's army friend. Holden wasn't her friend, nor could he ever be, not during this investigation, anyhow. It would compromise his work, because he'd want to trust she was telling him all she discovered with the pageant and that just wasn't reality. Not with a reporter. He'd already learned that lesson.

Holden had his priorities, and Bella had hers.

"If there was another way to do this, instead of having to be with you 24/7 and staying at your place, I'd make it happen." He needed her to know that he wasn't taking the easy way out at her inconvenience.

Steady green eyes met his. "I know." Her mouth was a half-smile and she let out a sigh of surrender. "I've got one brother who's a rancher and one who's a cop. They both deal in reality every day, as do I. If I'm doing my job right, anyhow. You can stay with me, and I'll do my best to stay in your sights or whatever you need for my security. Because it's not just about me, Holden. This is about the pageant, its contestants, the women who really need the scholarship. I'm doing it for them."

"And for your best friend."

She nodded and he saw the glisten of tears in her eyes, but she didn't let one fall. Add stubborn to independent, passionate, intriguing.

"Yes. For Gio."

BELLA DIDN'T LIKE that in the span of six short hours she'd gone from being completely undercover, working her report as part of the pageant, to Holden knowing so much about what she was trying to accomplish. But after being attacked, warned off the pageant and now being unable to shake the sense of someone watching her, she gave in to what her brothers called her killer instinct. She had a gut instinct for a story and was good at sizing up character. Holden might never appreciate her vocation or support her article, but he wanted what she did. Answers, and no more people hurt.

"Let's get into your vehicle." He took charge the minute they left the diner. "We'll come back in the morning for mine. This way if anyone's trailing you we'll make it look like—"

"Like I'm picking up a stranger in the local greasy spoon." She unlocked the passenger door with her keys.

"This car is the oldest running antique I've ever seen." Holden's observation brought a smile to her face but she didn't reply until they were both inside her beloved twenty-year-old station wagon.

"This was my mother's car. She and Dad were killed in his car, in a crash. One of their family friends bought this one from our aunt and kept it in his garage until my brothers and I were sixteen, and the day we got our driver's licenses he drove it up to the house." She couldn't stop the giggle as she moved the gear, on the steering wheel, into Reverse. "Our aunt Amelia was fit to be tied, because she didn't want us being that independent so soon, but when she realized we'd be asking her for a lot fewer rides, she gave in."

"Sounds like your aunt had her own issues."

Bella nodded. "She did. I had little to do with her after moving out, when I went to college, but now looking back... I don't know. It couldn't have been easy for her, losing a sibling and gaining three kids, age ten, ready to head into the tween and teenage years, all at once. She wasn't much older than me when it happened."

"I saw on your license when you checked in at the high school that you're thirty-one. That surprised me. I mean, I know you're Spencer's age, but it still seems unbelievable."

"Why?" She turned onto the main drag through town and headed west, toward the small, quiet subdivision where she lived in an adobe-style midcentury house.

"You look about ten years younger."

"Until I open my mouth, right?" She shot a quick glance at his profile in time to see the quick grin. "I've been told I sound like an old soul, and my deep voice sure doesn't sound youthful."

"I think your voice is sexy as hell."

Heat that had shimmered on the surface of her awareness ignited and spread to her center, pooling in her most sensitive spots. "Uh, Agent? I don't think that's something you're allowed to notice."

"It's not. Sorry. Are you a smoker?"

"Nope, never have been. My voice was froggy as a kid, and I never outgrew it. Supposedly it's similar to my mother's, but I have no way of knowing. I don't remember her voice a whole lot anymore."

"Spencer shared about losing his folks, your parents. That's an awful break in life, to lose them so early."

"Yeah, it wasn't fun. What about you, are your parents still here?"

"Yes, they're happy empty nesters in Kansas City, Kansas. My mother is an engineer and works at the state power authority. My father is a government contractor. I grew up there, in Kansas, with my two brothers. We have that in common, two brothers."

"That's neat. Sounds like you had the perfect childhood." She tried to keep the envy out of her voice, but it was there in the tightening of her chest. Dang, the attack must be making her more emotional.

"Perfect? Wondering if either parent was going to lose

their job as the economy swung up and down? Watching one of my brothers turn to drugs when we were teens?" He spoke matter-of-factly, not with an iota of self-pity. She liked that Holden knew himself well enough to be able to do that, that he knew he wasn't the sum total of some of his life experiences. "It wasn't perfect, no, but it was pretty darn wonderful at times. Our parents always did the best they could for us, and now that my brother's sober we all get together a couple of times a year to hang out."

"That's pretty cool, if you ask me. Kansas City sounds appealing, being a larger city. Living in a small place like Mustang Valley can be a bit like being in a cultural bubble. Except we're lucky that Mustang Valley is in Arizona. By that I mean we have a confluence of cultures, including Native American and Hispanic. I learned Spanish in school from kindergarten."

"I wish I'd studied a second language sooner. I took German in high school, then Spanish in college. I'm not a natural at languages. I imagine since you're a writer, you are."

"I do okay. I haven't had the opportunities you have to see the world, though. That would be neat."

"Can't you do international reporting?" His query hit a sensitive spot in her belly, a vulnerable piece of herself she wasn't ready to reveal. If she landed this piece with the pageant, she'd very well receive the attention her work needed to propel her to the next level, which she hoped would be on a more national and eventually international stage.

"It's not that simple. It'll take me a while to get there."

He let it go and she relaxed her clenched jaw. Her

street sign appeared and she made the left onto the wide paved road.

"I didn't picture you in a standard suburban neighborhood."

"Don't count on it. Why do you say that, though?" She took her time driving around the park that she worked out in. Walking or running proved much less expensive than a gym, and she had a set of weights in her small home's second bedroom that served as her office, workout room and crafting space. It was a guest room, too, but since her brothers lived close by, no one stayed with her, except if her college friends were visiting. No one really had, except Gio.

"You strike me as independent and preferring your own space to having a next-door neighbor."

Darn it, he had a true talent. "You're a natural at profiling, Holden. I mean it." She turned onto a graveled road that lead through a grove of huge cacti.

"Are you taking us out into the desert?"

She laughed. "In case you haven't noticed it, you're in the middle of the desert. It's called Arizona." Bella took the last S-turn and pulled up in front of her house, then shut off the engine. She watched Holden, tried to see the view through his eyes, but it was dark back here as the sun had lowered to below her home's roofline, and the house looked like a dark rectangle surrounded by the glowing golden rays of the last of the day.

"Are you the only one out here?"

"Do you mean my house? Yes. I'm still on city water and utilities, but I get the sense of being out in the country. It's really not that far to the nearest neighbors, no more than a quarter mile in each direction. But I like how it feels more rural. It's a nice break from running around Mustang Valley and beyond each day, chasing down stories."

Holden turned and looked at her. "I didn't mention it because I didn't want to put you on edge, but I've been checking the rearview and side-view mirrors since we left the diner. No one followed us, which is a good sign."

Relief unfurled and the attraction her fear had tamped down surged. This was the first time she'd been alone in her car with a man in…she didn't even remember. The few men she'd dated on and off over the last several years had either driven, claiming their vehicles were more comfortable, or she'd met them out for a meal or other date.

"Yes, that's good news." She watched him, or rather, felt him in the dark. Her dash light had burned out over a year ago and she'd been too busy to replace it.

"So now I'm going to have to ask to do something you're not going to like, Bella." His deep baritone wove a sexy spell around her and she tipped her head back, just a bit. In case he was noticing her lips.

"Okay. What is it?" She smiled in the velvet night, liking the direction things were going.

"I've got to go through your house first, to clear it. Protocol." He opened his door and slid out of the car before Bella's tingling lips had a chance to realize she wasn't getting propositioned.

She scrambled out of the car and walked up behind him as he strode toward her front door, his handgun out and reflecting the porch light, which she had on a solar timer. Good thing she didn't want their relationship to be anything more than business.

Chapter Eight

Holden couldn't get out of the jalopy soon enough, away from the temptation he'd been fighting every. Single. Minute. Of this case. It was no use pretending the attraction wasn't there, because it was, in spades. Bella Colton hit all his physical buttons and worse, she had a terrific sense of humor.

Nowhere else to go but forward. He pulled out his weapon and heard Bella's approach behind him.

"Stay behind me, to the right, if you're not going to remain in your car."

"Of course I'm not. What if the killer is out here, and attacks me while you're clearing my house?"

He gritted his teeth. "No talking. Let me work."

She complied but he gave her thirty seconds. Her naturally curious nature wouldn't allow her to not ask questions, he'd bet.

The sandy gravel underfoot gave way to smooth red tiles that led to the front porch area, which was really a front patio. A small table and a chair looked untouched, as did the ground around the house. He used his phone's flashlight to see if there were any footprints or other evidence of a recent unwanted visitor.

"The front looks fine. Give me your key." He faced her, saw the resistance in her stance.

"I can unlock my own door."

"Bella." He stood in front of her, his hand out. "Our deal."

"Whatever." She grumbled the last, held out the small ring of keys and dropped them in his palm. Was she careful to ensure they didn't have any skin contact or was he reading too much into it? The fact that he was turned on by her didn't mean Bella had any such desire for him. Nor should she—he was here to protect her, find a murderer and then he'd be back to Phoenix. Where he had his life, his job, and no troublesome undercover reporter questioning his every move.

"Stay back until I get the door open and clear the first room. Do you have a front hallway or does it open directly into a room?" He scanned her front windows, all two of them, to try to see what the inside looked like.

"I have a foyer with a skylight, and then it opens into the great room. The kitchen, morning breakfast room and living room all flow into each other. I don't have a lot of interior walls save for the outer ones."

"Where's your bedroom?"

"There are two. The guest room is off the kitchen and the master bedroom is behind that, down a short hall. This is a ranch-style home, one level." She spoke as if he were a grade-school kid and he couldn't blame her. He was asking pretty obvious questions for a person who lived in Arizona. The homes were often ranch-style, meaning one level, to help with keeping them cool through the long, hot days. Even with air-conditioning it was impossible to keep a home livable when the temperatures soared well over one-hundred-degrees Fahrenheit. The local joke was that it was a "dry" heat. When the temperature hit triple digits, it was too hot.

"Got it, thanks. I'll be right back." He closed the few yards between them and the front door, unlocked it and slowly pushed it open, his pistol ready to fire. As the door swung open, inch by inch, he shone his flashlight inside until he reached around and hit the wall light switch. Sconces on either side of a mission-style framed mirror lit up, throwing a pale golden hue into the room. Bella had done her work and made the place a home, if the various decor touches were any indication. A fluffy white throw draped over a white fabric chaise lounge; in another corner a love seat boasted a spillover of throw pillows, all printed in bright, gregarious colors.

No sign of an intruder. But Holden didn't allow relief to take away the weight of responsibility from his shoulders. Not yet. Not until they caught and apprehended the suspect.

He methodically cleared out each room, confirming the house was indeed empty, before returning to where Bella stood on the porch. "All clear." He motioned for her to come inside. "Let's lock up the front door and you're free to move about. I'm going to check the back of the house to be sure you're safe."

SHE WATCHED HIS retreating backside and only then did she allow herself to sag against the kitchen pantry door. She'd been surprised at how hard Spencer and his K-9 Boris worked situations before, how very tedious and exacting law enforcement was, done right; but this revealed a whole new level of ignorance on her part that Bella hadn't anticipated. How many times had she heard Spencer say it wasn't about the firearms, or the physicality of the cop, but the intelligence? The ability to conduct their job under any circumstance?

Holden St. Clair knew what he was doing, displaying a tenacity for doing what was right, no matter that they both were bone weary and dog tired. He could have dropped her off, assumed she'd be fine until the pageant began tomorrow, but instead Holden was conducting an investigation of her home security as if it were the beginning of the day and he had all the energy to be as thorough as when he first woke.

She watched the light beam flash outside the windows, first near the living area and then around to the kitchen, before it disappeared as Holden walked the perimeter of her house. Bella tried to stay focused on the present and what she needed to do to prepare for tomorrow, but her mind and her body couldn't stop flashing back to moments ago in her car.

Embarrassment washed over her. She'd really thought he was going to kiss her. Had she misread his signals? The glances, held a heartbeat longer than with just any other colleague, the quick drop of his gaze to her lips? And the electric current of attraction she'd experienced when their fingers touched, was it even possible that something so potent on her part was one-sided?

"Bella!" His shout made her stand straight and cleared her mind of what she knew were inescapable personal rabbit holes. "Come here."

"Coming." She made for the back door, which he must have opened with the key.

He stood under the pale glow of the moon as it filtered through her pergola on the back patio. A quick glance at her large cushioned swing, myriad planters filled with cacti and other succulents, and her different garden sculptures showed nothing amiss.

"What is it?"

"Over here." He led them with the phone light to her air-conditioning unit. "Have you had maintenance or repair on your AC recently?"

"No."

"What about this crack to your foundation?" A long, jagged line ran from the stucco under her bathroom window and disappeared below the ground.

"It's from the earthquake."

"That's right—it didn't hit us in Phoenix as it did here. And the epicenter was close to the Colton Oil industrial area, am I correct?"

"Yes." Annoyance mingled with fear. Would Holden just get to the point?

"Any reason these footprints should be here?" He spotlighted several sets of large prints in the sandy earth around the unit's concrete-slab platform. Her gut heaved and she wanted to blame it on being tired but she knew fear when it hit her.

"Those have to be recent or they'd be gone already." Nothing stayed the same in the desert, not for long and not during a time that included enough breeze at night to blow away the fine sand. "Why would someone come here, though, to an air-conditioning unit?"

Holden snapped several photos of the prints, a few with his feet in the shot for sizing perspective. "I don't know. Unless—" He shone the light up to the three-foot-tall unit, and revealed that there was a good amount of dust atop the grate where the fan blew out hot air from the house.

"He climbed on top to look into that window." She

finished his speculation and looked up to the high windows that lined her master bathroom. "Even if someone could get up that high without a ladder, no one could fit through those windows." They weren't more than six inches tall, tops, though very long to allow maximum light in.

Holden pulled latex gloves from his jeans' pockets and she laughed.

"You've got to be kidding me."

"No joke intended. Just part of my job." He pushed hard on the top of the AC unit before hauling himself up. She watched from the ground as he felt along the edges of the windows as far as he could reach. His movement stilled as his fingers rested on the same spot he had paused the first time he visually examined the frame.

"What is it?" Shivers raced down her spine and she crossed her arms in front of her, looked around them at the surrounding garden and wild property that backed up against her neighbors on either side, and acres of empty desert to the rear of the house. It had been her safe haven ever since she'd saved enough for the down payment to purchase the house a few years ago. She'd never felt vulnerable or at risk here.

Until tonight.

Holden tugged on something, then fisted his palm and jumped to the ground, far away from the footprints. "I need to look at this inside, in proper lighting, but I'd say someone is very interested in catching glimpses of you in your shower." He opened his hand to reveal a tiny box with a lens.

"I'm going to be sick." She said it before thinking.

"I mean, not really, but the thought of this—I can't do this right now."

His firm, gloved hand grasped her forearm. "Hang on, Bella. It's okay. You're not alone—I'm here. And the good news is that your stalker is nowhere near here right now, most likely. If they wanted to watch you in person there wouldn't be a camera and I'd have found them inside or lurking on the property. I'm going to call Spencer and have him and his K-9 inspect the area for scent, but we should be good to go for tonight."

"Meaning?"

"We'll be able to spend the night here, and then head to the pageant in the morning. It's already past eleven, and I need to be at the school a full hour before the contestants arrive at eight."

"I don't even know if I'm a contestant yet." She'd forgotten to check her inbox; the pageant director, Mimi, had told them they'd find out whether they qualified by nine o'clock tonight. A quick dive into her emails on her phone revealed a message. Her hands shook.

"Well?" Holden stood patiently next to her, as if whether she got into the pageant was important to him, too. Of course, she figured she'd be the best kind of bait for the serial killer, if there was one and if he'd now focused his sights on Ms. Mustang Valley.

She clicked the message open, skimmed the preliminary niceties, and let out a whoop. Relief and a sense of euphoria she did not expect washed over her, easing some of the tension that finding out about the camera had incurred.

"I take it you're in?" His enthusiastic tone was as surprising as her reaction.

"I am. And you're correct, I report at eight o'clock."

"Then we'd best get your beauty sleep going."

"You're crazy to do this, Bella." Jarvis sat at her kitchen island later that night, his hair gleaming under the pendant lights.

"As crazy as Spencer was to call you out here tonight? Really, you two don't need to babysit me. I already have a federal agent at my beck and call." Holden was outside taking evidence as Spencer and Boris patrolled her backyard. It was half past midnight and Bella wanted to sleep for a day.

"You should always let us know what you're up to, sis. You know we're going to find out one way or the other. Word doesn't take long to travel in Mustang Valley." Jarvis ran his fingers through his hair. "And you're working fast even for you if you've already got this agent doing your bidding." His words were harsh but Jarvis's tone was kind, loving even. He was the best brother, as was Spencer, and Bella didn't for one minute take either of them for granted. Yet she had, by not mentioning her intention to run for Ms. Mustang Valley.

"I'm sorry, Jarvis. It's best for me to keep things as low key as possible when I'm doing investigative work."

"I know that, sis, but Spencer and I are your only family. We need to know, so that we can be on the lookout for anything suspicious."

She poured them each a tall glass of ice water, and filled glasses for Holden and Spence, a mixing bowl for Boris that she placed on the floor. "I appreciate that, but this is a very insular community I'm delving into. Gio's passing made me realize that a lot of my grief is over not having been able to prevent her death."

"So you think digging up the past will help you with that?"

She shook her head. "It's not about me. We can learn from the past. If I do this right, I'll find evidence that this pageant committee and board have been negatively influencing young women's health and eating habits and shut that behavior down."

Jarvis's brow went up, the way it did when she tried to get one over on him in a board game. Whereas Spencer would blatantly call her out on anything he thought she was lying about, Jarvis took a more circumspect view of things. Of life, especially.

"That's a tall order, sis, even by your standards. Let's say you do find evidence—though what that'll look like is beyond me, short of finding a memo that states, 'Starve yourself or get kicked out.'"

"I have to do this, Jarvis. Gio deserves it. All the women who enter these contests deserve to know the truth about what they're participating in."

"It seems to me someone isn't happy about you getting involved."

"No one knows I'm doing this as a reporter, except for Spencer's friend Holden, whom you met when you came in."

"He's a good guy, Holden St. Clair."

"You know him?" A thread of self-pity wound its way around her heart. "Why didn't anyone tell me about him, who he was?"

Jarvis smiled. "Spencer did. You knew the name once you met him, didn't you? How did you meet, at the school?"

She nodded. "Yes. He was the security guard when I checked in. I didn't realize he was Spencer's friend, though. He's undercover. I guess I shouldn't have said that to you." The familiar heat rushed her cheeks and she prayed Jarvis didn't notice, or if he did, that he'd take it for her regret at spilling the beans. Not because she was already thinking of Holden as much more than her brother's friend.

Jarvis chuckled. "I'd have loved to see that. And don't worry about telling me—I'm a vault."

"You are."

"What do you wish you'd seen, and what are you a vault about?" Spencer looked at Jarvis as he, K-9 Boris and Holden walked into the kitchen. Spencer removed his hat and placed it on the counter. "Boris, drink." The dog's lapping filled the quiet.

"Oh, nothing. Just how Bella's getting away with being a pageant contestant when we both know how much she hates pretending to be anything other than herself."

She risked a glance at Holden and found another reason to blush in the way their gazes locked, as if they'd been working together for longer than a day. As if…as if there was something happening between them they weren't ready to acknowledge.

Holden blinked, shuttering the desire she'd seen in his eyes. He let out a laugh and the other two men joined in. The masculine rumble at once grated on Bella's nerves and comforted her. She knew her brothers only wanted her safety but they tended to lean over into the minding-her-business category. Holden had already told her he was going to basically be her bodyguard and protector for the duration of the pageant. A need to establish her turf twisted up through her exhaustion.

"Give me a break. Going undercover for this piece is

the same way I get any story. It's called doing my job." She emphasized her words, hoping her brothers took her words at face value. Holden, too. He couldn't find out how much he'd affected her since they'd first met. How much he distracted her now, standing in her kitchen close to midnight, a day's worth of beard on his impossibly square chin. At least it didn't highlight his cleft as much, one of his more annoying features. "And while I truly appreciate all three of you looking out for me, I'm a grown woman with a concealed-weapon permit." She walked over to the far kitchen cabinet, opened it to reveal her gun safe.

"Your weapon's in there?" Holden spoke first.

"Yes." She nodded. Let him chew on that. "I'm a perfect shot, too."

"She is," Spencer chimed in. "We thought Bella was going to join MVPD at one point."

"Maybe you should, if you're putting yourself in this kind of danger with your journalism." Jarvis nodded sagely and she wanted to punch both of her brothers on the arm.

"I'm glad you have weapons training, Bella, but no weapon will defend you locked in a safe." Holden's observation came just as she realized the same.

"You're right. Are you suggesting I carry it while working the pageant?"

"Ah, no. I'll be on-site the entire time you're there. Or anywhere."

"I'm counting on you, Holden," Spencer spoke up.

"We both are," Jarvis joined in.

Bella watched the testosterone exchange between her brothers and Holden and decided it was all too much, too late. She picked up her phone for a distraction and saw the email, sent only minutes earlier, from the pageant director. After she read it, she interrupted the men's ongoing discussion on how best to keep her safe.

"Uh, guys?" She held up her phone for them to see the email. "I have to be onstage tomorrow morning at eight. Which gives me a six-o'clock wake-up. You all decide what you need to do to save me, whatever, but I'm going to bed. Night-night."

She turned and left, hoping that no one would tell her she couldn't sleep in her own bed tonight. More than at any other time, Bella needed the comfort of the familiar.

As her head hit the pillow she realized that Holden felt way too familiar to her. And she'd only known him for one day.

This was going to be her toughest investigative report to date, and it had little to do with a serial killer or the loss of her best friend.

Chapter Nine

"You decided to let me stay in my own home. Why?" She greeted Holden as he walked in from the backyard, none the worse for sleeping outside all night. At least, that's where she assumed he'd been, as Jarvis was still sacked out in her guest room.

"If at any time last night or this morning I thought you were in danger, you wouldn't be here. But with your two brothers helping out, we secured your property no problem."

"But you couldn't have gotten much sleep."

He walked over and helped himself to the pot of coffee she'd brewed. "I'm not the one who needed the beauty sleep."

His musky scent mixed with the aroma of the brew and she all but swooned. How easy it was to forget that her two favorite scents—coffee and male—made for a delicious morning wake-up.

Not that kind of wake-up, though. Hadn't she learned from the nonkiss last night?

"I don't need it, either." She sat down at her small table and swirled the creamer with a small spoon. "Where did you sleep, by the way?"

"Mostly on the front porch. Your hammock is a perfect spot, and I only heard a few critters roaming about."

"Did you notice the prairie dogs at dawn? There's a family of them in my front yard."

"I didn't, but I'm guessing Boris warned them off."

"Hmm, yes." She'd forgotten that Spencer and Boris had made their rounds last night. It'd be easy to blame it on the late hour, long day, being attacked; but she didn't waste the energy kidding herself. Holden St. Clair was the distracting factor.

Holden took the seat across from her at the bistro set and she almost laughed. His large frame barely fit on the wrought iron chair, and the table seemed to shrink in his presence. Unlike her awareness of him.

"Let's go over the ground rules again, Bella."

"Rules?"

He nodded, sipped his black coffee. "Yes. For me to agree to your participation in the pageant. And the guidelines your brother agreed to."

"Spencer isn't my keeper." She blew a strand of hair from her eyes. "I appreciate that he's law enforcement. He and Jarvis have always been protective of me, a great thing for a sister. But we're all adults and there's nothing legally stopping me from competing."

"There is if I expose your motive for entering the pageant."

"You wouldn't." But looking into his dark eyes, noting he'd shaved and the cleft on his chin seemed sexier than she'd remembered, she knew he would. "I'll never get the truth about this pageant—which could have bigger significance, legally—if you give me away."

"I'm not going to do that, Bella, but we have to agree to the precautions that will keep you alive."

"You make it sound so dire." She was trying to be casual, to appear as though she could take whatever pageant involvement threw at her. But she couldn't ignore the quivering in her belly, the wobbly feel to her knees. Bella was scared.

"It is. Or will be, soon enough."

"How can you be so certain? You don't even know if the man who attacked me is the same person who murdered those other women. Or if those victims were killed by the same person."

"Actually, we've had DNA evidence begin to trickle in." It'd been a month since the last murder, in Tucson, and they had some evidence being revealed. "There was matching DNA at both murder sites."

"One a poisoning and one gunshot, right?" She recalled reading the initial reports of each murder as they came across the local online paper's front page.

"You're informed."

"It's my job. Plus I've been paying attention to the pageant scene over the last several months."

"When did your friend pass?"

He remembered their conversation in the staff room. It meant he hadn't been treading water, using the time to win her over to his point of view, or reveal what she knew only for his benefit. It might even mean he cared.

Scratch that—it's his job to remember. To observe.

"Almost a year ago." It felt like yesterday and ten years ago at the same time. "She was very sick for the last year, and dragging for the previous five. I can honestly say I haven't seen her as the Gio I once knew for at least seven years or so."

"All from malnutrition, due to her eating disorder?"

"Mostly, yes." Bella didn't want to discuss Gio's long

battle with mental illness, the struggles to get her friend in to the right professionals, from psychiatrists to therapists, all trained to expertly treat a young woman for the severity of her eating disorders, anxiety and depression. By the time Gio found a treatment center that worked well for her, it was too late. She'd starved herself so much that the nutritional depletion to her brain had destroyed her ability to see herself as she really was and not through the lens of body dysmorphia.

"You must have seen a lot with your friend, while she suffered like that." His compassion brought tears to her eyes.

"You speak as if you understand what Gio went through."

"No, I don't have any experience with eating disorders, but my grandfather had cancer and after over ten years of fighting it, died last year."

"I'm sorry, Holden."

"Thanks. It's always hard losing our loved ones."

"Yes."

They sat in peaceful silence and it didn't escape her that this was what she'd always thought other people had, what they deserved, when they found that one person to go through life with. Quiet and a simple acceptance of one another's presence.

But she had done little in her life to earn a whole lot of quiet moments, and rest wasn't something she wanted. Not until she got to the bottom of what had triggered Gio's life-ending issues.

"You get that there's a killer who's most likely involved in this pageant, and sees you as their next victim, right?" Holden's words underscored the frivolity of her imagination. So much for quiet respite free of worry.

"I do, but frankly, I don't have a lot of memory of being attacked." Her hand went to her throat. "I heard his weird voice, then yours, and then it's a blank spot until I was in the ER."

"It's normal for your mind to block out unpleasant memories. And being attacked is traumatic."

"True." She put her hand on his. "I've got this, Holden. I know you're the security and law enforcement expert. I trust you and I'll do whatever you tell me I need to, to stay safe and help you keep everyone else safe." She removed her hand. "Is that what you wanted to hear from me?"

"Do you mean it? Because I need you to know that it's paramount that you don't go anywhere alone with anyone until we catch the killer."

"I do."

"But?"

But she wasn't going to let anything keep her from getting this piece filed with her boss. She smiled at the man across the table from her. The man who'd spent a night in her home, something few besides her brothers had. A tug of regret deep in her gut reminded her that she'd been neglectful of her romantic life as of late. Time enough for that later.

"No buts." She stood. "I'll tell Jarvis we're leaving, get my bags and then we have ten minutes to drive to the high school."

Holden took her mug from her and walked to the sink, turned on the faucet and rinsed both cups. Bella didn't stay to watch him perform the morning ritual. The last thing she needed was to imprint the image of Holden moving about her kitchen as if he belonged there.

As if they were more than a reporter and FBI agent, both undercover.

THIS WAS ALWAYS the most exciting part of any chase. Well, except for when the victim realized they were going to die and had no way to prevent it.

The grin was impossible to hide, but if anyone from the pageant board noticed, it'd be easy to pass it off as being happy to be involved in the thirtieth Ms. Mustang Valley Pageant.

Yesterday had been scary—it all could have ended because of one stupid move. Fortunately Bella Colton was fine and from all indications it looked like she'd be back today. Bella had made the final cut and was going to be pitted against the twenty-three other beauties, but none as pretty or enticing as the green-eyed woman with fiery red streaks in her hair. It'd be better if she had her whole head of hair in a bright red. Maybe that was something they could remedy as part of her preparation to be sacrificed.

"Ten minutes." The announcement came over the school's antiquated public address system and the voice sounded tinny in the space behind the stage where so far, no one had ventured since yesterday.

It was the perfect vantage point.

"WE CAN'T HAVE you walking back and forth on the stage while we're trying to take the girls through their choreography." The woman leading the contestants through their opening-group-number dance steps left nothing to interpretation in her angry voice. Holden had completed his sixth circle of the large room, from the back of the auditorium seats to onstage, behind the several rows of curtains that could hide anyone all too easily.

Holden stopped in his tracks, turned and faced the tall, attractive woman who'd so far as he could tell done nothing but agitate her other pageant board members. Selina Barnes Colton was the ex-wife of Payne Colton, an oil tycoon in charge of the billion-dollar Colton Oil corporation who basically owned Mustang Valley. Selina was still on the Colton Oil Board of Directors as its VP and director of PR, and had zero problem throwing her weight around town according to Spencer, who'd filled him in on every pageant board member and judge.

"Just doing my job, ma'am." He kept to his security dude persona, not wanting to give her the tiniest hint that he had more right to be here than she realized. "I'll stay out of sight as much as I can, and be quiet."

"Not good enough. The girls need to feel safe in this space—am I right, ladies?" Selina tossed her hair over a bared shoulder, her figure model thin in tight-fitting clothes. Two dozen women stood in a group onstage, in various types of dance outfits. He'd memorized all of them, and constantly counted heads to make sure no one had crept off or worse, disappeared. A pair of emerald eyes flashed at him and he had to bite the inside of his cheek to not respond to Bella's wide grin. She was enjoying watching him take on a Colton Titan. But while the other contestants vocally supported Selina with calls of "Yeah, that's right," and "Listen to Ms. Colton," Bella remained silent.

"I'm here at the request of the state pageant director, ma'am."

"You're telling me that Bud Langston hired you directly and you're not here as part of Mustang Valley High School's staff?"

"Yes, ma'am." Holden had no problem playing whatever role he had to in order to get his job done. But Bella's glances communicated her impatience with Selina's trauma-drama tactics. He needed her to remain passive to Selina's theatrics, so that they could both gather as much information and evidence as possible.

"I think having the security guard where we can see him is a good idea. There are a lot of crazies around these days who prey on pretty women." Bella wasn't a mind reader. Or if she was, she'd ignored him.

Selina spun on her too-high heels and faced down Bella. Holden's hand clenched and he forcefully kept himself from stepping forward. He was going to have to handle this protective instinct toward Bella better. His drive to serve and protect was a part of him, but this sense of needing to know that Bella was in no way in any type of danger went deeper. To a place inside himself he didn't want to journey to, not now, maybe not ever.

To the place where he could get his heart broken again.

"That's enough, Ms. Colton." Selina's head swiveled as she addressed the rest of the crowd. "No worries, we are zero relation."

"Distant," Bella contradicted her and Holden wanted to whoop. His stomach constricted. Where was his agent self? He was here to catch a murderer, not cheer a potential victim on as she verbally sparred with a not-so-nice woman who seemed to think the world revolved on an axis named Selina.

"Wait a minute, you're related to one of the judges?" a contestant piped up, clearly annoyed. Her brunette hair was in two ridiculously juvenile pigtails and she wore an incredibly revealing leotard whose V-neck cut to her navel. Holden had thought this pageant was on the more conservative side but not for this contestant. "That's absolutely not fair. I demand that this woman be disqualified. No one related to the pageant board, judges or director is allowed to compete."

"We are not related at all, trust me." Bella spoke with authority, but it was clear to Holden that the belligerent woman wasn't going to let it go.

"What, do you spell *Colton* differently? Because from what I'm reading on both of your name tags, you have the same last name. And everyone knows that if you're a Colton in Mustang Valley or anywhere in Arizona, you get what you want." The overdone-leotard woman was on a roll, and several of the contestants murmured their agreement, nodding their heads and folding their arms in front of them. Holden knew the moment could prove an opportune distraction to detract from a killer, so he kept vigilant, walking slowly around the perimeter of the theater, never letting Bella out of his peripheral sight.

"*Puuullleeeze*, we're from completely different branches of the family, and we're not even blood relatives." Selina didn't want to be associated with a lowly blogger like Bella, it seemed. Holden stopped fighting his emotions and settled for keeping them hidden from the pageant contestants. At least the focus was off him and his job.

Except, he couldn't keep his focus off Bella and it wasn't for pageant reasons. Suddenly she wasn't a potential victim; she was Bella, the woman he was getting too close to, too quickly.

Chapter Ten

"Selina's correct—we're not related. The man she used to be married to, Payne Colton, is very distantly related to me on my father's side, but from a different branch of the Coltons. Trust me, I'm from the wrong side of the tracks. Isn't that right, Selina?"

Bella looked at the woman she'd only seen in tabloid stories and at the most prestigious social functions in Arizona. Selina Barnes Colton didn't limit herself to what she'd once called *the hick town* of Mustang Valley any more than she had to. As the second and former wife of the Colton patriarch, she somehow had maintained her pull on the board of Colton Oil and was known for her take-no-prisoners methods with the press. Bella had tried to score an interview with her for the Lifestyle section of the *Mustang Valley Gabber* but Selina's assistant had turned her down flat, stating that *Selina only talks to national syndicates.* Whatever.

"If that doesn't convince everyone here that I'm not going to give any favorite points to Isabella, I don't know what else will." Selina's gaze was hard as coal on Bella but her smile was wide, her expression catering to the other contestants. "I've been involved with the pageant for the last decade, and I assure you my integrity is impeccable."

Several of the contestants mumbled around Bella but she ignored them. All she cared about was the ability to stay in the pageant. She'd barely gotten here and now was threatened with removal because Holden had walked around the stage one too many times. He really needed to chill out with the security-guard routine. She'd talk to him later about it.

"Let's keep the rehearsal going. If any decisions need to be made about our judges or contestants, we'll take care of it at the pageant board level. And from my perspective, there is no conflict of interest here. Let's begin again. Selina, from the top." Señora Rosenstein, whom Bella still saw as her Spanish teacher and not a member of the Ms. Mustang Valley board, tapped her phone and the auditorium was filled with the sounds of seventies disco. The group re-formed into place and for the next hour went through step after step, turn after turn, working the opening number to look like a dance routine from that era. Bella thought it was a lame way to open a pageant but her expertise was reporting, not gyrating the way Selina suggested they all do.

She noticed one of the lighting techs, Ben, off to the side, watching them. He was always sure with a smile, a quick hello. Nothing to concern her, but she made a mental note to mention it to Holden later. Maybe they needed to add Ben to her short list of Señora Rosenstein and Selina Barnes Colton. Everyone was a suspect until the killer was caught.

The music and routine soon became rote and Bella was able to observe each contestant around her, as well as the judges and board members who were present, watching every lift and spin. Somewhere among them was the person or persons who had conjured up the requirements that the winner of Ms. Mustang Valley be impossibly thin, and able to wear a size Bella last saw in middle school, if ever.

"Remember to make eye contact with the judges and smile!" Selina's raspy voice sounded over the music, the microphone taped to her cheek a bit overdone as far as Bella was concerned. Who was the star of the show, the contestants or this demanding woman known for her willingness to shove whomever she had to out of her way to maintain the spotlight?

"Watch it, Colton." It was Bella's only warning before her knees slammed to the floor, thanks to a well-placed leg that tripped her forward. Bella scrambled back up and looked at her bully, whose face was straight ahead as if nothing had happened. Recognition washed over her. Becky Hoskins, her high school nemesis.

"Hey, I'm in the same place as you, Becky. Just trying to win the scholarship." Her mental list of suspects grew to four with Becky's nasty attitude. The woman had bullied both her and Gio in high school. What did they say about bullies—that they rarely changed? But did it mean they became killers?

"Sure you are. We heard your pity story yesterday but give me a break. I've never heard of a poor Colton." Becky's mean-girl attitude hadn't improved since tenth grade. Even her physical appearance was the same; she was a slim brunette with her hair tied up in a high ponytail and exaggerated eyeliner.

The music abruptly ended and the stage was filled with the sound of labored breathing and shuffling feet.

"Hey, in the back, do you two want out of the pageant? Because we can arrange that, pronto."

"Selina's such a—"

"We're fine, Selina. Just making sure we get the steps right." Bella spoke up, knowing that Selina wasn't paying attention to anyone but herself as Bella danced through the number like a pro. Holden stood at the back of the stage and she risked a look back at him. He didn't move a muscle but the sparkle in his eyes conveyed that he was enjoying the show. Heat that had nothing to do with the physical exertion of the last hour crept up her throat, her cheeks; and her backside warmed where she imagined Holden's gaze.

This was not the ideal way to conduct an investigation, or to stay focused on being safe as she'd promised Holden. Not to mention the pact she had with her brothers to always pay attention and be aware of her surroundings. They'd made the promise to one another after their parents died because of their father's reckless driving. Their dad hadn't been known as a great guy; in fact, he'd not made much of himself and had made their mother's life miserable. And theirs. No way was Bella ever going to let her brothers down. Their bond had gotten them all a long way from sad days living under Aunt Amelia's thumb.

"Don't make us stop again. Everyone, take ten and be back here ready to go another hour." Selina's order broke through her conscience inventory and the other Colton woman walked off the stage as if she'd completed a solo dance routine on Broadway, but when she was on the floor in front of Bella she waggled her finger. "Isabella, come with me."

Don't go anywhere alone with anyone.

Holden's words echoed in her mind as she slowly walked to exit the stage. What was she going to do if Selina wanted a private talk elsewhere? It would be too obvious for Holden to follow them. Maybe he was right and she should have carried her weapon. But where would she holster it? There wasn't a concealing place on her as she wore yoga tights and tank top.

Selina stopped a few rows into the theater seats and faced Bella. Relief relaxed Bella's muscles but she tried to at least look halfway interested in what her distant, nonblood relative was about to say.

"What do you need, Selina?"

"I'll tell you what I need, Izzy." Selina's disdainful use of a childish name might have been unintentional, but it sounded mean. "I need you to back off and be quiet. There's no way I'm ever going to show any favoritism toward you. Got it?"

Bella got it, all right. But she couldn't say anything, not outright, not as a contestant, and certainly not while so many pageant personnel were listening.

"I'm sorry if I gave you the impression of expecting anything other than impartiality, Selina. Trust me, I'd never expect special treatment from you. I'm from the other side of the Coltons, remember?"

"How dare you question how I got where I am." Selina's nostrils flared and it wasn't particularly attractive on her already overly made-up face. No amount of contour cream could erase her ugly expression, stamped with anger. "I've earned every bit of my current status. Check the Colton Oil stock value. It's quadrupled since I was appointed to the board, and my PR skills are second to none in Arizona. You know how I got here? Hard work and brains. You should try it yourself, Ms. Mustang Valley Gabber."

Bella bit the inside of her cheek to keep from blurting out that she wasn't here as just another contestant and that Payne had given Selina an in at Colton Oil. "Reporting is a noble and important job, whether it's for the *New York Times* or the *Mustang Valley Gabber*. I'm not going to justify my career to you."

"Just see that you don't make the other girls think you have a leg up. Hmmph." Selina walked away as if Bella was no more than a speck of dust she'd had to flick off her shoulder. It would have been satisfying to inform her that none of the contestants were *girls*, but full-grown, adult women. But she couldn't risk getting kicked out of the pageant before she'd even begun to do her research.

Bella waited until the older woman was out of the auditorium before she headed for the staff room, where many of the contestants were sucking down water.

"What did she say to you, Colton?" One of the contestants sneered at her and Bella pasted the same smile she'd used with Selina on her face.

"She reminded me that this is a fair process and my last name has no effect on my scores."

"Here you go, Bella." Another, kinder contestant with dark hair offered her a water bottle from the refrigerator.

"Thanks." The cold bottle felt great against her forehead, her nape.

"I'm Marcie." She smiled, her patience and kindness a welcome respite from the cattiness of the morning.

"Bella."

"Don't let them get to you." Marcie unscrewed her water top.

"Who do you mean by *them*?"

"The ones who never make it to the top, but manage to ruin every pageant experience they possibly can. Like Selina. She used to compete, years ago, but never got any farther than Mustang Valley."

"How do you handle it, all the criticism?"

"I remember why I'm here. I need the scholarship." She was beautiful, with cornflower-blue eyes. "It's unlikely I'll get it this year, or even next, but my dance routine for the talent portion keeps improving and I get more confident with each try."

Bella wondered if this woman knew Gio, but she'd met most of Gio's pageant friends over the years, all of whom had dropped out by age twenty-five or so. Marcie appeared too young to have run with that crowd.

"How long have you been in pageants?" Bella worked at sounding casual, as if she needed a friend in this tough competition. What she really needed was a good source on the inside.

Marcie's gaze shifted up and to the left as she thought. "Mmm, about three years now. I started right after high school. I've got a great job with Mustang Valley Health First, the insurance company. But I want to do more. Like you, I'd like to become a nurse, or even a physician's assistant."

"Couldn't you apply for a scholarship through your workplace?" As soon as she asked, Bella bit the inside of her cheek. Marcie could throw the question back at her. *You're a contestant.* How did Holden do undercover work all the time? It was one thing to pose as a pageant competitor for this piece, where everyone knew she was also a blogger. But Holden had to pretend to be something he absolutely wasn't. And he'd had to take guff from Selina Colton, the wicked witch of Arizona from all accounts.

Marcie shook her head. "My company only pays fifty percent of tuition. I need to support my mom and younger siblings. My father died two years ago and my mom has MS. She just had a flare so it's been a rough year. I can't afford to lose the hours at work right now." Bella reminded herself that she'd give the scholarship to the runner-up if she found herself in the unlikely position of being crowned Ms. Mustang Valley.

"How are you managing work with the pageant?"

"We're lucky that all the rehearsals and practices are on the weekends and evenings."

Still, doing the mental math and comparing her own heavy work schedule to Marcie's, Bella knew it was a major effort to handle both.

"Don't look now, but you've got a sexy guy heading your way." Before she could reply, Marcie slinked off and Bella turned.

"Can I have a word with you?" Holden's presence filled up the room, or maybe it was her impression only. The rest of the women continued chatting and comparing notes on the day's routine.

"Sure." Was he going to say something about the obvious chemistry between them? She'd felt his gaze on her through the entire morning routine, and now, this close to him her skin tingled with his nearness.

This all had to be due to the high school building. It was saturated with the hormones and pheromones of students past and present, affecting her reaction to Holden.

She followed him out of the staff room and onto the stage, but in the far back, behind the heavy black curtains.

"It's stuffy back here." She made a show of tugging at

her tank top, and immediately hated herself for it. Now was not the time to go all girly on Holden.

"What did Selina say to you?"

Sadly, her instinct was on-target. Holden hadn't drawn her away for a quick romantic rendezvous. She ignored the rush of disappointment and let her arms drop to her sides.

"I'm surprised you weren't able to hear the show she put on for everyone. She made it clear that I'm not getting any special favors for being a Colton." She snorted. "I never have, for the record."

"We'll talk about that later. The next time someone asks to speak to you privately, make sure I'm within earshot."

"You're saying you weren't?"

"I couldn't get there soon enough without blowing my cover, or looking like a stalker. I saw you talking, though, and trust me, if I had to get in a shot, I would have."

A chill ran up her spine and it was hard to ascertain if it was fear, awe of his ability to talk about something so deadly with ease, or her unrelenting sexual attraction to him. Bella didn't like mixed romantic signals, even from herself.

"Good to know." She looked at him and his eyes narrowed.

"What?"

"I've added two people to my suspect list. Becky, one of the contestants, bullied both Gio and me in tenth grade. Her attitude hasn't changed. Selina's insistence on running the practices, even though there's a professional choreographer assigned to the numbers seems odd to me. And then, another person caught my attention. It's probably nothing, but one of the lighting techs, Ben, is always smiling at all the women, and he watches us from the side of the stage. I thought lighting techs were supposed to be up on the scaffolding, or in the tech booth?"

"I've noticed him, too. I'm keeping an eye on him, and the other techs, as well. Trust me, Bella. Trust me enough to do as I ask."

"Okay." A warm sense of belonging filled her. But to what? Holden? She hardly knew him.

You know him better than a lot of people.

A series of claps sounded from the other side of the curtain.

"Break time is over, ladies. Back at it now, please." The announcement sounded far off, as the speakers for the school's address system hung facing the theater seats, away from the stage.

"I need to go." She turned away from him, toward stage right.

"Bella, wait." His hands grasped her forearms and she sighed.

"What?" Exasperation tinged her voice and she didn't care. "I've got to get back without anyone seeing me near you."

"Which is why you need to circle back the other way." He tugged and she expected him to move to the side and let her pass through the curtained tunnel, toward the waiting group. Instead he allowed her momentum to bring their bodies against one another.

Shock of the best kind reverberated from where her breasts flattened against his chest, down to her belly, which settled on his pelvis. He let go of her arms and waited, let her decide the next move.

Bella had experienced her fair share of relationships,

had enjoyed the occasional surprise kiss with an attractive man. But no other man made her heartbeat do the tango before he'd ever touched her. She did the next practical thing and wrapped her arms around his neck, pressed her lips to his.

With zero hesitation she was immediately in the embrace of a man whose passion ran deep, if his kiss was any indication. His lips were firm and decisive, his tongue's masterful strokes leaving no question about his intent.

Holden wanted her.

His hands were on her buttocks, lifting her up and to him, and Bella couldn't get close enough to his hard arousal. She pulled back from the most delicious kiss of her life but before she could speak Holden's cheek was against hers, his moist breath against her ear.

"It's not one-way, Bella. We both want it. But it can't happen, not now, not here." A quick soft kiss to her cheek and he turned her around and gently nudged her toward her destination.

THE KISS WAS his best mistake to date, one he couldn't do the postmortem on until the case was over, the killer behind bars. Holden was grateful for the backstage darkness as he'd needed a few minutes to settle himself after that scorching thirty seconds in Bella's arms.

He agreed with Bella that the suspect pool was widening. But he knew from experience they could still be on the wrong scent. Was Bella's attacker someone they hadn't considered yet, someone protecting the Ms. Mustang Valley Pageant?

He couldn't call in to headquarters while he was monitoring the pageant practice. Frustrating, but a reality of his job.

When he got back to the stage area he counted the contestants and came up one short.

Leotard lady.

He immediately swung back around toward the restrooms, thinking she'd taken a quick run before Selina began her drill-sergeant tactics again. But seeing a blonde woman speaking intently to Bella stopped him. It was Leigh, a known member of the Affirmation Alliance, a local group Spencer suspected of shady practices—maybe even a cult. His pulse hammered at his temples as his protective instinct surged. Bella was vulnerable at the moment, having been attacked only yesterday and then having her home invaded by him, Spencer and Jarvis last night. Add MVPD's forensics team working outside, and it could only add to her stress. He took a couple of steps toward the group, then stopped. It would be too obvious to interrupt their conversation now. He'd have to catch Bella at lunch and warn her.

As he kept an eye on Bella and Leigh, he understood how people were attracted to the Affirmation Alliance. Their motto of "be your best you" and the promise of no more worries about anything but success would be tempting to anyone, but especially someone who was in a slump, whether it was due to work, health, or a combination of both. But it was too perfect, offering life satisfaction simply by joining the group. It had all the makings of a cult. Leigh might appear sincere, and maybe she was, but her repeated vacuous statements gave him the creeps. It didn't hurt that Leigh was the perfect image of a blonde bombshell with her platinum hair in curvy lengths around her porcelain, doll-like face, and her curvaceous figure would turn any guy's head.

Except Holden's. He seemed to only have eyes for a certain redhead these days, and worse, she was a reporter.

Chapter Eleven

"Okay, that's a wrap for the morning." Selina spoke with suffocating authority. She held up her hand. "Hang on a minute, though. I have an announcement from the pageant board. The judges have agreed to allow Bella Colton to remain in the contest since she and I are not related at all, and you all can no doubt already ascertain that I'd never give anyone an unfair advantage. You're all on the same level playing field here."

Several murmurs and a snide glance from Becky played out. Bella remained still, refusing to give in to Becky's emotional immaturity.

Selina clapped her hands together as if applauding herself. "That's that. You have forty-five minutes for lunch, ladies. May I remind you that there are only two weeks until you walk across this stage for the last time, with one of you garnering the crown of Ms. Mustang Valley. Ask yourself if the extra carbs are worth it, my friends."

If Bella had a coconut cream pie in hand she'd plant it on Selina's face. Bella could ignore that the woman was bossing her way around, shoving the choreographer to the side so that she could run the show, so to speak. But the admonishment to basically starve themselves was over the top. Was this how it all started, with a committee member basically telling the pageant contestants not to eat?

"I'm hungry. How about you, Marcie?"

Marcie blinked. "I'm always hungry. But you heard Selina. No pain, there will be a lot of gain." The petite woman looked down woefully at her rounded figure. "If I even look at a slice of bread I gain weight."

"That's not true, Marcie. We all need good nutrition. We're burning a ton of calories with all of this prancing around. C'mon."

Marcie's shorter legs hurried to keep up with Bella, who headed for the staff room. She had her heart set on devouring the turkey on rye she'd packed at zero-dark-thirty this morning.

"Mind if I join you?" Delilah, a willowy platinum blonde, fell into step behind them. "There are some scary ladies in this crowd, let me tell you."

"How do you know we're not two of them?" Bella couldn't help but wonder why the stunning woman who'd given the best reason for needing the scholarship would be intimidated by any other contestant.

"Trust me—I've competed against almost everyone here at one time or another. The nicest people can become ugly when so much money is at stake." Bella admired Delilah's composure and pragmatism. She'd given a heartrending speech about having survived cancer as a child, and needing the scholarship so that she could become a pediatric oncology nurse, her dream job. She'd not been able to attend college right after high school as her family needed her to go to work right away when her father became one-hundred-percent disabled in a mining accident.

"Tell me something, ladies. Does this pageant always encourage its contestants to starve?" Bella had to take this chance to get some answers.

Marcie shook her head. "I don't think they're telling us to starve."

"All pageants suggest eating healthy food, getting rid of the processed." Delilah shrugged. "It's not unique to Ms. Mustang Valley."

"Huh." Bella tried to appear mollified but her mind was doing cartwheels. This added credence to her thoughts that while she was certain Ms. Mustang Valley hadn't helped Gio in anyway, it might not be factual to state that this particular pageant had caused Gio's illness. As with all investigative reporting, she had to accept what appeared to be truth, not bend the facts to her opinion. It didn't make it easy, for sure. Not when Gio had suffered so much.

The other two women took Bella's silence as a sign the conversation was over and they all agreed to take their lunches to the school cafeteria and eat together at one of the long metal tables. A few of the other contestants were there, too, but sat separately and far enough away that conversations couldn't be overheard.

Bella saw Holden from the corner of her eye as he first walked around the cafeteria, checked the exterior doors to make sure they were locked and then lingered in the kitchen area which was visible through the various windows for different food services. It made her feel safe but also concerned her. What if the killer went after someone else while Holden's attention was on her?

"We know one another and have been through what, Marcie, five or six pageants together?" Delilah opened her bag to reveal a huge bowl of lettuce and not a lot else. Looking at the rabbit feast made Bella's stomach rumble.

"Seven if you count the Ms. Mustang Valley Holiday short pageant last year."

Delilah laughed. "When you decorated sugar cookies as your talent."

Marcie groaned and looked at Bella. "It was a total disaster. I thought it'd be easy-peasy. I bought several premade, plain cookies that were shaped like cacti. My plan was to paint them green for Christmas and blue and white for Chanukah, then add appropriately colored sprinkles."

"And?" Bella sipped her water.

"And she didn't realize that someone had put her frosting in the freezer the night before."

"Why would they do that?"

"So that I couldn't spread the frosting quickly, as you can imagine I needed to when we only have three minutes for our talent portion. It was awful. The cookies crumbled under the globs of sticky frosting that behaved more like a big, marshmallowy mess." Marcie's distress was still evident in the downturn of her mouth.

"I'm sorry, Marcie. It's hard doing the talent, I take it."

"It's not about the talent part, or that I failed miserably. What still makes my blood boil is that someone sabotaged me. I've never done anything to keep another contestant from doing her best. It's not my style." Marcie's cheeks were pink and her eyes sparkled. "If I ever figure out who it was, they'll be sorry."

Bella's hand froze over the bag of potato chips she'd brought as a side dish to her sandwich. "What do you mean?"

"She means she'll give them the Marcie dressing-down." Delilah sprinkled more vinegar on her greens and mixed it all with her plastic fork. "When Marcie gets going, no one's immune."

Marcie giggled and Bella discreetly expelled a breath. Still, she'd have to mention it to Holden. She knew a serial killer could come across as normal. Charming, even.

"I hope it doesn't come down to you telling someone off." Marcie's story had also been touching, about how she wanted to go to the community college to earn a business degree so that she could expand her hair styling job into her own salon.

"It won't. What I didn't say when we were giving our reasons for running for Ms. Mustang Valley is that I escaped an abusive marriage five years ago. I'd planned to go to school and had saved the money, in fact, from taking every extra wedding and prom appointment possible for over three years. My ex took the money and blew it in the casino, and on drugs."

"I'm so sorry, Marcie, that's awful." Bella reached across the table and grasped her hand.

"Delilah helped me get out of my house when my ex was at work."

So that explained the friendly bond she sensed between Delilah and Marcie.

"And you helped me when I was sick."

Guilt sucker punched Bella. "I knew you both in high school but never took the time to get to know you better. I wish I had."

"You didn't need anyone—you had your brothers, and you were always with Gio. We were all in awe of how protective your brothers were of you."

"I never saw it that way, but it makes sense now. I could have used more girlfriends, as my aunt was difficult at best. But you're right, I was tight with Gio." Darn it if her voice didn't hitch.

"I was so sad when she passed, Bella." Marcie's eyes moistened and reflected compassion. "She was such a sweet soul."

Delilah nodded. "Gio talked me off the ledge more than once. I get stage fright and if not for her I wouldn't still be competing. She was a doll."

"You mentioned earlier that you think Ms. Mustang Valley is like other pageants as far as encouraging the contestants to stay 'healthy.' As in, skinny. Has any other pageant ever suggested to you or someone you competed with that you need to lose weight? I'm trying to keep my mouth shut but I have to admit, with this being my first pageant, it's annoying to have Selina tell me to watch my carbs."

Marcie and Delilah exchanged knowing glances. Bella interpreted it as an understanding that she was clueless as to how the industry worked.

"Honey, when don't pageants tell you how you need to look?" Delilah motioned at her lunch. "Do you think I really like this much arugula?"

Marcie giggled. "I ignore it, as you can see." She nodded at her almost empty bowl of cold pasta salad. "The truth is that most local pageants aren't about physical beauty as much as they are about talent and aspirations."

"Except for Ms. Mustang Valley." Delilah's voice lowered dramatically. Bella's stomach tightened and the hair on her nape rose. She recognized it as her reporter's intuition.

"What do you mean?" She tried to make light of cleaning up her lunch refuse, not wanting either woman to hold back.

Delilah's brow rose. "It's known in Arizona pageant circles to be the worst as far as physical judging goes. And for some insane reason, the women who began their pageant careers with Ms. Mustang Valley hold it up as the holy grail, the one pageant that will make the biggest difference in their lives."

Interesting, but not enough to frame her article. "That makes sense since it's the only one that offers a full four-year scholarship to MVCC." MVCC was the largest community college in the area and boasted almost two dozen four-year career degree programs, while most just offered associate's degrees for two years of study. She'd discovered how much the college had expanded since she'd graduated from high school when she'd done her preliminary research for the Ms. Mustang Valley contest. And almost wished she had a chance of winning, so that she could have the thrill of giving the scholarship to the runner-up.

"It's more than that." Marcie's expression was grave. "It's almost as if they sign some kind of contract when they compete in this pageant."

"We all do." Bella had grimaced at some of the language, but it wasn't as bad as she'd feared.

"No, not the contract you signed for this year's Ms. Mustang Valley. They used to have to sign a lot more away, including any proceeds from commercial deals that came their way as a result of Ms. Mustang Valley, even if they didn't win."

"Isn't that standard?"

"Not at all, not anymore." Delilah kept her voice low. "There was a contestant one year in the same contest as Gio, Marcie and me, at the Ms. Saguaro Cactus pageant. She didn't win the crown but did receive a contract to appear in a national ad campaign for toothpaste—she had the brightest smile! At first she was so excited that she'd be making enough to not only put herself through college but her two sisters. Until—"

"Until the Ms. Mustang Valley contacted her and reminded her that she'd signed away rights to any monies when she'd entered her first contest, the Ms. Mustang Valley the year before." Marcie hadn't been able to contain herself, apparently, as she interrupted Delilah.

"How long ago was this?"

"Almost ten years now, I'd say."

Bella did the mental math. She wasn't positive but she was pretty certain Gio's first pageant had been Ms. Mustang Valley. And the way Gio had emphasized that the evidence of misdeeds was in the paperwork to this particular contest was interesting, but again, not enough to form a true exposé.

"You don't look like you believe us," Delilah spoke up.

"I absolutely believe you. I'm trying to match it with what Gio told me." On this, at least, she could be totally up-front with the women.

"You mean Gio signed one of those first contracts?" Marcie's face scrunched with puzzlement. "I don't remember her ever getting a contract related to the pageant."

"I'm not talking about that, but there was one advertising deal that Gio landed years ago. I'm wondering if something at the Ms. Mustang Valley Pageant, or someone, forced Gio to begin an unhealthy pattern of behavior that led to her eating disorder."

"If you're looking for that, just look around, Bella." Delilah seemed frustrated. "As much as Marcie said the pageants don't care about that impossible beach-body look, Ms. Mustang Valley winners are always very thin and fit a certain profile."

"Like what?"

Marcie nodded. "Yeah, Delilah's right. I've never known anyone with an ounce of extra weight to win this pageant."

"Yet they might win other Arizona pageants, but owe this pageant any financial gains?" Anger surged, making Bella hot and cold all at once. Was this why Gio had never treated herself after landing a lucrative contract that included her face on the bottle of a popular beach-hair-care product? Gio had won the contract from the Ms. Mustang Valley pageant the year she'd been a runner-up for the crown, before the MVCC scholarship had become the sole award. Had she not seen any of the proceeds? As her best friend, Bella felt she should know, but she and Gio didn't talk about their finances much, if at all. Would Gio's parents know?

The implication that Ms. Mustang Valley had contributed much to Gio's pain was clear to Bella, but it still wasn't enough for her report.

"If you're trying to find out why Gio had an eating disorder, that's complicated, honey." Delilah spoke with authority. "I've been there myself, and trust me, it's not a black-and-white situation. Sure, the pageant might encourage a smaller physique, but it always boils down to personal choice."

"Does it, though?" Bella wasn't going to let this sit. "Just as someone with cancer doesn't have a choice about getting it, the person with the eating disorder doesn't have a choice in how their brain chemistry works. If they're encouraged to lose weight in an unhealthy manner, it can trigger a latent tendency." Bella agreed, and saw that combined with not receiving all the money due her from the hair product ad, Gio had myriad reasons to fall into a depression.

"Right. So how can you prove that the pageant caused anyone's body dysmorphia or bulimia or anorexia?" Marcie stood. "We have to get back to the stage."

Bella threw her napkin into her paper bag. "It just sounds odd to me, is all. That the contestants of Ms. Mustang Valley have a higher rate of reported eating disorders than any other pageant in the state."

As soon as she spoke, she realized she'd gone too far. Either woman or both could easily see that she was investigating the pageant. Yet neither so much as batted a false eyelash as they made their way through the wide, dark high school corridors lined with lockers, back to the staff room and attached backstage. Bella supposed they were back in their mental game, rehearsing the dance steps and thinking about what they had to do next to secure the top spot.

They were near the last turn toward the staff room when a locker door burst open and a huge *boom* sounded with a bright white flash, reverberating through the floor and Bella's feet, landing her on her bottom next to Delilah and Marcie, who had also been blown back.

Marcie's scream sounded far away, more like a squeal, but with her ears ringing and almost blinded by the flash, all Bella could think about was getting away from the explosion.

"This way!" Delilah grabbed both of their arms, tugged them back, away from what Bella now saw was a large cloud. Too late, she realized it was more than an explosion—there was a cloud of something hanging in the air and her eyes began to sting. They'd been gassed.

HOLDEN HEARD THE explosion at the same moment he saw the locker spring open. He'd been trailing the women on their way back from the cafeteria, annoyed that Bella had gone so far away from the main group all for the sake of her story. Nothing was worth her safety, not when she was the target of a serial killer.

He saw the filmy cloud appear from the locker and immediately went into biohazard-emergency mode.

"Don't breathe—hold your breath!" He did the same as he raced toward them, reaching the three just as Marcie's body hit the deck. Bella had scrambled to her feet and begun to run away, along with Delilah, and he pointed toward the end of the hallway as he held his breath and threw Marcie over his shoulder. His eyes burned and teared but he had only to get them to the exit doors, approximately one hundred feet away, and out into the fresh air.

His entire focus should be on the safety of everyone but all he felt in the moment was relief that Bella was okay, or at least would be, once clear of the detonation site. He'd never had such a visceral reaction to a citizen he was supposed to be protecting before.

They barreled through the double doors and an alarm immediately sounded, which he knew would summon MVPD.

Marcie began to cough and sputter as he lowered her to the ground, and Bella immediately supported the woman around her shoulders, squatting down to Marcie's level.

"You're okay, hon. Let it out." Bella looked up at

Holden and he wanted to take the anxiety, fear and anger from her. But he couldn't, no one could, until they found the perpetrator. He didn't even know if this was the same criminal who'd attacked Bella, or if it was also the serial killer.

The case grew more tangled with each incident. Not unlike his feelings for the woman whose beseeching glance tore at his insides.

"Are you okay, Bella? Delilah?" He checked each response, and nodded at Marcie. "I'm pretty sure it was tear gas. You'll feel better the longer you're away from it." As he spoke, he became aware of the hot sun beating down on all of them, the lack of breeze. "Let's all move to under the stadium seating." The rest of the pageant contestants and board were pouring out of the staff room. He suspected the gas was tear gas, from all the reactions so far. It'd be difficult for anyone but the US military to obtain anything more toxic. But he wasn't going to allow anyone near the detonation site until he was certain.

"Over here, under the bleachers." He called to them and motioned toward where the other three huddled, in the shade. Sirens sounded and he figured he'd have backup in another minute.

As the women headed toward the football arena he called Spencer.

"Talk to me, Holden."

"Detonation in a hallway locker, right near the staff room. Similar to a flashbang but it shot out of the locker so quickly I couldn't assess it. Gas, most likely tear gas, followed. Bella and two other contestants were the targets. Marcie was knocked out from the percussion but is coming around. Bella and Delilah are safe, and I'm about to take a head count. Send the EMTs to the football stadium. I've directed all evacuees to head under the bleachers for shade."

"We're turning into the school now. Talk to you on-site." Spencer disconnected as Holden spotted the first of the several response vehicles he expected.

Holden counted the personnel as they exited the building. All were accounted for save one. He counted again, matched faces to names, and his stomach sank. While Leotard Lady, real name Debra Juarez, was back, and looking quite shaken, another one of the contestants was missing.

Chapter Twelve

"Anybody see Becky?" He'd memorized the list and knew the woman who'd given Bella a hard time earlier, about being a Colton, was the missing person. So far, she fit the profile of the killer more than his other suspects, but his training kept him from jumping to any conclusions about anyone.

Selina Colton shook her head, walking over to him. "No, and I haven't seen her since before our lunch break. She and Bella, Marcie and Delilah are missing."

"Bella, Delilah and Marcie are under the bleachers. Marcie's going to need medical attention. Stay with them and wait there for the police and EMTs."

For once Selina didn't argue and walked off toward the rest of the group.

Holden called Spencer.

"I've got to go back inside to find Becky. She's the missing person. The rest of the pageant contestants, and the board, are at the football field bleachers."

"Wait for backup, Holden."

"I can't—she could be unconscious." Or worse, if the serial killer had something to do with this. Spencer knew it, too. "You're right behind me, anyhow."

"We are. I'll send a team into the school, through the

doors you exited. You take the stage and staff room, until we get there. Be careful, Holden. This guy's playing for keeps."

"Roger." He shoved his phone back in his pocket and drew his weapon. The side stage exit door was still wide open and he made sure to prop it with a wedge he found just inside the door. The more air that got into the building, the better. He didn't notice any fire related to the explosion, so that was one stroke of luck in all of this.

It didn't take long to clear the stage and auditorium, followed by the staff room. He didn't go back into the hallway where the tear gas could still linger, as the door between the staff room and corridor was closed and had left the staff room behind the stage clear. Whoever had rigged the locker knew enough to enable a remote detonation. It wouldn't take a rocket scientist but this criminal wasn't unintelligent, either.

Still no sign of Becky, though. There were two spots left, the steps that were used to access below stage for special effects, and the deepest places backstage, where all that normally stood were old props. Holden circled back to them, checking every niche behind the long stage curtains, weapon held in front of him. Satisfied that no one remained on the stage, he crept to the small stairwell nestled at the far right backstage.

And found Becky, her brunette ponytail askew, lying still at the bottom of the seven steps.

"Drink up, everyone." The EMTs handed out bottles of cold water and Bella gratefully gulped from hers. Marcie was being attended to, and she and Delilah had checked out okay as did the rest of the pageant members.

Except Becky.

"I should have waited until we were all together before we left the stage," Selina verbally berated herself. Selina faced off with Bella. "Did you push her?"

Her words hit Bella in her gut and it took every ounce of her self-control to not verbally lash out at Selina.

"How dare you accuse me! Was it you?" Selina's eyes widened and if she had talons, Bella knew the other woman would have dug them into her. Bella waved her hands in a surrender gesture before Selina's fury erupted.

"Forget I said that. You and I couldn't have hurt Becky, am I right? None of us could have known what happened to Becky—we were nowhere near the backstage stairs, not one of us, right?" Bella made eye contact with each person in the group, contestants and judges alike, as they stood around in a wide circle, eager to hear the dialogue between her and Selina. One by one, they each looked at the person next to them, and shook their head in confirmation that they'd been together. Within a minute, everyone had been accounted for and determined to be nowhere near the backstage doors at the time of the explosion.

Bella nodded. "Exactly. None of us is to blame. It was more important to get everyone out of the building after the explosion than to go back and search. That had to be left to the professionals." Bella hoped Selina got the hint. Bella had no time for her drama. The murderer was giving them enough of it. She knew Holden wouldn't say it was the serial killer for certain, but she had no doubt it was, even though Becky's hair didn't fit the profile. Only hers did, with the red highlights. Why would anyone else put the pageant through all of this? And wouldn't an explosion be the perfect way to distract everyone, especially Holden, enough to kidnap one of the contestants?

But "one of the contestants" was supposed to be Bella. She fingered her hair, which had fallen out of its ponytail. Her red hair was a beacon to the killer. So why hadn't he tried to grab her in the chaos of the explosion and tear gas? Why did he go after Becky?

It impressed her that Holden was so certain it was tear gas. He'd had in-depth training at Quantico, she knew, but still. Bella wouldn't know the difference between tear gas and a heavy fog until her eyes began to water.

She'd escaped the effects of the tear gas, as had Holden and Delilah. But Marcie's eyes were still streaming tears and her skin was a ruddy shade. A fierce sense of protection welled inside her gut. Bella had only known these women, her competition, for two days and yet she felt they were part of a team.

Even Becky, for all her bluster and meddling.

"Look!" Delilah stood beside her, gaze glued to the scene at the open stage doors. EMTs were running across the small field, carrying a board. They disappeared into the building and Bella's stomach dropped. "They've probably found Becky. I hope she's okay."

"Me, too." But while she was concerned about Becky, Bella couldn't keep from worrying about Holden. What if he'd encountered the killer in the school's hallways and been hurt, or worse?

And why was she so invested in a man she'd met a little more than twenty-four hours ago?

You already know that answer.

She'd watched friends fall for someone they barely knew. She'd also seen her brother Spencer fall hard for his now-fiancée, Katrina, in a very short amount of time.

When it came to finding the person you cared about more deeply than anyone else, time didn't seem to be a factor. One day or one year could be equal. But she wasn't falling for Holden.

No, Holden was the agent in charge of a special investigation. She was an undercover reporter hoping to avenge Gio's too-early death and to advance her career, truth be told.

It wasn't the time for even a brief fling, much less contemplating whether she'd met her match.

Bella was good at logic. It was all part of being a top-notch blogger and reporter. But logic and common sense blew apart into tiny shards that pierced her heart when she saw the EMTs emerge from the school with a woman, Becky, strapped to their board. At least Becky had color in her cheeks and appeared to be trying to talk, a good sign. Relief began to ease the tightness in her shoulders. Holden walked several steps behind, talking to Spencer as he led Boris to a spot to go to the bathroom.

The sight of Holden behaving completely normally lifted the rest of the tightness in her muscles. Was it normal to be this relieved, this joyous, that Holden was totally fine?

Probably not.

She was in trouble, and not just from a killer.

"It's important that we take twenty-four hours off to search the school and clear any remaining explosives." Spencer spoke in front of the group of pageant officials, contestants and stage techs huddled under the stadium benches. "Seeing that you've all already been out here for too long, it's time to call it a day and go home."

"Wait a minute." Selina spoke up, her face flushed but otherwise not showing an iota of stress. Holden hadn't appreciated how she'd been so rude to Bella but he had to give the woman credit for composure. "You can't stop the pageant. We'll just have to move it to another venue until you declare the building safe again."

"I'm afraid that's not going to happen, either." Holden stood next to Spencer. They'd already gone over how to handle this expected reaction. "We've got the security in place here to monitor the pageant. It will take at least two weeks to find and set up security at another place in Mustang Valley."

"You're a security guard. I'll take direction from MVPD, thank you very much." Selina was back in full-blown pill mode.

"Mr. St. Clair is a qualified security expert." Spencer vouched for him, unable to reveal their ties or Holden's true identity. "He's right. Either take a full day off and continue the pageant preparations the day after tomorrow, or cancel the whole thing now."

Grumbles and complaints rolled through the small group but didn't last. Either they were all wiped from being out in the Arizona heat or frightened enough by the day's events to go along with whatever Spencer suggested. Holden watched them all carefully, and kept a hand on his phone in case his handler texted or called with information on Selina. Holden had asked him to check where she'd been during the two pageants that involved killings.

"What happened to Becky?" Marcie stood near Bella, in the spot Holden wished he were—close enough to touch her.

"Becky's got a severe sprain, maybe a broken ankle."

Spencer took his ball cap off and ran his hand over his sweating brow, then replaced it. He wore full protective gear, dressed in a tactical response uniform. Boris, his impressive K-9, was in the air-conditioned MVPD K-9 SUV. "She was regaining consciousness as the EMTs moved her to the ambulance."

"Fess up, Colton. Did you push her?" Laurel, a woman Holden had noticed seemed to stay quiet until one of the pot-stirrers like Becky spoke up, accused Bella to her face.

"I wasn't anywhere near the back stage doors all morning, in case you didn't notice." Bella held her own.

"Then it had to be you." Laurel turned to Selina. "You Coltons don't like being found out. There's no doubt you're going to give Bella extra points for being a relative. Becky had the ovaries to call you out."

"I've never been out of your sight all morning. Unless you weren't paying attention to the choreography?" One hundred and ten degrees in the shade and Selina kept her cool.

"That's enough." Mimi stepped in front of the group. "This isn't about the pageant anymore. It's about the safety of all of you, and the security of the school building. We're breaking until eight a.m. the day after tomorrow. I suggest you all practice the two routines Selina has already given you, and use the time to work on your talent portion."

"I can set us all up on videoconference. Anyone without a personal computer or laptop, talk to me and I'll have one sent to your home." Selina finally used her Colton bank for good. "I'll see you virtually tomorrow morning." Selina started for her car and a few of the contestants followed.

Bella walked up to Holden and spoke to him and Spencer privately. "I'm going back to my house to cool off. I can take Boris with me if you want, Spencer."

"You're going nowhere on your own, Bella." Holden tried to keep the growl out of his voice but he was working from a primal instinct he couldn't remember ever feeling before.

Heat flashed in her eyes, the visceral connection between them palpable.

"I can drive myself to the dang police station and wait while you two do whatever you need to here."

"Bella, go home with Holden. He's not part of the sweep." Spencer looked at Holden with understanding. He knew better than anyone how stubborn his sister could be. "We've ascertained your house is clear last night, and I've had a unit there all day, with two additional officers patrolling your property. Your house is safe as long as Holden is with you. I can't risk you going anywhere else, Bella. You could lead the killer to innocent people."

Bella's eyes widened, her cheeks pink with anger. "Wait a minute. You're blaming me for the explosion, for Becky's nasty fall?"

"Of course he's not." Holden knew he had to share in the line of fire with Spencer. "There's a criminal here, possibly a serial killer."

"You mean *probably*, don't you?"

"I can't confirm anything yet."

"Give Holden a break, Bella. Now's not the time to get all reporter on anyone."

"Oh, that's rich, Spencer. You telling me how to do my job."

"I just want you to be safe, sis." Spencer must have

heard the hurt in Bella's tone. Holden wanted to take her away from all of this, to another state, another country. Anywhere but here, where the omnipresent sense of danger lurking wouldn't shake.

Bella's posture softened a smidge. "I know. But I have a job to do, too, you know. I can't do it from my house, no matter how safe. I have to figure out where the files from the Ms. Mustang Valley archive have been taken. I need to go through them, see if any of the suspects I'm looking at have evidence in them."

"Who are you looking at?" Spencer looked at Bella, then Holden.

Bella told him about Becky, Selina, Hannah Rosenstein, and Ben the lighting guy.

"You're right, sis—you need the information they contain. Someone on the committee knows where they are, and probably what's in them."

"Bella's already done a lot of the same background research that we did in our field office. But we still don't have motivation or corroboration on the suspects that are on the Ms. Mustang Valley committee."

Holden took a step closer to her and placed his arm around Bella's waist. He saw Spencer's brow raise. He didn't care. They were working a life-or-death operation and he suddenly didn't care what his best friend or anyone else thought about the nature of his relationship with Bella. His grandmother had told him that some connections were visceral, inexplicable. His attraction to—and protective instinct toward—Bella fell into that category.

Bella looked up at him, met his gaze and held it. If he was able to trust that it wasn't just wishful thinking on his part, he would say he saw a flicker of trust in her eyes. Trust in him.

"Do you think so?"

"I do. And if anyone can get someone to spill, you can. It just won't be over the next thirty-six hours." He turned to Spencer. "I've got your sister's back, Spencer."

Spencer nodded. "I know you do. I'll make sure the patrol remains in place regardless. For both of your sakes."

Holden had to fight the urge to keep his arm wrapped around Bella's waist and pull her to him as they walked across the wide field to the parking lot. He opened the door for her and then got in the driver's side of his nondescript sedan.

"Please try to see it from my point of view. This is my only chance to get this story right, and I'm coming up against brick walls in every direction." Bella spoke the moment his butt hit the car seat, and he had no doubt she was hyped up on adrenaline.

He put the car into gear and drove out of the school lot. "There are other pageants in the area, aren't there?"

"None is as important as this one, from all Gio told me. It's Ms. Mustang Valley where Gio got her start in the pageant business, and when she said her eating disorders began. I should know, as I tried to get her into a doctor six years ago, after that year's Ms Mustang Valley. For some reason, Gio's illness always flared around the time of this pageant."

"You never noticed she had issues before then?" She'd mentioned that she and Gio had been friends since grade school.

Bella sighed. "Not at the time. We did everything together, from summer camps to sleepovers. I thought Gio never ate differently than the rest of us, and she told me herself that her problems with body image and food began when she entered this pageant for the first time. Looking back, I suppose her problems may have began many years earlier than I originally thought."

"How many times did she compete in Ms. Mustang Valley?"

"Eight. Until last year, actually, when her physical appearance began to visibly suffer from the bulimia. There was a point when no amount of clothing or cosmetics could hide the toll of the bingeing and purging. It affected her mental health far longer, but it wasn't as physically visible until it was too late." He shot a look at Bella's resolute profile, the passing desert scenery serving as a colorful backdrop. The timelessness of her beauty struck him and he forced his gaze back to the road.

"It had to be incredibly difficult to watch that. When did she tell you she had a problem, or did you figure it out first?"

Bella shook her head. "That's just it. It was insidious. I had no clue at first, years ago. But gradually her symptoms began to add up to me. Her depression, bouts with anxiety, her obsession with food. Then I noticed her teeth were yellowed. Gio always had a bright smile and I asked her if she was smoking. She laughed and said no, it was from an antibiotic she'd taken as a kid. But I knew that wasn't true. Her mother spoke to me, as she was worried, too, as was her entire family. They thought I'd be able to convince her to go to the hospital. Gio had blown off their concerns. I begged her to get help, even offered to drive her to a clinic for treatment of eating disorders. Gio refused, said she'd fix it herself. Now I realize that we were both in denial of how lethal her illness was. Her mother called me a couple of months later and asked to meet me. She told me Gio had entered rehab and was in treatment. I couldn't visit her for the first part, but I did go several times to visit, when allowed."

"But that rehab time didn't do it for Gio?"

She let out a bitter laugh. "No. That's the hard part. Just like a drug addict or alcoholic, it can take several attempts to achieve a level of health that is sustainable. Gio went through treatment five times, and it looked like she was going to make it the last time. She gained weight and went back to work."

"But?" He turned onto her driveway, nodding at the MVPD officer in the cruiser on the street.

"It didn't hold. Less than two years later she was gone."

He turned off the engine and faced her. "You don't still blame yourself, do you?"

"How can I not? Sure, I've read the literature, spoken to my own therapist about it." She bit her lower lip as if regretting her admission. "I go to a counselor regularly, about once every other month. I used to go weekly after my parents died, and then again when my aunt died and my brothers and I were on our own. Despite our last name, none of the larger-than-life Coltons so much as invited us to dinner."

"That's rough. Let's go inside." He didn't want her to get warm again and the AC's effect was dissipating quickly.

"Sure, but Holden?"

"Yeah?"

"Thanks for listening. You have a lot on your mind with this case, and I'm sure the last thing you expected was to listen to a sad story."

"No problem."

No problem? He got out of the car before he said something equally ridiculous.

Bella was ahead of him and waited while he opened her door, following him only after he'd cleared the house.

As the front door closed she headed for the kitchen. Without preamble she opened the refrigerator and pulled out a pitcher of water and filled a large tumbler with an Arizona State logo. Bella gulped until it was empty, and immediately refilled it. Only after she'd finished half of the second did she stop and look at him.

"Do you want some?" Her face was flushed and large splotches of wet dotted her white tank top, dirtied from the explosion. Her breasts pressed against the light material and her skin glistened with perspiration. He rued the presence of her sports bra, which prevented him from seeing the outline of what he imagined to be perfectly round, rosy nipples.

He wished her sweat was from a long round of love-making, of bringing her to climax, and not from her being dehydrated.

"Yeah." He wanted "something" all right. But it wasn't anything he had a right to ask for.

She put the plastic insulated cup down. "Holden."

"Pour me a glass, Bella."

"Here you go." Bella handed him a glass and he carefully accepted it from the bottom, avoiding any physical contact. He was using every skill he possessed to keep an erection from becoming obvious.

But nothing was enough to dowse the fire Bella lit. If

he did something stupid, like kiss her, how much would he regret it?

"I've got to get a shower." With no further preamble, Bella turned and fled toward her room.

Chapter Thirteen

Bella was always mindful of water usage and made her showers short and functional whenever possible. But today had been a zinger and she needed to cool off. It wasn't from the hot sun, dance practice or running to escape the locker explosion, though.

Her body was on fire for Holden.

"Stay on course." After shutting off the shower she grabbed a towel and scrubbed herself dry. Nothing was enough of a distraction from her treacherous libido, though. Why hadn't she taken up with that pro baseball player who'd asked her out twice this past spring?

Because his brains didn't match his wallet, he didn't ignite the flame she wanted lit. Instead of regret at the road not taken, she was relieved that she wasn't attached to anyone. She was free to pursue any man she chose.

And for tonight, she chose Holden. May as well own up to it. Without further thought, she donned her silk robe that barely hit her upper thighs and belted it snugly around her waist, liking how the material provided just the right amount of support for her small breasts. Grabbing a condom from her nightstand, she slipped it into her pocket and went out into the kitchen and great room.

Holden lay on the sofa, stretched out to his full

length. She placed him at six-three or six-four, as Spencer was six feet tall and Holden was taller than him. Padding across the wide-planked flooring in bare feet, she stopped no more than a foot from him. His arms were crossed and his head lay to the side, facing the back of the couch. She could make out the curve of his ear and the shadow of his short-cropped hair on the side of his head.

"Holden?" She whispered his name, her belly tightening as she anticipated his touch. Since he'd kissed her literally senseless behind the stage curtain, all Bella thought of when she looked at him was how it would feel to go beyond the kisses and into the full depth of Holden's lovemaking.

At first she thought she heard wrong, that maybe he'd said an endearment instead of her name. Until she leaned over him, straining to hear, and recognized that Holden wasn't talking.

He was snoring.

HOLDEN WOKE TO the aromas of coffee and bacon, two of his favorite scents. Second and third after the scent of female, which now took a place behind the scent of one particular woman.

Bella.

He looked at his watch, an antiquity he refused to give up even though most agents relied on their phones. He'd slept eight hours solid after Bella went back to her room, waking only when his alarm vibrated every two hours for him to do a house check. He trusted MVPD and the officers patrolling the yard to keep them secure, but he still wanted to check the inside regularly.

It'd taken every iota of bearing he had to not move

when Bella came into the room. He'd started to doze off but immediately alerted when he heard her steps, then picked up her scent. A soft floral scent, belying the tough-skinned reporter image she projected. Mingled with what was undeniably her scent—musky, sexy, the epitome of feminine. Pure Bella.

It felt like it had been years instead of days that he'd had to keep his arms crossed, make himself not reach for her, grasp her waist, pull her to him, have her straddle him and allow him to press his erection against her until she writhed and they went back to her bedroom. Because he was going to make love to her in her bed, all night long.

Just not last night, or tonight, or anytime that he was on duty with the serial killer case. It was a rookie mistake to get involved with a civilian during an open investigation. He wasn't about to compound it by risking her safety.

"You're finally moving. Here's your coffee." She greeted him from the kitchen but stayed there, didn't come close to him again. He felt like a class-A jerk.

"I was up every two hours, checking around." He stretched, got up, walked to the counter. "Thanks."

"I'm making eggs, if you want some." She deftly cracked a brown egg against a clear glass bowl and looked at him.

"Sure, but only if you'll let me make lunch."

"Your job is to protect and serve, not cook." She added more eggs, tossed in salt, pepper, cayenne and whisked them into a frothy concoction with a fork. Her defensive posture reflected what he'd feared.

"You know I wasn't sleeping last night."

"Yeah. Got that figured out." She ignited the burner

under a large pan, melted butter, poured the eggs. All without looking at him.

"It's not that I don't want to—"

"Spare me the integrity routine, Holden. My brother's a cop, remember? I know the rules as well as anyone. You can't get involved with someone during a case, especially one like this with the stakes so high. And you're protecting me, so you don't want to get distracted in any way, especially that way. Even if we did decide to pursue a connection it's pointless, in the long run. You live two hours away in a big city—I'm here in Mustang Valley. You're a big bad federal agent and I'm your nemesis, a reporter."

"You're a blogger." Wasn't that reporting light?

"A blogger and a journalist who is trying to get a job as an investigative reporter. Geesh, Holden, you still grimace whenever the word *reporter* comes up. What is your exact problem with the news media? It has to be more than what you told me in the diner."

"I don't have a problem with the media. The public needs information and it's the best way to deliver it. My problem is that I don't appreciate anything but the truth when it comes to reporting." He paused, then decided to just say it. "And I am not impressed with the dishonesty reporters utilize to get their story."

"Hmm." She moved a spatula around the pan, scrambling the eggs into fluffy clouds. He noticed the sexy robe from last night—he'd peeked—was replaced by yoga capris and a tank top. Her hair was up in a high ponytail and she had zero makeup on. And was more startlingly beautiful than ever.

Discomfort had him lean against the counter, eager to figure out what she was thinking.

After she dished up the eggs, she slid a plate and fork to him and took her plate around the counter. They sat at the same small table as yesterday.

Holden had no idea how it'd happened, but one day felt like years. As if Bella had always been a part of his life. What did Grandma St. Clair used to say? That it only took a minute when it was the right one? She'd say that whenever she told the story about meeting Grandpa in Paris right after World War II.

Was Bella his match?

"Stop it." She sipped her coffee, ate a few bites.

"What?" He decided to dig into the food before he said something more inflammatory.

"You're trying to figure out why I'm not exploding at your nasty dig toward reporters. I don't know a lot, Holden, but I do know that it's never smart to generalize or label. I'm not some jerk trying to get a story by hurting anyone or lying to them."

"You're undercover, though, pretending to be in the pageant."

She set her mug down a little firmer than necessary and her coffee sloshed over the edge. Her eyes were fire as she looked at him while sopping up the spill with her paper napkin.

"I'm not pretending to be anything, Holden. I'm in the pageant, a bona fide contestant."

"You mean to tell me you're going to take the scholarship if you win?"

She snorted, then giggled, then burst out into a belly laugh. "Holden, you are hilarious. Do you really think there's any chance of me winning this competition? Have you even looked at the other women who are close to my age? They've been doing this far longer and have the system down." She wiped her eyes with her hands. He'd made her cry, all right. To him, she was the clear winner in any competition.

"It's a fair question."

"It is. And if I won, I'd pass the scholarship on to my runner-up. But I have no reason to think I'm even in the top three. Gio used to say that by the end of day one it was pretty clear who the top five were. Trust me—it's not me."

"Who do you think it is, then?"

She tilted her head. "Marcie, because she's been around and has all the right answers, Delilah because she's Delilah, Leigh because even though she's odd, she's always on-brand, and maybe Becky. Do you know what's going on with her?"

He nodded. "Spencer said she's broken her ankle. It twisted when she was shoved down the backstage stairs. She's out of the pageant."

"Okay, so someone else is number four. And five could be any of the competitors, but definitely not me. The pageants haven't had a debut contestant final in the last ten years."

"You got this from Gio?"

She nodded. "Yes. Frankly, I have enough to write an exposé of the pageant industry in Mustang Valley, maybe even Arizona, from all that Gio's told me. But I can only corroborate it with her mother. It's not enough. And for the record? I think Leigh's a shoo-in to win. She's a little over-the-top with her positive-thinking preaching, but I sense she has a heart of gold. She has the enthusiasm needed to win." Bella's candor and total unselfconsciousness tugged at something deep in his chest. A small part of the glacier that was otherwise known as his heart broke away. He couldn't hold back what he knew had to be a silly grin.

"What's so funny?"

"Aww, nothing. Just thinking about how glaciers calve icebergs."

"Some the size of small continents lately." She alluded to climate change, but like a true reporter didn't reveal how she felt about it. Which made him respect, and like her even more.

Like or lust?

He definitely was attracted to Bella—insanely so. But for the first time in forever, he was also impressed by a woman's sense of honor, integrity. Nothing like his ex.

"Now you're frowning, Holden." He liked how his name sounded on her lips. Crisp but a loving roll to it.

"I'm thinking I may owe you an apology."

"Why is that? Are you done?" She nodded at his empty plate, then carried it to the sink when he raised his hands.

"Thanks." He grabbed their mugs and glasses and set them on the counter. "Breakfast was delicious."

"You're welcome." She pulled out latex gloves and he took them from her.

"I'll clean up. You cooked—you're done."

"It's not necessary—"

"Please." He didn't budge, didn't let his gaze drift to where the tank top bared her shoulder and the lone angel drawn on it. An angel the size of a tiny fairy rested on her skin, its pink wings and hair unmistakably feminine.

"Fine. But tell me why you're so against reporters while you clean up."

She was so close, her scent teasing him as it had last

night. Washing dishes was going to be his most difficult task to date on this case.

At least it kept his hands busy, and off Bella.

Chapter Fourteen

Holden was looking at her with those bedroom eyes again. Did he realize it? Or was that expression purely a physical reaction to the chemistry that smoldered between them? Before she had a chance to consider asking him, he threw a dishtowel over his shoulder and went to work filling the sink with sudsy water.

"There's room for a dishwasher but since it's just me I haven't been in a hurry to get one."

"You don't need one. I'm here." He flashed his smile and she leaned a hip against the counter to keep from swooning toward him. Hopefully she appeared casual, not overly interested.

"Thanks. So, about your reporter hate?"

"*Hate* is the wrong word. My grandmother always said not to use it unless you really mean it."

"Is she still here?"

"No, she passed away a couple of years ago. Ninety-nine years old and still tending the same ten acres I ran around on as a kid." A wistful expression rolled across his face. "Funny, that's the second time I've thought of her in as many days."

"I've been thinking about my mom lately, too. Maybe

it's the pageant, or having our lives threatened?" She tried to make it light but the words were heavy.

He finished up and faced her. "I've had one or two scary situations. Most of my work is actually pretty boring, much more than, say, Spencer's job as a sergeant and a K-9 handler. I'm not around the public each day, only when an investigation calls for it. It's easy for me to end up in the office every day, all day, for long periods as I do research and search archival evidence for clues. But the few times I've thought I might be facing death, yeah, I've had thoughts of my loved ones. I think it's natural."

"I can't say I've ever thought my life was being threatened until today with the explosion. The attack yesterday remains pretty much a blank still, other than what I already told you I remember. I'm not thrilled that someone planted surveillance equipment on my property, either, but again, that's creepy, not life-threatening."

He regarded her steadily. Not willing to look away, she allowed the heat to rise, to circle and settle in her most sensitive places. Was this when Holden was finally going to break down and do more than kiss her?

"About your question. Yes, I have a good reason for detesting reporters." At what must have been her annoyed expression he held up a hand. "Most reporters. Okay, some reporters. My ex Nicole Drew was a reporter. I went into the relationship knowing it, and ignoring it for the most part. I had no reason to judge her or her profession."

"Until?" She sensed his hesitancy to spill the truth. As if he was ashamed, or didn't want to betray his ex's confidence.

"Until I found out she was using me to get the information for an important story. The story? It involved another case I worked on. She tried to manipulate me to tell her classified information."

"I'm sorry that happened to you, Holden. That's rough."

"Rough isn't all of it, believe me. I am a total believer in free speech and the public's right to know where their tax dollars are going. But not when it comes to the security of an ongoing case, or an innocent civilian's safety."

"That can be a hard line at times." She thought about how her presence in the pageant might be what was drawing the attacker or killer out, but she didn't want to quit until she got her story. Was that what Holden was talking about?

"Yes and no, Bella. Would you put someone's life at risk for a story?"

"Isn't that what I'm doing? Putting everyone at risk in Ms. Mustang Valley because I have red streaks in my hair and I'm not quitting? Would you have to spend any time away from the pageant or school if I weren't still in the contest?"

"No, I'd be at the school for most of my time. Which isn't always the answer, to be at the event venue. Killers go for live bodies, not buildings. Today's explosion was an exception, a distraction so that no one would see Becky get shoved down the stairs. I'm convinced it wasn't an accident—she's been in Ms. Mustang Valley eight of the last ten years. She graduated from Mustang Valley High, your classmate if I'm correct. There's no way she'd miss those stairs."

She watched him speak, saw the depth of emotion behind his words. Holden was the epitome of dedication to duty and if she wasn't already hot for his smoking bod, she'd be drawn to his honesty and intensity. Totally.

"Have you heard any more about what Becky remembers? Does she know who pushed her?"

He leaned back and picked up his phone, tapped and scrolled for a few seconds. "Yes. But no, she doesn't know who pushed her. According to Spencer, she was grabbed from behind, heard a scary voice tell her "Leave Colton alone," and then she was dragged to the stairwell. The last she remembers are hands on her back, throwing her into the pit. No one heard her scream because of the explosion."

Chills pricked at her nape. "That's horrible! And sounds exactly like the person who attacked me."

Holden nodded. "Agreed. But there's nothing we can do about it right now. Spencer and the rest of MVPD are all over the school, combing the area for evidence of any kind. The surveillance equipment we found here didn't have any prints but my officemate is searching for possible retailers."

"That's a needle in a humongous haystack." She couldn't imagine narrowing down what had looked to her like a standard surveillance camera to one particular retailer.

"Yes, but you never know. We catch criminals best when we're working all the angles."

"I'm sorry you can't be in the thick of it, Holden."

"But I am. I couldn't be at the school now, or I'd risk blowing my cover. Too many of the agents and local MVPD know me and might unwittingly reveal my true identity. I've got my laptop and I can access some sites, though not most of the ones I'd need. I'm okay with being here, Bella."

"Tell me the same in twelve hours. We're still not leaving until tomorrow morning, are we?"

"Nope. You are correct." The smoldering look was back in his eyes.

"Thanks for telling me why you don't like reporters. And I'm sorry about your ex. I can't tell you I'm not willing to do whatever it takes for the truth, though. I have done whatever I need to for a story before, and entering Ms. Mustang Valley is no exception."

He cupped her face in his hands. "You are nowhere near my ex." His breath was hot on her skin, making her lips tingle. He laughed and the chuckle vibrated through his chest, which she felt as her arms were braced against his torso. It was longing in the best way, this ache that wrapped around her. "I can't think about her when I'm looking at you, babe."

"Holden." She wanted to say something, let him know that she wasn't looking for anything other than to explore this insane desire between them. Instead she closed her eyes and wished for the stars.

Please don't leave me frustrated again.

"I haven't been able to stop thinking about kissing you again. Forgive me for overstepping my professional boundaries, Bella, but I have to have you." He lowered his lips to hers and just as on the back of the stage, her skin turned hot and her insides melted into liquid want. She reached around his waist, grabbed onto his T-shirt and tugged him as close as the embrace would allow.

Holden's tongue took every liberty with her mouth that she was willing to surrender. The moans in her throat were impossible to stem, and she almost cried out when he moved his hands lower to her hips and brought her snug against him. His need and response to her was evident and she moved her hips against his erection, needing the contact.

"Babe." He lifted her as if she was no heavier than the frying pan and placed her on the counter bar. Face-to-face, they looked at one another. His eyes were half-lidded. His hands rested on her thighs, heat searing through her workout bottoms.

"Are you sure, Bella?"

"Definitely." She leaned forward and pressed her lips to his, licked their outline with her tongue. "Don't tease me, Holden." His whiskers scraped against her skin and he fully opened his mouth to her.

Bella reveled in taking the lead, and loved that he let her. But kissing him wasn't enough. A deep part of her acknowledged that she'd never get enough of Holden St. Clair but she couldn't spend energy on the thought. Getting up close and the most personal possible with him was everything.

She wriggled her hips until her bottom was all but hanging off the counter edge, and lucky for her Holden let his arms and hands work again. He grasped her cheeks much as he had backstage, but this time, alone, certain of no intrusion by unwanted observers, he lifted her to him, his hands running the length of her hamstrings. She wrapped her legs around him as if they'd done this before, as if they already knew one another as intimately as she longed for.

HOLDEN FINALLY EXPERIENCED what he'd suspected. Bella's skin tasted as sweet as it looked. He took his time, licking, kissing, teasing every inch of her lips and mouth. When she tilted her head back for his access, he buried his head between her breasts and one by one, kissed the very tops of them, to where her tank stretched across her chest.

"That's positively delightful," she murmured as he moved his hands over her, down her back, making circles in the two indentations he found at the base of her spine.

"You're the delight, babe." He wanted so much from her, wanted to drink from her lips and the hot spot between her legs.

"Mmm." She leaned up and gave him a playful bite on his neck, and when her tongue flicked out his erection became painful.

"I'm not going to last very long if you keep doing that." He captured her lips again and moved his tongue against hers until she whimpered her pleasure. Her nipples were visible under her bra and shirt, and it turned him on that he'd done this to her.

"I need to touch you, Bella." His voice shook with need and for the first time since he'd met her he didn't care what she thought, how he appeared. All he wanted was this moment, with Bella.

"Touch away." She trailed more kisses across his jawline.

Tracing the edge of her yoga tights he worked his fingers, then his hand, under her clothing. His pulse pounded in his ears as he felt the soft tufted hair, the heat under his fingers.

"Look at me, babe."

She opened her eyes and he thrust one, two fingers into her heat.

"Oh. My. Gosh. Holden!" She said his name with such intent he almost lost his control. Instead he focused on her pleasure, moving his fingers, exploring the newness of Bella.

Her gasps and moans led him to her pleasure points, to the rhythm that satisfied her.

"Let go, Bella. Take it."

She responded with a wiggle of her hips, a cry of passion. Holden had never held a sexier woman in his arms.

BELLA GASPED FOR BREATH, unable to do anything but rely on Holden's strength as he held her against the counter. The orgasm had rocked her, and he'd only used his fingers.

What was it going to be like when they were joined?

"Your room?" He kissed the base of her neck next to her shoulder and she melted against his erection.

"Yes."

"Condoms?"

"Yes."

They continued kissing as he slowly walked her across the kitchen and down the short hall to her bedroom. She slid down his body as her legs lowered to the floor, hanging on to his neck while his arms supported her, kept her from crashing.

With little fanfare they both disrobed until they stood in front of each other completely naked. Her gaze soaked in his muscular edges, the scars on his ribcage, the patch of hair over his sex. He'd driven her to an erotic point she'd never been before. There was nothing but this moment with Holden.

"I'll get, get the—"

"Wait. Let me look at you." He was breathing heavily, but stilled long enough to grasp her hands, to drink her in. His gaze trailed heat along her face, down her throat, across her breasts. As it lowered, her desire rose, and she didn't think it could become more insistent. "You're beautiful."

"You, too." Her voice was as hoarse as his, and they

hadn't done a whole lot more than kiss yet. Her body shook with need, and she was glad the wanting was stronger than what lay under her passion.

Fear. Fear of the ferocity of their connection. No love-making had ever affected her like this before.

"Where are the condoms?" He was moving toward her nightstand, and at her nod he opened the drawer and took out her box of condoms, the box she'd only opened last night.

"Lie on the bed, Bella." He donned the condom with ease and waited for her to lie down, which she did with relief. Her trembling knees weren't going to support her much longer.

Holden knelt over her, his knees coming to rest between her legs, and his forearms supported him on either side of her head. She tried to think of something funny to say to break the moment but words failed her. She, the writer, blogger, investigative reporter, was at a loss for words as she was about to make love to a man she'd only met two days ago, yet didn't know how she'd lived without him until now.

When he continued to look at her, she smiled and reached her arms around his neck. "I can't take it anymore, Holden. Please, please take me." She tugged on his neck and she watched him lower his head, watched until his lids covered his eyes and she, too, closed her eyes.

It was all feeling now. Lips against lips, tongues wrapping and touching, skin against skin. The rough calluses on his palms ran paths down the outside of her thighs as he lowered his erection onto her, and then with one last deep kiss, plunged into her.

"Oh!" The intimate contact knocked the air from her

lungs, sent tingling sensations across her skin down to her toes. It was so very, very good with Holden. Delicious.

"Hang on, babe." Holden began to move, first filling her fully and then pulling back no farther than he had to, to her great gratitude. She needed him inside her, to never leave, to keep the rolling wave crashing against the sands of her heart.

"Holden!" She couldn't stop the climax that hit her, but it wasn't enough for him. He kept moving, then reached his hand between them to touch her in the most perfect spot until she experienced an orgasm unlike any other.

"Bella." Holden cried out her name, joining her in the exquisite pleasure.

Bella wanted to hear him say her name again and again.

Chapter Fifteen

Bella left Holden as he dozed atop her sheets and dove into the bathroom for a quick shower. It was enough time, though, to collect what was left of her thoughts. The sex with Holden had been so much more than she'd imagined, and definitely more than she'd bargained for. Electric, elemental, primal.

Life altering.

Do not go there.

She couldn't. There was the pageant, Gio's honor and a killer that Holden was after. Probably another criminal, too, if some of the attacks turned out to be those of a lesser villain. Maybe everyone who made it to be a contestant was put under surveillance. She'd have to ask Spencer about it later. He might not be able to reveal anything about an ongoing investigation but he could let her know what petty crimes had occurred during Ms. Mustang Valley in years past, couldn't he?

She opened the bathroom door and found Holden still stretched out on the bed in all of his sexiness. Her body immediately reacted and she forcefully focused on the exit.

"I'll be in my office." She gave Holden a quick smile before she left and went into the other bedroom that she'd converted into her writing space when she purchased the place over five years ago. She had to get out of her bedroom, away from Holden's naked bod, or she'd never check in to the videoconference session.

Would that disqualify her from the pageant?

"Give me a sec before you go." He deftly dressed, as if taking a woman to bed first thing was a daily occurrence. With a pang she realized it might be. How much did she know about Holden, really?

Enough to know that her brother wouldn't have become friends with him during his service, much less maintained the bond years later. And she'd watched Holden in action all day yesterday. He was a professional who put justice and safety of all civilians first. Otherwise he would have left her, Marcie and Delilah to get out of the building on their own while he tracked down the culprit.

"Hey." He was dressed in his white T-shirt and jeans again, and standing next to her. "Where did you go?" So he'd seen her drift off.

"I was thinking about how great you were yesterday. You made sure we were all safe. Don't you regret not going after the bad guy?"

He frowned, tilted his head. "I didn't have a bad guy to go after. At least, not in my face. It wouldn't have mattered though, because whoever it was had already made their way backstage and taken Becky. I want to point out that it's a good reason to eliminate Becky as the killer, but Selina and Ben might still be involved. I'm sorry Becky got hurt, but all three of you could have been gravely hurt or worse, if there'd been a connected fire. Then we'd have had four casualties instead of one."

"Said like only an FBI agent can." She tried to grin

but her lips trembled and tears filled her vision. What the heck?

"Hey, come here." He pulled her to him, crushed her against the broad piece of wall that was his chest. "You've been through so much. You're a trooper—you haven't so much as complained. Let it out."

She wasn't one for spilling tears on a guy's shoulder, but it was Holden's shoulder and he was wearing a nice soft cotton T-shirt that felt so comforting under her cheek. "Sorry." She sniffed.

"Nothing to apologize for. The stress has to come out one way or another."

The meaning in his words took a heartbeat or two to reach her brain. She pulled back and looked up at him. This close she had to crane her neck back, he was so tall.

"Are you saying that, that—" she pointed at her bed "—was like a stress-relieving ball? I'm not sure how I feel about being compared to a squishy heart-shaped toy."

His eyes smoldered with a sliver of what she'd witnessed only minutes earlier.

"For the record, I don't hook up with women I work with, agent or civilian. And if I had any smarts I wouldn't get involved with my friend's sister."

"But?" She realized that it already had become second nature to coax details out of him that she was certain he'd rather keep close, private.

He looked away, and she saw the pulse ticking on the side of his jaw. Its visible, rapid staccato was incongruous to the air of total control and order he projected. When he turned back she saw the emotions that matched in the depths of his dark, dark eyes. Wonder. Passion. Regret?

"What happened did because we're both attracted to one another and have been through a heck of a lot of dangerous scenarios in the past forty-eight hours. But don't mistake me, Bella. I'd want you just the same, just as much, if we'd met on a tour bus to Smithsville." His mention of one of the oldest and most worn-out tourist attractions near Mustang Valley made her giggle. Smithsville was as corny as it got, with a fake Wild West ghost town and cheap souvenirs. Old-fashioned carnival games and rides completed the ridiculous ambiance.

"Smithsville? I haven't been there since second grade, on a terrible field trip with a teacher who told us she wanted to be a zoo keeper but couldn't get into vet school."

"How do you remember those details?" The lines on his forehead deepened with what she'd come to understand as his *Get out!* expression, when he found whatever she said incredible. Or maybe unbelievable was more like it.

She shrugged. "I've no idea. Spencer has the same talent, ever since we were little. He memorized all the commercial jingles and cartoon skits from our favorite shows."

"You're correct. Spencer was the best navigator to have in a platoon as he never forgot a landmark. We didn't need satnav during training when we had Spencer with us."

"Yup, that's my brother." She hoped her light banter hid how much she was moved by his reminder that he'd served the same time as Spencer. She'd always hated Spencer could have faced combat during his military stint. To know Holden, too, had served and risked the same chance of being sent to a war zone froze her insides.

She'd have never met him. And now that she had, she wasn't thrilled that his job was so dangerous, just like Spencer's.

Gio, girlfriend. Don't forget Gio.

"Is Jarvis like that, too?"

"In a lot of ways, yes." She missed Jarvis, even though he lived in Mustang Valley, too, but on a ranch in the crew quarters. His long days, every day, made him busier than even Spencer. She had a full schedule, too, but at least she had the option of working from home as needed. "Look, I've got to get in on the meeting that starts in five minutes or I could be kicked out of the pageant."

His gaze immediately shuttered and he looked like the security guard she'd met when she checked in. "Keep the door open so that I can have a bead on you at all times."

"Aye-aye, sir. Or is it *roger*?"

He didn't respond but for a growl in the back of his throat. It reminded her of how his voice had gotten deep and rumbly while they made love.

Yeah, she needed to make the video meeting.

HOLDEN CIRCLED THE entire inside perimeter of the house for the umpteenth time in an hour, waiting for Bella to be done with the pageant training session. He heard Selina's voice ring out from the laptop speakers, counting as he imagined Bella doing the coordinated dance moves. Holden wasn't a dancer or into performance art but he imagined it wasn't much different from orchestrating a takedown operation. Everyone in their place at the right time, knowing exactly how and why they would execute their moves. Plus have a backup plan.

He didn't look in on Bella because he didn't trust himself. After the best sex of his life how could he?

It's more than sex now.

Indeed. He looked through the living room window, saw the cruiser parked beyond a grove of cacti. Two MVPD officers patrolled the property, and he saw one or the other as he made his interior rounds, through windows. It couldn't last very long, the response from MVPD. They were overworked as it was, with recent events in town now including looters who'd taken advantage of homes damaged in the recent earthquake, investigating the attempted murder of Payne Colton and keeping tabs on the Affirmation Alliance Group. He knew from his background checks on each contestant that Leigh, the woman going out of her way to speak to Bella during the pageant practice, was a part of the mysterious group.

He had to find who was sabotaging the pageant before MVPD called the protection off Bella. Before the killer got to her, or any other contestant.

"Bella, your posture is totally off." Selina's voice blared out from Bella's office and he wanted to tell Selina just how incredible Bella's posture had served them both earlier. Making sure she was safe inside the house, he went outside to do a perimeter check. He knew that MVPD was patrolling the outer edges of her property, but Holden needed to see the house entry and exit points, make sure they were secure.

In case you want to make love to Bella again?

"Keep it in your pants, St. Clair," he muttered to himself as he again checked the bathroom's window locks. It bugged him that there was a high clear window in Bella's bathroom. He texted Spencer and asked him to bring either sticky opaque peel-on covering or curtains. He didn't care which, but he wanted to know that no one could see inside the house.

Be there in five.

His reaction to Spencer's immediate reply surprised him. Shouldn't he be grateful for the break from his position of constant vigilance? He could talk to Spencer while Bella continued her modified pageant practice, knowing that there was an additional LEA on-site in case the killer came back.

Instead he had a serious case of guilt. He and Bella were adults, and his decision to break his professional protocol to be with her was solely his. And Bella's decisions were her own, too. But—and it was a big but— Bella was his buddy's sister. No escaping that. And if Spencer caught a hint of what had gone down this morning, he'd be up in Holden's grill.

Which he totally deserved, but didn't want to have to deal with.

His phone vibrated and he answered his supervisor's call. "Holden."

"We've got DNA confirmation that it was the same killer in both previous pageants." His boss wasn't one to waste time on preliminaries, which Holden usually appreciated but this case had more meaning to him.

Bella.

It was as if his boss had punched him in the gut. He sucked in a deep breath, fighting his nerves. Fighting the fear.

"Copy that. Any clues as to his identity?"

"We don't know if it's male or female, but the pattern

seems to fit a male killer as he's always picking female victims who bear a resemblance to one another."

"He's making up for a lost love."

"Or nurturing pain from a loss that was never processed. Like a mother, or former girlfriend or wife. Both victims had red hair and green eyes, so we're looking at a mother figure with the same."

"Did anyone else get hurt at those pageants, contestants who survived?" Holden had to ask, even though it showed a hole he'd missed in his own research and investigation.

"Yes. In each case, anyone who had a visible problem with the victim was either assaulted or had other criminal activity that appeared aimed at them. One had a car stolen, abandoning her at a diner in the middle of nowhere. Another incident involved the death of a contestant's dog."

"What had the contestant done to warrant their pet being killed?"

"They criticized the victim. Apparently our killer is very defensive of his targets."

Holden breathed in and out in a steady rhythm as he'd learned to do to keep his anxiety at bay. The thought of Becky being shoved down the stairs on the same day she'd verbally sparred with Bella made him nauseous. "It sounds like positive confirmation that it's the same guy, then." He told him what had happened with Becky, how Becky had given Bella a hard time two days ago.

"We're close, Holden. Don't let up, and we'll have the killer before the end of this pageant."

"Yes, sir." After they disconnected, Holden took a minute to look at the blue sky, the small yard that backed up to pure desert beauty. No wonder Bella enjoyed liv-

ing a little farther out from town. This spot had a quiet
peacefulness he missed while living in Phoenix.

A treasured quiet shattered by a monster.

Chapter Sixteen

Holden had suspected it was the serial killer that plagued the other two pageants, and now he had proof, or as close to definitive evidence as he'd have until he apprehended the bastard. The same DNA had been discovered at both murder sites, indicating the same killer. He didn't have DNA evidence processed from the Ms. Mustang Valley pageant yet, but he wasn't waiting on it. The fact that Bella was his next target was clear enough. From the camera he'd found on her window to the attack on first her and now Becky, the killer was following his or her own profile to a *T*.

Bella. He had no regrets about making love to her that morning, but it had been too risky. If anything had happened while he'd been distracted…

You knew you were safe, protected. MVPD had been there the entire time. Still, Bella was more than a woman he was attracted to in a very big way. She was his friend's sister. He owed the truth to Spence—that he'd let his dick run the show that morning. Of course, that put Holden at risk, because Spencer was likely to clock him when he found out he'd put personal pleasure over mission requirements.

Before he had a chance to come up with the best way

to let Spencer know that he had made sure the other LEA were in place before he made love to Bella, he heard the crunch of steps on the crushed seashells and gravel.

Spencer rounded the far corner of the yard, his expression resolute. They were on the eastern edge of the house and property so there was still some shade thrown by the house, but it was rapidly narrowing as the sun traveled across the sky.

"Hey." Spencer nodded. He was alone, with no sign of his dog Boris or the curtain Holden had asked for.

"Good morning. Did you find something to block out the view through the bathroom-shower window?"

"I did—it's in my SUV. I wanted to talk to you alone first, without Bella hearing us. Is she inside?"

"Yes. She's busy on a videoconference for the pageant, in the spare room, so we can go inside if you want." It was at least twenty degrees cooler in the house.

Spencer shook his head. "Not right away. First, give me the rundown on what you have so far."

"Not as much as I'd like, but I do have some new information from my office in Phoenix." Holden outlined where they were so far, including the description of the explosion he'd gleaned from Bella and the other women. He told Spencer about finding Becky at the base of the backstage stairwell, and that she was expected to make a full recovery. "I'm waiting for you to tell me we can resume pageant activity at Mustang Valley High. Or do you think we need to move it?"

Spencer shook his head. "No, we're not moving it. My chief talked to your boss, too, and they're in agreement that this might be the only chance to catch the serial killer. At least it looks like we can take Becky off the suspect list. Although, frankly, I'm not ruling out anything."

"You think Becky threw herself down the stairs?" Holden knew it was possible, but considered it unlikely. It would have been too difficult for Becky to set off the bomb at the same time.

"It's always possible. No matter, we're going to go ahead with the pageant. We've got the high school locked down tight now. I'm concerned that if we move it anywhere else, it could leave a hole for the killer to sneak through."

Holden's gut twisted. "I don't like where this is going, Spencer."

"You think that I do? Bella's my sister, man." He didn't say what they both knew, he didn't have to. The killer had his target on Bella. She fit the profile perfectly with her green eyes and red hair.

"I can put a call in to get a substitute, a look-alike." But Holden knew that the FBI didn't operate as it was often portrayed on television or in the movies. Finding an agent who matched Bella's description wasn't easy, and they didn't have enough time. Plus it would involve letting the entire pageant know that Bella was out, some stranger that looked like her was in. Even if they cut in the contestants and board on the undercover op, it wasn't safe. It risked spooking the killer, too.

"We both know that won't happen in time, don't we?"

"Yeah." Holden crossed his arms in front of his chest. "I have to think about how we're going to work this when we go back to the school. I'm pretty certain the killer is behind the attacks—who else would it be? But I don't like that he's actually a part of the pageant, and that we haven't figured out who it is yet. We've yet to confirm that any one person has worked all three pageants."

"I hear you. I'm working on a difficult case myself." Lines appeared between Spencer's brows.

"Yeah?"

"Are you aware of what's going on in Mustang Valley with the other side of the Coltons? The rich side?" Spencer grinned and it reminded Holden of the laughs they'd had downrange. Humor was imperative when facing life-or-death situations each day, and Spencer's had helped him through.

"I'm up to speed on the fact that Ace Colton was switched at birth, that no one knows by who or why. And the man he thought was his father, Payne Colton, remains in a coma, correct?" Holden had almost forgotten about that case, as he was so wrapped up in the pageant killer.

"That's right." Spencer shifted his weight, his concern evident. "We finally tracked the email sent via the dark web to Colton Oil that spilled the beans on Ace Colton not being a biological Colton. It was from a man named Harley Watts's laptop, and he admitted he sent the email, as ordered by his boss. He was about to tell us who exactly he worked for, but then he had a visitor and clammed up."

Holden's nape tingled. "Who was the visitor?"

"Have you noticed the contestant Leigh Dennings?"

"Blonde, pretty, always super nice—to a fault. Yeah, I've noticed her." He'd cringed as she'd spoken to Bella the other day. "She's with the Affirmation Alliance Group, right?"

"Yup. She's a big follower of Affirmation Alliance Group, AAG, one of their 'welcome managers.'"

"Right. I've heard of AAG, and have read quite a bit of backstory on them. I've been keeping an eye on her, but frankly most of my attention is directed at keeping Bella safe and catching the killer." He had two large interests that drew him to apply for the FBI: serial killers and cults. This particular case should be his dream LEA op, but instead he'd found himself more worried than intrigued.

It was a different way to work a case when he cared about someone he was supposed to be protecting.

He cared.

Did he care for Bella or would he feel the same about any woman he was attracted to right now?

"So you know that AAG is dangerous, Holden?"

"I do. I've warned Bella to be careful around Leigh, who seems very nice and welcoming, but—"

"But you know she'll suck the spirit out of you and she shares everything she's told and overhears with her superiors in the group. It's creepy at best, a cult at worst. I don't want Bella anywhere near her." Spencer sounded like the protective brother he was.

"Near who?"

Bella's voice came from the back patio, where she stood with two iced glasses of water.

"Is your rehearsal session over?" Holden smiled his thanks as he took the large tumbler, gulping down the cold nectar.

"Answer my question. Who were you talking about?" When Holden didn't reply, she focused on her brother. "Spencer?" Their sibling bond was evident, as was her irritation at her brother for not speaking up.

Holden had served alongside Spencer Colton and trusted him with his life. He'd never seen Spencer as much as blink in the face of danger. Yet he appeared to have hit a wall—his sister.

"I can't talk about an active investigation."

"Holden?"

Green eyes he'd seen lit from within as he moved inside her, bringing her to a second climax, looked at him with exasperation. And a hint of warmth that hadn't been there a day ago. "Let me guess. You're talking about Leigh."

Holden exchanged a glance with Spencer.

Bella rolled her eyes. "I already know you're investigating AAG, Spencer. They've come up at *Mustang Valley Gabber* more than once. It's hard to miss an always-positive, be-your-best-you kind of group when it shows up in our small town. Spit out whatever else you know, Spencer."

"I don't know anything new, unfortunately. But that doesn't mean you can trust Leigh. I wish you'd quit this ridiculous pageant." Spencer wiped his brow and Holden felt the sweat pouring down his back. They needed to move this inside soon.

"As long as you intend to remain in the pageant, Bella, you need to be very careful around her. We don't know her motives." Holden knew Bella didn't like anyone telling her what to do, but he had to be honest with her.

"I used to think the way you both do, about Ms. Mustang Valley. About all beauty pageants. But they're not all about looks when they have scholarships available, and when there are more scores in relation to talent and essays and answering questions." A red blush highlighted her smooth skin, her determination etched on her expression.

"Sounds like you've been drinking some Ms. Mustang Valley drink that's brainwashed you, sis." Spencer wasn't moved by his sister's beauty.

"That's not fair, Spence, and you know it. I'm the biggest skeptic of all three of us." Holden instinctively knew she wasn't referring to him but to her brother Jarvis, Spencer and herself. "But since I've gone through the application process and have made it to the contestant phase, I've seen different sides of the pageant."

"Such as?" Spencer's incredulity was hilarious but Holden thought better of laughing aloud while the siblings were hashing it out.

"The women competing for the scholarship really need it. They are doing this to better themselves, Spencer. It's no different than when you and I fought like heck to get into college and then to find a way to pay for it."

"Except we didn't have to parade around in a bikini to get our scholarships, or suck up to a bunch of tight-lipped snobs."

"No, we didn't, but we knew we had other options, and it worked out for us the first time around. It doesn't happen for a lot of people, Spencer. Definitely not the initial time they apply." Bella's passion stirred a deep longing in Holden. For a partner, sure, but for more. Something lasting.

"You may be right." Holden couldn't tell if Spencer didn't want to upset Bella any more or if he really was believing her. He suspected it was a combination of both. "But you still need to be very careful around Leigh. She's associated with a dangerous group, and that makes her a suspect."

"You don't think she's a murderer, do you? And are we sure there's a murderer or are we talking more of someone who gets off on scaring and injuring people? I know the DNA proved the other two murders are linked, but maybe we don't have the same person here."

"Murderer."

"Serial killer."

Holden's reply melded with Spencer's and he watched Bella's eyes widen for an instant before she regained her composure.

"Well, at least you two agree. Here I thought going after Selina Barnes Colton's backstory was going to give me an extra juicy piece to work on, next to my exposé."

"Both stories could get you hurt or worse, Bella. At least wait until we identify the killer." Spencer was on a roll. "What's so wrong with staying put at the *Mustang Valley Gabber*? You've built up a good readership and you like it, don't you?"

"I want more. I can do more. I'm going for a bigger job. If it were Jarvis looking to do something besides his ranch work would you be giving him such a hard time?"

Sensing a standoff between the two, Holden cleared his throat. "I don't know about the two of you, but I'm sweating bullets out here. Why don't we go inside?"

"You two go. I've got to get back to work. Let me get the curtain out of my car." Spencer stalked off and Bella shot Holden a questioning glance.

"Curtain?"

"Yeah. I asked him to bring me something to block the view through your bathroom window."

"The one with the camera." He saw her shudder. "You really think it's the killer, don't you?"

Integrity warred with the need to protect her from all harm, psychological as well as physical. Her vulnerability was guarded with her defensive posture, but he knew the softest parts of her, the treasure that the killer wanted to wipe off the face of the earth.

Bella's safety was paramount. She deserved nothing less than the truth.

"I'm positive it's the killer."

THEY THOUGHT THEY were smart, holing up at her house. The cops weren't going to make the job easier but the challenges were often the most exciting parts of the life-style of a professional killer. The only thing more fun was watching the girls die.

They were stupid, stupid girls for entering a beauty contest. The redheads rarely got as much attention as the blondes. Didn't Mommy always say that? She'd never been paid any attention by Daddy, who ran out when Mommy had a two-year-old to raise. The memories of lurid fights were still there, no matter how young the brain had been.

Mommy needed someone to help her die and that's where the best lessons were learned. Bella Colton would join the rest of the redheads that had died with love and affection, all because of what Mommy taught as she lay on her deathbed, unable to be cured of the awful dis-ease that took her.

Soon, Bella, soon. I'm coming to save you from this awful life. Your death will be so, so peaceful. After I get you all to myself.

Chapter Seventeen

"I'm craving a steak." Bella eyed the menu, her only protection between her and Holden. His aura wrapped around her as he sat across the Formica table on the opposite booth bench, his legs too close to hers.

"Get whatever you want." He'd already perused the menu then shut it without much prevarication.

"Are you sure? I mean, I don't want to take advantage of the government tab."

"It's not on the FBI—it's on me."

That made it sound like a date, except Holden wasn't playing the part. She'd angered him when she'd pushed to get out of the house late this afternoon, and she didn't blame him for being annoyed with her. If it were her guarding him, she wouldn't want him to leave a building that was surrounded by MVPD officers and wired with extra security systems that Spencer had Jarvis install today.

"I'm sorry, Holden. I know why you wanted to stay at my house, but after you told me that I'm definitely a target, that you know it's a killer, I couldn't stay there one more minute. The killer's been to my house, my home." She picked her menu up again. "At least he didn't get inside the house."

"No, there's no indication that he did." Holden looked at her with his dark, dark eyes and she wished they were back in her bedroom. Instead they were out of Mustang Valley and having a late dinner at an upscale shopping strip several miles away, hoping to get a mental break from the weight of the case.

"Thanks for coming here."

"Is it a place you go often?" He looked around at the southwestern-chic surroundings, the soft lighting even in the early afternoon, the linen tablecloth. She sucked in a breath when his gaze landed back where she craved it. On her.

"No, not really. I mean, I like it here, but I've only recently started to earn enough to come here whenever I want to."

"You seem very successful for a reporter. I'm told it's a brutal business."

Again with the allusion to his ex. She wished Holden had never met that woman. "All writing is difficult to make a living at. It's the way it is. But I hold my own, and if I can manage to get the kind of job I want, I'll be doing very well."

His face stilled and she saw it as a warning sign. A red flag that she was encroaching his offensive.

"You have to have a passion to do your job."

"A passion? I see it more as the desire for the truth. Always the truth, no more, no less."

"At any cost?"

"That's an odd question. It depends on what the story is. The pageant story, yes, I feel I'm willing to do whatever it'll take, because Gio gave her all to this system, in the worst way. Now, if I can glean some dirt on Selina in the process, you bet I'll take it and run with it. But

Selina Barnes Colton isn't worth staying in the pageant for. Definitely not worth being stalked by a serial killer."

His face had turned to stone, reminding her of the sandstone cliffs she enjoyed hiking whenever she escaped north to Vermilion Cliffs National Monument. At least the cliffs reflected the setting sun. Holden revealed nothing. Wherever his thoughts had gone was a dark place.

The waitress took their orders and they remained quiet as their drinks—sparkling water for her and a cola drink for him—were placed on the bistro-style table that was covered with a white tablecloth, a nice touch in an otherwise casual dining atmosphere.

"Do you have any idea when we'll go back to the school?" She ran her fingers on her sweating tavern glass.

He shook his head. "It's up to MVPD to give the all clear. They're working with us, of course, and I don't anticipate it'll take much longer."

"I'd imagine it'll be a mess, from the explosion."

"Naw. It looked bigger than it was. The explosive was very small—it was how and when it was detonated that made it so scary, and loud. The tear gas was for added effect but didn't damage anything in the vicinity."

"Yet if any of us had been closer it could have killed us."

"Getting hit by the locker door, yes, technically it could have injured you. But the tear gas was the real weapon. And surprise."

"Yes."

They changed the topic to less lethal topics, to include what each planned to do when the case was closed, the killer caught.

"I need some time out in the desert, under the stars." Holden had a dreamy expression on his face.

"You mean, away from Phoenix?"

"Yes. I enjoy being on my own, backpacking through state and national parks. There's too much light pollution in Phoenix to enjoy the night sky."

"I get that. I like to birdwatch, and the desert is a great place to do it. I'm lucky I can watch as much as I do from my back patio. But I hear you on the hiking—it's great to exercise while soaking up nature."

"Have you ever camped?"

"Out in the wilderness, like you? No." She met his gaze and his intent was unmistakable. Holden meant, had she ever made love in the night, under the stars. Heat pooled between her legs as she imagined sharing a sleeping bag with him.

"I'd love to take you with me sometime."

"Well, that might not be for a bit, considering we have a killer to catch, right?"

Holden didn't answer but kept his smoldering gaze on her, promising pleasure without even touching her.

She welcomed the arrival of their food, wanting a distraction from the memories. It wasn't enough that she and the other contestants, save for Becky, had made it out all right. She would not rest until the killer was caught.

"Spencer wants me to get an undercover agent to fill in for you."

"No way." She chewed her food, pointed her fork at Holden. "You know me well enough to figure out my body language. If I think I'm in trouble, I'm going to let you know. And this killer is smart, or they wouldn't have gotten away with two previous murders and all the crimes around them."

At his stunned look, she grinned. "I've been doing my own research, Holden."

"Clearly." He took a bite of his sea bass and she watched his Adam's apple bob with each swallow, saw the stamp of masculinity in his strong jawline. Her lips tingled with the memory of kissing that very line of bone, using her tongue to make him groan with desire.

They'd been incredibly compatible in bed.

"Tell me again about your ex. Why you hate reporters and have never changed your mind about them."

He set down his cutlery, sipped through the straw for a moment. When his gaze met hers, she noticed the fine lines at the edges of his eyes. Her fingers itched to smooth them. "You tell me, Bella. You're the one who's putting her life at stake to get the answers you want to avenge your best friend's death. A death, I might add, that was the result of her choices over the years."

"That's cold. No one chooses to be sick with an eating disorder or any other mental illness."

"You chose to write about it." He took a long swig of his soda. "Tell me you'll write anything other than what you've already decided will be the story."

Indignation rushed over her, and she was grateful for the semi-fancy restaurant or she'd recook his fish right here, with a votive added in for pleasure. "I do not prewrite my stories. That's the epitome of the worst kind of reporter. It's not reporting—it's creative writing."

"You mean to tell me you've never embellished story details to get a better headline?" His derision scraped against the trust she had felt building toward him.

"No, I haven't. Sure, the *Mustang Valley Gabber* isn't the *Wall Street Journal*, but our, my work ethic and personal ethics have stayed the same."

"Yet you want to ask me what I know about Selina Barnes Colton." His lack of empathy was chilling. What had triggered him?

"Of course I do, if you know her or anything about what's going on with Payne Colton. You can see why I would, don't you? It could be foul play that landed him in a coma. How do we know it wasn't Selina behind it?"

"We don't. But I've found the press to be a bit rabid over a man who's been good to his community his entire life."

"Many wealthy people's companies have given lots of money to charity."

"Answer me this, Bella. If you found out that I knew the story behind Selina but couldn't tell you about it, what would you do? Would you try to force it out of me?"

"I'd do my journalistic duty to get the information from you, yes. You can't blame me for trying to do my job!"

"I can if it compromises an active investigation."

His resolute expression struck a chord with her. What had she been thinking, going to bed with him last night? She didn't know him. Maybe Spencer vouched for him, and Jarvis thought he was a good guy, but the side she was seeing now wasn't the man she'd thought she'd known.

How can you really know someone after only a few days?

"I need to use the restroom. Excuse me." Before he stood up and tried to tell her he needed to follow her, as part of his protection role, she darted into the hall behind the bar, where the rooms were located.

Bella couldn't believe it but she had to get away from Holden before he saw what his words did to her. This wasn't like her, to get emotional over something a man said to her. She'd had a rough start in life, and she was thirty-one, not some adolescent being chastised by her first-ever boss. Still, Holden's words had stung, burrowed under her thick skin and found what she valued most.

Her passion for finding the truth and writing it into a succinct report.

After she splashed some cold water on her face and gave herself time to calm down, she headed toward the dining area. Laughter spilled from a room farther back in the café and she saw a big sign with gilded letters that welcomed a baby shower party.

Standing by the sign were Marlowe and Ainsley Colton, her distant cousins. She couldn't stop from staring. Marlowe's stomach was huge, and Bella vaguely remembered that she heard she was pregnant and engaged. But that had been months ago and Marlowe appeared near the end of her pregnancy, or maybe she was having multiples. Each of the women wore springy dresses and sandals—Ainsley's were high spikes while Marlowe's were lower and chunkier, offering her more support—and were laughing, their heads close together. A tight pang of exactly how alone she was when it came to the Coltons made her wish she knew them better. Why had her parents disengaged from the family? And why did Aunt Amelia keep up the same type of emotional walls that made Bella, Jarvis and Spencer the estranged cousins?

As if her presence drew their attention, they both looked over, spotted her and turned toward her at the same time. Panic gripped Bella but she found herself walking toward them, smiling.

"Bella! It's so nice to see you." Ainsley spoke first, and Bella couldn't help but notice how all three of them were petite.

"Yes, it's been so long." Marlowe's soft smile showed none of the malice she'd remembered as a kid, from when they'd be at a Colton reunion on Rattlesnake Ridge Ranch. No one had ever played with her or her brothers. Bella had used the time at the picnics to wander through the immense home, imagining she was a princess and it was her private castle. It had always been her, Spencer and Jarvis. Which had served them all well, and she loved her brothers with all her heart. But it would be nice to know more family.

"We were so sorry to hear about your friend Gio." Marlowe never lacked for grace. As the current CEO of Colton Oil, she was a consummate diplomat. But her sincerity felt genuine.

"You knew?" She let out a nervous laugh. "Of course you did, it's Mustang Valley, after all."

"I wanted to go to the funeral, to support you, but I never really knew Gio and it seemed the wrong time to reconnect with you." Ainsley's eyes were moist. Was she that concerned about Bella's loss?

"That's nice of you to say that." An unexpected and unusual shyness enveloped her. Maybe the events of the last few days were finally catching up with her. Deciding to run for Ms. Mustang Valley, meeting Holden, getting attacked, surviving the explosion—how had her life become an action movie instead of the usual steady one she'd built to support her writing routine?

"I mean it." Marlowe put a hand on her forearm. "We may not see one another very much but we're all still family."

"Agreed." Ainsley nodded. "As a matter of fact, wouldn't it be nice if we made this happen on purpose? Meeting each other, I mean."

"It'd be lovely to have you up to the Triple R." Marlowe pulled out her phone.

"That sounds good." Bella figured they'd never really want to hang with her. She was from the wrong-side-of-the-track part of the Coltons, the sister of triplets whose parents had left the clan years before their untimely deaths. Still, she went through the motions of exchanging contact information before they said goodbye.

When she slid back into her seat, she discovered Holden's plate was empty and her food cold.

"You okay?" His gaze was full of concern, and that muscle tic on the side of his jaw was jumping around. "I was about to come knock on the door."

"I'm good. I ran into two distant cousins."

"Oh? Did they have some dirt on Selina for you?"

And they were right back where the conversation ended, when she'd needed to leave the table.

"I have no idea. I didn't ask." She sipped her water. "I'm not against helping an ongoing investigation. In fact, I think that reporters and LEAs do their best work when it's together. Take the robberies we had in Mustang Valley a few years back. I usually am assigned to write fluffier lifestyle pieces, about homes and lives of the more affluent residents. But I was able to convince my editor that exposés on the victims of the crimes, detailing how hard they'd worked to get where they were, would be popular to our readers. Everyone wants to know about their neighbors, especially if it's perceived they're living the 'better' life. While interviewing one particular family, it came to light that the husband had an estranged stepbrother who was actively addicted to opiates. Since two bottles of painkillers were part of the stolen goods, it allowed MVPD to connect the dots and figure out who the thieves were."

"That's unusual, Bella. You know better than I do how rare it is for law enforcement to work with the media."

"You're wrong, Holden. Maybe with bigger agencies like the FBI it's not common, but at the local, small-town level, everyone works together to make things happen."

"You may be right." He motioned to her plate. "Are you going to finish that?"

She sighed. "I've lost my appetite, frankly."

"You need to eat if you're going to have another re-hearsal later today."

"I'll get something at home." But the thought of returning to her house filled her with anxiety. It was usually her refuge and now, even with police presence and Holden, it was more like a prison. "Don't take this wrong, Holden, but I'm not keen on going back to the house."

"I don't blame you, but you're safe there, Bella. I won't let anything happen to you."

"It's not that. It's the reality of a serial killer, a mon-ster, being so close to me, to where I live and breathe."

"We don't have to go straight back. When's your next video practice session?"

"Eight tomorrow morning." Selina had said she'd meet with them again after they had time to rest and study the routines she'd dealt out this morning.

"It's not even sundown yet. We've got some time."

"For what?"

"It's a surprise."

HOLDEN LIKED HOW he'd gotten a smile out of Bella when he'd told her their destination was a surprise. She'd been far too serious when she'd returned to the table. Truth be told, he knew it was his staunch dislike of reporters that had put her in the foul mood.

Would it have killed you to go easier on her?

No, it wouldn't have killed him but if he wasn't on that sharp edge of awareness that a case like this necessitated, her life would be at risk.

He glanced at her as he drove onto the highway, heading west. She sat relaxed against the seat, her eyes closed. He hoped the AC and lull of the drive had put her in a decent nap. It was so hard to tell with Bella—her moods and bearing changed with the wind.

And dang it if he didn't love every bit of the challenge of keeping up with her.

"Why are you staring at me? Keep your eyes on the road," she murmured in a sleepy voice and he grinned.

"There isn't much out here but roadrunners and prairie dogs."

"We don't want to kill any innocent bystanders." She stretched and snuggled into the seat more deeply. "Don't wake me 'til we get there."

"Okay." He promised himself he'd keep his gaze on the flat highway, the mountains and blue sky in his peripheral vision.

Holden had never skipped out of an op before. And he wasn't now, not technically, as keeping Bella safe was his top priority. That, and luring in the killer.

At Bella's risk.

Guilt sucker punched him for the second time in a day, but it had nothing to do with Spencer or their bond that would last a lifetime. His emotional discomfort had everything to do with the beautiful woman reclined in the passenger seat beside him, trusting him enough to keep her eyes closed and to nap on the way to an un-known destination.

Maybe he needed to learn how to trust, too. He could trust that Bella wasn't using him for information for her exposé. She hadn't sought him out, hadn't even known an FBI agent was undercover at the pageant.

The sun set as he pulled into their destination. He'd driven here without thinking, knowing it was safe as he was certain they hadn't been followed and he checked in with his Phoenix office and Spencer at MVPD regu-larly. His phone was connected to both to provide con-stant GPS location.

He'd reported that Bella needed a break from her house and it was a good security move to get her away from town for the night, until the pageant practice re-sumed at Mustang Valley High, as determined by Spen-cer. He'd received zero pushback on taking Bella away from either his boss or Spencer.

"Where are we?" Bella must have felt the road change and was sitting upright, peering through the windshield.

"My favorite getaway." He waited for her to register the other cars and people milling about with binoculars and cameras, each equipped with a long lens.

"Wait—is this Carr Canyon?"

"Yes. I'm a member of SABO." The Southeastern Ar-izona Bird Observatory was a favorite amongst locals and tourists alike, and it had provided him with much-needed respite from his heavier cases. He had a feeling he was going to need to escape into his birding after this investigation wrapped up, too.

"I've done so many articles on them over the years. Have you ever been to one of the hummingbird bandings?"

"Only once, but I'd like to do more. With the long drive from Phoenix I can't get here as often as I like, but it's always great when I do."

"So what are we going to see tonight?" She followed his lead and got out of the car and walked around to the back with him. He opened his trunk and handed her a ball cap, reflective vest and binoculars. He donned his birding vest over the black T-shirt, and retrieved his favorite camera.

"It's a long shot that we'll actually see anything, but we'll hear the owls. I'm taking my camera but it might be fruitless."

"I love owls. There's a family of screech owls in a clump of dead saguaros behind my house. I feel like they're my personal watchdogs at night—sometimes I hear them fussing when the neighborhood teens are playing flashlight tag."

"Are you sure that's all they're doing?"

"No, but I'm not their mother." They both laughed and headed toward the top of the trail, the walk steep as they were in the mountains.

Holden had tried to hang on to his belief that Bella had to be an opportunist because she was a reporter, just like Nicole, his ex. But as they headed into the canyon's depths it occurred to him that unlike his ex, Bella was all about grasping all the joy life had to offer. And she wasn't a martyr about being a serial killer's target.

Bella was the woman he'd dreamed of finding. Why did it have to be now, during such a dangerous op?

Chapter Eighteen

Bella surprised herself with how easy it was to forget their acrimonious dinner conversation and allow herself to enjoy the nighttime walk with Holden. The moon was full and she was able to make out his features with little trouble. It was always a bonus when she could see a handsome, sexy man as he spent time with her.

"We lucked out with the moon." She looked at large white cactus blooms on the sides of the path. "The angel blooms are practically glowing."

"Yeah, they are, aren't they?" He moved his hand to her lower back, rubbed in soothing circles. It was a peaceful bubble, just the two of them. Until a family with several young children walked by.

"The full moon explains the crowds. I never realized how many folks would show up to hear owls and look at flowering cacti." She turned away and began to walk farther down the path.

"Birding's an early-morning and late-night sport during the summer here, as you know. We're lucky it's still cooler." Holden hopped easily over a grouping of rocks and turned to hold her hand as she leaped from the four-foot precipice back to the ground. When her feet hit the sandy, graveled surface, he didn't let go but instead intertwined their fingers and continued walking.

Bella knew she should pull her hand back, keep up staunch boundaries with Holden. He'd already proven to be the best lover she'd ever known and if she wasn't careful the end of the pageant was going to mean more to her than losing a crown.

"Tell me why you really signed up for the pageant, Bella."

"I already have. I want to find out the truth about what happened to Gio. And I believe this pageant board has skeletons in its closet."

"What if you don't find them?"

"Then I'll have to figure out something else to investigate."

"So your ultimate motivation isn't about Gio." Spoken quietly, his words held no judgement or criticism.

"It's twofold. I want justice for my best friend, yes. And I want to move on from the *Mustang Valley Gabber* and secure an investigative journalist position at a more prestigious publication."

"Is there a paper or news organization you're targeting?" His voice was low and sexy and she wondered if he realized how attractive he was. How many FBI profilers could switch from badass agent to serene birder all in the same day?

"Not really. I wouldn't want to have to leave Mustang Valley, and with most organizations I can work from home except for when I have to travel for a story. But I'm not opposed to leaving, either."

"I've stayed here, in Arizona, I mean, and a couple of times I was worried I'd thrown my career away with some of my job decisions. But so far it's all worked out.

Unfortunately for all of us, there are enough cases to keep the Phoenix field office in business for the next decade. It's a good thing for me, personally, as I've been able to stay here and be closer to my family."

"Did you grow up in Phoenix?"

"I did, in a suburb of it. It was so hard to be away from my family and everything I'd known when I went in the army and then ended up downrange. That's when I met Spencer."

"Did you realize you were both from Arizona? And southeastern, to boot?"

"Not at first. I learned more about him after he shoved me out of the way of friendly fire during a training event."

"He never told me or Jarvis that."

"He wouldn't, would he? Spencer is that kind of hero."

Understanding dawned. "That's why you're so close—you were with him during that one training exercise." She mentioned the location and even in the dark, with the moonlight she was able to make out the grimace on his face.

"Yes." Nothing more was needed.

"Holden, I know it's awkward, but about this morning…" She halted on the path. They were far ahead of the crowds as their pace had taken them to a more remote location. Stars sprinkled the outer edges of the light shining off the moon and she suddenly wanted to come back here with this man and see all the stars.

"Hey." He tugged on her hand and she took the two steps to be up against him, where the feel of his breath as it stirred the wisps of hair on her temple lit the fire that burned only for him. "It's fast for me, believe it or not. I never meant to make love to you like that, this soon. You deserve to be wined and dined first, at least."

"So you thought about it beforehand?" She'd feared it was a spur-of-the-moment decision for him, an opportunity.

"Touché." He wrapped his arms around her, their bulky binoculars and cameras the only items between them. "I just accused you of being an opportunist for doing your job—I suppose I had that coming to me. Yes, I've thought about taking you to bed since the minute you walked into the school."

She shivered with desire in the cool desert night, and wished there were no pageant, that the serial killer were made up, and that Gio were still here.

Gio.

Instead of feeling the usual guilt that she wasn't doing enough to search for what had really killed Gio, a wave of exhaustion swept over her. "I wish we'd met under different circumstances, too." But even if they had, he lived in Phoenix, two hours away. Was she ready for a long-distance relationship? Was he?

"We aren't going to figure out what's going on between us right now, Bella. There are too many things competing for our attention. I suggest we enjoy the moment."

"I couldn't agree more." She moved to continue their walk but he pulled her up short, cupped her head in his palm and lowered his lips to hers. As before, her body responded immediately to his caresses, and her lips tingled with the passion they shared.

As her breathing grew more rapid she held on to his shoulders as tightly as possible. It was like floating in water that was over her head and Holden was her safety, his tall, lean length all she needed or wanted to stay alive.

When he stilled and lifted his head, she nearly whimpered from the withdrawal of heat from her mouth.

"Shh." His insistent order made her freeze, and fear began to shoot cold arrows through her heart. No, not now. How had the serial killer found them?

"What?" She trusted him implicitly. If anyone could save them, it was Holden.

"Do you hear it?"

She stilled her breathing and tried to tune out her rapid heartbeat. Fearful of hearing heavy footsteps, she almost missed it. But then, through her fears and reaction to this man, she heard it.

Hoooooot.

"A pygmy owl." She'd memorized the birdcalls years ago, for the article she had mentioned to Holden earlier.

"Yes. With juveniles. Listen." Sure enough, after the mother or father's long call, tiny, more "chirpy" sounds split the silence. Relief rushed in, followed by something she'd never been able to grasp no matter how long she'd ever dated a single person.

Trust.

IT WAS TOO EASY. Did they think they couldn't be followed, found, wherever they went? It would be easier if she were alone but no worries. He'd taken out other men who thought they were protecting the women, too.

They weren't in the house, which was a shame. He'd been able to break through the MVPD patrols with little trouble, once night fell. The feed from the camera he'd put over her bathroom window had disappeared, and he figured the police got it since he didn't see it from the perimeter of the property. He couldn't get close enough right now, but as soon as he knew they were back in the house, together, he'd get her.

And she'd pay for running away tonight.

THE NEXT MORNING Bella's phone woke her before dawn and she automatically answered, thinking it was one of her brothers. Holden had resumed his position on her sofa after they'd returned, assuring both of them that MVPD had her house under a basic lockdown. There was no safer place for her at this point.

"Hello?"

"Quit the pageant. You're in over your head." The same distorted voice that she'd heard before her world went dark in the staff room, backstage. Wide awake now, she bolted from her bed and moved in the darkness out of her room, into the hall and into Holden's granite physique.

"Who is it?"

She continued to listen, but the caller had disconnected.

"It was the same person as before. They hung up." Trembling began and, to her consternation, deepened in intensity. "It—it—it was him."

"Shh." He pulled her into his arms, held her tight. "You're safe. I'm here."

"I used to be so tough, but now I'm a puddle after a stupid prank call."

"Hey, you're not out of line to be afraid. This call wasn't just another crank call, but from a lethal killer. I'll have my handler see if he can get anything from the phone company."

"Thanks, that's reassuring me about now." She smiled

through the tears that ran down her face, her reaction to anger and frightening circumstances. She let his shirt absorb her tears, and didn't feel an ounce of guilt about it. It was safe, here in Holden's arms. "Sorry, I'm an odd duck when it comes to expressing my emotions. When I get really angry, I cry, which can come across as being overly emotional. The same thing happens when I'm afraid. But when Gio died, I couldn't muster a tear for days, weeks even."

"It was too deep. The hurt. I get it." He kept holding her and she heard his heartbeat since one ear was pressed against his chest. His breathing slowed, deepened. He let out a long sigh. "When Spencer and I were serving, we saw a lot. I'm not sure how much he's told you."

"Enough. He's told Jarvis more, I think, because both of them have always felt more protective of me than each other. They're not being jerks or misogynists, just good brothers."

She felt him nod, and his embrace tightened reassuringly. "If Jarvis is anything like Spencer, then yes, it's because they care very much for you."

"So during your work with the FBI, what have you seen that bothered you the most?"

He shifted next to her, as if seeking more contact. "Most cases aren't as bad as you might imagine. But when they are, they're rough. Anything involving kids is pretty much the worst. Sometimes I hit emotional overload. I know I'm there when I can't compartmentalize or shove down the horror. I've cried like a baby more than once."

"That's crying like a man, Holden. Accepting life on life's terms, even when it's awful."

"Yeah."

They stood in silence for several minutes, and to Bella it was as if they'd always been here. Together.

She pulled back. "I've got to get dressed. I imagine there's going to be another video session this morning."

"Actually, no. I was going to let you sleep a little longer, but I talked to Spencer about an hour ago. It's a go for the high school. Pageant practice resumes this morning."

"I didn't think Selina or the pageant board were going to give us Sunday off, not when all we'll have for the next three weeks are evenings." She was actually sorry that the pageant was only going to be for a few more weeks, with the final festivities at the end of the month. It meant she had only three weeks with Holden, before he went back to his life in Phoenix. Back to being an FBI agent, far away from Mustang Valley.

"You can ask for another agent to guard you if you want, Bella. You don't have to be tied to me for all three weeks."

"But you won't let anyone else have the final say in my safety, will you?"

"No."

"And we've gone past the point of acting as if we don't share more than this pageant and wanting to catch the killer. Right?"

He nodded. "Right again."

"Then I'm fine with you staying here. There's nowhere else I can go without bringing the threat with me, be it a hotel or even Rattlesnake Ridge Ranch, if I were ever invited there." She heard the self-pity in her voice and resolved to do whatever she had to do to erase it. Martyrdom had been Aunt Amelia's gig, not hers.

"I know it's scary. But you're right—wherever you go we'd have to start over again as far as your security."

"Then let's leave it as it is."

"I won't distract either of us again, Bella." His level gaze wasn't entirely convincing as there was a flicker of heat in its depths.

"It's a two-way responsibility, Holden. You didn't make or even convince me to do anything I hadn't wanted to since just about the time you opened my bag to check for contraband."

His color deepened and major dimples formed on either side of his mouth but he didn't widen it into a grin.

"We're only going to hurt one another in the end."

"I agree." She shifted on her feet, knowing she needed to get dressed or at least get a large mug of coffee. But she couldn't bring herself to walk away. As if it would truly mean the end of anything personal with Holden. "But, we can both agree that we're friends of a sort, can't we?" The plea in her tone made her cringe on her behalf but it didn't stop how she felt.

She needed to know Holden was her friend.

A flash of white in the dim hallway reassured her. "There's no way I couldn't be friends with my buddy's sister."

So she was back to being Spencer's sister. At least that meant they were still talking, and back on neutral territory. Away from the heated desire that threatened her heart as much as the killer threatened her life.

Except unlike her wish to see Holden apprehend the murderer, she didn't seem to care if her heart was on fire.

HOLDEN KNEW HE was being a jerk. No question. He'd just brushed off the woman unlike any other he'd ever known. But it was for her safety, the security of the entire investigation.

And the tightness around his heart every time he remembered why he was here, to catch a killer, served as a reminder that he was getting too close to Bella.

While Bella got dressed he took a cup of coffee out to the patio and placed a call to Spencer to pass on some information MVPD needed for the ongoing investigation against AAG. It was already hot, even in the shade of her terra-cotta-tiled roof, but he needed to be outside, to see the desert wake up.

"You're up early for a G-man." Spencer's teasing was a welcome relief after drawing the grim boundaries he needed with Bella.

"Don't worry, man, I'm going back to bed after this."

Spencer's silence had him replaying what he'd just said. "Oh, geez, Spencer, I didn't mean with your sister, for heaven's sake." Guilt slapped his conscience silly.

"It's pretty apparent that there's something going on between you two."

"I promise, I won't let anything happen to her."

"I know that. I trust you, always have." Spencer paused again and in Holden's line of work, he had learned that pauses were where trouble lay. "Bella's not had a lot of luck with guys, Holden, and I don't want to see a broken heart when you go back to your job in Phoenix."

"Copy that. I won't hurt her, Spencer." Holden couldn't say any more without betraying what he and Bella had shared. No matter how it ended, how it had to be now, what they'd made together was special, private. Sacred.

Sacred? He'd gotten in deeper than he'd thought.

"I wasn't referring to Bella, Holden. I meant your heart. Bella's been a heartbreaker since middle school." Spencer laughed. "In case you haven't noticed, she can hold her own against almost anything. I don't want her to have to do that, though, not with a killer."

"We're on the same page, then. Listen, I called to give you what our office found on the Affirmation Alliance Group and its leader, Micheline Anderson."

"You know MVPD got the charge to stick against Harley Watts, right? He's been charged with threatening the Colton Oil structure by sending a classified email over the dark web."

"Yes, my handler mentioned that. Another thing that's come up that I think you'll be interested in is that there are indications that Micheline might be planning some kind of mass-destruction event, like a mass suicide."

Spencer's low whistle pierced their connection. "You mean like a Jim Jones poisoned-fruit-drink kind of thing?" Holden wasn't surprised that Spencer recognized the reference. Law enforcement officers often studied the mass suicide orchestrated by the cult leader Jim Jones in Guyana, in 1978.

"Yes, exactly. And an eerie connection is that Jim Jones's spouse was named Marceline. It seems awfully close to Micheline, especially as neither are common names."

"You don't think she took this name on purpose?"

Holden sighed. "No clue. I've learned not to put much stock in coincidence, though. Not in our line of work."

"I hear you. Thanks for this, Holden, and please thank your office colleagues, and your supervisor. This saves me a lot of digging, and we'll be sure to keep Micheline and AAG under tight surveillance."

"Good to hear." He saw Bella walk back into the kitchen through the sliding patio door. "I've got to go. Ms. Mustang Valley waits for no one."

Spencer's chuckle reached him before he disconnected. Eager to get his head back in the game, he took a moment to remind himself why he'd come to Mustang Valley. To apprehend a killer. To prevent further murders. But Bella's safety had become priority number one. Long before Spencer had requested it.

Holden shoved aside anything that remotely felt like an emotional response to Bella and focused on the case.

Both of their lives depended upon it.

Chapter Nineteen

"You're off by a half beat, Bella! Marcie, Delilah, stop letting her mess you up, ladies." Selina's voice cut through the soundtrack, a disco tune that required everyone to do three turns in a row, followed by a quick two-step. After their second week of evening rehearsals, it was the pageant's third all-day Saturday practice.

Bella clamped her mouth shut to keep from responding with some very unpageantlike words. But that made her even more out of breath, and she felt her face heat with the effort.

"Don't let her get to you. We're almost done with all of this." Marcie spoke through several more steps, her face flushed, too.

"She's not. Trust me." The number ended and Bella took the opportunity to walk off to the side of the stage to where Holden stood.

"How can anyone think I'm going to receive extra points from her?" She gulped from her water bottle and didn't miss how his gaze drank her in. Her body reacted by sending heat everywhere she'd tried to shut down these past two weeks as he'd slept on her sofa each night. She'd had to deal with him being around all the time, including following her to the *Mustang Valley Gabber* headquarters a few times. It was fortunate from a security perspective that she was able to work from her laptop, and remain at home for much of her imposed "exile" from independent living. To be fair, she enjoyed Holden's company and they'd gotten to know each other better.

It wasn't a stretch to realize they'd indeed become friends, as she'd hoped.

But they'd avoided a repeat of their one night together. She was relieved and frustrated by their mutual agreement to avoid any further bedroom activities. They were adults, after all. Yet a big part of her wanted to bring that up, remind him that they could enjoy a physical relationship without worrying they'd expect too much from one another when it ended.

At least, that's what she'd thought before she got to know him so well.

"Keep your cool and remember to not let them see you sweat."

"Funny." Her clothes were soaked with perspiration and had been all day. "At least this is the last bit of today's rehearsal."

"Still, we can't take any chances. Be aware."

"Got it." She didn't want to be short with him but each night Holden had gone over what he thought she needed to do, to survive any possible attack by the killer. Stay alert, aware and always ready to run.

"I know you do." His confidence in her buoyed her when she would have wondered just why she was doing this in the first place. So far she'd uncovered nothing nefarious about the Ms. Mustang Valley Pageant, and in fact had learned that it took a lot of work and dedication for the competition to continue year after year.

Was Gio's mother right? Had Gio's talk near the end been delusional, brought on by her advanced disease?

"You're frowning. Need to talk about it?"

"Not here. Maybe later." But what would she tell Holden? He'd take her admission that there was nothing the pageant could do to prevent Gio's illnesses as surrender. She wasn't going to ever claim being a reporter was in vain.

"Bella."

"Yes?"

"You're doing great. You'll get your story, don't worry." His smooth tone hid the depth of thought and intuition its accuracy required.

"How do you do that?"

"Do what?"

"Know what I'm thinking, what I need to hear?"

He gazed at her thoughtfully. "With you, it's easy."

"Break time's over!" Selina's command was her bidding, at least for another week. The ex-wife of Payne Colton still commanded a room as if she still was married to the state's richest man. Bella wondered how Payne's current comatose condition, affected Selina personally. It had to be difficult to be on the Colton Oil Board of Directors and not have the chairman present, knowing he might never return. Payne had been her husband once, after all. But as much as Bella had tried to talk to Selina alone, or asked others if they knew more about her, she hadn't been able to dig up any more dirt on the Colton Oil empire's current situation. Spencer had told her in the strictest confidence that there was big drama going on as to who the eldest biological heir to Payne's legacy was, but she wouldn't be able to use that for a report unless she heard it from a different source.

Which left her with doing what she came here to begin with—Bella needed to find the original records of the Ms. Mustang Valley Pageant that had been in the file cabinet.

"Okay, ladies, thank you for such a great day. I'm going to leave you with Dawn Myers, Mustang Valley's own winner of several pageants and the winner of Ms. Mustang Valley ten years ago. Please welcome her and follow her lead on how to get through your talent portion."

Crap. Bella had written on the original application that she'd be presenting a verbal essay on why reporting mattered in today's world of insta-news and social media. But she'd done nothing to prepare in the meantime. While many of her competitors were staying up late working on their talents, she'd been writing assigned articles for her paying job.

And lying awake too late, wondering what Holden was doing in the other room besides guarding her and laying his long, sexy body on her poppy-red sofa.

"Bye, Selina." Dawn was a perky blonde whose hair was in a twist, her figure still perfectly trim in white capris with a slinky sleeveless pale pink silk top. Bella wondered how she stayed looking so cool in the heat. Air-conditioning made life bearable in Arizona year-round, but it was still roasting outside in the sun.

For the next hour, the contestants were each grilled on their talent portion. Bella mentally prepared as much as possible, but when it was her turn to walk on and stand center stage without her colleagues she felt every bit the ingenue.

"Hello, everyone. I'm Bella Colton, and I am so fortunate to be able to earn my living doing what I'm most passionate about—bringing the truth to you, the reader, no matter how difficult it may be. Since I'm used to public speaking, I've picked poetry reading as my talent. I've chosen a poem—"

"Stop, stop!" Señora Rosenstein ran up to the edge of the stage, her cell phone in hand. "There's been a terrible accident!"

Bella looked around for Holden, and met his gaze with trepidation. Was this another distraction from the killer?

"What is it, Ms. Rosenstein?" Marcie stepped forward.

"Selina's car has flipped off the highway at the bend just out of town, on the way to Rattlesnake Ridge Ranch."

A collective gasp made the hairs on Bella's nape raise, and she fought to keep her feet planted. All she wanted was to run to Holden's arms as she had the night she'd received the crank call. It'd been easy to think the killer had changed his mind, that's how quiet the pageant had been.

"Is she okay?" Becky, who was still watching the pageant activities albeit with crutches and only as an observer, spoke from a theater seat in the front row.

Holden walked forward down the main right aisle. "I've just spoken to MVPD Sergeant Spencer Colton. Selina appears to be completely fine, just shaken up a bit. She walked away from the crash. She's being evaluated by EMTs."

"What caused the accident?" Bella asked.

"We won't know until a full investigation is completed."

Murmurs turned to panic amongst the women.

"This is crazy. No scholarship is worth this."

"What's going on, really?"

"I heard that there were murders at two other pageants." Leigh spoke up, her usually singsong voice shaking. "But remember, we can all be our best selves in the most trying circumstances. This is our chance to join together, to rise to be our best selves."

"Do you really believe your own lies, Leigh?" Becky, on crutches and standing next to the stage, was clearly not in the mood for fluffy sayings when they were all at risk.

"There's no reason to believe anyone here is a target." Holden didn't meet Bella's gaze. "I'm just pageant security, but we're surrounded by Mustang Valley PD, and the officers are conducting regular inspections. No one can get in here who isn't a part of the pageant."

"But what if there's a killer amongst us?" Delilah asked the same question that had given Bella nightmares all week.

"We're not going to allow negative energy to affect the positive motivation we all have to win this pageant, are we, ladies?" Dawn spoke up, her background in motivational speaking evident. "This is scary—I'll grant you that. But we've got MVPD on our side, and I'm willing to be here today to do the work. How about you?"

Bella was stunned at how quickly the panic turned to enthusiasm with the group. It wasn't the sticky-sweet platitudes from Leigh, either. It was genuine.

Pageant women were strong, and had reason to fight for their privilege to compete. They all wanted to improve their lives, and education was a valuable ticket.

LATER THAT EVENING, Bella faced what she thought of as her firing squad. Holden, Spencer and Jarvis sat on her crimson sofa and looked at her with a gravity she wasn't certain she could ever remember her brothers having before. Holden was almost always serious, especially about this case, so his granite expression didn't surprise her.

She sat in her recliner, a birthday gift from her brothers last year. It was one of her favorite places to write, but at the moment it felt more like an interrogation seat.

"What gives, guys?" Her brothers had already been in her driveway when she and Holden pulled up.

"Selina's brakes were cut." Spencer went for the jugular. "This matches all the information that Holden has on the killer. He goes after anyone who insults his target. Selina and Becky both criticized you. At the last pageant he cut brakes, too."

"And we're closing in on the time when he usually strikes. He likes to do scare tactics beforehand, but kills during the last week of pageant preparation, no more than three days out from the final performance." Holden's eyes held concern, but something else. An apology for not telling her these details sooner?

"When did you find this out?" She kept her focus on Holden.

"I found out about Selina's brakes while you were going through your talent portion this last hour. I've known about the killer's MO since I arrived in Mustang Valley but wasn't able to share everything."

"Yet you didn't mention it in the car. The part about Selina's brakes."

"There was no point. I thought you'd need your brothers here for support, and I wanted you to be able to ask Spencer any questions, too."

"What's different now? We know there's a killer, and he's after me because I made the unfortunate decision to streak my hair red." What had possessed her to do it? Not that it would have discouraged the serial killer, she suspected. He'd have found a target one way or the other. At least this way Holden could protect her, and she could protect herself.

"You should come stay with me at the ranch, sis. You can disappear until this blows over." Jarvis looked at her. "No one gets on or off the Triple R without having to pass their incredible security system."

"What, and stay with the other hands in the bunks? No offense, Jarvis, but I'm, we're thirty-one, not thirteen."

"Whoa, that's not nice, sis. And you'd be able to stay in the big house, that'd be no problem if I asked."

"I know you have to live in a bunkhouse as a ranch hand, but I wouldn't be comfortable there or in the Colton mansion. You know that, Jarvis. We're not from that cut of Colton. Why are you still working on the ranch, by the way?"

"Hold it." Spencer stood up. "This isn't about Jarvis and his career, or about me, or Holden. This is about you and your safety. I know you've already refused to quit the pageant, and we can't make you, but Holden and I agree that there needs to be an undercover MVPD officer working to distract the killer."

She looked at Holden. "You told me it would take too long to find someone. We only have days left until the pageant finals." Until the killer tried to end her life. Shudders shook her but she crossed her legs, folded her arms in front of her, hoping none of them noticed.

"An FBI agent, yes, it would take too long. But Spencer has an officer who can do it."

"No."

"Bella, this isn't your decision."

"Hear me out, Spencer. I'm the one who entered the contest to get information, remember? And not just for Gio. I can help you close this investigation and catch the killer like no one else, being a contestant. I'm not quitting. If you let your undercover cop come in now, it'll spook the killer. Sure, it'll keep me safe but we won't catch the murderer and it will put more women at risk. That's the point with serial killers, right? Catch them or they're going to do it again. And again."

Jarvis shook his head. "I'm sure glad I've stuck to horses and ranches these past months."

Spencer looked at Holden. "It's your call, Holden."

Holden met her brother's gaze for a long stretch. It was impossible to tell his thoughts as his stone expression was back in place. She was once again facing Agent St. Clair instead of the Holden she knew and had come to care deeply for.

What?

Before she could analyze her thoughts, Spencer was pacing the room, shaking his head.

"Gosh dang it, Bella. You never, ever, can agree to do what's easiest for you! This isn't a race through the desert, though, or deciding on whether to double up on your majors." Spencer referenced her decision to major in both journalism and environmental science in college. All while working as a barista to keep her student loans to a minimum. Her brothers had been in school at the same time, of course, and had watched her work herself into a bout of exhaustion that had taken the first six months after graduation to get over. But she'd landed her degree and the job at the *Gabber* within a month of each other. It didn't feel like five years of work at the

Gabber, though. It'd passed so quickly, because she really did love her job. But she'd enjoy writing more hard-boiled reports even more.

"Don't throw it on me, Spencer, I'm not the killer!"

"We're down to the wire, folks." Holden looked at her. Did her brothers feel the connection between them? "You're not going to quit, so I say we do all we can to catch the killer before he does any further harm." He stood. "I'd rather you left the pageant, too, frankly. But you've already refused to, twice, and I have to catch this bastard."

"Tell me again—when did he strike the last two times?" Jarvis was clearly at a disadvantage, not being in law enforcement.

"Within the last few days leading up to the start of the pageant."

"Where we are now." Bella finished Jarvis's thoughts for him, wanting her brothers to accept her decision to stay. She needed them to leave, leave her alone. She had a pageant to prepare for, and *Gabber* work to catch up on. "I'm not going to lie to either of you. I'm scared. Of course I am. But it's not like I haven't been before, when I've been working on investigative pieces."

"I thought Gio's report was the first one you were going for?" Spencer challenged her.

She let out a sigh to give herself time. But there was no way around admitting her career failures. Except this time it was in front of Holden.

"I've tried to get information on a lot of different subjects. I want to move to the next place in my reporting, in my career. The *Mustang Valley Gabber's* been great, and it's certainly paid my bills for the last several years.

But I've been doing investigative work, writing up draft reports, for the past year."

"So why didn't those articles get published already?" Jarvis stood, ran his hand over his head. "Do you really need this particular story, sis?"

"The other stories haven't published because I wasn't able to get relevant information. And at the rate this investigative piece is going for me, my exposé for Gio's sake won't publish, either. I'm at a stalemate until I find the pageant's archival records to verify which pageants each committee member served on, and if there are any indications that Ms. Mustang Valley really did cause Gio's illness." But even as she voiced her needs, she already knew the answer. There was no way one pageant, one event, could cause the kind of illnesses Gio suffered from. Not singlehandedly. And she'd learned a lot working in this pageant, enough to know that the majority of pageants as well as contestants were in it for the right reasons. Scholarship, community, empowerment. Still, for Gio's and her reporter credentials' sake, she had to close the loop. "Gio told me they were in a file cabinet in the staff room but I was attacked before I was able to look inside. When I returned, the drawers were all empty."

Jarvis let out a low whistle. "Is this worth your life, sis?"

"It's not about me. It's about Gio." And all the women who'd ever competed in a pageant, but especially the alumnae of Ms. Mustang Valley.

"You'll be able to write about the killer, once the case is closed." Holden turned to her brothers. "If Bella's not willing to quit, then at least she should have something for her sacrifice."

Bella was stunned by Holden's words. Sure, she could write about the serial killer investigation, and it would prove a promotion-worthy article. But he'd never admitted it to her, never gave her a clue he'd be willing to bend his FBI rules to allow her inside information that she'd be free to report on.

"I'd have to be careful, to protect the court case."

"Which I'm certain you will. You're a professional." Holden didn't hold back in front of her brothers. Not one bit. He closed the gap between them. "I completely trust you, Bella. I need you to trust me. It's the only way I can promise to keep you alive."

Chapter Twenty

Holden's gut twisted as he said the words, as Bella's brilliant green eyes widened and the blush on her cheeks deepened. Holding her hands, facing her, he knew what he had to say next.

"I'll protect you through every bit of this, Bella, as I have so far. But going forward, there probably aren't going to be any more warning signs or incidents perpetrated by the killer to throw us off his trail. The next move will be to take you out."

She nodded. "I know that. And I do, Holden. I trust you." She squeezed his hands and he squeezed back.

To their credit, neither Colton brother groaned or made a rude comment. Which appeared to move her more than the prospect of facing her attacker again.

Everyone knew this was a matter of Bella's life or death.

"This isn't a crackpot criminal, Bella. You're dealing with an evil we don't usually find in Mustang Valley." Spencer stood and looked at Holden. "I trust you with my life, buddy, and know I'm trusting you with Bella's."

Jarvis didn't say anything and Holden didn't blame him.

"I give you my word, nothing will happen to your

sister." He meant his words, but couldn't fight his own worry over Bella's involvement in such a dangerous pivot-point.

Holden had to keep it together, because zero FBI backup was in the area and MVPD was spread thin.

"I'm going to walk your brothers out. Stay here until I get back."

"I need a shower. Or is that off-limits?"

"Fine. Get one but make it quick and don't leave the house, not even to go out on the patio."

"Got it."

He caught up to the brothers and fell into step next to them until they were at Spencer's K-9 SUV.

"I'll keep you posted." He spoke to Spencer, as informing Jarvis about the investigation wasn't protocol. He knew Spencer would keep Jarvis informed.

Spencer nodded. "I know you will. I'll let you know what I do, Jarvis."

"Sure thing. See you, Holden." Jarvis got into the passenger seat and waited while Holden and Spencer talked outside.

"Thank you for the extra security on-site at the school and here." Holden couldn't do his job if MVPD didn't do theirs.

"Yeah, well, whatever it takes, right? Let's get this bad guy once and for all, Holden." Spencer looked up at the deepening sky, the stars that were shining across the earth's canopy. "It's not unlike the long hours we pulled waiting for the drill sergeant to ream our butts, is it?"

"Not much different at all. Except I've been managing some sleep each night, thanks to MVPD and you."

Spencer snorted. "I know you, Holden. You never sleep while the enemy's still on the prowl."

"Yeah, well, at least I can catch a nap here and there. That's more than we ever did in the Army."

"It is." Spencer opened the driver-side door. "Let's hope this doesn't go on for the rest of the week."

"If he does what he's done in the past, the next two days will be key." Holden had studied the timelines of each murder, the pageant preparations leading up to it. Ms. Mustang Valley was right on time for the murderer's schedule. He expected an attempt on Bella's life in the next forty-eight hours.

Spencer shifted on his feet. "Not to change the subject or make it seem like I'm not invested in my sister's stalker, but I have another case to ask you about. I need a favor."

"Anything. Shoot."

"You know about AAG, and that Leigh, one of the contestants, is heavily involved in it."

"Right. She's still ingratiating as all get-out, always telling Bella and the other contestants that they are all beautiful winners and can do it no matter what." Holden managed a short laugh. "We probably owe her, in a twisted way, for keeping the pageant going and the contestants coming back in the face of danger."

"I'd hold off on your praise. AAG is not right, I'm certain of it. And I've had reason to look into its founder, Micheline Anderson, after we talked about her. Turns out she didn't exist as a person until forty years ago." Spencer looked at him intently, clearly waiting for Holden to put something together.

"Okay, so she's forty years old?"

"No, nothing like that. Micheline isn't a day under sixty-five. But her birth date, or appearance on the planet, coincides with the disappearance of Luella Smith, the nurse at the hospital who likely switched her baby for the one we know as Ace Colton. Look, here's a photo of Luella Smith from forty years ago." Spencer tapped onto his phone and handed it to Holden.

"Wow. Save for the darker hair and glasses, this woman's the spitting image of Micheline." He'd observed the AAG founder at the pageant practices, sitting in the audience with the smattering of other relatives, friends and parents who stopped by to see how their loved ones were doing.

"Exactly. I questioned her about what kind of history she had, before forty years ago when it all goes dark for her. She told me that she was in the witness protection program until now, and can't talk about it. I thought that was odd, because you can't divulge if you've ever been in the program but I didn't want to call her on it right then. I want her to think we're clueless as to her motives."

"Good thinking. No, you're not supposed to ever reveal if you've been in the witness protection program." Holden referred to the Bureau. "I can ask a colleague who helps administer it to look her up."

"That'd be great!" Spencer's relief was palpable. "I appreciate it."

"But remember, I'm not privy to the protection's program information, not on an official level. Whatever you find out is yours—do with it as you need to."

"No, no, that's not a problem at all. I owe you, buddy."

Spencer's phone sounded and he looked at Holden. "I've got to take this. I'll be in touch."

"Same."

Holden turned back and was almost to the front door when he realized what mattered most to him in this moment wasn't the investigation and getting to his next rank in the FBI.

It was the woman in the modest adobe house.

Bella.

"Holden, hold up!" Spencer's voice shook him out of his revelation as he trotted up to him, phone in hand.

"What's up?"

"That was the head of the MVPD forensics team. The lab results are in and we have an ID on the prints that are on the file cabinet."

"Whose are they?"

"Becky's. She's voluntarily turned over several boxes of paper files from the pageant. She admitted that she didn't want the pageant to become fodder for tabloid gossip, which is what she said she considers the *Gabber* to be. She suspected Bella was reporting on the pageant the minute she signed up as a contestant." Spencer had a look of disgust on his face. "All Becky had to do was read the *Gabber.* She'd see it's a reputable news source."

"Those are the files Bella has been searching for." Holden felt a sense of pride. Bella had trusted her gut, and Gio's information, and she'd been correct. The pageant's archives had been in that file cabinet.

"We can have them to her as soon as we get through the red tape. Will you tell her?"

"Tell me what?" Of course Bella was standing in the threshold. Holden tried not to glare at her. "What? I'm not outside, not completely."

As HOLDEN REPEATED what Spencer had told him, she felt both men watching her, gauging her reaction.

"Becky?" Bella couldn't believe it. And yet, she'd

never seen her attacker. "Holden, is it possible that Becky was the attacker you talked to?"

Holden frowned. "It's possible, yes, but improbable. I remember the assailant as wider, more muscular."

"This doesn't explain how she fell, or who pushed her, or how the explosion was set off at the same time, or even why she'd want to kill the victims."

"If she was pushed. It's possible she jumped, faked being pushed. But I've never had a case where someone intentionally hurt themselves, to distract from the real crime. Becky really wanted to win the pageant." Spencer shook his head. "Nothing is as it seems in this case."

"That's exactly what the attacker said to me." Holden's mouth was a straight line, white around the edges from pressing his lips together.

Chills assailed her. Holden was the one person she counted on to know what the heck was happening.

"Spencer has an officer at her place now, questioning her. She's already turned over several boxes of pageant files. Spencer said you'll have them as soon as he takes care of the administrative and legal details."

"Is it possible that we don't have a serial killer, but a woman who is for some reason bent on keeping the history of Ms. Mustang Valley a secret?" She had to ask the obvious.

Holden expelled a breath. "Possible, yes. Probable? No."

Spencer shook his head. "I'm a local cop, you're the serial-killer expert."

"The majority of participants are really just trying to get ahead. It's often their last hope. We have no reason to think Becky didn't want the same. So of course she wanted to protect the files, and the pageant—she didn't want it shut down." Bella blurted out her thoughts before she thought twice about it. Both men turned and faced her. Standing on the threshold, she saw Jarvis sitting in the SUV with Boris.

"That wasn't your opinion when you signed up for this." Spencer's exasperation made her wish she'd kept her mouth shut. He had enough on his shoulders with Payne Colton still in a coma from a gunshot and the shooter still on the loose. Not to mention the other everyday myriad petty crimes that kept MVPD busy on a slow day.

"It's my job to keep my opinion out of it. I'm learning as I go along." She paused, afraid to ask the next question. "Can you get me the files as soon as possible? I'm willing to come in to the station and copy them myself."

"I'll see what we can do, but my first priority isn't an old stack of paperwork, Bella."

"That's fair. I get it." Still, if she could have the files, her exposé would be complete.

"Keep us informed, Spencer." Holden looked distracted.

Spencer nodded and walked back to the SUV.

As soon as she shut the door, Bella followed Holden into the kitchen where she watched him start a pot of coffee.

"Isn't it a little late for caffeine?"

"Normally, yes. But it's going to be a long night."

"Again." She rounded the counter and stood next to him. "I'm sorry that you haven't been able to get much sleep."

"It's my job. This isn't the first time I've had to go without. It's always worth the final results."

"It seems a high price to pay, your health."

"Lack of sleep is manageable, short-term. But most cases aren't solved as quickly as we're hoping this will be. It's not like on television or in the movies. I've worked as long as three years on a single case before connecting the dots well enough to not only get the criminal, but to ensure the case is solid for the prosecuting attorney."

"I know it's not like the movies, trust me. Spencer is my brother, remember? I also know that you're being modest. It takes an incredible amount of tenacity to hang in there, day after day." She knew; reporting was often the same.

"You're trying to show me that you do the same thing, Bella, but it doesn't equate." His tone was cooler than it had been since he'd first made it clear he wasn't a fan of reporters almost three weeks ago.

The most revelatory few weeks of her life. Not that she had time to process it all right now.

"I'm not trying to manipulate you into believing something you never will. If I have something to say to you, I'm direct. You should know that by now, if nothing else." Heat rushed her face and she turned away, damning the tears that threatened to fall. Anger at herself for falling for this unreachable man combined with frustration at reaching the end of the pageant with not a heck of a lot of exposé material, save for whatever the archival files Becky turned over might have, had made her a hot mess. Plus the fact that maybe it was time she faced some hard facts about Gio's illness and its causes. She might never have that answer, and she had to figure out what to focus her reporting on, besides Ms. Mustang Valley pageant wrong-doing. The pressure of it welled inside, adding fuel to her tears of frustration.

Think.

There was plenty to draw from with all she'd learned as a contestant, albeit undercover. The scholarship award was particularly noteworthy, as the motives for each contestant to win were deserving of their own story. The other topics she'd inadvertently learned so much about were eating orders and mental illness. There was never enough light shone on them, as far as she was concerned. She'd figure out a story topic, even though her emotions were making it seem impossible at the moment.

"Hey, hang on." Holden reached for her and she dared herself to look up at him. "We're at the tough part here. It's normal to feel like it'll never end."

"Stop it with your constant stream of FBI platitudes. I know what I'm feeling and while it's probably hard for you to believe, you can't read my mind." She watched his face as she challenged him and where she expected an answering anger she saw heat...of a different kind.

"Bella. When are you going to get it that much of my—what did you call them, oh yeah, *platitudes*, are my way of staying on the straight and narrow, where I have to be to do my job?"

"Your job is to catch a killer and you've given yourself the additional assignment of protecting *me*. Unless you see me as the ideal lure for the murderer."

"Never." He pulled her up against his chest, her breasts flattened by the sheer masculine wall, and lowered his mouth to hers. Hadn't she just told him she was direct with communication? Holden had the direct part of physical communication down.

His kiss turned into their kiss as they didn't waste time on preliminaries. Mouths opened, tongues swept, breathing hitched. Desire rose and pooled in the most delicious, torturous way as Holden's hands caressed her cheeks, her throat, then grasped her breasts with un-abashed need.

"Holden," she moaned against his mouth and he began to kiss her jawline, her throat, as his hands moved over her belly and down to the molten hot spot between her legs. Her knees felt as impermanent as the desert sands, the quaking he caused making her hang on to his massive shoulders. "I can't take this much longer."

"Then don't, babe." He lifted her into his arms with zero fanfare and walked into the living room where he deposited her on the sofa. Her question must have been in her gaze as she looked at him, marveled at how her fingers had tousled his hair, her kisses had made his lips fuller, his eyes half-lidded. "It's safer out here."

"Okay." She sat up. "Let me get—"

"This?" He pulled a condom from his jeans front pocket and grinned.

"Were you expecting this?" She'd thought she'd never experience his lovemaking again, not during the inves-tigation and definitely not if he really couldn't stand her profession.

"Never expected, but hoped." His words were as hot as his tongue and fingers, setting her already flaming want into a full-raging inferno.

Unlike the other time they'd made love, she wanted to undress him. He shucked out of his T-shirt and she got on her knees, the sofa cushions buckling underneath. "Let me." Kissing his chest, licking the skin through the tufts of his chest hair, she heard him sigh, groan. She unbuckled his belt, unbuttoned the single jean fastener. Unzipping his jeans was the single most sensual mo-ment she'd ever had. Her reward for going slow, slow,

slow was grasping his erection and freeing it, pushing the pants down with her other hand.

"You next." He sucked in air as he spoke, and the huskiness of his voice made her aware of how wet she was, how ready to be one with him again.

"Holden, I want to—"

"I know, babe, but we're short on time here." He pushed her back to her feet, lifted her top up and over her head, peeled her leggings off. She stood in front of him wearing a sports bra and lacy thong.

"I do have matching underwear, I swear."

He chuckled but it was strained. Never had she been with a man who so clearly wanted her as much as she did him.

"Babe, I'm not interested in your bra-and-panty sets." He squeezed her breast through the thin stretchy material, lowered his head and sucked on her nipple. As she cried out with need he lifted the bra up and off, then kissed and suckled each nipple, the feel of his tongue against her bare skin driving her close to the edge. And she still had her thong on.

"Holden, I—"

"Come here." He grasped her thong and pushed it down, his fingers doing what she was certain was some secret move to her most private parts. As soon as she was naked, he sheathed himself then lay on the sofa. "Come here."

His hands on her hips to guide her, she propped her hands on his shoulders and leaned over, her knees on either side of his pelvis. He moved his grasp to her buttocks and pulled her down atop his erection. The sudden heat and fullness sent her into preorgasmic miniquakes, her body shaking beyond her control.

"That's it, babe, take it, take it." He spoke as he gyrated underneath her, moving the way that made her gasp, sigh, and with a definite swirl of his pelvis, scream.

He didn't wait for her climax to end before he began moving hard and fast inside her, forcing her to cling to him, holding on for what she thought an impossible second orgasm.

His forehead was bathed in sweat and it turned her on more to know she'd made him feel like this. She'd helped drive him to this point, the same place she was. Where whatever it took, they were going to come together.

"Holden, I'm going to come again." She couldn't stop moving against him, meeting every thrust with a downward swing of her hips, the swell of her climax surging, threatening to take her down with Holden's next move.

"That's it. Babe!" He thrust up and shouted as she screamed. But the intensity of their mutual climax didn't drag her down at all—it lifted her to the highest places imaginable.

Chapter Twenty-One

"We can't stay like this all night." Bella spoke against his chest as he moved his fingers through her hair, brushing it off her damp brow. They'd taken a full fifteen minutes to come back to Planet Earth and he'd reveled in every second of it.

And silently thanked MVPD for having the outside security down pat.

"We could, but it might get sticky." He laughed and loved that she let out a little giggle, too.

"Ewww." She rose to look at him and he'd never seen such a beautiful shade of green. "Now you sound like a guy and not—" She stopped.

"What?" He helped her off him and then stood next to her.

"Let's finish this in the bathroom."

"The guest shower." He didn't want her near her shower until they either caught the killer or were certain Becky had been the criminal all along. They padded, naked, down the hall. Holden took his gun with him, his only concession to the reality of their situation. His thoughts were on getting into the shower with Bella. Two minutes later they were under the cool spray.

"What were you going to say, when you said I

sounded like a guy?" He was massaging her scalp as he washed her hair and the way she leaned her head completely back let him know that she trusted him. It was a sacred space and he didn't take it lightly.

"You are bigger than life. It'd be easy to think that, that I'll never meet someone like you again."

His hands stilled and he turned her around.

"Babe, it's not me, or you. It's what we become together. Us."

"But you don't like reporters."

"And I live two hours away."

"We have different career goals."

"We do."

They remained quiet as they stood together under the spray, then took turns drying one another off.

"So this was it?" Her voice was steady and he admired how pragmatic she was. He felt like he'd been kicked in the gut multiple times, except the memory of their lovemaking made it impossible to feel much of anything besides completely content.

"Bella, I—"

Suddenly, the sound of gunfire rang through the night, coming from the other side of the house wall. He pushed her down onto the floor, covering her with his body. He listened, but silence descended. Reaching up to the sink while still protecting Bella, he grabbed his phone and called Spencer.

"Inside the house, we're under fire. Where's MVPD?"

"We're on it, Holden. Take cover until I find out where your patrol is." Spencer's frustration bit through his words.

He left the phone on speaker and placed it on the sink, next to his weapon, which he grabbed and flipped the safety off. "We're in the guest bathroom, northern side of the house. I've got my weapon and we're going to stay put until you tell me it's clear."

"We have to get dressed." Bella's voice was low, meant for him.

"Quick, let's get clothes from the bedroom." He'd left a bag in the guest room and knew she had her workout and out-of-season clothes in there. The bedroom was between them and the center of the house, where they'd have the most protection from bullets. "I think the MVPD patrol was disabled. There's no other way a shooter got past them."

They were dressed in thirty seconds flat, and as he zipped his cargo shorts and Bella tugged on bicycle shorts, gunfire again rang out.

Bella didn't need him to push her down this time— she was already flat on the floor, between the bed and closet. He'd been in only one other live shooting and he'd relied on what he'd learned in Quantico at the FBI Academy. "Stay down, and let's get into the center of the house."

"Do you think it's the killer?" Bella spoke as she shimmied on her belly down the hallway.

"Don't go any farther. Stay between the two walls." He sat, his back against the wall, weapon loaded and aimed at the ceiling until needed.

Bella copied his posture, and he again was impressed with her composure under duress.

"What do you think is going on?"

"I don't know." Spencer hadn't, either, which was a red flag.

"What if—" She was cut off by a loud, splintering sound. "The kitchen door!"

"Stay here." He ran up to the edge of the wall, weapon first, and peered around the boundary. It was dark and he was unable to see anything but a large shadow of a person on the other side, kicking in the door. The motion-detector light had been shot out, no doubt.

"Stop or I'll shoot!"

A barrage of bullets through the shattered door window was the only reply. Holden's only recourse was to fire back. As he held his hands steady, he got off six, seven shots, waited for the attacker to either drop or flee.

Rapid footsteps faded into silence, and he waited. The front door was one hundred and eighty degrees behind him, so he positioned himself to be able to answer fire from either entrance.

Sirens sounded in the distance, the wails soft but persistent. He had at least five more minutes before the house would be surrounded by responding MVPD. What had happened to the patrol unit in front of the house, and its officers, remained unknown but experience screamed at him that the killer had owned up to his role tonight.

"Holden!" Bella's scream had him turning to the left, looking down the hallway. She was scrambling to her feet, trying to run to him, as a figure similar to the one he'd seen in the staff room stood at the end of the hallway, weapon aimed at Bella, who was now behind Holden.

"Stop or I'll shoot!" Holden kept his weapon aimed at the killer. The intruder seemed to consider his options before he leaped sideways and disappeared into the master bedroom. Holden shoved Bella back, into the kitchen. He saw she held her handgun, which he'd asked her to keep by her side when at home. "Keep your weapon out—watch both doors."

He was down the hall and cleared into the bedroom, where all he found was the window wide open, gauzy drapes hanging both in and out of it, billowing into the night. Running to the open window he knew what he'd find—nothing. As he peered out, he spotted a MVPD officer in tactical gear as they rounded the corner of the house.

"He took off into the desert!" Holden yelled, pointed at the heavy brush that made it easy for the killer to disappear. The officer nodded and Holden heard mumbles through their helmet as the officer spoke into his or her microphone. The officer ran to the back of the property, followed by another, who'd entered the backyard. Bella's garden backed up to the desert and the perfect escape for a criminal who knew their way around the southeastern Arizona scrub.

Holden swore, the words inaudible to his own ears as the sirens roared and cruisers screeched to a halt, surrounding Bella's house. The killer had eluded him once more.

Bella.

Running out into the hall he let out a huge breath when he saw her standing in the apex of the entryways and short hallway, her defiant posture underscoring what attracted him to her in the first place. Not her beauty, nor her sensuality, but her strength.

Bella was the strongest woman he'd ever met, and that was a big deal, as until now he'd always counted Grandma St. Clair as the toughest.

Beams of light splayed across the living area from the windows and partially-cracked-open door. Bella was safe.

For now.

"YOU CAN STAND DOWN, Bella." Holden's voice reached her ears but she couldn't stop from standing on alert, her arms raised with her weapon ready to fire. Only when his hands touched her shoulders, ran down her arms to hug her from behind, did she lower her arms and engage the safety. "You're safe."

She leaned against him, not caring that it was only minutes since she'd promised herself she wouldn't so much as touch him for the remainder of the pageant, no matter how much longer she had to rely on his protection. There was no hope for them past what they'd already shared, and she wasn't about prolonging her own agony. Her resolve seemed trite in light of the shootout, and while her brain registered that she'd been intimate with Holden for the last time, her body needed the physical reassurance of his hold to confirm that they were both alive.

They'd survived.

"That was wild." Her words came out higher pitched than usual, not unlike a cartoon character. Giggles erupted, joining the trembling that shook her.

"You're going on adrenaline. It'll pass." His voice, his warm breath, was against her left ear and she had to fight to keep from turning her head the few degrees it needed to put her mouth to his. To escape into the heat they alone shared, far away from the threat of immediate death at the hands of a determined monster.

"This will never pass, Holden."

He didn't respond and she sensed he knew what she meant. Their combined attraction and connection wasn't trivial, and was made of the fiber that bound couples together for a lifetime.

But their lives were too different, too separate. Even

if she were willing to choose a career he'd be more accepting of, and she wasn't, not for any man, Holden had made it clear that he wasn't about long-distance relationships. The two hours between here and Phoenix wasn't impossible to manage but she knew he wasn't talking about mere miles.

Holden meant their worldviews and values were too far apart to navigate. To make holding on worth it.

"Listen, Bella, if the intruder is the killer, if he'd captured you—"

"He didn't. You were here."

"But I might not always be. Do you know what to do if you're taken hostage?"

She looked up at him. "Stay alive."

"Yes, but there are some techniques we know are worth employing. Keep the kidnapper talking, try to draw them out. And don't let them take you to a different place if you can at all help it. Promise me you'll do that." He wanted her to promise not just for her, but for him. Because he wasn't sure he'd be able to live without her.

"I'll do it, promise. But with you around, no killer is getting to me."

He wished he was the man she thought he was. With Bella, he felt invincible.

Footsteps stomped outside, and someone pounded on the kitchen door.

"MVPD. We're coming in. Stay still with hands up." The female voice that sounded from the other side of the kitchen wall, on the patio, was Detective Kerry Wilder, whom Bella knew well through Spencer.

"Kerry, it's Bella Colton. I'm with—"

"FBI Agent Holden St. Clair." Holden's voice was loud and commanding next to her, and she started to relax. "The shooter took off through the desert, heading toward the edge of the neighborhood."

"Roger." Detective Wilder's next commands were rapid and Bella imagined Kerry was telling the team with her to disperse into the desert. "Stay put until I come back." Kerry's voice reached them from the other side of the kitchen door. Bella saw several shadows swipe by the window as the tactical team ran for the desert.

Holden and Bella stood in the quiet of the kitchen, and she reveled in the strength she drew from being in his arms. It was almost possible to believe they might be near the end of this nightmare.

Until the shadow of a police helmet passed the kitchen window. "It's Detective Wilder, I'm entering your kitchen through the door."

When Bella took full stock of Kerry in full tactical gear, her nerves forgot about relaxing. It was impossible to tell it was Kerry, as she couldn't see the woman's flaming red hair, obscured by a dark helmet complete with night-vision goggles. Kerry reached a gloved hand through the broken kitchen door window, turned the dead bolt and opened the battered door. She carried an automatic weapon and Bella registered the magazines of rounds clipped to her body armor.

Kerry lifted her helmet visor, sending the NVGs above her head, too. The flash of her familiar blue eyes sent waves of relief through Bella. Followed immediately by quakes of nausea. Where was Spencer? Had one of the bullets hit her brother?

Sweat beaded her upper lip and she forced breaths in and out of her mouth, not sure if she was going to pass out or throw up.

"At ease, folks. We've cleared the outer perimeter, and we've got several officers chasing on foot. You won't be staying here for the rest of the night, though."

"Is, is Spencer okay?" Holden wrapped a firm arm around her shoulders and she shrugged it off. Whether she got sick or crumpled to the floor, she had to do it on her own. Holden wasn't her personal support system.

"I'm good." Spencer walked in from the backyard and stood next to Kerry. "You're going to need a new kitchen door, sis."

Chapter Twenty-Two

Three days later, Holden and Bella arrived at the school together for what would be the last pageant practice. Against her wishes, Bella had to stay at different places each night after the break-in to thwart the killer. The assailant at her house had knocked the police offers out with tear gas, similar to what happened after the high school locker explosion. So they knew it was most likely the same person but exactly who was still a mystery. They couldn't rule out Becky as a suspect, even with her admission of not wanting the pageant to end if the files were examined by a reporter or the police. It made Bella nervous, knowing Becky might try to hurt her mid-finale.

Holden had remained at her side the past few days, but like her, never crossed the romantic involvement line that they'd silently laid down before the killer injured two MVPD officers. Bella kept telling herself it was for the best; it would make the last time she saw Holden that much easier.

If only her heart dealt in logic.

"This is really heavy, and hot." She wore body armor under the evening gown she'd chosen. The short-sleeved, round-neck navy blue dress was the simplest and most modest style she'd ever worn, but it did the job of hiding the Kevlar vest. And also made her look twenty pounds heavier, in her estimation, but she had no illusions of winning the pageant.

"You've got tonight and then the pageant tomorrow to sweat it out. After that you'll be free." Holden strode next to her, his looks heightened by the tuxedo that he wore. The pageant board and Selina in particular had requested everyone be in the same attire they'd wear for the actual pageant. Since the final event was being live streamed via the *Mustang Valley Gabber*'s website, Selina and the technical-production team wanted the optics and blocking to be perfect.

"When do you go back to Phoenix?" She bit her cheek as soon as she asked. So much for keeping it platonic and easy between them.

"As soon as I catch the killer."

"What if you don't?"

"It's my job to. What I came here for."

She caught the undercurrent. He hadn't come here to meet her, get involved with his buddy's sister. Irritation that had nothing to do with the Kevlar armor made her chin rise, her anger sharpen.

"As I came here to get my story. I'm still waiting for MVPD to turn the files over to me." She'd tried to get them released sooner but Spencer had made it clear that his team had to go through them first. With the demands of the pageant security, plus chasing the assailant at her house to no avail, there hadn't been time to read several decades' worth of pageant files. Bella didn't doubt Gio but she also had to face facts. Gio's mind hadn't been operating at one hundred percent near the end. Her memory could have been faulty, but again, Bella needed the files to verify her theories. She'd done further research on the women who'd come forward with their eating disorder and mental illness stories, and while they'd all competed in Ms. Mustang Valley, none of them blamed the pageant. To a fault. They all stated that they'd had a tendency toward mental illness or eating disorders before ever joining a pageant, and the sometimes frenetic activity and perceived pressure may have triggered their illnesses. But none would state that the pageants, or any one thing, had caused their disorders.

"Bella, do you have enough for your story?" Holden stopped short of the front steps. The lowering sun cast streaks of violet and fuchsia across the Arizona sky and reflected a light in his mahogany eyes and made her heart hurt. He'd had the same spark when he'd looked at her naked.

"Maybe. But not really, no. Not until I read the files." A clump of hair fell in her eyes and she shoved it aside, ignoring the crackle of too much hairspray.

He chuckled. "You never did figure out how to get your hair to stay up, did you?"

"I like to wear it down. It's not my fault the pageant requires more than one hairstyle throughout the night." Straightening her spine, she squared off with him, ignored the devastating contrast between his skin and the white crispness of the tuxedo shirt. Or how the black jacket material made his eyes appear impossibly seductive.

"You haven't answered my question." Spoken as softly as the endearments he'd whispered in her ear before he made her come in full technicolor splendor. Yet the current of his dislike of her profession remained.

"I will have a story at the end of this, yes. It might

not be what I'd hoped for or expected, but I don't have a choice. If I want to go further with my career, become a bona fide investigative journalist, I need to produce. If this isn't the story to move my career needle, there'll be another."

"Let me guess—you've finally found some dirt on Selina and the hold she has held over Payne Colton for years?"

Did he know his words were like an owl's talons? Cutting deep, causing irreparable damage?

"Maybe." She had no such thing, but wouldn't admit it to him. Holden had gone back to being her adversary. "And just think, I didn't have to pry it out of you with more sex." Without further comment, she turned and bolted for the entrance. It was too agonizing to see if her words had landed anywhere as soft as his had.

Right in her heart.

HOLDEN FOUGHT AGAINST pulling Bella up against him, holding her and kissing her until they both forgot why they had to throw down their respective gauntlets. Why they had to so effectively deny each other the pleasure they'd found in one another's arms. And more—they'd found friendship, understanding, agreement between them. An intimacy he'd never experienced. And it wasn't due to the intensity of this case, the constant threat of a methodical killer.

It was Bella.

He had no time or energy to spend on a failed relationship. She'd made her position clear. Bella had her entire life here in Mustang Valley, and would only ever leave for a new job. Judging from her diligence to meticulous research and the articles he'd read under her column in the *Gabber* and on its website, she'd receive offers from all over the country, if not the globe after her pageant story published. No matter what she chose to write about, Bella had a voice that demanded to be heard and stories that deserved the readership a major newspaper would bring.

"Okay, ladies. You all know what we're here for tonight. We'll take it from the top, with the opening number." Selina, garbed in a sparkling, formfitting multicolored dress, stood onstage with a gold microphone, her bright red nails like talons on its neck. Holden wouldn't miss this woman's drama, or the pageant itself.

You'll miss Bella.

He scanned the stage as the music began and the lights focused first on each contestant as she walked across the stage. He followed the beams to where the lights were affixed to scaffolding brought in just for the pageant. The school's theater lights were manually operated from a control booth in the audiovisual room above the theater seats. The scaffolding lights were remotely operated, too, but he knew there were two techs up in the rafters affixed to the metal structure, there to maneuver some of the special effects, to include a net of balloons that would drop when the new Ms. Mustang Valley was announced.

He counted one, then two of the techs, in place as prescribed.

"You're looking awfully dapper for a G-man." Spencer stood next to him in the theater, grinning as if he'd discovered Holden's deepest secret.

"It's for the pageant. Selina demanded it."

Spencer guffawed, the noise swallowed by the loud music booming through the theater as the contestants moved through the opening dance routine. Holden's gaze never left Bella's form, and he didn't see why she was so unhappy with wearing body armor. To him, it only made her look more the warrior that he already knew her to be.

"Do you really think the killer's still even in Mustang Valley?" Spencer spoke from the side of his mouth as they both watched the stage.

"I wouldn't be here if I didn't."

"It seems stupid. If he really wanted to kill Bella, he would have."

Spencer's comment was salt to the self-inflicted wounds he'd been nursing the last few days. And the long nights in three different hotel rooms around the area, where he'd slept on a bed next to Bella's, while the entire place was in lockdown with plain clothed MVPD officers and two rookie FBI agents who'd been sent in to help out.

"Aw, crap, Holden, I didn't mean to say—"

"Yes, you did. I left your sister in the hallway and never thought about the fact the killer had disabled two officers and would enter through the master-bedroom sliding door."

"You're not perfect, Holden. You kept the killer from coming into the kitchen. If you hadn't, you'd both be dead."

He shoved his self-loathing aside, spoke out of the side of his mouth as he kept vigilance on the stage.

"We're both still here and I have a killer to catch. Bella can defend herself as needed." Not that he'd ever let it get to that point. "I'm certain he is still here, a part of the pageant. His MO is to take his time, draw out the actual murder. You've read the same reports I have."

"No, I haven't. You have more access than I do with the other two murders—they're out of my jurisdiction."

"Trust me on this. The killer is still here."

And he was going to catch him.

BELLA SQUATTED DOWN behind stage left to adjust her ankle holster. Her dress was long enough to not reveal the weapon, but she didn't want any of the leather to show, either. Holden had watched her affix it to her leg, and it had been difficult to keep her mind on the investigation and the killer who was after her with him looking at her so closely.

"You holding up okay?" Holden had materialized as if from her thoughts.

She stood and even in her heels only came up to his chin. "I am. To be honest, I'd really like this to be over once and for all." She was tired of fighting her fears, and the knowledge that the end of the pageant meant the end of ever seeing Holden again was getting to be too much for her already-worn-out emotions.

"I'm sorry it's not already finished for you."

Was he referring to the killer or their unrelationship?

"Everyone center stage, please. Last call before the final number." Señora Rosenstein was filling in for Selina while the woman changed into what she said was *the best costume this pageant has ever seen.* Someone needed to tell her that she wasn't a contestant.

"Do you really think the killer is still even in Mustang Valley?" She and Holden spoke in hushed tones as they stood on the stage, under the lights, waiting for the last instructions.

"Yes."

Holden's grim expression told her what she dreaded.

The killer was that cold, that measured in his attack plan that he'd do anything to get his way and have the murder be to his liking. His depraved needs.

Funny, she'd willingly entered a contest she didn't believe in, only to find she had more in common with all the other women that not. Bella understood how Gio had seen the pageant community as an extended family.

The memory of Gio reminded her that she'd not gotten far at all on her exposé. Suddenly it didn't matter. What mattered was the safety of these women, of all the future Ms. Mustang Valley contestants. Anger flared and lit a flame she'd always carried but had never allowed to empower her like this before.

"Holden." Her voice was loud, and not only did Holden turn to her but so did the entire pageant.

"Excuse me!" Selina had returned.

"Shut up, Selina." She turned back to Holden and lowered her voice to a whisper. "Look, we have to make this happen on our terms, not the bad guy's."

Holden opened his mouth to probably tell her to be quiet and let him do the find-the-serial-killer bit, but she saw the opportunity for what it was. Bella leaned up and wrapped her hands around Holden's nape, pulled him to her and kissed him with all her might.

He stiffened, and while he didn't push her away he didn't tug her in close, either, as he had before. Bella paid it no mind—she was after one thing.

To entice the killer.

The other pageant participants tittered, gasped and *awwww*ed until they all broke out into a loud round of applause. Only when she was certain no one involved in the event could have possibly missed the kiss did Bella pull back.

Holden's eyes glittered with cold fury. He leaned in, though, and for a moment she thought he was going to kiss her again.

"What the hell, Bella?" His voice low and lethal, he asked his question against her ear.

"The killer wants me. This is the surest way to draw him out." She felt Holden's breath hitch as she whispered back. "I'd rather have him come for me tonight than tomorrow during the actual pageant finale, with a few thousand civilians in the audience."

"I don't know how you got the impression that the stage is your personal rendezvous spot, but it's not. Please do your job, Holden, and Bella, you've come too far to get disqualified now."

She stepped back but Holden's hand still had a grasp on her wrist. She turned and looked at him. "What?"

"Don't forget what I've taught you."

He released her and disappeared behind the stage, where she knew he'd be on alert, patrolling, waiting for the killer to make his move. As she walked to her spot to wait until her time to give her talent portion— the recitation of a poem written by a reporter two centuries ago—she wished she could hang with Holden in the dark. Just one more time before they parted ways and never saw one another again.

Chapter Twenty-Three

Holden looked under the stage, and through the entire backstage, with zero evidence of a killer or anyone else. Becky moved through the routine of the pageant numbers like any other contestant, and she never once appeared to be doing anything but what everyone else did. She didn't have a weapon on her—every contestant had been searched and put through the metal detector as part of the extraordinary security measures. Everyone, it seemed, was either on the stage, in the orchestra pit below stage front, or up in the lighting scaffolding. The pageant board members were all seated in the audience seats in rows one and two, save for Selina. She continued to cue each contestant to come forward to answer their questions and then perform their talent portion, just as they would on finale night.

Marcie began to sing the Broadway tune he'd heard at least twelve times during the previous practices, and he felt his insides tighten with adrenaline-fueled anxiety. He was always wound tight before an op went down, if he was aware of it. This time it was so much more than an op, or taking out a serial killer, no matter how hard he tried to believe it wasn't.

This was all about Bella and saving her. Sure, he'd

catch the killer in the process, and while it wouldn't hurt his career progression to do so, it wasn't what mattered to him most.

He wanted Bella at his side all the time, not just as the woman he was ordered to protect through the investigation and eventual apprehension of a serial killer.

Holden watched Bella walk across the stage when it was her turn but didn't allow himself the luxury of appreciating her beauty or grace, even in the cumbersome body armor. If the killer attacked before he had a chance to react, it would mean Bella's life.

He cursed himself, wished he'd insisted she drop out of the Ms. Mustang Valley Pageant. It was beyond agony to know that at any moment she might be hurt, or worse.

The only thing keeping him sane was that the level of security imposed by Spencer and MVPD was the best it could be. He prayed it'd give him enough time to save Bella, if and when the killer struck.

When Bella finished the poem, which he hadn't paid attention to, intent on observation, she walked offstage toward him, before turning to go to the staff room. He knew she was going to change for the last number, as were all the other contestants.

He scanned the light scaffolding and his heart stopped. Only one tech was atop the metal structure instead of the two who were always present throughout the entire pageant. A movement in his peripheral vision made him turn to the left. He immediately spotted a man dressed in jeans, black top, and most chilling, a mask. He recognized the clothing as that of one of the lighting techs, Ben. Ben stood with his hand on the main stage light switch. Holden hit the comms unit on his chest and alerted MVPD, already surrounding the building as a precaution.

Precaution had turned to deadly intent.

"Stop!" Weapon drawn, he ran toward Ben, perpendicular to his course, planning to cut him off before Ben got any farther. Before he reached Bella.

The stage went black and Holden was plunged into darkness.

A piercing scream split the air.

Bella.

"Shut up or you're dead now, bitch." Ben's voice was so close, above the cacophony of screams from the contestants. Holden reached for his phone, intent to use the flashlight function. As he enabled it a heavy blow to his head made everything go dark.

"YOU'RE MINE NOW. Stay quiet and I won't kill your boy toy." Ben, one of two lighting techs, had her by the hair, the barrel of his gun pressed painfully to her temple. He was forcing her to walk through the school's dark, empty corridors. He didn't falter, as if he'd practiced this escape route. As if he meant business.

Keep him talking. Do not let him move you.

Holden's words were her guiding light, gave her a sense of purpose.

"What did you do to him? And why do you want to hurt me?"

He yanked hard and she saw splatters of light across her vision. Sirens outside and the school fire alarm inside sounded; the emergency lighting came on, giving the hallway a dim but serviceable light.

"I said for you to. Shut. *Up!*" He pushed her into the wood shop, forcing her to land on her knees. His foot landed on her lower back and she almost passed out from the agony.

Stay conscious. Don't worry about your kidney.

Scrambling to move away from him as he turned and locked the door, then hauled a workbench in front of it, she looked around the room. The only other exits were the windows, an entire wall of them, through which she saw the blue-and-red lights of the LEA surrounding the building. The only other way out was a bay of double doors where the lumber was delivered. She recalled that it was a loading dock in the back of the school.

Ben didn't seem as worried about her escaping at this point, as he focused on fortifying the door. Which meant only one thing.

He was going to kill her here and now.

Please, please, Holden. I need you.

"HOLDEN, WHERE DID he take her?" Holden opened his eyes to his best friend standing over him. Spencer's voice came through a deep fog. He ignored the monster headache that originated from the back of his head. Groggily, he stood, and was ready to make for the staff room.

"She's not onstage, Holden." Spencer put his hands on Holden's chest, stopped him. "Think, man. Where would he take her? We've got the other contestants and judges secure in the breakroom, but since the lights went out no one saw where he took her." Spencer confirmed the safety scenario they'd practiced with the contestants earlier this week, just in case, which had them gather in the breakroom if it was too dangerous to risk exiting the building. "The entire school is surrounded. He's not going to get out of here alive."

"Then he'll kill her, if he hasn't already. I need you to make sure no one gets out of this building. I'm going to find her." Holden felt like another person was saying the words. It couldn't be true. He couldn't lose Bella. His head cleared and he had to move, had to save her. He began to run.

There was no sign of Bella or Ben anywhere, and he strained to listen for a scream or voice but it was impossible with the school's emergency alarm clanging. The hallways seemed like one long row of tiled floors after another.

Until a sparkle caught his eye.

Several sequins lay scattered across the floor, in front of the industrial-arts-classroom door. Bella had sequins on her evening gown.

He paused, not wanting to risk barging in and forcing the killer to do anything stupid out of surprise. There were two doors, and he knew that one opened inward, the other swung out into the corridor. It was to allow for maximum-sized furniture and equipment to move through it with ease. The door that swung inward had a window, and as he peered inside he saw the door was blocked by a pile of wood—and he saw Ben's back, turned to pick up more wood to pile on. Bella lay crumpled at the base of the teacher's desk in the front of the room.

Please be breathing.

He quickly texted Spencer what he saw and then made a decision that would mean Bella's life or death. If she was still alive.

She's alive.

She had to be.

BELLA WANTED TO scream for Holden to run away when she saw his figure through the classroom-door window. But she had to move very, very slowly, while Ben continued to pile wood atop the workbench. She noted that the bench had wheels, and she hadn't seen him lock them.

He wasn't such a smart killer, after all.

Slowly, inch by inch, she got to all fours, then her knees, then when Ben went farther back in the classroom to get more lumber, she surged forward and with all her might pushed on the workbench. It didn't move an inch.

A sob escaped her, a fatal mistake. Within a split second Ben had her by the hair again, and was screaming in her face. His spittle hit her skin, his face flushed with rage. But his eyes remained flat. Cold. Unemotional.

He was going to kill her.

A loud *crack* stopped Ben in his tracks, and like an automaton he dropped his hold on her hair and kept his arm around her neck as he turned his head toward the noise.

Holden leaped into the room sideways, the bench now at a sidewise angle, his weapon pointed at Ben's head. But Ben had already pulled her around in front of him as a shield.

"Don't make a move or I'll kill both of you." Ben's voice was full of rage and intent. "Put your gun down."

"Drop her. I'm an expert shot." Holden's hair was mussed, his tuxedo a mess; he was her avenging angel. But it was too late.

Bella didn't make a sound, but her gaze never left Holden's. He was focused on Ben, never wavering.

"You won't get her. She's mine. You don't deserve her. You don't know how to treat a woman." Ben yanked on her hair, rubbed his cheek against hers. She wanted to close her eyes tight but everything depended on this moment. On how she and Holden communicated.

An explosion, then the back cargo door blew open. She felt Ben startle next to her, not as much as she was sure she had, but it was enough. She dropped to her knees, giving Holden a clear shot.

Holden fired.

HOLDEN WATCHED IN slow motion as Ben dropped his weapon and collapsed to the ground. He wouldn't be getting back up. Without hesitation he ran over to Bella as MVPD and EMTs surged into the classroom. She stood halfway up to meet him.

They clung to one another for a brief, endless moment until Spencer burst into the classroom, followed by several other MVPD officers.

"Stay here—I've got to get his confession." Holden kissed the top of her head and walked over to where Ben lay on the ground. Spencer had already kicked his gun out of arm's reach but Ben was too weak for that. Spencer had just finished reading Ben his Miranda rights. Holden had to act fast. He looked at Spencer. "Be my witness."

"Got you."

Holden knelt down next to the man who'd terrorized three pageants, killed two women, and almost killed Bella.

"I'm FBI Agent Holden St. Clair. Do you have anything you want to say?"

"I only did this for my mother. She didn't want me to love anyone but her, but it was so lonely after she died."

"What did you do, Ben?"

"I just wanted my mother closer."

"Did your mother have red hair, Ben?"

"Yes, and her green eyes were so beautiful. Just like the beautiful women in the other two pageants, and Bella." A sneer moved across Ben's face as he focused on Holden, seeming to remember that Holden had stopped his efforts to take Bella. "I was so close. You ruined my chance with Bella. She looks the most like my mother did."

"Did you hurt Becky and Selina, Ben?"

"It's their fault. They went after the prettiest in the pageants. I had to protect my women from them. Becky and Selina were mean to Bella. I wanted them dead for what they said to Bella. But they lived. If I had more time... They tried to kill my mother." Ben's voice was whisper thin, his breathing very shallow.

Holden and Spence exchanged glances over Ben's prone form. They'd caught the killer. He'd somehow looked at each victim as "his," and while they were alive, conflated them with the memory of his mother.

"Let us in, officers." Two EMTs swept in, and started to work on Ben. Holden stood, as did Spencer. They'd gotten what they needed from the murderer. Ben stopped breathing and CPR was administered, but after several minutes it became clear that Ben was no longer a threat to anyone.

Holden's work was done. He needed only one thing now.

Bella.

"BABE, YOU DID IT." He lifted her to her feet and hugged her tight. Then pushed her back, looked at her face, her body. "Are you okay?"

She nodded slightly. "I am, but my scalp's going to be sore for the next few days."

"That bastard will never bother you again."

She went back into his arms, rested her head gingerly on his shoulder. "No other woman, either. We'll be able to have the pageant finale in peace, at least."

"Bella!" Spencer was next to them, and Bella turned to him. Watching the siblings hug, a sense of deep longing hit him. He wanted to be part of Bella's family. He wanted to be her family.

But she needed room to finish her exposé, and he had his own work to do. He'd disabled the threat but there would be a long after-investigation and reports to fill out. Law enforcement learned from each case and relied on accurate documentation.

More EMTs showed up, and escorted Bella away to check her over. Spencer turned to him. "You okay, buddy?"

"Yeah, why?"

"I've never seen you cry at a scene, man."

He wiped his eyes. "There's a first for everything." Including the realization that what you've been working for isn't everything. Not even close.

Chapter Twenty-Four

One week later Bella scanned the audience from her vantage point on a stage bleacher, during the opening number. MVPD had asked the pageant committee to delay the final night of the competition until the following weekend to allow for cleanup and investigation closure. She fingered the tiny owl charm on the silver bracelet that had arrived two days after the shootout. It had been gift wrapped with a note in bold print.

> **Hope you find peace again. Gio would be proud.**
> **Thanks for being such a great partner.**
> **Holden**

It was the last she'd heard from him. As each day passed she came to accept that it signaled the end of whatever they'd shared.

"Welcome to the thirtieth annual Ms. Mustang Valley Pageant and our final night of exciting competition!" Selina's voice boomed over the sound system and the funky music she'd insisted upon and the crowd roared. As much as Bella had signed up for this for such different motivation than to win the crown of Ms. Mustang Valley, she couldn't help but react to the adulation and enthusiasm from the audience. She waved from her bleacher spot onstage toward where she saw Spencer and Jarvis sitting, both hooting and hollering as they clapped. They still didn't know what kind of exposé she was about to publish—no one did. She'd written it all last week. The pageant files from Becky had told her nothing about the pageant committee, except that they'd handed down nutrition and fitness plans to the contestants.

Becky had been afraid Bella would misconstrue the diet plans and make it look as though the committee had told Gio personally to starve herself. Bella wasn't surprised by what she found and didn't find. It had been a hard won conclusion, but the plain truth was that eating disorders and mental illness were complicated, rarely caused by one event or instance. Triggered, yes, but from what she'd read in the archival files, Ms. Mustang Valley hadn't remained in the dark ages about beauty pageants and in fact had always called itself a scholarship contest. Bella had to admit she'd been too ready to find fault when she started this investigation, and had learned a valuable lesson to always keep an open mind, even when trying to justify a beloved friend's untimely death. Bella knew she was lucky to be healthy and alive, and once she accepted what she'd really learned through this entire ordeal, the Ms. Mustang Valley pageant's files had ended up fortifying the article she did write. There would never be enough attention given to eating disorders or mental illness. This report gave her a platform to shed more light on both, from a personal angle.

Holden remained MIA the entire time she worked on finishing her report. "He has so many loose ends to wrap up, you know," Spencer had told her. But she knew there was more to Holden's absence. Her worst fear was substantiated by him not showing up at all. She figured Holden realized that what had looked like a budding relationship wasn't going to go any further.

Still, she searched the faces of the crowd, as many as she could see from her vantage point on the bleacher step and through the stage lights. Hoping against hard reality that Holden was here.

Leigh Dennings had her own cheering team in other Affirmation Alliance Group members who sat together in the first several rows. Micheline Anderson was in the center of the group and Bella wondered if Spencer or Holden had seen her. Holden didn't appear to be present, but she knew Spencer would let him know Micheline had shown up.

The grief over losing the relationship she'd never had a chance to appreciate or enjoy without threat of immediate death threatened to make her sob onstage, in front of several hundred of her best friends.

Only for Gio did she hold it together. She may have lost Holden, but she still had her life to live. This wasn't the time for self-pity.

HOLDEN HAD THE pageant streaming on his laptop as he took care of all the personal business he'd neglected over the past month. A month spent searching for, and finding and ultimately taking out a disturbed serial killer. Ben's musings about his mother, before he'd died on the high school classroom floor, had proved true. She'd been a redhead with green eyes, and according to Ben's elementary school records his mother had abused him repeatedly. He'd been in and out of foster care, always returning to her side and no doubt more abuse. He had no regrets about that, except for the surviving victims' families who would never see justice carried out in a court of law.

Streaming from unclassified, insecure internet at the Bureau was strictly prohibited, so he'd saved his bills and personal correspondence until tonight.

The stream wasn't as clear as he'd wished; while he knew which tiny figure was Bella onstage it was only because he'd witnessed all of the practices.

No, he had no regret over the case and how it had worked out. But he did wish he'd been able to express to Bella what she meant to him. It didn't make sense to begin something he couldn't follow up on until he closed the case.

Until he knew he was worthy to ask her to consider to be his partner.

The television sound was background as he double-checked utility bills, caught up on laundry. Vaguely he registered that the talent portion had begun. When he heard Selina's voice, unmistakable even with a shaky internet connection, announce the next talent portion, he stilled.

"Ms. Bella Colton tells us what matters most to her in a very special personal essay." Selina's intro revealed none of the acrimony she'd shown to Bella during the rehearsal period. He had to give the ex-Colton credit; she earned her PR director pay grade in spades.

"Good evening, everyone." Holden sat down in front of his laptop, unable to move as Bella spoke.

"It's been a dark journey for our pageant, and for all of Mustang Valley, as well as Arizona, as we've endured the threat of a vicious criminal. But unlike the sad endings we're seeing too much of these days, there is a happy ending for Ms. Mustang Valley. For all of us.

And there is peace of mind for the surviving victims of this awful killer."

Bella went on to talk about how she'd entered the pageant looking for information on her best friend's struggles with bulimia and major depression, but instead found a community of strong, intelligent women who fostered empowerment she'd never felt before.

"I've picked a poem to read for my talent. Some of you might know it; it's by a journalist from a long time ago but still holds true today. Its title is 'To Jennie' but for me, it's 'To Gio.'"

To Jennie

Good-bye! a kind good-bye,
I bid you now, my friend,
And though 'tis sad to speak the word,
To destiny I bend

And though it be decreed by Fate
That we ne'er meet again,
Your image, graven on my heart,
Forever shall remain.

Aye, in my heart thoult have a place,
Among the friends held dear,-Nor shall the hand of Time efface
The memories written there.
Goodbye,
S.L.C.

"S.L.C. was Samuel Langhorne Clemens, also known as Mark Twain. I want to add that I've learned one other thing these past weeks. True love comes in many forms, but when it does, it's unmistakable and always worth fighting for. Thank you.

She looked straight into the camera as applause boomed over the audio and while Holden couldn't make out her exact expression, dang the low-quality feed, he didn't have to."

He heard Bella. He'd figured out some things himself over the course of the pageant investigation. Bella wasn't his ex, and she was a woman of integrity. Her reporting reflected that.

And he realized he'd never make it without her. But he had to get this case wrapped, and see if he could get moved to the Tucson Resident Office. If not, they'd work out the commute between Phoenix and Mustang Valley. Whatever it took.

"Trust me, babe. I couldn't agree more." He knew it was silly, speaking to Bella's image on the television, but it made him feel that much closer to beginning the rest of his life with her.

The last remaining piece of the puzzle would be to see if she agreed to his plans.

BELLA WAITED ONSTAGE with the other contestants while the finalists were named. She wasn't surprised to not be amongst the final five, and waited with anticipation as it came down to Marcie and Leigh, who held hands center stage.

"And this year's Ms. Mustang Valley is..." The winner of last year's contest stood at the podium, hands shaking as she tore open the sparkling, large gold envelope, another Selina touch.

"Leigh Dennings!"

Marcie smiled graciously and hugged Leigh, who smiled wide and accepted her crown, placed on her head by the previous winner. Leigh walked to the microphone.

"This wouldn't be possible without knowing I can live my best life today, and every day! If you want to know how I did it, you're welcome to the next meeting of the Affirmation Alliance Group. Find us on your favorite social media platform."

Bella looked out and tried to meet Spencer's gaze, but he was already on his cell, no doubt reporting what he witnessed to Holden. Her breathing slowed, almost stopped as she faced her truth.

Spencer and Holden would always have their friendship and working relationship. Bella wasn't in the picture at all any longer.

"CONGRATULATIONS, SIS." JARVIS and Spencer stepped out from under the school's front awning as she exited. Jarvis handed her a large bouquet of sunflowers. "These are from both of us."

"Thanks, Jarvis." She hugged him. "It was sweet of you to come tonight."

"Hey, what about me?" Spencer gave her his classic bear hug and she hugged him back, too.

"We want to take you out. To congratulate you for making it through the pageant alive." Jarvis kept a straight face until Spencer laughed and Bella punched Jarvis on the shoulder.

"Funny. I appreciate the offer, but I'm beat. Can we go out for something to eat next week?" The reality that Holden really hadn't come to see the last night of the pageant finally hit her and she was bone weary. If she couldn't be with the one person who'd made a major difference in her life these last weeks, she wanted to be alone and reading a novel.

"Are you sure? There's sure to be a big party at the diner." Jarvis grinned and she smiled back at her brother.

"You've been quiet through most of this, Jarvis. Except when you kept telling me I was crazy to sign up for the pageant. What's going on with you? Have you dug up the old family secret you think is at Rattlesnake Ridge Ranch? Or are you going to admit it's for naught and go back to being your businessman self?"

"It's not for naught, but I can't talk about it yet. Let's just say I'm close. Besides, I like ranch life more than I realized I would."

Bella turned to Spencer. "Do you believe this?"

Spencer shrugged. "I didn't believe you'd signed up for Ms. Mustang Valley, but you did. Anything's possible."

"You didn't think I'd make it out alive, did you?"

"I never doubted you would. You had the best man watching you."

Tears threatened but she didn't want to let her brothers see how deeply Spencer's words affected her. Not yet. Maybe not ever.

"Thanks for your belief in me. I'll catch you both next week."

All she wanted to catch tonight was sleep. If it was an escape from facing her true feelings, and the grief over losing something that had never taken off, then so be it.

It was one thing to have the right man next to her, to guide her and protect her through a tough situation. To expect he'd be around afterward was pushing it.

But she refused to blame herself for feeling how she did. Holden had been a special chapter in her life. She'd come too far in life and in this past month to accept anything but the truth from herself.

Two weeks after the pageant, Bella made her way through Mustang Valley Hospital with a huge bear balloon and an arrangement of chocolate-dipped fruit. The pageant and its aftermath had brought her both joy and sorrow. The sorrow she wasn't ready to face just yet, but figured she had a lifetime to mourn losing Holden to his career, and hers.

The text that she'd received as she pulled up to the hospital helped buoy her steps. She'd been offered an investigative-reporter position with the county paper, the *Bronco Star*. She'd been so excited she'd immediately changed her job status on all of her social media accounts. If Holden wanted to find her, to see what had happened with her career, thanks to the pageant, he could. The county publication, still in print but with a robust online presence, fed into several major national news outlets. After years of hard work and an especially brutal previous month, Bella had realized her dream.

If it wasn't as great as she'd expected, because she'd lost a lot to get here, too, then so be it. She couldn't allow herself to be sad over Holden leaving her life. If she started down that emotional path, she wasn't sure she'd ever find her way back to the joy she'd thought she'd lost when Gio died.

Today she found joy in being reunited with her extended Colton family. As Marlowe had suggested, she'd met up with her and Ainsley for coffee a few days ago. Marlowe had been very uncomfortable, and Ainsley said they all thought the baby was going to make an appearance at any minute. When Spencer let her know that Marlowe was in labor and had been taken to the hospital from her work office, Bella had experienced a radiant sense of quiet happiness that she could only attribute to family.

Another reason to work on letting Holden and her feelings for him go. Their connection had no "quiet" part to it. It wasn't all sexual passion, either, but an intense bond she couldn't explain.

The hospital-room door was open and she walked into a world of flowers, pale blue ribbons, baskets chock-full of baby needs and a radiant Marlowe sitting up in the hospital bed, the newborn at her breast.

"Oh, I'm sorry!"

"Don't be silly. We're family. Have a seat." Marlowe's mother, Genevieve, smiled and moved over, offering Bella the easy chair closest to the new mother. Bella was struck by Genevieve, Payne's third and current wife. The woman's grace while enduring so much personal suffering thanks to her husband's shooting and coma was awe inspiring.

"I wasn't sure what to bring, so I opted for food." Bella placed the balloon arrangement on the crowded bedside table and held out the platter of bright fruit.

"OMG, let me finish this side with him and I want one of those chocolate strawberries."

"I thought you had to avoid caffeine when you nursed?" Genevieve spoke up, her gaze glued to the baby. Her grandson.

"One little bit won't hurt." Marlowe grinned at Bella.

"He's so beautiful." She looked around the room again but as she'd first determined, Bowie wasn't here. "Where's the happy father?"

Bella watched as Marlowe lifted her son from her

breast and proceeded to burp him. The little peanut complied almost immediately and all three women laughed. A warmth of belonging and peace filled Bella. This was living life to the fullest, as Gio would have wanted her to do. Enjoying each and every moment.

Marlowe laughed. "I sent him to get a shower, and to bring back some real food. Would you like to hold him?" Marlow held out her bundled babe and Bella tried not to blanch. "Um, I've never really been around such a new baby."

"It's fine. Here." Genevieve took the baby and handed him to Bella as she sat in the chair. "Keep his head supported, yes, like that, and just enjoy his precious little face." The grandmother love radiated from her.

"Thank you." Bella stared at little Reed Colton Robertson, and allowed herself the simple pleasure of holding him.

"We read your piece in the *Mustang Valley Gabber*." Marlowe spoke as she readjusted her bedclothes. "It was fantastic, and what an honor to your best friend. Gio would be so proud of you, Bella."

"Thanks. I appreciate that." She'd decided to write about why she'd initially joined the pageant, her change of heart about the lack of pretentiousness, save for Selina, and why pageants that offered scholarships and ways for women to improve themselves were important. "I've learned a lot from volunteering at the MVED clinic. They're always looking for volunteers, if you're ever interested."

"Thank you. I like how you gave all the resource links for people seeking help for eating disorders and how you explained that while Gio had suffered from an awful disease, it wasn't possible to blame it on pageant culture per se. It was so wonderful how you presented Ms. Mustang Valley as an opportunity for every woman. You handled it so well, Bella." Genevieve's sincerity made the lump in her throat grow.

"It's my job to tell the truth." She adjusted Reed so that she could look into his sweet, tiny face. "Right, little dude? Truth and trust. It's the only way."

"You forgot one thing there, cuz." Marlowe lay back on the bed, beginning to wind down.

"What's that?" Bella handed Reed to Genevieve. It was time for her to depart. New moms needed their rest where they could get it, she'd read.

Marlowe smiled, close to drifting off. "Love."

LATER THAT NIGHT, Bella opened the front door to her two brothers, each wearing dress shirts and jeans.

"This is a surprise. What's going on? Come in." She walked back into her living room and shut off the crime series she'd been bingeing. It was too difficult to watch her favorite shows, mostly romantic comedies. The happy endings were still hard to stomach.

"We've been trying to reach you for the last three hours, sis." Jarvis took the lead while Spencer tapped on his phone. Police business was never over.

"Oh, sorry. I turn my phone off when I get home. It's the only way I can unwind from my job." And stop obsessively checking for a text or call from Holden.

It hadn't happened in over three weeks. It wasn't going to. Why torture herself more?

"Do you want something to drink?" She noted that Jarvis had a cooler in hand. "Or did you bring your own?"

He smiled enigmatically. "This, dear sister, is a surprise."

She mentally checked the date. Not their birthday,

not a holiday she'd forgotten in the flurry of the previous weeks.

Spencer shoved his phone in his back pocket. "That was Katrina. She and Boris will be by in a bit."

"Okay..." She looked down at her old T-shirt and jean shorts. "Do I need to change? Oh wait, is this about celebrating for you and Katrina?"

Spencer slowly shook his head. "Nope."

"It's about you and I, Bella." The voice reached to her core and she turned toward the figure who walked up behind her brothers.

"Holden!" Confusion and a tiny flicker of something else—hope—rained on her. "What are you doing here?"

Spencer and Jarvis stepped aside to allow Holden a clear path to her. He wore a pale blue dress shirt, black jeans, cowboy boots. With one hand behind his back, he looked everything and nothing like the FBI agent she'd fallen for.

She'd fallen in love with. Tears began to spill down her cheeks and she sniffed.

"I wanted your brothers to be here, because I know how important they are to you." Holden pulled his arm around and handed her a huge bouquet of multicolor flowers, with a single spiky creamy bloom in the center.

"Thank you." She touched the center pale yellow flower, smiled. "An angel cactus. Just like—"

"The ones in Carr Canyon." He looked over his shoulder at Spencer, who stepped forward and took the bouquet from her hands so that Holden could grasp them.

"Holden, I—"

"Bella, it's my turn to talk. I'm hoping we'll have all the time in the world to work out the details of where we'll live, how we'll handle two careers—congratulations on your new job, by the way, I couldn't be prouder—but right now, I have one question to ask you."

Holden bent down on one knee, still holding her hands. She was vaguely aware of her brothers standing behind him, giving their silent blessing to the event. But all she could see were Holden's dark, dear eyes, looking up at her with complete trust. And the truth.

"I love you, Bella Colton. Will you marry me?"

"Yes, Holden St. Clair. I will marry you—I will!" She tugged him up, and to the applause of her brothers she met her fiancé's mouth and let herself fall into the most delicious kiss of her life.

* * * * *

COMING SOON!

LET'S TALK
Romance

For exclusive extracts, competitions
and special offers, find us online:

f facebook.com/millsandboon

🐦 @MillsandBoon

📷 @MillsandBoonUK

Get in touch on 01413 063232

MILLS & BOON

THE HEART OF ROMANCE

A ROMANCE FOR EVERY KIND OF READER

MODERN

Prepare to be swept off your feet by sophisticated, sexy and seductive heroes, in some of the world's most glamourous a romantic locations, where power and passion collide.
8 stories per month.

HISTORICAL

Escape with historical heroes from time gone by. Whether y passion is for wicked Regency Rakes, muscled Vikings or ru Highlanders, awaken the romance of the past.
6 stories per month.

MEDICAL

Set your pulse racing with dedicated, delectable doctors in high-pressure world of medicine, where emotions run high passion, comfort and love are the best medicine.
6 stories per month.

True Love

Celebrate true love with tender stories of heartfelt romance the rush of falling in love to the joy a new baby can bring, a focus on the emotional heart of a relationship.
8 stories per month.

Desire

Indulge in secrets and scandal, intense drama and plenty o hot action with powerful and passionate heroes who have it wealth, status, good looks…everything but the right woman
6 stories per month.

HEROES

Experience all the excitement of a gripping thriller, with an romance at its heart. Resourceful, true-to-life women and s fearless men face danger and desire - a killer combination!
8 stories per month.

DARE

Sensual love stories featuring smart, sassy heroines you'd wa best friend, and compelling intense heroes who are worthy
4 stories per month.

To see which titles are coming soon, please visit

millsandboon.co.uk/nextmonth

JOIN US ON SOCIAL MEDIA!

Stay up to date with our latest releases, author news and gossip, special offers and discounts, and all the behind-the-scenes action from Mills & Boon...

 millsandboon

 millsandboonuk

 millsandboon

might just be true love...

MILLS & BOON

HISTORICAL

Awaken the romance of the past

Escape with historical heroes from time gone by. Whether your passion is for wicked Regency Rakes, muscled Viking warriors or rugged Highlanders, indulge your fantasies and awaken the romance of the past.